Scattered Stones

Michelle Kelly

Scattered Stones

Michelle Kelly

A catalogue record for this book is available from the National Library of New Zealand.
First published 2018
Ryegrass Publications

www.ryegrasspublishing.co.nz

PO Box 99-204, Newmarket, Auckland 1023, New Zealand

IBSN: 978-0-473-44912-4 (Softcover)

IBSN: 978-0-473-44913-1 (Kindle)

IBSN: 978-0-473-44914-8 (iBook)

The moral rights of the author have been asserted.

Book design and format: Pamela Bestwick

Cover Design: Elina Shikhimova

Cover Photograph: Kelley Woods

Proofread/Copyedit: Marilyn Bridger.

DEDICATED TO

Rebecca Mary Butler Cutten
2 October 1962 - 12 June 2018

Rebecca, my friend, who passed away before
Scattered Stones was published.
Sadly missed, always cherished.
Rebecca, this one is for you.

It's been a pleasure, a challenge, and a passion writing this novel and I believe it's a story that was meant to be told. It's my hope you enjoy the journey as much as I have enjoyed being a part of it.

Michelle

ACKNOWLEDGMENTS

Special thanks to...

Elina Shikhimova for the cover design.

Marilyn Bridger for proofreading and editing
(Any mistakes are Michelle's for titivating after the fact).

Pamela Bestwick for assessment & publication.

Moureen Hartley (Mum) for endless encouragement.

Kelley Woods for the $300,000 photo for the cover – thanks mate!!

&

Terry for his incredible patience, love, and support.

Contents

Chapter 1　　　　Unwashed Memories

The air was filled with sandflies and the sound of the mighty, rushing river. Pat slapped at a sandfly on the back of his neck, splattering blood. Heads bent close together, Pat and his father, Jim, worked the cradle, their hungry eyes searching for gold. Sleeves rolled up, hats low on their ears, wearing thigh-high boots, the pair sifted the river with pick, pan and shovel.

Pat's eyes gleamed; a nugget the size of a small pea lay on the matting in the bottom of the cradle among specks that glittered like stars. They had won a tremendous haul since pegging out *The Redemption*. Yet, up until now, the majority of the winnings had been spent on rebuilding the Welcome Home, which was destroyed by fire when Charles Butler had attempted to kill Ma. Now the building work was finished, and the hotel up and running again, perhaps there would be money left over, money that could be used for the finer things in life. For Pat, the finer things were wine, women, and song. Ah, the memories, Pat thought wistfully. Aye, he missed chasing a bit of skirt, the opium dens, and drinking till he dropped. And damn it, he missed Tiny.

Jim clapped his hand on Pat's muscular shoulder. He grinned. "We'll be as rich as kings, son."

Pat wished Tiny were there to share in their good fortune. Smiling sadly to himself, he remembered the last time he and Tiny drank together. It was the night before the Big Flood. The night they thought they'd have a feed of wood pigeon. After a day spent on The Arrow with little to show for it, they had retired to their tent, leaving the side flaps open to let in the breeze.

They were resting on their cots when Tiny spied the bird sitting in the Lucky Tree. Perched on a crumbling ledge above the river, and growing at a perilous angle which would mean certain death should anyone try to cut it down, it had been spared the usual fate of being turned into firewood or pegs.

Tiny sat up, reached for the rifle, raised it, took aim at the bird, and fired. The pigeon didn't budge, but as if fascinated by the fire and smoke it blinked and continued to stare at Tiny from its lofty perch. Tiny went outside to meet the courageous bird, raised the rifle, and fired again.

"You missed," Pat scoffed from the safety of the tent. "You cock-eyed buffoon! You couldn't hit an elephant if you were right in front of it."

Once again, Tiny took aim. There was a loud bang. Again, the shot missed. The curious bird blinked but didn't move. Seven shots later, Tiny was out of powder and out of sorts.

"Throw the rifle and you may well hit the overstuffed budgerigar," Pat chuckled, amused.

Cursing his bad luck, Tiny threw the empty rifle back in the tent. "Come on," he'd said to Pat, "we may not eat tonight but by God we'll drink."

Together they set off to Fox's township. The pair were great mates, both being red-headed Irishmen who loved to drink. Tiny was a bear of a man with fingers the size of sausages whereas Pat was tall, all bones and cunning.

At *The Oak*, Tiny complained to Ned the barman, that he'd wasted no end of good powder on an enchanted wee beastie in the Lucky Tree.

"Perhaps he was lucky because he was sitting in the Lucky Tree." The barman tried to jolly Tiny out of his bad humour.

"Or perhaps Tiny's a rotten shot," Pat said, elbowing Tiny in the ribs.

"Damn bird was laughing at me," Tiny muttered darkly. Taking another slug of brandy, he emptied the bottle in a single draught.

Chalking it up, Tiny ordered nobbler after nobbler until he was roaring drunk, and Pat's knees were beginning to buckle.

"Bloody bird was laughing at me!" cried Tiny, thumping his fist on the bar.

Aware of a presence behind him, Tiny turned to see Constable Brick standing there. Arms folded, face stern, the constable looked down his long nose as if summing up how drunk Tiny was, and more importantly, whether he'd be able to take him.
Adding curses for emphasis, Tiny told the constable his story.

Grasping Tiny by the elbow, the constable said, "Come along, man, you've had more than your fill tonight."

Tiny shrugged him off like the nuisance that he was. "He's one of the little people, I tell you." He belched, his fumy breath overpowering.

A deep frown appeared between the constable's thickset, bushy eyebrows. In a stern voice, he said, "Thomas Heenan, I'm arresting you for drunk and disorderly behaviour, and for using obscene language." Then as if he was coaching a small child, he said softly, "Come along peaceably now, Tiny, that's the man."

With no jail to house miscreants, the only method of securing a prisoner was the log. The log, with its thick chain and fettle, was situated on the outskirts of town. Resigned, Tiny went quietly, leaning on the constable for support. Together they negotiated the path. Pat did not pick a fight with Constable Brick as he didn't fancy time on the log, but he wasn't going to let his best mate suffer alone. He followed them out into the street. He saw a passed out drunk with a bottle of cheer tucked under his arm lying outside the billiard rooms. Pat plucked the bottle from him and continued on his way the pilfered bottle in his hand, and dodging horse manure, he stumbled along Buckingham Street.

Above the log, there was the shade of a lone tree that the prisoner could huddle under. Anyone who dared to chop it down was under the threat of being chained to the log themselves. Compliant, Tiny allowed himself to be chained without argument. He muttered curses as the shackles were placed on his wrists, then slumped heavily on the ground like a sack of coal.

Constable Brick scowled. "Right, man," he said in a deep rumbling voice, "sleep it off. And, if you give me no further trouble by singing, swearing or causing any other disturbance tonight, I'll release you come morning." He patted Tiny's shoulder.
Tiny frowned up at him thinking the man's eyebrows looked like two fat hairy slugs. Satisfied, the constable reattached the keys to his belt then walked stiffly, slightly bow-legged back towards town.

Melancholy, his legs sprawled at right angles in front of him, Tiny, leaned against the log and stared at his fettered hands. Pat collapsed beside him and offered Tiny a swig from the almost empty bottle. Thanking him, Tiny drained the last drop. In companionable silence, they used the log as a rough pillow and stared up at the star-studded sky. Stupefied by drink, Pat felt his heavy eyelids close but Tiny continued to peer up at the night sky as if looking for the angels. Just as sleep was beginning to cloud his vision, he caught sight of a wood pigeon, its head on its breast, asleep in the tree. The pigeon opened one eye and winked. Tiny's fingers found a stone, he threw it but missed, the chains preventing his aim being true.

Outraged, Tiny got to his feet. The log was pulled out from under Pat and he landed face first in the dirt. Pat spat, and rubbed the haze from his eyes. Astonished, he watched as Tiny hoisted the huge log onto his shoulder. Like a Scotsman with his caber, Tiny dragged the log up Buckingham Street making a furrow in the dust.

Pat got unsteadily to his feet. Banging the dust off his hat, he put it back on his head and followed his mate into town. Tiny used the log like a battering ram and pushed open *The Oak's* saloon doors. He dragged the log to the bar where he dropped it. It landed with a thud on the flagstone floor, bouncing twice before coming to rest.

Demanding another drink, Tiny told the shocked barman, "Damn bird was laughing at me."
The following day arrangements were made to build a permanent jail.

Pat's smile faded as his thoughts turned to the night of the Big Flood. He remembered waking to the sound of a rumbling that grew into a deafening roar. A torrent of water burst around the narrow bend in the river, sweeping away everything in its path, and their tent with it.

Pat woke to find himself amidst the broiling flood waters, and though he tried desperately, he could not find Tiny. And that was the last he ever saw his best mate. That day, due to the many landslides the river changed direction, and the claim they'd worked together as partners was nothing but a washout. Not that it ever yielded much more than a pennyweight. Devastated by loss, Pat's heart was so grieved he had wanted to die too, but something, or someone, always made him cling to life, however tenuous his hold on it might be. After all, his Da returned from the dead; perhaps there was still hope for Tiny.

To hide his tears, Pat, scooped up a handful of chill water and scrubbed his face. God, he missed Tiny.

Pat's hand trembled as he plucked the pea-shaped nugget from the matting and held it up to the receding light. She was a beauty. He glanced sideways at his Da, it never ceased to amaze him that his father trusted him with the gold. A bag of gold on his person was a mighty big temptation. Da said it was to make up for the lost years. Pat knew Da sought to make amends, but while Pat was working on forgiving, he would never forget.

Pat's memory haunted him whenever he thought of that fateful night in '63. The blizzard killed many, some were blown clear off the mountain, some buried where they fell, under several feet of snow. Not knowing if Da was dead or alive, and unable to face the family, Pat didn't return to Dunedin. Instead, he hid in taverns or opium dens trying to forget. But his mother wasn't the kind of woman who would sit idly by and wait. After several weeks, she packed up the family and came looking for them. With one horse between six, the family trekked from Dunedin, and when they arrived at The Arrow footsore and tired, they found Pat in *The Royal* toasting his dear father's memory with his new mate Tiny.

Reluctantly, Pat, told his mother that he'd lost Da on Old Man. Branding him a coward, his mother left him to work his claim with

Tiny in peace, and with the gold Da had sent back prior to his disappearance, she bought the Long Gully Pub from a widow who was eager to sell. His three sisters, Annie, God rest her soul, Meg, and Kitty helped Ma run the hotel, while his younger brother, Dan, went off to stake his own claim at Moonlight, a place so rich they now called it The Jeweller's Shop, and his youngest brother, Jack, worked down at The Head of the Lake Timber-mill up until the accident. Now, he was a blacksmith in Queenstown.

Whenever Father Whooley visited, he always reminded the family not to be too hasty to see Jim change. He said, change would come, in time, with love and patience. The new priest was nothing like that old hypocrite Father Francis, who was so full of hellfire and damnation that you could almost smell the Lake of Fire with every breath the man took. That self-righteous old git refused to give Annie the last rites because he'd heard her child was a bastard. Pat's gut twisted in anger.

Da had returned, but he had lost Annie, and Tiny, and some days his grief threatened to overwhelm him.

Meg had to shade her eyes from the blinding sun which poured through the schoolhouse's open window, but the moment she'd seen him riding over the brow of the hill, she knew who it was. Yankee Brown had a peculiar riding style. Hoping to flee before he arrived, Meg hurried outside to lock the schoolhouse but to her dismay, she heard the thundering of horse's hooves rapidly approaching, and she knew she wouldn't make it. The horse and rider stopped. Meg fumbled nervously turning the key in the door. She turned.

Yankee swung down from the saddle and stood beside his horse. He patted Lucky's neck while studying her with his cool blue eyes.

Doffing his broad Southwester, Yankee smiled. "Miss Margaret."

Meg couldn't pretend she didn't see him; nor could she escape, for behind her was the sanctuary of the schoolhouse which he had just seen her lock and before her the path which he now blocked. Trapped, she gasped for air while he looked calm and relaxed. He may have been a whaler's son but, Yankee had a ruggedly cocky air about him that made folks believe he was born for better things. Tall and handsome, he was lean with broad shoulders, and sandy hair that framed a noble face and matched his moustache and beard.

Refusing to give him the satisfaction of knowing his nearness affected her, Meg lifted her chin and met his gaze. "Mr Brown." His hair and beard had grown.

Hat in hand, he took a step towards her. "How's the school ma'am?" he drawled.

Meg took a step. "Well, thank you," she answered primly.

He made a great show of putting his hat on and nodded. "Aye, you look well an' all," he agreed gazing down at her with open appreciation.

Meg sought a suitable response, failing to find one she left it hanging.

He took another step; his hobnail boots heavy on the gravel. "As for myself, I'm doing mighty fine. Thanks for asking, Miss Margaret." He waited letting the words sink in.

She forced a smile. "So, I've heard." Her brother, Dan, had been quick to tell her. Surely he hadn't come all this way to brag. He looked a little thicker around the middle, his eyes less hollow. He'd been eating well. What was it about him that rattled her?

"Mighty fine indeed," he repeated. He hooked a finger in his braces.

There was that jauntiness again, that devil-may-care attitude, the way he could laugh at anything. It needled her.

Yankee lifted his chin. "And Mr Burns? How goes his venture?"

Her eyes narrowed. He was deliberately provoking her and she resented him for it. News travelled fast, and just as she knew he was raking in gold at the Jeweller's Shop, Yankee would have heard rumours about The Alliance. They were only just setting up the sluicing company, tunnelling was going well, but the sourcing of equipment for more extensive mining operations such as dredging, were looking costly and the transport too difficult. William's grand schemes were beginning to cause ill-feeling between him and Lord Asterly, who was of the opinion a dredge or a battery wouldn't pay its way. William begged to differ and was adamant that he should be allowed to experiment.

Once, in a temper, William hotly declared to Meg that Asterly was as shy as a maiden when it came to business. He thought he should be allowed to take risks that they could well afford to take. The miners were beginning to take sides and it looked as if the partnership could be dissolved. The tension between Lord Asterly and William was obvious to all, and for Meg, still living under the Asterlys roof, it made life difficult.

Lucky stretched her long neck and ripped the grass at Meg's feet.

"I don't really know," Meg said, telling a bare-faced lie. "I leave the business up to them. I am," she looked at him pointedly, "only a woman after all."

"Aye," he grinned, giving her the once over, "but what a woman."

Yankee's arrogant flirting irritated her further. "It's been," Meg paused trying to think of a suitable word, "ah… a surprise to see you Mr Brown," she said coolly.

He cocked an eyebrow. "A pleasurable one, I hope?"

Ignoring him, Meg continued, "I offer you my hearty congratulations on your most remarkable success." She gave him a perfunctory nod, signalling the end of the conversation.

Yankee stroked his beard. "Aye, it is truly remarkable. I can hardly believe it myself. Have to pinch myself most days."

He was so self-assured she wanted to throttle him. "Well, I must be on my way." Meg waited for him to move aside but Yankee didn't budge. Planting his feet astride he stayed riveted to the spot. He let go the reins and allowed his horse its head. When she attempted to go around him, he caught her by the sleeve.

"I love you," he said quietly dropping the façade. The softness of his voice penetrated her eggshell heart. She could feel the warmth of his fingers through the fabric of her dress. Fearing he would see the uncertainty in her eyes, Meg kept her head down.

"Have you accepted Burns' proposal?"
Meg nodded, not trusting herself to speak.

His face fell. "Why?"
She simply hadn't found a reason to refuse.

"Why do that, when you know I love you?" He placed his finger under her chin and encouraged her to lift her head. She did so reluctantly.

His cool blue eyes studied hers. "You love me, don't deny it?"

Meg's thoughts were crashing violently one upon another like the waves on a West Coast beach. The arrangements had been made, and Kitty had almost certainly finished the dress. Everything was ready. It was too late, much too late.

Meg shook her head. "I'm sorry," she said backing away. Sidestepping past him, she hurried down the path, her pace quickening with each step.

"You're making a terrible mistake," he called after her.
Head held high, back ramrod straight, Meg walked on briskly.

"I plan to take a wife," he shouted, his voice carrying on the warm breeze.
She stopped, then walked on willing herself not to look back, or run.

The horse's retreating hooves sounded like a drumbeat in her ears. Meg waited till she was sure Yankee was far enough away that he could no longer see her, then she made a mad dash through the long grass up to the graveyard. The iron-gate clanged with a hollow ring as it shut behind her. Reaching the simple white cross with its blood red rose, not caring if she soiled her long skirts, she crossed herself, fell to her knees, and fastened her hands in prayer.

The tussocks, rocks and scrubby low-lying trees clinging to the shingle banks went past in a blur of green, gold, and grey. It was as if the river was racing him back home to Moonlight. Bent low over his horse's back, Yankee rode for all he was worth. He knew he shouldn't ride Lucky hard over the rough terrain but he needed an outlet. He wanted to challenge Meg, make her see reason but Meg was a stubborn mule and any attempt to change her mind would only make her more determined.

Last year, she had said things like, she didn't want a miner for a husband. Didn't want a man with wanderlust in his veins who would disappear with the next big rush. So, he bought Riverstones Station. And because she said she didn't want to live in a dirty hovel raising children like rats, he made sure there was a decent homestead on the property. Hiring a manager and farmhands had taken time and effort and meant many trips to visit his investment. Getting farmhands was hard work since every man and his dog wanted to earn a quick fortune on the goldfields, but he'd managed it. He was about to ask for her hand in marriage when word reached him that while he was busy doing all that to please her, Meg had accepted that splay-legged, arrogant peacock's, proposal. It was a bitter pill to swallow to try and please a woman only to have it blow up in your face.

He passed people coming along the track but didn't slow down or stop to pass the time of day. He was angry and didn't know what to do about it. He'd travelled up to Skippers especially to ask her to reconsider – and, if he was honest, to brag. But money and property weren't enough when what he wanted most was Meg. Beautiful, spirited, stubborn Meg, with her nut-brown hair, big brown eyes, porcelain skin, and cherry lips. To him, she was as fresh as summer rain and as sweet smelling as lavender oil, and he wanted her to be his wife.

But instead of being pleased to see him, she looked like a startled doe, wary and ready to take flight. She was afraid of him, yet he'd never done anything to harm her. No, all he'd ever done was love her, yet she spurned his every attempt, preferring instead that stuck up, trussed goose, Burns, with his charming tongue and flashy ways.

He slowed his horse to a walk as a thick blanket of melancholy came upon him. What was the use of all his money if he didn't have someone to share his fortune with? He felt her rejection as keenly as a stab from a red-hot poker. It stuck in his craw he had gone to all that trouble for nought. He might as well drown his sorrows with the drink as her heart would never be his.

Pink, violet, and yellow lupines lined the track like a glorious guard of honour. The sun was warm on Kitty's young freckled face and a soft breeze tickled a few red curls loose from the confines of her bonnet. Kitty had a talent for dressmaking, but her mother being a practical woman did not hold with finery where it was not needed, so Kitty wore a simple grey day dress, for as her mother said, to wear anything else in this environment would be a sin.

She carried her parcel carefully so as not to wrinkle or spoil it. Lady Asterly had kindly invited her to stay the night, and her mother being in a congenial mood had allowed her to go, without Grace. Being away from the endless chores was a small taste of freedom to relish. Not one to believe in idleness, Kitty's mother believed it was better to wear out than rust, and if Mary Healey had anything to do with it, no one would ever rust.

The letter in her petticoat pocket felt like it was burning a hole in the fabric. To ensure Ma didn't get wind of it, Kitty knew she must to slip it to Dusty away from the hotel, and quickly, or the placement would be gone. Granny McNab offered to write the letter of recommendation but was afraid Mary Healey would strip the skin of her bones for interfering. Granny was not a relative, but a kindly old widow who lived with her bachelor son over at Greengate. Granny recognised Kitty's talent for sewing and encouraged her in it. No, Kitty decided, there was no point getting Ma all riled up for nothing, other girls would apply and she might not be offered an apprenticeship, but Mary, Mother of God, she wanted it.

She neared Pinchers Bluff, a harrowing stretch of road. A packer's life was a dangerous one, there were places where one wrong footfall could send you to your death. She checked the position of the sun; Dusty should be along any time soon. He was a funny wee fellow, wizened and gritty, he loved his horses more than people but he delighted in a good gossip and loved to pass on a juicy morsel or two.

Suddenly a horse and rider appeared and came thundering towards her. Kitty backed into the rock face and turned her head as the horse and rider passed by in a choking cloud of dust. She coughed and blinked as the dust settled. Blame fool could break his neck, Kitty thought, peeved.

She dusted herself off and continued on, her head busy with thoughts. What if she was offered a place – what then? She'd have a time of it convincing her mother to let her go. Kitty saw the dust and heard the jangle of horses' harnesses long before the pack ponies came into view. Dusty was out front holding the leader's reins, his trusty ponies following faithfully behind, heads bobbing, their backs swayed from heavy loads.

Heart hammering, Kitty took the letter from its hiding place and held it in her hand, ready.

"Whoa there," Dusty called to his girls. The ponies stopped, raised their heads, and huffed, examining Kitty as if they expected some treat to be produced.

"Miss Kitty," Dusty said, touching a hand to his battered black hat. His bushy silver eyebrows met. "Where are you off to young lady?"

"Morning, Dusty, I'm going to visit Meg. I've finished her wedding gown," Kitty said, holding the parcel out to him.

Dusty smiled showing a row of yellow stumps. "You're rare good with a needle Miss Kitty. I'm sure you've done a fine job of it and all. Why you ought to be a seamstress." Not a man given to excesses so a compliment from him was to be cherished.

"Why thank you," Kitty replied, pleased. She took a deep breath; it was now or never. She lowered her voice to a whisper. "Ah, Dusty, I have a letter. I wonder if this could be kept just between us."

Dusty took exception to the inference. Heckles raised, he declared, "All the mail is safe with me, miss."

"I wasn't implying..." Kitty hastened to add but was interrupted.

Suspicious, he squinted at her, "Here, it's not a love letter, is it?"

"No." Kitty was shocked. "No, Dusty, I promise it's no such thing." Hand on her heart, she said, "It's a surprise for my parents, is all."

His leathery face softened, "Oh that's all right then, give it here I'll put it with the rest of the mail."

"So, if there's a return letter..." she lifted an eyebrow.

"My 'orses won't breathe a word," he teased, tapping a finger to his nose. Taking the envelope from her, he deposited it in his mail satchel and refastened the leather straps. "Don't you worry none, your secret is safe with me, Missy," Dusty assured her, the old twinkle back in his eye. "Righto, I can't dally about here all day, I must be on my way. Congratulate Miss Meg for me, she's caught a good one there I'll wager. Still," he said, running his fingers through his long scraggy whiskers, "I expect I'll be seeing her myself, as she'll be ordering special things for the nuptials, eh?"

"I'm sure she will," Kitty replied.

Kitty watched Dusty's animals follow him around the bend and disappear from sight. Glory be she'd done it! Now, all she had to do was sit tight and wait, and hope the waiting didn't kill her. With a nervous skip in her step, Kitty continued on her way.

Meg absently fingered the petals of the red rose that blossomed on Annie's grave. A thorn scratched her; she sucked the spot of blood on her finger. She sat in the graveyard for a long time and prayed hard, prayed to all the patron saints in Ireland, and to any who would see fit to work on her behalf but there was only an eerie silence from the hollow blue sky. Not even a whisper of comfort from the long grass. The loss of her sister seemed even harder to bear these days when she so desperately needed a friend and confidant. Why did Annie have to die? Meg's prayers littered her heavy heart. Confused, she sat back on her heels and buried her head in her hands. Was Yankee right? Was she making a mistake?

She thought back to the first time she had met Yankee. He had come to the hotel with her brother, Dan. He was handsome and made her laugh. She thought he was interested in Annie. Besides, she had always told everyone she'd never be silly enough to marry a miner, and would probably never marry at all, but instead enjoy a teaching career and die a spinster. Yet whenever Yankee Brown was near, she was nervous and acted like a tongue-tied fool. Somehow he made her feel – vulnerable.

Yankee had driven her up to the Asterlys after her big fight with Ma, he'd been thoughtful and kind. He'd protected her the night of the big storm, he'd held her close and told her he loved her. The truth was she was afraid of him. He was a miner with wanderlust in his veins. He might disappear one day, like her father had, but not return. Meg believed if you loved someone with your whole heart they could hurt you beyond repair. Granted, he'd bought Riverstones Station on the other side of the lake, but he had station hands and a farm manager to work it while he chose to remain on the fields but what was to stop him going to the next big rush? The digger's life was a transient one, and many had left as soon as they heard news of the strikes being found in the West Coast. Why had he stayed? Had he truly stayed because of her?

Meg felt like a small boat tossed on stormy seas. Perhaps if she saw William she would know she had made the right decision. She brushed down her skirts and hurried back to the Asterlys homestead. She ran up the path, the stairs, and burst through the door. Startled, Lady Asterly put a warning finger to lips, signalling that baby Henry had just gone down.

"Sorry," Meg apologised.

Worried by the harried look on Meg's face, she asked, "Is everything all right my dear? You look like you have seen a ghost."

Meg pressed a hand to the grabbing stitch in her side. "William," she puffed. "Is William, up at the mine? Do you know?"

Lady Asterly shook her head. "Sorry my dear, I don't know." Lady Asterly steered Meg into the sitting room and to the nearest chair. "But you look like you could do with a nice cup of tea. I'll tell Lottie to put the kettle on."

Meg fell into the large gold-velvet armchair and gripped the ornate arms as if they were her anchor. Lady Asterly settled herself in the armchair opposite and studied Meg while she waited for Lottie to bring the tea.

Meg glanced up when she heard the rattle of cups as Lottie wheeled the tea trolley into the sitting room. She would have liked to strike up a friendship with Lottie but the girl was the most nondescript, sullen person, Meg had ever met. Deathly pale, she moved around the house as silently as a vapour. It was like Lottie had no soul, she never laughed or smiled, she just existed.

Lady Asterly waited patiently for Lottie to leave the room, then she poured the tea. Meg didn't know how Lady Asterly did it, but before you knew it, you had bared your soul to the bone. Meg prepared herself to resist Lady Asterly's kid gloved interrogation - the little woman could prize a pearl out of an oyster just by looking at it with her soft dove-grey eyes.

Kitty pressed on, she waved out to a few diggers as she passed, some waved back, most didn't notice her. There were numerous scars cut into the hills from machinery. Some sluicing guns were now operating on the terraces on the other side of the bank, and huge jets of water rocketed into the air.

At the waterfall called Bridal Veil, she cupped her hand and drank a couple of mouthfuls of chill water. If they accepted her for the apprenticeship, what then? What if they didn't? She closed her eyes trying to shut out the pain. They must say yes. Shaking off the dark thoughts, she continued on. She crossed the hastily constructed lower bridge and climbed the hill to Asterlys Terrace.

The Asterlys homestead was grand compared to the ramshackle cottages and huts that were scattered like a gambler throws dice. Gold fever running rife in their veins, miners gave little thought to their own comfort, while they had breath in their bodies, their only waking thoughts were to win as much gold as they were able.
Kitty climbed the front porch steps, stopped at the top, caught her breath, and knocked.

"Katherine!" Lady Asterly cried opening the door. "How lovely to see you."

"Thank you for inviting me," Kitty smiled.

"My pleasure," Lady Asterly assured her beckoning her inside. Putting the parcel on the wall stand, Kitty removed her bonnet and gloves.

Excited, Lady Asterly squeaked, "Is it?"

"Yes," Kitty replied, beaming with pride.

"Wonderful!" Lady Asterly clasped Kitty's hands in hers, and whispered in her ear, "The cake is iced."

In the background Kitty could see Lottie moving about as silently as a shadow. Kitty wondered if some terrible tragedy had befallen Lottie, and she could not bear to speak of it. Kitty picked up the parcel and followed Lady Asterly into the sitting room, where Meg sat glumly staring at the rug.

Meg lifted her head. "It's nice to see you, Kitty."

"And you, Meg," Kitty returned. She loved this house. Kitty looked admiringly around the room, even with a new baby in residence the place was spic and span. There was only the one servant, but Lady Asterly was a perfectionist and liked everything neat and tidy, and in its proper place. The fireplace had been polished with black-lead and shone like ebony. Gold-velvet armchairs sat either side of a pink velvet chaise lounge, and tapestry footstools were placed to the side, while a bear rug with its yawning mouth, lay stretched out on the floor before the fireplace. Silver and china treasures were beautifully displayed in highly polished walnut cabinets. White lace dollies and ornate fine porcelain vases stood proudly on top of a small round walnut table. Beautiful hand-painted china and brass lanterns hung from the ceiling. Lady Asterly's own handiwork adorned the walls and chairs. Everything was tasteful and in harmony with its surroundings.

"You must be tired, take a seat, my dear. Would you like a fresh cup?" Lady Asterly offered, her hand hovering over the teapot.

"Yes, thank you," Kitty replied. Turning to Meg and ceremoniously presenting the parcel, Kitty said, "I brought you your gown."

Meg stared at the parcel on her lap.

"I hope you like it." Kitty took a seat besides Meg.

"I'll love it," Meg answered, bleakly.

Kitty frowned, puzzled by Meg's reaction.

Lady Asterly poured the milk and added sugar, gave it a quick stir then handed Kitty the cup and saucer.

Kitty sipped her tea and glanced out the latticed window. "Where are the children?' she asked.

Lady Asterly smiled. "They went to the bakery with their father a little while ago they should be back soon." Lady Asterly raised her eyes to the ceiling. "And the baby, bless his heart, is sleeping. He suffers dreadfully with colic, poor dear."

"Poor darling," agreed Kitty.

"How are your parents, are they well?"

"Fighting fight," Kitty grinned.

Lady Asterly smiled discreetly.

"And Grace?" Meg asked.

"Walking," Kitty boasted as proudly as if Grace were her own.

"That's wonderful," Meg exclaimed, surprised.

Kitty giggled. "Ma doesn't think so - she's had to move everything up higher to keep Grace from getting into it. You can hear Ma muttering 'wee besom' all over the hotel."

Meg widened her eyes at her sister in disapproval. Kitty mouthed an apology.

Meg gently untied the string and peeked inside the tissue paper. "Oh Kitty," she breathed.

"Why don't you go to your room, and try on the gown while the children are away," Lady Asterly suggested. "You won't get a moment's peace when they return."

Kitty plucked at Meg's sleeve. "Yes Meg, come on."

A loud squawk came from upstairs.

"Oh dear, there's little Henry now, he's not been down nearly long enough." The crying grew louder and Lady Asterly hurriedly left the room.

Meg's room was out through the back door on the left-hand side of the porch. Kitty adored it. Kitty felt a pinch of jealousy. Meg was so lucky. There was a sash window with cross over lace curtains and sage-green velvet drapes, a double bed with a fine sage patchwork quilt, and a nice wooden dresser on which stood a blue china washbasin and pitcher, and at the far end of the room stood a large oval mirror. Kitty pulled the drapes to and Meg began to undress.

"Long white gloves and it will be perfect," Kitty said, tying the sash in place. The dress fitted perfectly. It had a high lace collar and lace cuffs, a white ribbon sash around the middle, three tiny embroidered rosebuds across the bodice, and pearl buttons down the back. It was a gown fit for a princess and with Meg's long slender frame, dark hair swept up in a bun, she looked beautiful.

Kitty stepped back and cocked her head to one side. "Oh Meg," she sighed, pleased.

Meg stared at herself in the mirror. "Thank you, Kitty, it is lovely. The detailing is just right and the lace not overdone." She took a deep breath and placed her hand on the washstand to steady herself.

Alarmed, Kitty's asked, "Are you all right? Do you feel faint?"

"Nerves," Meg answered turning away from the mirror. She placed a hand on her stomach and breathed deeply trying to calm herself. "I don't know if I'm ready to be a wife, or if I'll be a good one."

An invisible hand squeezed Kitty's heart, she chided herself for having such mean thoughts. Hugging Meg, she said, "Don't be silly, you'll make a wonderful wife and mother, you know how to cook and clean, and you are great with children. Besides," Kitty smiled as she added, "you are the best teacher in the district."

The corners of Meg's mouth twitched into a smile. "It's not hard to be the best at something when you are the only one."

"Precisely," Kitty laughed, her bright eyes shining.

They returned to the sitting room where they found little Henry, red-faced from crying, sitting on Lady Asterly's lap chewing his wooden rattle, dribble freely running down his chin.

A few minutes later Lord Asterly arrived home with the Asterly girls, little Miss Amelia and Miss Mabel. They entered the sitting room, their hands and faces thick and sticky with toffee.

Horrified, Lady Asterly shooed them away. "Look at you!" she scolded. "Like street urchins the pair of you. Go wash your hands and faces, then you can come back and say hello to young Miss Healey properly."

Hesitant to venture further, Lord Asterly stood in the doorway. "Good day, Miss Healey," he said stiffly with a slight bow.

"Good day," Kitty replied, amused. Lord Asterly might be in charge of men at the mine but his wife was the mistress of the home.

He excused himself saying he had some business to attend to at the mine. "I'll be back in time for supper," he told his wife, making a hasty escape.

Faces freshly washed, the girls came back and presented themselves to their guest. Amelia, being a shy, quiet child, hung back, watching from a distance, but little Mabel as curious as a kitten, coyly wormed her way closer until she was happily sitting on Kitty's lap.

"What do the letters say?" Mabel asked poking a chubby finger at the engraving on Kitty's signet ring.

"*Gentleness and Mercy*," Kitty told her.

"The other Miss Healey has one too," Mabel said pointing at Meg.

"Aye, hers says *Faithful and True*. Our father had them made for us," Kitty told Mabel. "Our other sister's one said, '*Goodness and Kindness*.'"

Mabel looked up at Kitty and frowned. "Where's your sister? Is she at home with your mother?"

"No, Annie's with the angels now," Kitty said quietly.

"Oh," Mabel's face fell. "Our brother, Benjamin, died too. He fell off the flying-fox and drowned. He's hiding in a hole in the ground and won't come out. Is your sister in the ground?"

"Yes, but that's just her body, she's with the angels now."
Meg flashed Kitty a warning look. Kitty had her own curious set of beliefs and was free with them. Protestant, Lord Asterly tolerated Catholics in his house as long as they didn't share beliefs.

"Did she take her ring with her to Heaven?" asked Mabel.

"No," Kitty replied trying to think of a fitting answer. "Our mother is keeping it safe until Annie's daughter, Grace, is old enough to wear it."

Mabel was about to ask more questions when Lady Asterly interrupted, "Mabel dear, please go and get your slate and show younger Miss Healey how you can write your letters."

"I'll draw a picture of your sister with the angels," Mabel promised, wiggling off Kitty's knee.

Mabel drew pictures while Amelia played a tune on the pianoforte for Kitty's entertainment. Mabel loved the novelty of Kitty being at the homestead and chatted away merrily filling the air with so many words that Kitty almost had to beg her to stop. Lady Asterly came to the rescue by telling the children it was time to wash for supper.

Supper was served by Lottie, who silently went about her chores. And Meg was almost as morose. Throughout supper, Meg remained distant, other than occasionally reminding the children of their manners she barely participated in conversation. Kitty had expected Meg to gush with praise over her gown, instead, she scarcely said a word.

"What's wrong?" Kitty whispered when Lady Asterly's back was turned.

"Nothing," Meg replied with a shrug.

Kitty felt a stab of disappointment. Meg didn't trust her. Thought she was too young to understand, no doubt, well she was old enough to feel hurt and she felt hurt now. Meg should have been delighted with the beautiful gown she'd made her, she'd put so much time and effort into its creation, if not her heart. Being around Meg tonight was as depressing as the darkest day in winter, and the fact that Meg wouldn't confide in her only served to irritate Kitty further. Clearly, Meg had decided she was too young to understand matters of the heart. Well, Kitty thought piqued, she knew what it was to love someone and not have them love you in return.

Desperate for air, Kitty escaped while Meg got the children ready for bed. She needed to talk to Annie. It was approaching dusk when she trod the familiar path to the graveyard. The moon hung like a sliced silver platter in the sky, the ground beneath her boots was damp and soft. Kitty took a moment to compose herself, she believed the dead deserved the dignity. Sometimes she missed Annie so much it felt like a deep ache. Their father said, Annie was too good for this world, and for that reason she had been taken from this world to be with the angels in the next. Kitty thought God was punishing them for the lie. Annie should have been the one enjoying seeing Grace take her first steps, and Annie should have been the one marrying William.

Kitty pushed open the gate and closed it quietly behind her. Careful not to disturb the dead, she tiptoed across the shadowy graveyard towards the simple white cross bearing the wrong name. Kissing her fingertips, Kitty touched the top of the wooden cross as if hoping to reach across the great divide separating the living and the dead. Kneeling on the cold, hard ground and taking a smooth round quartz stone out of her pocket Kitty placed it on the grave, crossed herself, and clasped her hands in prayer.

Kitty went through her rosary praying her normal recitations, then said aloud, "Forgive me," the words were caught by an invisible hand and thrown like a pebble across the thin night air. "I know it's a sin but I...I'm..."

"Kitty? Miss Kitty?" called a voice she recognized.

Kitty's mouth fell open. Was it a sign? Had Annie sent her a sign?

"Yes?" she answered turning quickly. She scrambled to her feet and smoothed down her crumpled skirts.

The gate opened, and clanged shut, footsteps hurried to her side. William Burns stood beside her. Tall and immaculately dressed, William was a handsome man with his dark hair and well-groomed goateed beard, mature looking for his twenty-three years.

He touched a hand to the rim of his top hat. "Miss Kitty what are you doing here at this time of night? It's not safe." But before Kitty could answer, he said, "Does your mother know where you are?"

Annoyed at being scolded like she was a naughty child, Kitty took a breath. "No, my mother doesn't know I'm here Mr Burns, however she does know I'm staying with the Asterlys tonight."

"But you shouldn't be here," he protested. "It's not safe."

Kitty tried to explain. "I needed to talk to Annie - alone. You do understand, don't you?" Of course, he did.

His expression softened. "I come here sometimes when I've got things on my mind," he admitted. "But this is not the time for a young lady to be visiting a graveyard. The Otago Hotel is nearby, not to mention the sly grog shanties, too many men under the influence of the drink and ...," he trailed off not wanting to alarm her. "It's best we be getting you back to the Asterlys." He tucked her arm in his and herded her towards the gate.

She held onto his arm and allowed him to lead, and waited while he opened the gate for her. He walked briskly and Kitty had to take two steps to each of his long-legged strides. They walked along the path back to the Asterlys house. When they reached the top step, he let go of Kitty's arm, straightened his jacket, knocked, and waited.

Meg opened the door and was surprised to find them on the stoop, preoccupied with getting the children to bed, she hadn't noticed Kitty slip out.

William removed his hat and tucked it under his arm. "How are you my dear?" he asked bowing slightly in deference.

Meg's smile did not quite reach her eyes. "Fine" she lied. She wondered if she should mention Yankee's visit. Maybe she should leave it be, but what if someone else said something?

William allowed Kitty to go inside first, then followed. They crowded the entrance way.

Meg said, "Did Kitty tell you she delivered my wedding gown today?"

He raised his eyebrows at Kitty. "No, she did not."

Kitty waited expectantly, hoping for Meg to tell William how much she loved it.

Bemused, Meg said, "And now here you are delivering Kitty."

He nodded grimly; his face serious. "I found her wandering like a stray puppy in the dark, and thought best return to the fireplace, where she would be safe and warm."

"I was visiting Annie," Kitty mumbled. She could feel her bottom lip starting to jut, and a fine pout developing. She wanted to say she's better company than you Meg but held her tongue.

"Thank you, William, it's thoughtful of you, isn't it Kitty?" Meg prompted.

Angry she was being coached, Kitty murmured her thanks.

"Would you like to take tea with us?" Meg asked, looking questioningly up at William.

"No thank you, Margaret, but perhaps you would care to join me outside on the settle?"

Meg hesitated. Turning to Kitty she said, "The Asterlys are in the sitting room reading the children bedtime stories. Lady Asterly is a fine storyteller, if you hurry you'll not miss the end."

Kitty disappeared into the next room, closing the door abruptly behind her.

William presented his arm. "Shall we?"

Meg draped her shawl around her shoulders and stepped outside. William followed, closing the door gently behind them.

Stars were beginning to pinprick the night sky. The settle on the veranda was cold and uninviting but it afforded some privacy. William's leg brushed hers as they sat down.

"Is everything all right, my dear?" William asked, his arm resting on the back of the settle. "Are you ill?"

"I'm fine," she assured him. She turned the question. "How are you?"

William lowered his voice. "I don't know what's wrong with Asterly. He's been particularly obstructive of late. I've been pushing for a dredge operation but he's against it, he thinks it would be unsustainable." He sighed. "He says getting the equipment here would out-weigh any benefit but I beg to differ. We have been arguing ever since. Just as well the sluicing is going well or I would...", aware she wasn't listening he broke off. "Does that trouble you?"

"No." She gazed down at her hands resting tidily on her lap, her father's signet ring on one hand and William's on the other. She took a deep breath then the words came out in a rush. "William, are you quite sure you want to marry me?"

"Nothing surer," he smiled, his arm coming to rest on her shoulder. Checking to see no one was around he drew her close. "How can I convince you?" he whispered in her ear. "Tell me what to do and I'll do it." When Meg didn't reply, he ploughed on, "Haven't I agreed that you can continue to teach, even though people might think I cannot support a wife if I send her out to work?"

Meg shied away. Adopting her haughty voice, she replied, "Teaching gives me great satisfaction, William. Education makes a difference in my pupils' lives, it gives them choices."

William nodded. "I don't doubt it my dear," he said catching her hand bringing it to his lips. "But when we have children of our own Margaret, I'd like you to mind them." He let her hand fall.

Meg bit her lip. She wanted children, of course she did, but there was plenty of time wasn't there? She was only coming seventeen. She shivered. For there to be children, there would have to be intercourse, and then should she get with child she might die in the delivery, or the child might, pregnancy was dangerous business. Annie had not shared what it was like to make love other than to say it hurt. Annie was sent away until the time to give birth was near. After Grace was born, she bled out and died. The world felt a darker place without her. Grace was beautiful though, a little piece of Annie left behind to help make their loss easier to bear. She drew her shawl close.

"You're cold, come we should go inside."

"A ghost walked over my grave is all," Meg assured him. And a ghost had. She had seen a vision of Annie with her slick dark hair fanned out on the starched white pillow, her crying newborn babe tucked into the crook of her arm, and blood - everywhere. Childbirth killed Annie, what was to stop it killing her? Panic began to beat inside Meg's ribcage like a trapped bird. What if she died trying to give birth to William's children? What if, like Annie, she died before her seventeenth birthday?

Meg's thoughts drifted back to her meeting with Yankee. What she should have said? What she should have done? Worry continued to gnaw at her like a rat refusing to leave a scrap.

She twisted the engagement ring on her finger. Her signet ring said 'Faithful and True'. She had accepted William's proposal and the honourable thing to do would be to see it through. William was a good man and she admired him. Was it enough?

William leaned closer. "What's wrong?" he asked. A large moth flew in his face he batted it away. "Don't you like the dress?"

"It's beautiful. Kitty did a grand job."

He sat back, frowning. "Is it the preparations then?"

"No, no it's all going well. Lady Asterly is enjoying the challenge of organizing the picnic, and Ma is letting her have her way. That in itself is a miracle," Meg admitted, smiling despite the growing knot of worry in her stomach.

Tired of guessing, William got to the point, "Then, what is troubling you?"

"Yankee Brown came to visit today," she said, gazing into the distance.

"Oh?" William's arm tensed. There was a long drawn out pause. "And?"

"Nothing." Meg avoided his eyes. "I just thought you should know."

Jealousy pricked, William's voice was short when he asked, "What did he want?"

Meg shrugged. "Nothing, other than to tell me he plans to wed."

William's shoulders relaxed. "Oh. That's good news."

"Yes, I think so," Meg watched as moths drawn to the light of the outside lanterns danced a deadly dance, perhaps they were mating, and dying.

William gave her knee a gentle squeeze. "See, I told you that everything would turn out all right in the end."

She desperately needed to confide in someone, visiting Annie's grave was not offering any solace these days, and Kitty wasn't old enough to understand. No, Meg decided, for want of anyone better, it would have to be her mother, for as much as she hated to admit it, Ma knew her better than she knew herself. "I'd better go inside, the Asterlys and Kitty will be wondering…"

"Not without a kiss," William said. Lifting her chin, he pressed his lips to hers.

Meg pulled away and abruptly stood up. "Goodnight William," she said quickly, and vanished inside.

Perplexed, Burns lingered for a few minutes frowning at the closed door. It had been a strange evening. After a day spent arguing with Asterly, he had been on his way to the Otago Hotel for a drink when he stumbled across Kitty, alone in the cemetery, and then Margaret's behaviour towards him was…odd, cold even. It made him feel uneasy. He shook his head trying to dispel the worm of worry. Seeing the lights of the Otago hotel winking in the distance he tapped his top hat twice so it settled nicely on his head, and feeling the pull of the tavern, he walked down the forked path and took the track on the left.

The nerve of that weasel Brown turning up here unsettling Margaret like that. He comforted himself in the fact he had won Margaret's heart fair and square. She had accepted his proposal and that was that. But for the life of him he couldn't understand why Margaret doubted his devotion? He had not compared her to Annie since the day they met.

The moment he met Annie; he was enchanted. He waited a respectable time before coming to Long Gully to declare his love for the young widow, and ask for her hand, only to be told Annie had died two months prior. As he'd gotten to know Margaret he soon realized although they looked similar, they were very different in nature. Annie was gentle, as graceful as a swan and as peaceful as a dove. Margaret might look delicate, but she had strong opinions and was as determined as an ox. He smiled recollecting her father saying, they were like the two local waterfalls, Gentle Annie and Roaring Meg.

There were times he wished Margaret wasn't quite so headstrong, especially when it came to educating the miners' children. He feared she would get too attached to her pupils and because Asterly was resisting his ideas they may have no other choice but to sell up and move on. It was probably best not to mention that until after the wedding - Margaret wouldn't want to leave the school, or her family behind. There was not long to wait, a few weeks and they would be wed. As he drew nearer the Otago Hotel his spirits lifted at the sound of the honky-tonk being played on piano. He entered the lively, noisy tavern and hung his hat on the peg. His rival Yankee Brown was engaged! Now that was something worth celebrating. Yes, by God he'd drink to that.

Chapter 2   Bruised

Marnie lay in a wretched heap on the cold wooden floor. She should have known better. They were never going to let her waltz out the door. The moment she mentioned Jack's name she could tell she had made a grave mistake. Madame raised her arm and struck Marnie hard, leaving a stinging imprint on her face. Marnie held her smarting cheek, her blue eyes filling with tears.

Hands curling into fists, Madame summoned Bill. Rumour had it that Bill was the Madame's son but no one knew for sure. A simpleton, Bill was a bull of a man, all muscles, no neck, and little brain. He kept the girls and patrons in check, and Madame kept him. Together they dragged Marnie into Madame's chambers, where Bill gave her a beating like no other. Small and slightly built, Marnie was no match for the muscle-bound bully who delivered her punishment. Hands protectively covering her head, she cowered, whimpering in the corner, hoping the end was near. Experience had taught her that it was best to stay down and keep quiet, and never answer back. Her right eye was swelling shut, her bottom lip was thick and split and she feared he may have cracked a rib. Frightened to move, she gasped in pain.

Bill stepped back and waited for further instruction. Arms folded across his expansive chest, he barred the door. There was no hope of escape. Her dark eyes flashing, Madame called down all manner of curses upon Marnie's head, and forbid Marnie to see, or ever speak to Jack Healey again.

"Do you understand?" Madame shrieked, her large bosom heaving.

Sobbing, Marnie nodded.

"Take her to her room, and make sure she stays there," Madame barked at Bill.

Marnie's tears blinded her as she struggled to her feet. She pressed her hand against the tongue-and-groove wall to steady herself and walked the narrow passage with Bill close on her heels. Reaching her room, Marnie twisted the brass doorknob, as she opened the door Bill gave her one last shove for good measure which sent her sprawling. She lay in a crumpled heap on the floor, eyes closed trying to shut out the pain. Marnie heard the door close and the key turn in the lock. She crawled to the rag mat. After a few minutes, she pulled herself up onto her bed where she lay curled in on herself like a sleeping fern frond, arms protectively wrapped around her belly.

Marnie hadn't expected much out of life. When news of gold broke, her family travelled from impoverished Ireland to lawless Ballarat when she was a child. Her father never struck it rich and they lived a destitute existence. Her mother died in childbirth, and the babe with her, leaving Marnie the only child from her parents' union. Blonde with big blue eyes, small and sweet-natured, Marnie had been cursed with prettiness. From the age of seven her father taught her things children do not tell. At ten her father died but she never shed a tear in mourning at his passing. Madame found her starving and sleeping rough on the streets and took her in. Madame fed her and groomed her, even paid for her passage to New Zealand. Marnie felt a strange sort of loyalty to a woman who made a lot of money from her body, of which Marnie saw none. Madame told Marnie she was keeping it safe for her. Still, she lacked for nothing - she was fed and clothed, and had a roof over her head. Customers gave her expensive presents, mostly perfume and jewellery, and she was everyone's favourite, for Marnie knew when to dimple, when to laugh, and how to please as Madame had groomed her well. She knew everything but how to live outside the four walls of her plush prison.

Holding in the hurt, Marnie realised she must forget such useless pipe dreams like marriage; for a girl like her it was too much to ever hope for. Broken, she cried herself to sleep.

Mary's wrist ached, it always did when it was going to rain. She broke it the night Charles Butler tried to kill her. Sometimes in her nightmares she could feel the heat of the flames and the madman's hands around her throat. She shuddered trying to bury the thoughts of that horrific night.

Some had it on good authority that Charles Butler had escaped to the West Coast but the Law had yet to find him and bring him to justice. And now, not only were they charging him with attempted murder but numerous other crimes as well. Victims had been found scattered about the canyon with a pick axe sized hole in the back of their skull, but new to the area and unknowns, no one claimed them as a relative so they were buried in paupers' graves in the nearest cemetery.

"There'll be rain soon, I'll wager," Mary told Grace, who was happily playing at her feet.

A sudden deluge hit the ground with ferocity and was gone just as quickly. Rain was bad for business - the track became a thick, greasy mess and kept the miners in their tents. Weather in the Canyon was extreme, blistering hot one minute, biting cold the next. Miners used every waking minute to eke gold out of the river working from daylight till dusk, but when the sun disappeared behind the mountains, they came to find comfort and companionship at her hotel.

It almost destroyed her when Charlie razed the hotel to the ground, but Jim promised to rebuild it for her, it was a solemn promise, and one he kept. The hotel boasted eight rooms, but Kitty and Grace shared one, she and Jim another, Pat had a room at the back, and there was a hut they kept especially for the priest when he was travelling through, so that only left five rooms to let. At present, there was no one staying at the hotel which meant less work, but an empty stable meant less income.

Mary loved the life, she enjoyed the men, the raw easy-going banter, but most of all she loved them spending their hard-earned winnings at her establishment. Most nights, the hotel was full of men wearing serge and moleskins, a mix of nationalities ready to slake their thirst, toasting their good fortune or cursing their bad luck. Most were happy if they had their mates by their sides and enough coin in their pockets to imbibe. She knew how to lift a man's spirits after a day spent in freezing water by a smile, a word, or a wink or two. Yet they all knew she was not a woman to be trifled with, she commanded respect and got it.

The patrons were surprised when Jim Healey returned from the dead. They assumed she was a widow, and she'd said nothing to make them think otherwise. Jim never worked behind the bar, nor joined them for a drink. Rumours were rife, and she'd heard some. Folks said it was because he feared he'd be overcome by the demon drink. Word about Lake County was that the young priest had a lot to do with the restoration of their estranged marriage. And they were partly right, the priest had been instrumental in melting the bitterness she felt towards her husband, but if she were honest it was because Jim had stopped drinking, and despite everything, she loved him.

The hotel kept her busy, and that made her happy. Maybe it was just because there was a lack of drinking holes in the area, and she served good grog. It didn't matter the reason why they frequented her hotel, just as long as they did. Satisfied the Long Gully pub should enjoy its usual patronage, Mary let the curtain fall.

Grace hid amongst the folds of Mary's skirts playing peek-a-boo. Mary smiled down at her little granddaughter. The wee one was a delight, but her dark hair stuck straight up like an upended broom, and no amount of licking and spitting would make it sit. The child had a look of her father about her but Mary chose not to see it. Grace's father would never come for her — married with three legitimate children he wanted his bastard to remain a secret. She made sure he paid dearly for what he'd done to Annie and the price of silence was a monthly maintenance payment made to a solicitor's office in Dunedin. There were rumours that Annie hadn't married a man called Tom O'Callaghan, but no one dared to challenge Mary to her face.

"Come on little one, there's work to do," Mary said, tucking the child into her hip.

Mary was sweeping the kitchen when Kitty came through the side door, her sodden bonnet dangling limply from her wrist. Her hair was dripping wet and her skirts muddied and soaked through. A twist of red hair hanging rakishly over one eye made her look disreputable.

Mary glanced up at the clock. "You are home early," she said, surprised.

Kitty shook the drips from her hair, took her boots off, and stood in a puddle of wet stockings. Grace bravely toddled to her as fast as her pudgy, unsteady legs could go. Kitty scooped Grace into her arms and planted a wet kiss on the baby's soft, warm cheek. Grace squirmed and giggled with delight.

Despairing, Mary put the broom aside. "Pssht, now the baby is wet as well," she grumbled.

"She'll dry, won't you, love." Kitty put Grace down, held her steady for a moment then let go. Grace fell on her napkin-cushioned bottom with a soft ploomph.

"Here, dry yourself," Mary said chucking Kitty a towel. "You should have taken your oilskin? Do you want to catch your death?"

Voice muffled by the towel, Kitty replied, "I didn't expect it to rain."

Kitty went to her room to get changed and Grace crawled after her. Mary smiled, wherever Kitty was, Grace was not far behind. At fourteen there were times Kitty showed responsibility beyond her years, yet at other times she could be as flighty as a tomtit. Mary shook her head. For the life of her, she couldn't figure out how the same ingredients went into the recipe but each child came out entirely different. Out of her five surviving children, Kitty was the youngest, and the image of herself when she was young. Now the older girls weren't there to help, Mary relied heavily on Kitty, and kept her busy with the washing, cooking, and cleaning. Idle hands were the devil's playground and she wasn't going to give Kitty time to get into any mischief. Mary's heart grew heavy, if only she'd kept better watch over her children then Annie would be alive today. She shook off the ghosts and started to prepare dinner.

Kitty helped, and soon the glorious aroma of freshly baked bread and rabbit stew filled the kitchen. Hungry, Grace kept getting underfoot. Kitty was quiet. Unusually so. Something was wrong. Jim often joked that Kitty could happily talk the leg off a three-legged pot.

Using the long-handled paddle, Mary took the bread out of the oven. "You haven't said much. How was your visit?"

Kitty popped Grace into the highchair. She checked the sides of the tablecloth for evenness as if it was suddenly of great importance. "There's not a lot to tell," she replied.

Perturbed, Mary asked, "Did Meg like the gown?"

"I'm not sure," Kitty answered truthfully.
Grace impatiently banged her spoon on the highchair's wooden tray.

Kitty placed the bowls on the bench. "You can ask her yourself; she'll be here tomorrow."

"Oh?" Mary looked up sharply. "But it's not Sunday."

"Well, there you go, Ma," Kitty grinned. "Maybe Meg is trying to be as unpredictable as the weather."

Pat and Jim went back to the hotel, stripped off, and left their wet things to dry on the back porch. Ravenous, and wearing little more than their undergarments, Jim and Pat traipsed into the kitchen, tired but happy after a good day's pickings.

Jim kissed Grace's soft downy head in passing, and glancing over Mary's shoulder to see what was cooking, he patted his wife lightly on the bottom.

"Smells good, Mary, me love, so good in fact me nose carried me all the way home."

Mary waved the tea-towel at him. "Get away with ye, silly old fool."

Jim clutched his chest as if he was mortally wounded.

Mary scolded him saying, "You'll put some trousers and a clean shirt on before you'll sit at my table, James Healey," turning to Pat, hands on hips, she said, "and that goes for you too, Patrick Healey."

They knew better than to argue when their full names were in use so they disappeared to their respective rooms to change. Exasperated, Mary sighed, the pair of them were alike in many ways. Pat was as spindly as a spider, all arms and legs like his long-limbed father, but his hair was red where Jim's was dark. Although they hadn't been working The Redemption long, the trust growing between the two was heart-warming. But Pat wasn't over the loss of his sister, or his best mate Tiny, but occasionally there was a flicker of humour on his fiddle-face that gave Mary a glimmer of hope that, in time, he'd return to his old light-hearted self.

Hands and faces washed, changed and ready for supper, the men took their places at the table. Mary dished up. They waited till she was seated before clasping hands and bowing their heads in prayer. Jim thanked the good Lord for keeping them safe from harm, and for the food they were about to eat, before cheekily adding, "and for the blessing of not only a fine-looking wife, but one who can cook so well." He winked at Mary who rewarded him with a smile.

Hunched over his bowl of stew, Pat ate like he thought someone might try and steal it from him.

Mary passed the basket of thickly buttered bread to him. "Kitty says Meg's visiting tomorrow."

Pat frowned. "Why?" he asked, his mouth full.

Jim looked at Mary, his brow furrowed. "It's not Sunday tomorrow, is it?"

"No, it's Saturday," Kitty replied, breaking off a crust, she handed it to Grace who greedily rammed it into her mouth.

Mary reached for the salt shaker. "Meg probably wants to spend as much time as she can with us now before her marriage."

"Or maybe she's running away," Kitty said softly.

Mary sharply turned her head. "What makes you say that?"

"Nothing." Kitty shrugged. "Just a feeling."

Grace let out a high-pitched squeal. Mary shovelled a spoonful of apple and custard in the child's mouth to keep her quiet.

Pat sniffed and wiped a finger under his nose. "I reckon she's wants to get away from the place. I hear Burns plans are causing friction. I hear the business partners are like two sticks of gelignite left in the sun."

"That's none of your business," Mary snapped. "You'd best keep your mouth shut and your nose out of it."

Pat tore off a hunk of bread and wiped his bowl clean, he was silent for a moment then said, "Well then, what is Meg worried about, Ma?"

"I don't rightly know but I'm prepared to get to the bottom of it," Mary told him.

Jim patted Mary's hand, "Don't you worry your pretty little head about it, darlin', I'll have a wee word in Meg's ear tomorrow, and find out what's troubling her, all right?"

"Jim Healey, you think you are the Lord God Almighty and can fix the world and all its problems," Mary shook her head at him but she was pleased none the less. Meg and Jim shared a special bond. She glanced up at the clock. "Quick, eat up! There's dishes to be done."

Life spent on the river was tough so Mary made sure the men forgot about the hardships of the day when they entered her hotel. They bet on cards, played billiards, laughed and drank to their hearts content. Some played the accordion, the fiddle or a tin whistle, and could belt out catchy tunes. Tonight, Billy Chicken was playing the squeezebox with great gusto, while his mate Little Tom clapped and tapped his hobnailed boots in time, and Sprat crowed like a rooster in what he thought was singing. Mary gave the men good grog, danced reels and jigs with them until they could dance no more.

As the clock neared midnight, Mary rang the bell and shouted, "Almost closing time boys!" There was a surge towards the bar as they ordered last-minute drinks before they were chased out into the inky night. Footsore, Mary closed up. Bolting the door, she fell against it exhausted, thinking she'd never felt happier.

Jim waited until he heard the bell and the last patron being shooed away into the night, before he appeared in the tavern. Together they straightened the chairs, did the dishes and wiped down the tables. Always mindful to keep the drink away from Jim, Mary emptied the dregs into a bucket of slops and quickly disposed of them into the pig bucket. Jim reckoned the pig was never sober. One by one, Mary trimmed the paraffin lanterns. Using a candle to light the way to their room, she carried the holder at arm's length, the spilling light made their shadows long and thin on the dark panelled walls.

"How were the takings, love?" Jim asked, following her up the hallway.

"Fair enough, it was a rare busy night," Mary replied. "I had to douse Sticky with a bucket of cold water, he was passed out under the billiard table again."

She opened the door to their bedroom. Their room was bathed in warmth, the fire glowing in the grate cast shadows that moved around the dark panelled walls like long ghostly fingers. Mary lit the bedside candles. Jim untied his heavy boots, pulled them and his woollen socks off, he wriggled his cramped toes.

"I'm looking forward to hitting the hay," he said, not bothering to undo the buttons on his shirt he tugged it off over his head.

"You and me both," Mary agreed. "And If that blinking rooster crows at four again, so help me God, it'll be in the pot."

Stepping out of his trousers, Jim put them over the arm of the chair, and fell into bed. Resting his arms behind his head he sighed, a contented man. He couldn't help marvelling at how things had changed in a short time. Last year, he slept in the stables for fear Mary might kill him with a cast iron skillet if he dared to set foot in the hotel. He wished he was cured from his need for the drink, for the pains Mary took to keep him from it bruised his heart. He knew it would take years to earn her trust again, if ever. He hoped little by little trust would come.

Mary pulled the pins from her unruly hair and it tumbled past her shoulders in a mass of springy ginger curls. He loved her hair, it crackled, like her, it was fiery and wild. He watched as Mary undressed slowly in the soft yellow candlelight.

"What are you thinking?" she asked, threading her arms through her linen nightgown.

"Come here little darlin' and I'll show you what I'm thinking," Jim answered, turning back the covers.

Mary climbed into bed beside him. His fingers drew slow lazy circles up and down her thighs, his touch featherlight on her milky skin.

As Mary was drifting off to sleep, she kissed him and murmured, "You've a persuasive way about you James Healey."

Holding her close, Jim tucked a wayward curl behind Mary's ear and lovingly kissed her cheek. Mary's breathing was soon a slow steady rhythm. But Jim was restless and couldn't sleep, worried, he kept wondering what was up with his wee Meg.

It was still dark when Marnie awoke. Most of the brothel was sleeping. Careful not to disturb her snoring customer, she lifted his heavy arm off her, and slipped out of bed. She gingerly touched her right eye, it was swollen shut and tender to the touch, but the bruising was coming out. After quietly dressing in the dark, she tiptoed downstairs. She could just make out the silhouettes of men lying, snoring, on the lavish furniture in the downstairs lounge. Believing it would be bad for business to be seen to be inhospitable, so as long as they didn't vomit on her fine furnishings' Madame let them be, and didn't turf them out. However, she had no trouble getting rid of any whom didn't have any coin left in their pockets.

Thinking of the overstuffed baboon she'd rolled away this morning, Marnie sighed. He hadn't minded her looking a bit roughed up. For six long months Jack had been spouting tales of love, telling her he wanted to marry her, and take her away from all this. But he was just a boy. And, if they got away, far enough away that they wouldn't be caught, he was only starting out in his trade as a smithy, how could they survive? There was still such a shortage of women on the goldfields men didn't seem too worried by the prospect of having a whore for a wife. And, there were those who could afford to buy her outright from Madame, should she be willing to sell. Other girls had tried to escape, one had been so badly beaten that she had cocooned within herself and refused to speak. Another 'fell' off a cliff. Marnie shuddered remembering seeing the girl's broken body, the coffin was left open as a warning.

Tiptoeing across the bare floorboards she picked up her lace parasol from the mahogany coat-stand and gave Bill, who was sleeping by the door, a nudge.

"Can you open the door?" Marnie whispered.

47

Bill popped open one sleep encrusted eye and regarded her with suspicion. "Why? Where are you going so early?" He stretched, yawned, and scratched his backside.

"Madame's orders," Marnie lied. "She wants something special from the bakery for the Major for breakfast."

Bill grunted and fumbled with the keys hanging from his belt. Gathering himself to his feet he leaned against the wall for support. Unlocking the padlock, he pushed open the door. Heart skipping a beat, Marnie quickly ducked underneath his heavily muscled arm and disappeared into the empty street. She heard the door close behind her, then holding her aching ribs, she ran.

It was getting lighter. The sun was pulling away from the earth casting a soft golden glow upon the lake causing it to sparkle like cut crystal. The town would soon be rousing itself, and if she was coming, then she was late. Jack's stomach squirmed like a sack full of newborn kittens. Had she changed her mind? Daisy told him Marnie got a hell of a hiding for even suggesting leaving The Ladies of the Lake. That, Bill, the swine, had almost cracked one of her ribs and Marnie was forbidden to see or speak to him ever again. Daisy was sent to tell him to keep away. Devastated, Jack felt like all the colours in the world has faded to black. He ached with longing for the girl who stole his heart.

Then, two days later, Daisy popped her head around the Smithy shop door and cryptically told him, 'Little lady wants to run away. Meet her tomorrow at dawn, at the Bank of New South Wales corner.'

Jack was about to give up hope when he saw a winged shape coming out of the gloom. Wearing a hooded cloak and carrying something, a woman hurried towards him. He ran to greet her. Marnie fell into his arms. He embraced her. Wincing in pain, she let out a muffled groan. Apologizing, he released his hold and gently kissed her cheek. Her lip was split, her eye was a nasty purplish yellow. Fear bit him.

"Come quickly," Jack said, taking her hand. They hurried along the alleyway towards the smithy shop. He had to get her away from here, and fast, before they found her and took her back to the brothel. The first place they'd come looking would be his shop and if they caught her, then they'd really hurt her. To throw them off the scent he'd have to stay, and Marnie would have to disappear, far enough away that Madame wouldn't bother to try and retrieve her merchandise. The only place he could think to hide Marnie was the Welcome Home. He couldn't leave Queenstown, not yet, or it would look too suspicious. No, there was nothing else for it, he'd have to take Marnie to Moonlight, and ask Dan to deliver her to Ma. Then, once the dust settled, he'd travel up to Long Gully and make her his wife.

The building's walls were streaked with soot. The smithy shop smelt like damp dirt, horse, and musty leather. Tools were arranged neatly on hooks, and jars sat in rows on the rough sawn timber shelves. Ropes were coiled like snakes on the floor and harnesses hung from the walls. A water trough stood beside the square stone well in the corner, where a fire burned, a large bin of coal beside it, with a long-handled shovel at the ready.

Watching Jack saddle Mr Bennett's horse, Pepper, Marnie clutched her parasol tightly like a weapon. Pepper stood patiently as Jack buckled the saddle around his girth.

Marnie's ribs ached. She closed her eyes trying to shut out the pain. "Where are we going?" she whispered from the gloom. The horse's ears twitched as if he was curious to know.

Jack patted Pepper's neck. "To my brother Dan's. He'll take you to Ma's and I'll come get you as soon as I can."

"What?" Marnie cried, stepping out of the shadows. "You can't leave me! I ran away to be with you!"

Jack turned away, unable to bear the horrified look on Marnie's battered face. "If I leave now, they are sure to come looking at one of my relatives."

"But..." she objected.

"I need to stay here a little longer, and earn enough to get us safely away from here."

Marnie felt weak. Had she made a terrible mistake? Should she try and return to the brothel now, before it was too late? "I... don't want..." she gasped, struggling to find the words. "I want to be with you."

"You will be. Forget the notion of trying to ride side-saddle, you'll need both legs to stay seated," he instructed. "Foot."

Afraid, Marnie didn't know what to do. If she returned to the brothel, she might end up down some abandoned mine shaft somewhere. No, she couldn't go back, but she didn't want to go to Mary Healey's hotel either, she just wanted to run away with Jack, and be far enough away from her old life, in a place where no one knew anything about her. Jack might be young, and poor, but he was earnest, and he loved her. Desperate, she glanced nervously at the end of a coil of rope dangling from the rafters. She'd heard things about Mary Healey and none of them kind.

"But I need you," she insisted, clinging to him.

Kissing her softly, Jack said, "It won't be for long, I promise. It's for the best."

"Your mother will hate me!"

"She will not be best pleased," he admitted. "But darlin' you can charm a rattlesnake so I'm sure you'll have my Ma eating out of your hand soon enough. Besides, Da has a knack with Ma. He'll talk her round, you'll see. You'll love my little sister Kitty; she'll talk your ear off but she's lovely. I promise to come as soon as I can."

Marnie was close to tears.

"Foot."

She grunted as she placed her foot in the stirrup and hoisted herself onto the horse's back.

"I don't think you'll need the parasol," he said, amused.

"I might," Marnie replied indignantly. For some strange reason, she felt she must have something, that was hers, and hers alone.

Shaking his head, Jack rolled the parasol inside a blanket and secured it to the back of Pepper's saddle. Regardless if she would need it or not, they couldn't leave it behind, it would be evidence Marnie had been there. Leading the horse out of the smithy shop, he bolted and padlocked the large wooden doors behind them. Jack climbed onto the stone wall, mounted the horse, settling himself behind Marnie. Arm about her waist, he gave Pepper a sharp nudge in the flanks and urged the horse on. Marnie's head bumped solidly against Jack's chest as Pepper trotted along the lane. Jack was relieved to have Marnie safe in his arms but knew it was imperative to get her away from danger. They must make for Moonlight.

They were lucky, only the bakery shop lanterns were burning brightly, the rest of the town still was blanketed in sleep. The ride to Moonlight was not a long one but there weren't any proper roads, just tracks. Their heads struggling with fears, they rode in silence. Pepper was a faithful sure-footed workhorse not used to been ridden at pace, and the way was rough in places. Jack urged the tired horse on. The ground was narrow and uneven, Matagouri bushes reached out long thorny fingers trying to claw them as they passed. Marnie's ribs pained her, but apart from a grunt of discomfort now and then, she didn't complain.

Jack reined up beside a stone hut set a little way back from the river. There was a wooden sign tacked on the hut's door.

"What's the sign say?" Marnie whispered.

'Stone Hall.' Jack chuckled.

A dog barked, and Marnie tensed. Pepper snorted and pawed the ground.

"It's all right," Jack said, sensing her fear, "it's just Tu." He dismounted and gave Pepper a reassuring pat before helping Marnie down. He held her in his arms for a moment as if trying to impart courage.

The dog kept barking, and they could hear stirrings inside the hut. Someone shouted something in a native tongue. Surprised, Marnie glanced at Jack, her eyes wide with fright.

"That's Maori Harry, you'll like him," Jack told her. He tethered Pepper to the hitching post where two other horses stood, their tails swishing. They acknowledged the newcomer with a nudge. Pepper pushed between them and drank greedily from the water trough.

There was a ruckus coming from inside the hut. Someone swore. Marnie hid behind Jack as he knocked.

The door opened, and a black and white collie flew at them barking furiously. Terrified, Marnie froze. Barring his sharp pointed teeth, ears lowered, Tu crouched and growled. Jack gave Tu his hand to sniff.

"Come!" Dan commanded. The sheepdog obeyed and half crouched beside Dan, still eyeing the intruders warily as if daring them to make a false move.

"Jack!" Dan stepped outside. "What are you doing here?" Then he caught sight of Marnie. "What's she doing here?"

"She's with me," Jack told him, immediately on the defence.

A woman in their midst was a novelty for the diggers. Dressed, only in their long-johns, Harry and Yankee appeared in the hut doorway. Marnie couldn't help staring at the swirling tattoos covering Harry's face. Tall and powerfully built with long black hair and coal-black eyes, Harry was a formidable sight. Marnie stuck to Jack like she was pinned to his side. Maori Harry nodded, his dark eyes assessing Marnie's bruised face. Just as she was fascinated by his appearance, he was equally intrigued by hers.

Eager to be on the road, Jack was impatient. "Can we come in?" he said shortly.

"Sorry," Dan apologized, waving Harry and Yankee aside. "Yankee, put the billy on mate."

Yankee took Jack by the hand and gave it a good shake. "Good to see you again mate," he paused, "and nice to meet you…er…?"

"Marnie," she replied, managing a timid smile. Feeling self-conscious, Marnie realized she must look a mess with her smeared makeup, black eye and thick lip.

Yankee chucked a pair of moleskins and a serge shirt to Harry, which he reluctantly put on.

"I'm Yankee, and this here is Harry, and his dog Tu," Yankee said formally. He hopped about trying to put his trousers on. "Can't make tea for a lady in nothing but my underwear, can I?"

Hardly a lady, thought Dan, disgusted. He knew what she was. He had seen Marnie soliciting outside *The Ladies of the Lake*.

Yankee buttoned his fly and tied his red sash about his waist. "Am I fit for entertaining?" he asked, barefoot and grinning.

"The billy," Dan reminded.

"Hold ya bloomin' horses," Yankee grumbled. "We only got four mugs but don't worry mate, I'll go without." Yankee swung the billy over the open fire and stoked life into the embers. He reached up and got down four battered tin mugs off the rough sawn shelf. "Dan seems to have misplaced his manners, must have left them in his cot this morning."

In no mood for fooling, Dan glowered.

Marnie surveyed the dingy hut. There was a clay pipe which acted as the chimney, two tea chests served as tables or chairs. A sack cot in one corner and a ledge that acted as a bed in the other, and on the floor lay a flax mat and a grey woollen blanket. The hut was rudimentary but seemed to suit the men's purposes well enough. Dan motioned for Marnie and Jack to take a seat on the upturned crates while he sat on the stone ledge, his hands pressed on his thighs. Tail wagging, Tu sniffed Jack first, then Marnie. Afraid, Marnie pulled her hand away.

"He won't bite," Harry told her. Grinning, he added, "but I might."
The look of sheer horror on Marnie's face made Harry laugh.

"He's joking," Jack told her. He was feeling agitated, aware time was getting on and he must return before Bennett arrived at the forge.

After a couple of sniffs, Tu decided Marnie was more friend than foe and surprised her by lying down and resting his head on her feet.

"So, what brings you to Moonlight?" Dan asked.

"Utu?" Harry frowned across at Yankee.

"Huh? What's that mean?" Jack asked.

"Revenge or something like avenge," Yankee interpreted. "Harry wants to know if you want us to deal to whoever beat Marnie," he explained.

"Oh, no. Thank you, though. I just need to get her to safety." Jack got straight to the point. "I need your help, Dan. I need you to take Marnie up to Ma's. I can't go myself but I'll be up there soon as I can. Take her for me, please?"

Dan frowned at Marnie. "Why? Has she run away?"

"Yes," Jack replied, reaching for Marnie's hand, "with me." He continued to speak plainly, "As soon as we can we are going to wed, but first I need to throw them off the scent. I reckon they will come to the smithy looking for Marnie. They will expect to find her

55

there, but she'll be safe with Ma, and they won't know to look that far."

Dan looked at Jack like he was deranged, he blurted, "Are you mad? You want me to take her up to Ma's?" He shook his head. "She'd be safer back where she came from."

Marnie's fear was making her feel sick to her stomach. If they found her, they would kill her.

Yankee interrupted. "We've no cow so you'll have to take it black. Sugar?" he asked digging a spoon in a tin.

"Two please," Marnie replied, grateful for the diversion. Yankee added two heaped spoons of sugar to the tea and gave it a stir.

"Thank you," she said, taking the cup from his hand.

Jack indicated black was fine while Harry got his own, which smelt strongly of liquor. He sat cross-legged on the hard-packed dirt floor staring up at Marnie. Marnie dropped her gaze. Yankee handed Dan the remaining mug which Dan accepted with a nod of thanks.

A weighty silence fell. Yankee leaned against the far wall, smoking his pipe. "I'll take her up," he offered.

Dan shot Yankee a dark look then turned his attention to Jack. "You think Ma will..."

Jack interrupted, "I know she won't approve but she'll come around, eventually. Can you take Marnie for me, yes or no?" He couldn't hide the desperation in his voice. He must get back if he didn't return soon Mr Bennett might report his horse stolen.

"I said I'll take her," Yankee repeated.

"The hell you will," Dan snapped. "If anyone's going, it'll be me."

56

"Then you'll do it?" Jack breathed a sigh of relief.

"Aye, I must be as mad as you are, you silly young cockerel," Dan replied. Rubbing his hand across his stubbly chin he took a fortifying sip of tea; God help them all.

They clustered outside and watched as jack prepared to leave. He pressed his rosary beads into Marnie's hand, "Here, these will keep you safe," he told her kissing her. Then he clambered up on Pepper and rode away. With a sinking heart Marnie watched him disappear. Had he deserted her? Could she trust him? Or anyone? The sun was struggling to penetrate the low-lying clouds that shrouded the mountains in a thick mist, and she was grateful for the warmth of her fur-lined cloak. She tucked the rosary beads away in her cloak pocket and sat despondently on a log by the hut door, waiting. She felt like crying but knew she must stay strong, even if it was only to gain the men's respect. Tu sat beside her, his head on resting on her feet, his sorrowful eyes looking up at her. She reached down and patted the collie's head.

Dan packed his saddle bags and saddled his horse. Marnie decided the brothers weren't alike in looks. Dan's hair was dark and wavy and he had a stubbly beard that seemed reluctant to grow whereas Jack was lean, lanky, clean shaven, tall and red-haired. She guessed Dan was only a couple of years older than herself.

Dan shook his head as he secured Marnie's lace parasol inside the saddle blanket so it wouldn't be in the way. Where she was going, she wasn't going to need a lace parasol but a strong pair of hands. He resented having to be the one to take Marnie to Long Gully but there was no other way around it. He couldn't let Yankee go and have his heart broken all over again, and it wasn't right to involve Harry in his family's messy affairs. It was ironic that he was charged with the responsibility of taking this woman to his mother's hotel when he despised women like her. He thought any man seduced by such women were fools. His brother, Pat, consorted with harlots and charlatans and now here was his youngest brother planning to marry one! She could probably hide her background with some respectable clothing but her swinging hips gave her trade away. Jack was clearly besotted with the girl, but she was hardly someone he could take home to mother. God in Heaven, what was the young fool thinking?

Dan gave Marnie a leg up on Goldie, and once she was settled, he mounted and gave his partners a couple of last minute instructions before they moved off.

Yankee called after them, "You're going to miss a fine feed of Maori hen tonight boyo."

"You can have my share," Dan replied. He grinned. "I'll think of you when I'm enjoying a helping or two of Ma's Irish stew."

"You're all heart." Yankee clutched his chest as if pained.

Harry said to Marnie, "Remember if you need..." he smacked his fist into his palm.

"Thank you, I'll remember Harry," she nodded.

Yankee waved. "Take care, Marnie."

Mary inclined her head. "Thank you. Bye, Yankee. Bye, Harry." The men waved and Tu barked a farewell.

Dan held the reins in one hand, kept one arm about Marnie's waist, and used his legs to guide the horse.

Marnie was acutely aware of being an unwanted burden. She saw Dan's displeasure in the tautness of his body, the way the veins

58

in his neck stood out, and his jaw clenched. She didn't dare speak for fear of being rebuffed. She wished Yankee had been the one to take her to the hotel, he was nice.

As if reading her thoughts Dan broke the uncomfortable silence. "I couldn't let Yankee take you."

"Why?"

Dan sighed. "Because he's heartbroken, that's why. My sister accepted another's proposal. And he wants any excuse to see her again to try and convince her she's making a mistake. But when my sister has made up her mind she's harder to move than a mountain. She'll only hurt him some more, and then Harry and I will be the ones who to have to pick up the pieces. He's been moping for months now, Harry and I can't bear it any longer, it's like living with a corpse who won't have the good grace to lay down and stay buried."

Marnie realized she knew very little about Jack's family. She'd heard tales of Mary Healey, and she knew Pat, for he was a frequenter of the brothel, but she knew nothing of the rest of the family Except Annie, she'd met Annie once.

"Who is your sister marrying?"

"Meg's to wed, Mr William Burns, next month. Maybe then Yankee will stop mooning around like a lovesick cow and get on with the business of prospecting. Mind you, he's bought a sizeable chunk of land with his share of the gold so perhaps he'll go farm that. I hope he don't, for all my grumbling about him, he's a good mate, and I'd miss him."

"That must mean you are as wealthy as he," Marnie noted.

There was a cold silence. Marnie realised he thought her a gold digger ready to pluck any purse, it saddened her that just because she was a whore, he thought she was also a thief.

Searching for something to say, she said, "Yankee is a fine-looking man, he won't have trouble finding someone. "

"It's just as well you're spoken for then, isn't it," Dan replied, his tone cutting.

They fell silent again. Whatever she said would be wrong. It was best to say nothing. Marnie was worried, she had no idea what to expect, and she was scared. Had she jumped from the frying pan into the fire? Since the age of ten all she'd known was the brothel and she didn't know what to expect outside its four walls. She'd heard stories about Mary Healey and none of them had been kind. Even her sons were afraid of her. Marnie swallowed. This wasn't how she thought things would be but it was too late now, she couldn't go back. God no, she would never go back.

Chapter 3   Dead Man

Jack made it back to the forge before Mr Bennett roused himself for the day. Only the stable hand in the livery next door knew that Pepper had been ridden hard, but he promised not to mention it when sixpence crossed his palm. It was dark and smoky in the forge. Jack lit the kerosene lantern and hung it from the rafters. Stripping off his jacket, he rolled up his sleeves and donned his leather apron. He pumped the massive bellows to stoke life back into the embers, and once the fire was roaring, he heated horseshoes until they were glowing. He hammered them into shape on the large anvil, but his mind was fixed on Marnie.

He had been besotted with her from the first day they met. It was the day after his accident when the tree fell the wrong way and he wasn't able to escape in time. It was a blessing. He hated life at the timber mill. The sex-starved men saw him as young and girlish and ripe for the picking. He was afraid to turn in to his cot each night. He shuddered at the dark memories; he couldn't forget how they violated him. He'd wondered after being sodomised if he would be ever able to have natural relations with a woman. He thought he was damaged beyond repair.

It was Pat who collected him from the infirmary, and having had enjoyed some windfall, paid for their stay at the brothel until he was well enough to travel up to the hotel. Like an angel Marnie watched over him, she made him feel whole. She made him feel like a man, not a boy, and he loved her for it. She would be safe at Long Gully. His Ma might strike the fear of God into the hearts of men but she was a kindly soul underneath, even if you had to dig deep to find it.

Mr Bennett grunted, 'Mornin',' to Jack, and set to work repairing a broken wagon wheel. Bennett was a reserved man and apart from his bulbous nose he had a bland round face and careworn eyes. Bennett kept mostly to himself, and Jack thought it wise to keep his own counsel. His back to the doors, Jack didn't see Bill coming until he barged past, nearly knocking Bennett over.

Grabbing Jack by the collar, Bill lifted Jack off his feet, and slammed him hard against the wall. Stretched on the tip of his toes, Jack struggled for breath as Bill's fingers squeezed his wind pipe. Jack desperately tried to pry Bill's hands off but he had an iron grip. Bill pulled his knotted fist back, ready. Madame bustled in, in a flurry of lace and emerald silk skirts and demanded to know where Marnie was hiding.

"What's the meaning of this?" Mr Bennett snapped, coming to Jack's rescue. "For God's sake put the lad down he can't breathe," he cried.

Ignoring Bennett, Bill shook Jack again, banging his head against the bricks. "You heard the lady, where you hidden her?" he growled.

Jack struggled, trying to claw Bill's fingers from his neck. Turning blue, he felt like he was about to pass out.

Madame signalled Bill to lower Jack, "He can't tell you if he can't breathe," she said, practically.

Bill let go and Jack fell gasping to the flagstone floor.

"What the hell is going on?" Bennett demanded, his dander up and his blood pressure boiling, his face went as red as the tip of his bulbous nose.

The Madame gave the blacksmith an austere glare. Pointing her jewelled finger at Jack, she declared, "He's got one of my best girls." Bennett didn't react so Madame continued, "Marnie is missing." Sweetening her tone, she said, "Perhaps you have seen her?"

Outraged, Bennett said, "How dare you come in here spouting ridiculous accusations," he blustered. "The lad's been with me the whole time. If you don't leave, I'll call the constable and have you arrested."

Madame turned her attention back to Jack, "I'm warning you," she said her voice hard and cold, "If I find you're hiding her..." she bent down, got up close, close enough for him to smell she'd been eating onions, "I'll have you flogged. I'll have the meat stripped from your bones, boy. Do you understand?"
Labouring for breath, Jack wheezed.

"Out!" Bennett yelled, his anger erupting. When neither intruder made a move, Bennett walked over to the well of fire and using the long-handled tongs picked up a red-hot horseshoe from amongst the embers. Jabbing the horseshoe at them, he cried, "Now!"
Bill stood his ground, his arms folded across his massive chest as if daring Bennett to brand him.

"Come on, Bill," the Madame said tugging on Bill's heavily muscled arm. "This is not over," she warned Jack. "I want Marnie, and if you value your scrawny neck, you'll return her."

Chest heaving with indignation, Bennett chased them out the door with the firebrand. When they were gone Bennett threw the horseshoe aside, it clanged as it hit the long-handled shovel resting in the corner.

Jack took in great thirsty gulps of air as he struggled to his feet.

"Well," Bennett said steadying the lad. "Do you want to tell me what that was all about then?"

Jack shook his head trying to clear it. Through the large open wooden doors Jack could see Bill on other side of the road, waiting for him.

Bennett kept his voice low. "You can't stay here," he warned. "They're not going to stop until they find her."

Jack's heart sank, he had hoped to earn more to be able to give Marnie a better start in their new life together.

"I don't want no trouble, son," Bennett said his weathered face grave. "I don't want those ruffians burning my shop down, and they are likely to if they don't get what they want."

Jack couldn't argue because he believed it to be the truth. Madame and her thug weren't going to let him be. It was wrong of him to drag Bennett into this mess. Bennett may be a drunk, but he'd given Jack a chance, taken him in when he needed work, let him live in a hut at the back of his cottage. Jack appreciated the chance he'd been given; such kindness shouldn't be repaid with violence.

"If you'll - give me - my wages - I'll go, and not cause you more trouble," Jack wheezed.

Bennett put a hand on the young man's shoulder, "I'll miss you lad, you've been a fine apprentice but you understand, don't you?"

64

Jack nodded; his heart heavy with despair.

"I'll go to the bank you best wait till the cover of dark before leaving. Go out the back way then run like the blazes boy, and make sure that bally black-hearted bastard doesn't catch you." Bennett went out the large red wooden doors. "Back soon," he called over his shoulder, loud enough for Bill to hear.

Jack slumped down on the floor and put his head in his hands. If he made for the canyon in the dark, he'd have to stop and sleep rough in the best grassy area he could find and wait for daylight, he wouldn't want to risk walking off a ledge in the dark, or falling into the river and drowning. What he could take. Not much, his hat, coat, pocketknife and wallet.

But instead of money, Bennett came back with food. Handing Jack a bacon dripping sandwich, he told him to eat.

Jack looked at it doubtfully. "I don't think I can. I think he crushed my windpipe."

"Save it for a bit, you'll be fine," Bennett patted Jack's shoulder. He sat down on a barrel and stroked a hand through his straggly whiskers, "Ye know I've been thinking you mustn't leave too soon or they'll know you're guilty. Wait a while. Sleep here if you must. We got to come up with a better plan son or they'll skin your sorry carcass alive."

"That sounds like good advice to me," Jack agreed wholeheartedly. The last thing he wanted was to lead them straight to Marnie.

Bennett shook his head. "By God, I hope this girl is worth the trouble she's caused you lad," he said, taking a bite of sandwich.

Hand on heart, Jack said, "She is to me."

Yankee knocked, and waited.

A young woman opened the door a crack. "Yes?"

Surprised, Yankee removed his hat. "Hello ma'am. Is the priest in?"

"No, I'm afraid he's not," she apologized. "He's gone to visit his flock up at Macetown. I don't expect him back for a couple of days."

Disappointed, Yankee wrung his hat in his hands.

She opened the door a foot wider. "Have you travelled far? Would you like a cup of tea?"

Yankee ducked his head. "Ah...thank you kindly that would be grand."

"Niamh Boyle, the good father's new housekeeper," she told him.

"Yankee Brown," he said with a slow smile. "I take it the previous one got married?"

"How did you guess?" she flashed him a smile.

Opening the door wide she ushered him inside.

Petite, with her sandy hair pulled back in a bun, she wore a white apron over a simple grey day dress but she was a girl with keen blue eyes and a ready smile. Father Whooley's lodgings were small and cramped. Books filled the bookshelves of a small, simply furnished cottage.

While Niamh busied herself in the kitchen, Yankee took it upon himself to sit in the priest's chair. He stared out the latticed window trying to gather his wits. He'd spoken to Father Whooley several times about the ache in his heart that would not shift. He described to the Father as like having a stone in your boot that you can't get rid of. And how he thought he was going cockaloop since he couldn't stop thinking about Meg. He couldn't share his feelings with his best mate, since Dan was duty bound to side with his sister. Harry joked, that he should just throw Meg over his shoulder and carry her away, even that suggestion didn't provoke a smile.

But it helped to unburden his soul to the priest. Father Whooley listened patiently, and told him that the pain would ease in time, assuring him when he met another, he would be free of his feelings for Meg. He desperately wanted to believe that. Yankee smiled to himself, it was fortunate that the priest wasn't at home only his housekeeper was, a pleasant girl she was, and handsome enough too. Perhaps, Father Whooley was right. Perhaps this was just the kind of diversion he needed to keep himself sane. Niamh came into the living room carrying a tray, she lowered the tray so he could take his cup and saucer.

"Thank you kindly, ma'am, you're a true Christian." Yankee gave her a mischievous smile. He put the cup down on the side table.

"Milk? Sugar?" Niamh asked, stooping over the tray and looking expectantly up at him through her lashes.

"No thank you, but I fancy one of those delicious looking buns," he said, helping himself to a side plate and three buns.

"Healthy appetite," she noted with a smile. Placing the tray on a side table she sat on the opposite chair, teacup and saucer poised on her lap. "Baked them fresh this morning," she told him proudly. "There's not a lot to do when Father Whooley is away but I like to keep the place neat and tidy, and have the tins full for his return."

"I'm sure he appreciates you," Yankee said, taking a bite. "Mmm, mighty good ma'am, they're mighty good buns."

"It's Miss," she corrected, her blue eyes meeting his over the rim of her cup. "Thank you erm...Mr...?"

"Yankee Brown at your service ma'am. Master. I have to admit I'm rather pleased Father Whooley is not at home," he confessed. "Are you new to the area?"

Grinning, Niamh answered, "I arrived last week and I rather think I'm going to like it."

Meg arrived early Saturday morning with a basket on her arm.

"Hello Ma, gifts from the Asterlys for you." She pecked her mother's cheek and deposited the basket on the bench.

Mary lifted the tea-towel, and was pleased to find a batch of scones, jar of jam and pot of cream.

"Thank Catherine for me, won't you?" Mary had never expected to like the woman but Catherine Asterly showed a quiet determination and strength of character that matched Mary's own. Besides, with such a lack of women in the area, it was nice to have at least one friend.

Fidgety, Meg wandered about the room picking things up and setting them down again.

"It's nice to see you a day early, I wasn't expecting you until Sunday."

"I told Kitty I was, didn't she tell you?" Meg asked, surprised. She glanced up the hall. "Where is Kitty?"

Mary rolled her eyes. "Over at Greengate again. She's making a right nuisance of herself over there. Kitty takes Grace with her, and

Granny spoils Grace while Kitty sews. Sprat bought Granny a treadle machine, he reckons it softens the sound of her voice. He's always said his Ma has a crow like a rooster." Mary chuckled. "That's the pot calling the kettle black, you should hear Sprat's singing voice."

A small smile tugged at the corners of Meg's mouth as ran her finger along the sideboard.

Mary said, "Are you checking for dust? Don't think I'm getting soft in my old age; I make Kitty do all her chores before she goes. You should see her; she flies around here like the devil is chasing her."

"Sorry, Ma." Meg took her hand away. "I had hoped to see Grace. Kitty tells me she's walking."

"Don't be upset now, you'll see the wee one soon enough. She gabbles away nonstop, pulls herself up on everything, and waddles like a duck. And she's too quick - I have to watch her like a hawk around the fireplaces."

Meg wrapped her arms protectively about herself as if she was holding something in.

Mary lifted a plate down from the sideboard, she wondered whether to ask Meg outright what was troubling her, or to wait. Mary decided best to wait.

Finally, Meg said, "I think I may have offended Kitty."

Mary glanced up. "Oh? How's that then?"

Meg sighed. "I think she may have expected me to show more enthusiasm."

Mary nodded sagely. "I can see how that would upset her you know how she likes a fuss."

Changing the subject, Meg said, "Da and the boys have done a fine job of building the new kitchen, haven't they?"

"Aye, that they have," Mary agreed. She put a dollop of jam and cream on the scones.

Meg crossed the floor and peeked out the lace curtain. "Is Da about?"

"I don't rightly know," Mary replied. "He could be up at the claim." She cocked her head to one side. "But then again, I could be wrong. Kitty told us you were coming so he probably stayed close to home, like as not he'll be mucking out the stables. Have a look for him if you like, but I tell you any hint of food and he appears out of the woodwork like magic. The man has the nose of a fox. I don't know where he puts it all. It's not right he can eat all that tucker and stay as thin as the eye of a needle."

Meg sat on the kitchen stool, and dropped her head in her hands. "I need to talk to you, Ma."

Mary took a deep breath, braced herself and took a seat. Surely not again. "Are you in trouble?"

Meg's head jerked up and her brown eyes opened wide. "No!"

Mary sagged with relief. Reaching over, she patted Meg's hand. "Then for goodness' sakes girl, what's troubling you? A tooth doctor would have an easier time extracting the problem."

Meg glanced down at the engagement ring on her finger. The metal was burning her flesh. "I think...I think I may have made a mistake," she stammered.

Mary frowned. "What kind of mistake?"

"Oh, Ma," Meg cried, "I'm not sure that I should have accepted Williams' proposal."

Mary waved a dismissive hand. "Oh, darlin' it's just your nerves talking. I don't know what you've been told or what you believe will happen on your wedding night, but William will take good care of you. I don't expect you are blind ignorant as you've seen animals mating after all, but it's different with men and women in that ..." Meg held up her hand to silence her mother but unfazed Mary continued, "And if you're anything like me, you'll enjoy..."

"Ma stop!" Meg began to pace. "You don't understand. I like William well enough, he's a good man but..." She threw up her hands in despair. "Oh Ma, I'm confused."

"Love?" Mary snorted. "Love is an action, not a feeling." Suspicion skittered across Mary's mind. "Has Yankee Brown been to see you?"

Meg nodded miserably.

Mary was not one for mincing words. "You are troubled because your heart is not committed."

"I am committed," argued Meg. "I am engaged to William." Mary bit into light buttery scone and savoured the sweetness of the blackberry jam.

She swallowed. "Trouble is your heart and your head are at war with each other. Your heart tells you one thing and your head another." She licked the jam off her fingertips.

"I don't know what to do, Ma!" Meg wailed. "Tell me what to do," she implored.

Mary knew her daughter well enough to know if she advised one thing, Meg would do the opposite, besides, she didn't want to take the blame. "That's for you to decide."

Meg sighed. "Yankee's told me he's going to wed."

Mary lifted a cynical eyebrow. "And is he?"

"I guess so," Meg shrugged. "Why would he tell me otherwise."

Mary placed her hand on Meg's shoulder. "I'm sure Dan would have said something if that were the case."

Puzzled, Meg frowned. "Do you really think so?"

Mary nodded. "Yankee's only trying to hurt you like you did him. It is as plain as the nose on your face." Mary looked her daughter dead in the eye, "You need to decide – they are both good men."

Meg frowned. "But Yankee didn't ask me to marry him."

"He would have, if you hadn't accepted William's proposal, now wouldn't he?"

Mary put the kettle on to boil. Jim's familiar footsteps could be heard traipsing up the side steps. The door opened.

"Meg me wee darlin'," Jim cried. Flinging his arms wide he enveloped his daughter in a bear hug and swung her around the kitchen.

Meg gave him a wobbly smile as he set her down. "Da."

"It's grand to see you darlin'." He pinched her cheek. "I hope your wee sister told you we miss you something fierce. Of course, she did, that's why you're visiting us earlier than usual. Are you staying the night?"

Meg shook her head.

He waggled his finger. "I don't want you there on Sunday's listening to Asterly's sermons, you might get strange protestant notions in your head." He tweaked her nose. "You belong to the one true religion, remember that."

Meg grinned, her Da was irrepressible at times. She batted his arm lightly. "Oh, get away with you, Da. You know I'm true."

Spying the scones, Jim seated himself at the table, and cocked an expectant eyebrow at Mary.

"Fancy that, you're just in time for a cuppa," Mary told him with a wry grin.

"Ah splendid, I could drink the pot dry," he laughed.

Mary winced. There was a time he would have drunk the pub dry. The fear he might relapse was always there, just under the surface.

Meg joined her father at the dining table. Jim had finished two scones before Meg had even finished her first lick of cream. Mary filled Meg in with the local gossip then Meg told them about what she'd read was happening in America. Then they talked about the land wars in the North Island and how happy they were that they had settled in the South. Meg told her parents what was happening at Stony Creek, Pleasant Creek, Asterly Terrace, and beyond. She finished up by telling them how well the school at Skippers was doing. The Asterlys had agreed to allow their daughters to attend if the girls had extra tuition at home over and above the normal curriculum. The school roll was now up to twenty-one, eight of the children belonging to one family, most were girls as the older boys were required to work. Meg told them that one poor boy would walk for miles barefoot on an empty stomach, and arrive with nothing but a rabbit leg to eat, his only meal for the day, which he'd have to cook over the school house's potbelly stove.

"Poor little beggar," Jim sorrowfully shook his head.

Mary sighed. "We should count our blessings."

"I pop an apple or some bread in his hand now and then," Meg told them.

"That's good," Jim approved, patting his daughter's hand.

"Yes," Mary agreed. "Someone needs to show some kindness to the poor little chap, and I'm glad it's you."

"That's great news about the school darlin' but you must have forgotten to tell your face. What's wrong girl?" Jim asked. "You're as serious as the grave."

Mary pressed down on Jim's foot.

He frowned at her. "What? Am I not allowed to ask?"

"Yankee's been visiting," Mary told him.

"Oh." Unsure what to say, Jim picked up a scone and took a bite, chewing it thoughtfully. He opened his mouth to speak, thought better of it, and shut it again.

"I'm fine Da, really. Just a little unsettled is all. It's like Yankee's trying to show what a big man he is now he's a runholder."

"Aye, well they say a woman spurned is a terrible thing to behold, but I don't think Yankee Brown took being rejected too well either. And he's probably trying to make ye feel remorseful. But you're happy enough, aren't yer?" Jim asked, his face creasing with concern.

Suddenly defensive, Meg said, "Of course I am. I love William." Not meeting her father's eye, she brushed the crumbs from the table onto her plate.

"Well, that's as it should be," Jim said, relieved.

Her mother looked sceptical.

The teapot bobbed mid-air. "Another cup?" Mary asked.

"No thanks, Ma." The chair scraped as Meg rose. "I must be going. Give my love to Pat, Kitty, and Grace, won't you. It's a shame I missed them. Please tell Kitty I adore my gown."

Mary gave Meg a reproving look. "That's something you should tell her yourself."

Chastened, Meg hung her head. "Yes Ma, I will," she promised.

Jim volunteered to walk Meg back part of the way but she declined his offer saying,

"No, Da, you stay put. As much as I love you, I need a bit of peace and quiet, and I doubt you'll give me that. If you tag along you will fill the air with your tall-tales and I won't be able to hear myself think," she teased.

"Aye, well you're right there," Mary agreed. "He natters away like an old woman most days, makes me wish I was born deaf."
Jim pretended to be wounded, but his lopsided grin betrayed him. They went outside to say goodbye.

"All right me darlin' far be it from me to argue, or wear out your ears, have it your way, but for goodness sake girl, try and look a tad happier or you'll scare the birds."

"With all the blasting going on do you really think the birds would be scared of the likes of me, Da?" Meg set off up the track.

"Clever girl, isn't she?" Jim smiled at Mary.

"Yes," Mary agreed. "Lucky she takes after me. You are as green as your cabbage looking."

Peeved, Jim said, "I'll be splitting kindling if you want me." And headed to the wood pile.

Meg walked up the track with the basket slung over the crook of her arm. She knew her mother meant well and was trying to comfort her, but she didn't want her mother to explain the facts of

life. She had no idea what to expect, or what William expected of her, but the very thought made her feel ill.

Meg sighed. She didn't understand herself. If she truly loved William as much as she said she did, then why did the news that Yankee was going to wed upset her? She loved teaching. It made her happy but after they were married, William wanted her to stay home and raise their children. And hadn't that been what she'd been trying to avoid all along? And what if William suddenly decided they would leave the canyon? She loved it here in this scarred and barren land.

Meg stopped to rest at the fork in the trail. When Kitty left yesterday she was sour as a lemon, but occupied with her own troubles Meg couldn't be bothered to ask. When Kitty was upset, she would go quiet. Coming from a hot-headed Irish family, Kitty's austere silence was a far worse punishment for them than any angry outburst. Meg resolved that when she next saw Kitty, she would tell her how much she adored the lovely gown. That ought to cheer Kitty up.

Now, how best to get herself out of her own doldrums? This dark mood was all Yankee Brown's fault. If she hadn't seen him, she would have been perfectly happy. Of course, she was doing the right thing marrying William. Lady Asterly and Ma were right; it was just nerves making her skittish.

Reaching the turn off, Dan and Marnie began the ascent. The long silences stretched out unbearably.

Searching for something to say, Marnie remarked, "Your hut is named Stone Hall," and waited for Dan to respond.

Dan snorted. "That's Yankee's sense of humour for you. When we finished building it, Yankee said it was stronger than the rock of Christ and fit for gentry, so he christened it Stone Hall."

"Tell me about your family," Marnie said, hoping he would alleviate some of her fears.

"Aye well, I think you'll know Pat."

Yes, she knew Pat. "Yes, I do."

"He's living at the hotel now, and working The Redemption with Da."

"Pat's there?" she squeaked.

"Aye," Dan grunted. He and Pat didn't get on. Dan didn't approve of his brother's loose morals, and he despised the way Pat lived life as if it was one big, drunken party. After Annie's death they reached a begrudging acceptance of one another, and truth be told, Pat earned Dan's respect on the night of the Big Flood.

That night, Pat's bravery had not gone unnoticed. *The Witness*, *The Observer* and the *Wakatip Mail* were full of accounts trumpeting Pat's heroic deeds. Pat risked his scrawny neck to rescue men that were trapped buried alive under mudslides and debris. Seeing some swept away by the ferocious powerful current, Pat waded out, and encouraged others to form a human chain, which bore the men safely back to the banks of the river. He deserved a medal for such selfless bravery, not that he got one.

"Then there's Da," Dan continued. "We lost him for nigh on two years, and just when we thought him gone for good, he returned from the dead like Jesus Christ himself."

"Where was he?" Marnie chanced to ask.

"Wandering," Dan answered, deliberately vague.

Goldie shied as a rabbit shot across the track. Prancing sideways, she snorted and lifted her head. Dan fought to keep Goldie under control. Marnie gripped the pommel tightly as Dan held her firmly. The rabbit gone, Goldie settled, and walked on, shaking her head as if a fly had flown up her nose.

Dan loosened his grip. "Sorry, if I hurt you."

Convinced he hated her; Marnie was quick to assure him she was fine. In truth, her ribs were aching and her backside was saddle sore.

Dan continued, "My sister, Meg, lives up by The Terraces. She's the Asterly's governess, and the Skippers school ma'am. Her employers allowed her to set up a school for the miners' children. They are kindly folk and paid for the building of the school. And then there's Kitty. Well, she's is the biggest chatterbox ever born and she'll talk till your ear is about to drop off, but she's a fine wee seamstress for all that."

Marnie took a deep breath. "And your mother?"

His voice was solemn as he replied, "Ah yes, and then there's Ma." He paused then said brightly, "Oh but I'm forgetting our little Grace. She's my late sister Annie's child. She's a wee darlin'. Her hair sticks straight up like a hoar frost on a wire fence," he laughed. "She's been a comfort since her mother passed."

"I met Annie once," Marnie said softly, remembering the pale-faced, dark-haired young girl who had delivered Jack's love letter then disappeared like a vision. Even then, Annie looked as fine and fragile as bone china.

"Aye, was a terrible tragedy to lose her," Dan said, his voice tinged with bitter sadness.

They fell silent again. Now and then, Dan checked to see if she needed a rest stop. Marnie was in awe of the surroundings, treacherous and spectacular, the canyon was a grandiose sight. The way was narrow and steep and could make the bravest heart falter. The grey rock dust was a thick as fog in the air, and in the lungs. Beyond the road, the river was a turquoise ribbon that threaded its way through the golden canyon. Large, and threatening standing stones towered like giant beacons marking the way. Slowly, steadily, they made progress.

On the other side of the river, they could see Hell's gate. Chinamen dangled from ropes plugging sticks of gelignite into the rock to form a road. It was a perilous task, as unstable parts of the rock face could slip at any moment, and they could be buried alive under an avalanche of rubble. Marnie shuddered wondering how many dead men's bones were buried there.

Dan said, "Don't worry Goldie knows the track better than most, she'll get us there in one piece. What happens after that - well that I can't guarantee."

It was midday when the pack train rumbled to a stop. Mary went outside to meet it. She ticked off the supplies while Dusty stacked the goods neatly on the porch. Tea, sacks of sugar and flour, wood, blacklead, boot polish, lard, and thread. For a small thin gnarly man, Dusty was strong and fit. When he'd finished, Mary handed Dusty the bank notes she owed him. He smiled showing his yellowed teeth as his fist closed around the money. He tucked it safely away in his satchel and crossed out the debt in his ledger.

And with a final flourish said, "Oh yes and there's a letter for Miss Kitty. Is she about?"

Bewildered, Mary stared at the letter in Dusty's sun-blistered hand. Kitty had never received a letter in her life. Who could have sent her one?

Gathering her wits, she said, "No, Kitty's over at Greengate." She whipped the letter out of his grasp. "Don't worry, I'll see that she gets it."

"It's private and confidential," he insisted.

"She's my daughter," Mary snapped, giving Dusty a harrowing glare, "at fourteen, nothing's confidential."

Dusty knew Mary didn't like him. He thought it was because he'd been the one to bring her deserter of a husband back to her. But at the time he hadn't known the beaten bloodied man in the back of his cart was Mary Healey's husband. He'd found the poor wretch left for dead down at the turn off and being the good Samaritan he was, he delivered the beggar to Mary believing she would be able to tend to his wounds, should he live. He thought she blamed him ever since.

Dusty placed a finger to his battered hat and saluted. "I'll be on my way then," he said, taking the leader's reins.

"Good day to you," Mary replied curtly. She didn't like people who stuck their noses in other's business and Dusty was far too nosy for his own good.

Seeking clues, Mary turned the letter over but the seal was indistinct. Frustrated, she placed the letter on the table propped up against the flower vase so Kitty would see the moment she came in. Then she went outside and moved some of the lighter stores from the porch leaving the heavier ones for the men to shift later.

Mary was convinced time was standing still. She checked the clock again. Curiosity was eating her like a swarm of hungry sandflies. She would open the letter, read it, seal it again, and Kitty would be none the wiser. She was about to hold the letter over the steaming kettle when she heard a child's distant cry. Hurriedly putting the letter back on the table, she busied herself wrapping potatoes in newspaper to store in the cellar. Kitty came in the side door carrying a parcel under one arm and Grace in the other. Grace was red-faced from crying. Kitty put the parcel down on the bench and Grace on the floor. Grace started wailing again.

Mary used a rag to wipe the ink from her hands. "What's wrong with the wee besom?" she asked picking Grace up. Grace stopped; she rubbed her tired eyes. Snuffling, she cuddled into Mary's shoulder.

Mary kissed Grace's tear-stained face. "Shush, hush now," Mary said as she cradled Grace in her arms.

"Tired is all. Need a sleep, don't you little one?" Kitty smoothed Grace's wayward hair away from her face.
Grace hiccupped back a sob, and sucked her thumb.

"You missed Meg; she was asking after you."
Kitty was sceptical. Meg was so wrapped up in herself Kitty didn't think Meg could see past the end of her nose.

"Did you finish the veil?" Mary asked.

"Aye, all finished." Kitty said sagging with relief. "Hand-stitched."

"There's a letter on the table for you."

Kitty's eyes lit up. "For me?" she shrieked, snatching the letter from its resting place.

"Well, open it." Mary jiggled Grace on her hip. She peered over Kitty's shoulder. "What does it say?" she asked, eyeing it with interest.

"I'll read it later," Kitty replied, pocketing the envelope.

Mary wanted to scream with impatience but keeping calm, she asked, "Who's it from?"

"I won't know till I open it, but since it's my very first letter I'm going to savour the moment." Taking her leave, Kitty went up the hall and opened the door to her room.

Exasperated, Mary watched Kitty disappear. She whispered in Grace's ear, "The horrid child has reached the challenging years and is deliberately baiting me. Don't you grow up little one, I like you fine just the way you are."

Grizzly, Grace bored her pudgy fists into her tired eyes.

Mary sighed. "Come on, let's change that soggy bottom and put you to bed."

Kitty locked her bedroom door, and with trembling hands, she sucked in her breath and opened the envelope.

Dear Miss Katherine Healey,

We are delighted to inform you that you have been granted a three month trial apprenticeship at our Fashion house, in High Street, Dunedin.

Should we find your work acceptable, we will grant you a year's apprenticeship of which you are well aware of the costs.

We look forward to seeing you at 9.00am sharp on the 21th of
January at our premises in High Street, Dunedin.
Sincerely yours
Madame Juliette le Roux
Head Dressmaker and Designer
de la Parisanne Fashion Boutique

Overcome with the sheer wonder of it all, still holding the letter tightly in her hand, Kitty flopped on the bed as limp as a rag doll. Granny's recommendation had opened the door! God in heaven, how was she going to tell her mother!

Marnie was fading. She hoped the hotel wasn't far away, even her eyes felt gritty.

"Do you need to rest?" Dan asked for the umpteenth time.

"Is it much further?" She couldn't hide the hopeful squeak in her voice.

"No more than half a mile. See those smoke trails there?" Following the line of his finger, she nodded.

"That smoke's coming from the hotel's chimneys," he told her. Marnie's stomach clenched, soon she would meet the infamous Mary Healey.

She changed the subject. "Tell me, how did you meet Harry?"

"Ah Haerakia," he smiled, remembering, "His last name is as long as your arm and just as hard to pronounce. We call him Harry for short and he likes it well enough." Dan paused. "We met Harry the day Yankee tried to drown us. Yankee made two useless mokimoki, flax canoes," he explained, "and we were attempting to cross the lake when they sank. We were dragged to shore by Harry and his dog. Harry lit a fire to keep us warm, and he and his dog lay down with us to stop us from freezing to death. Since we owed him our lives, we asked him to go mates with us on our claim, and it was a good thing we did."

"Why?" Marnie asked, intrigued.

"We got claim jumped once. They beat us badly and ran us off our claim, but good old Harry rounded up his tribe and they sprung at them with clubs and adzes and beat the blighters to a pulp. Fearing for their lives, the blackguards scarpered and we've not been bothered since." Dan chuckled softly to himself. "Come to think of it Harry is always rescuing us. When his old dog died, Yankee and I bought him Tu as a present. He has been happier about that pup than he ever has been about his share of the gold."

"Is Tu a good dog then?"

"Yes, and a clever one too," he told her.

A little later, Dan said, "Do you know Maori legend has it that at the bottom of the lake there's a sleeping giant? They say that's why the lake rises and falls, they say it's the giant breathing."

"You're teasing me."

"No, it's true," he assured her.

They rounded the last bend, and Marnie caught her first glimpse of the Welcome Home. The hotel was a wooden building painted white with two large sash windows in the front and three on the side. It had a red corrugated iron roof, and five steps leading up to a large veranda. There was a hitching post and horse trough out front and stables on the right. Marnie took a steadying breath.

Dan murmured, "It's good we've arrived at opening time, Ma will be too busy to notice us."

"Isn't it always opening time?" Marnie asked, astonished.

"It is, but men don't come up from the river till it's nigh on dark. Ma kicks them out about midnight, she reckons nothing good happens after midnight."

The music coming from the hotel was lively. There were rowdy hoots and hollers and the stomping of hobnailed boots keeping time. Dan was relieved no one was outside on the veranda when they arrived. He went straight to the stables where he fed and watered his horse. Sitting on a pile of straw with her parasol resting across her lap, nursing her aching ribs, Marnie watched as Dan brushed Goldie down.

Dan shook his head. Marnie had left with nothing more than the clothes on her back and her precious parasol. Far be it from him to deny her the luxury of her one treasured item, but God only knew when she'd need it.

"I think it best if we go in the back way," he said glancing at the shortness of her dress which showed off her stockings and fine buckled boots. "Ma will be busy in the tavern but Kitty will feed us I'm sure." He sighed, knowing his mother would not take this inconvenience lightly. "I'm hoping Da will soften the way."

The more he spoke about his mother the more Marnie wanted to flee. Jack had sent her to this god forsaken place. Now she was trapped, with nowhere to go, and nowhere to hide. She wasn't even sure of the way back.

Dan pushed his hat further back on his head. "Right, here goes then," he said, leading Marnie around the back.

Kitty quietly closed the bedroom door, and was about to tiptoe away, when she heard a knock. Startled, she jumped. The door opened a crack and the chain rattled. Kitty covered her mouth to stop herself screaming.

"It's only me, Dan," Dan whispered through the gap.

Kitty raised the lantern. "Dear God in Heaven!" She placed her hand on her beating heart. "Daniel Healey, you scared me half to death," she scolded. Undoing the chain, she opened the door and let him in.

Dan put a warning finger to his lips. "I'm not alone."

"Is Yankee with you?" Kitty glanced past him.

"No." He stepped aside.

The cloaked figure removed her hood, revealing her long blonde ringlets and bruised face.

Fearing Kitty would jump to conclusions, Dan said, "This is Jack's lady friend."

"Jack's friend?" Kitty cried, aghast. "Then you must be...Marnie?"

Marnie's palms were sweating, she wiped her hands on her cloak. "Hello Kitty. It's nice to meet you."

"Well it's a surprise to meet you," Kitty replied honestly, studying Marnie's battered face.

Shedding his jacket, Dan hung his hat on the peg. Wary, he looked around. "Is Ma...?"

"Don't worry she's in the pub. Da's in the kitchen. Pat's gone over to Fox's for a few days to see some old friends." Kitty gave him a meaningful look.

Dan rolled his eyes as if he expected as much. "We didn't come to see him."

"Are you hungry?" Kitty asked.

"I am," Dan replied. "And I expect Marnie could eat her arm as well."

Marnie nodded, her pretty ringlets bouncing like springs.

Dan licked his lips. "And, I'm as dry as the inside of a furnace."

"Come on then, I'll see what I can find." Kitty led the way down the passageway and opened the door to the kitchen. Jim's chair was in the half shadow, he was dozing by the warmth of the fire, his unlit pipe hanging limply from his mouth. The draught made him shiver, and he popped one eye open.

Jim leapt to his feet. "Danny, my boy!" He rushed to greet him but stopped abruptly when he saw Marnie.

Self-conscious, Marnie shifted uneasily, staring at her feet wishing the ground would swallow her.

Dan coughed. "Hello Da." He gave his father a grim smile. "Da, this is Jack's lady friend, Marnie. She needs a place to stay."

Jim bit down on his pipe. Struggling to find words he finally managed to croak, "Ah Jack's...well...hello Marnie."

"Mr Healey," Marnie said, her eyes on the floorboards.

Kitty said, "Da, take Marnie's cloak, will you, while I fix them something to eat. I can hear their stomachs growling." Kitty disappeared into the larder and they could hear the clatter of plates.

Jim went to take Marnie's cloak but Marnie was reluctant to part with it. She was keenly aware that her scarlet dress was too bright, the bodice too low and the hem of her skirt too high.

"No, its fine, really," she insisted but Jim pressed her until Marnie finally allowed him to take it. Marnie felt like she was standing before the clergy naked.

Dan took his place at the table. Jim ushered Marnie into a seat at the table. Kitty returned with plates of cold mutton pie, and cheese and chutney sandwiches which she placed in front of them, then disappearing again, she returned with some apple cider for Marnie.

"What would you like to drink, Dan?" Kitty asked, lightly touching his shoulder. Dan desperately wanted to wash away the taste of the road with some strong spirits but didn't want to drink in front of his father.

"Ah, water will do nicely," Dan replied, seeking Jim's approval.

"It's all right son, if you want something stronger, have it," Jim told him. Jim desperately wanted something to fortify himself too. For the life of him, he wasn't sure how he was going to stop Mary erupting like a volcano when she saw what, or rather who, was sitting at her table. He could hardly hide Marnie on the property and hope to God Mary wouldn't notice.

"I'll have another cup of tea, thanks love," he called to Kitty.

Ravenous, Dan devoured sandwiches, two slices of pie and downed a glass of cider while Marnie daintily nibbled at hers like a little mouse. She washed her food down with a sip of cider, wincing as it stung her cut lip.

Kitty's face grew grave as she handed her father a mug of tea. "Da, there's something I need to tell you," she confessed. Taking the letter from her apron pocket she handed it to him. "I guess now is as good as time as any. I'll need you to break the news to, Ma, and the way I see it we might as well hang for a horse as for a sheep."

Jim took the letter, not a fast reader he took his time, but as he got to the bottom he realized Kitty meant to be going.

He looked at her, incredulous. "What's the meaning of this?" he asked. "Do you want your mother to die of an apoplexy?" He handed the letter to Dan.

Dan read it slowly, then stared up at Kitty, "You are not really…"

The door from the tavern opened and Mary entered the room. Kitty snatched the letter from Dan's hand and quickly hid it in her apron pocket. Mary was halfway across the room before she noticed they had company.

Mary's face lit up "Dan!" But froze when she saw Marnie.

Dan's chair scraped loudly on the wooden floor as he rose. "Ma."

Mary bristled, "Who's this? And what's she doing here?"
There was a wheeze of silence.

Finally, Jim said, "This is Jack's friend, Marnie. She needs a place to stay."
Mary's head swivelled from one man to the other and back again. The music in the bar stopped.

"Stay right where you are," Mary told them brusquely. She went back into the tavern. They listened as Mary barked orders, her voice easily travelling through the thin scrim walls. The accordion player started up again and this time was joined by a fiddler, once again there was the heavy stomping of hobnailed boots. Mary reappeared. Securing the door behind her, she leaned against it.

"Someone better start talking," she said, her green eyes sparking. Mary's voice was low but controlled. "This is a decent hotel. No place for a whore. I run a respectful establishment and I'll not have the likes of her within these walls."

"Now Mary," Jim said cautiously, as one does when trying to soothe a wild beast, but it was too late, Mary's dander was up and she wasn't about to be pacified by a few choice words.

Kitty blurted, "Jack and Marnie are to be married, Ma."

"What!" Mary cried, rounding on her daughter. "The hell he is!" she blustered, puffing up indignantly. "The boy's too young to wed without my permission."

Marnie was scared, her heart was racing. Mary Healey was a volatile woman and there was no telling what she'd do. And if Jack had lied about his age what else had he lied about? If he couldn't marry without their permission, had he ever intended to marry her? Trapped, she searched for a way out but Dan was standing against the door that led to the passage, and Mary blocked the other door. There was no escape.

"Now Mary," Jim lowered his voice. "You can see the girl's been beaten; she just needs a place to stay until she's mended."

"Don't you try that on with me, James Healey," Mary warned pushing him out of the way. "I know what you're up to." Arms tightly folded across her chest; the toe of Mary's boot tapped a steady rhythm on the floorboards. She smouldered with rage.

"Think about it Ma," Kitty said, carelessly wading into the fray. "We need an extra pair of hands around the place. Marnie will be able to help with the chores."

90

Rounding on Kitty, Mary pointed wildly at Marnie and declared, "Do you think that strumpet has ever done a day's work in her life? All she knows is how to lie on her back. She wouldn't know one end of the broom from the other."

Marnie was shrinking before their eyes. Jim came to her defence, placing a solid hand on Marnie's shoulder. She was as brittle as a sun-baked thread.

"Just a couple of days, Mary, till she heals, and then we can see what's what after that."

Mary advanced, stabbing a finger at Marnie, she said, "You'll burn that dress and those stockings."

Marnie kept her eyes lowered while Mary ranted.

"Kitty will fix you a bath, and you'll scrub yourself raw before you sleep between any of my sheets." With a face like thunder, Mary's gaze shifted to Kitty. "And since you're so damn keen to have her as a pet she can sleep in your bed, and you can give her something decent of yours to wear." Turning her attention back to Marnie she raged, "And you'll brush out those ringlets, and cover your head with a cap, and you'll not," she paused for breath, "go anywhere near my tavern, or let anyone other than family see you. No one is to know you are here. Do I make myself clear?"

Marnie nodded, her blue eyes blurring with tears. Mary went back into the tavern slamming the door so hard it was in danger of coming off its hinges.

"Well, that went better than I expected," Jim said, relieved.

Dan downed the last of his cider. Wiping his mouth with the back of his hand, he said, "Just wait till she hears Kitty means to desert. I hope to be long gone when that happens."

"Aye," Jim agreed, wishing he could as well.

Kitty led Marnie out the back way to the washhouse. Telling her to stay put, Kitty went back and forth to the pump to fill the tub, then took many trips to the kitchen to bring back hot water from the stove. The short tin tub was only half full but Kitty had endured enough fetching and carrying, and decided that the bath was deep enough. After checking the temperature, Kitty put a few drops of lavender oil in the bath water.

"Here's the pumice and soap," Kitty said passing them to Marnie. "I'll just go get a towel and dressing gown." She slipped out the door again leaving Marnie alone in the wooden shed.

The light from the kerosene lantern was soft in the otherwise cold and shadowy washhouse. Marnie was delighted with the prospect of having a bath. She was dusty from the journey and her hair felt greasy. She was perfectly aware she wasn't welcome at the Welcome Home. Dan was cold and standoffish. Jim was nice, and Kitty a darling, but Mary Healey scared her half to death. Jack better be true to his word and come for her soon, or she'd never forgive him for abandoning her in this God awful place. She gingerly lowered herself into the tin tub and enjoyed the warm water caressing her sore limbs. Her ribs ached, her eye was swollen shut, and her split lip smarted but she closed her eyes and sighed, the water felt amazing, like it had healing properties.

A fire graced the hearth bathing the bedroom in a soft golden glow. Looking like a heaven-sent cherub, Grace was sleeping in her wrought iron crib, her thumb thrust in her mouth, and her little padded bottom stuck high in the air. Kitty placed the flickering candleholders on the mantelpiece, and covered Grace with the quilt.

"The chamber pot is under the bed if you need it," Kitty informed Marnie.

Marnie nodded.

Quietly, so as not to wake the babe, Kitty opened the wooden chest at the end of the bed. "Here," Kitty said, handing Marnie one of her nightgowns.

Casting the robe aside, Marnie shrugged the white cotton nightgown over her head, threaded her arms through the sleeves, and tied the drawstrings under her bosom.

"Sit close to the fire so your hair dries quicker," Kitty suggested removing the fire guard. "I'll brush it out for you."

Marnie sat on the rag mat before the open fire while Kitty changed into her night things. Picking up her ivory hairbrush Kitty knelt behind Marnie, and humming softly to herself she began to brush Marnie's hair with long, slow, rhythmic strokes.

"You have beautiful hair," Kitty murmured, braiding Marnie's hair in a single plait.

Marnie's tone was bitter. "I'm surprised your mother hasn't insisted I shave my head."

Kitty placed a comforting hand on Marnie's shoulder. "Don't worry, Ma might be as prickly as a hedgehog but there's a soft belly underneath. It will be all right, you'll see."

Hugging her knees into her chest, Marnie stared miserably into the fire. If Mary Healey was going to give her a bed, she'd be earning her keep, and having done no household chores since she was ten, Marnie doubted her ability to perform them well enough to satisfy Mary Healey. If Jack didn't come and rescue her soon, she'd end up like a poor old workhorse, flogged to death.

Marnie gripped Kitty's hand in hers. "I'd be a whole lot happier if knew you weren't leaving. Don't go," she pleaded.

Kitty looked misty for a moment. "If I can, I must. Don't worry, Jack will come for you."

But when? When would he come? How long would she have to endure Mary Healey's cutting tongue? Marnie sighed. It was no use, she would have to make the most of being stuck way out here, that's if Mary Healey didn't throw her out on her ear. When Jack arrived, there was no way Mary Healey would let them marry, then what? Would they run away? Where would they go? How would they survive? What would they do for money?

Sensing Marnie's distress, Kitty attempted to cheer Marnie by saying, "Meg will visit."

"But she's to be married soon, isn't she?" Marnie replied gloomily.

"Yes," Kitty said sadly, looking suddenly vulnerable. She tiptoed over to the oval mirror and brushed her auburn curls.

Marnie felt guilty. Kitty looked fragile and she didn't know what she'd said to upset her. "Won't you miss your family?"

Kitty looped her curls up in a topknot and straightened. "I am fourteen. Old enough to leave home."

Marnie frowned. "Are you all right? You seem a little preoccupied."

"Tired, as I expect you are," Kitty answered with a tight smile.

Marnie was exhausted. The pain from her injuries, combined with the pent-up emotions of leaving the brothel, the journey to Long Gully, and her fear of meeting Mary Healey had sapped her strength.

"Let's go to sleep," Kitty suggested. "Everything is sure to look better in the morning."

Marnie doubted it. She slid between the starched sheets, Kitty got in the other side and pulled the patchwork quilt up to her chin, then snuffed the candle.

Kitty quietly said, "I miss my sisters. There aren't many girls my age in this area, so it's nice to have you here."

"Annie sounded lovely," murmured Marnie.

"She was," Kitty replied, her voice bruised.

Marnie was sincere. "You're very kind. You have been kind to me."

"We will be friends," Kitty decided. Moments later, Kitty asked, "Did you have any friends at the brothel?"

"Yes, I have friends but Daisy is my best friend. She's kept me sane. She's the reason I haven't killed myself." Marnie felt a pang of regret. She'd never got to say goodbye to Daisy, now she never would.

Kitty sighed. "You will miss her."

"Aye," Marnie's eyes grew moist.

Kitty whispered, "Do you have any sisters?"

"No, Daisy was the closest thing to a sister I had." Marnie blinked.

"Then we will be friends and sisters," Kitty said, smiling in the darkness.

Marnie could not speak for the lump in her throat.

Kitty spoke to the ceiling. "I'm worried. Meg left without Ma's blessing and it took Ma a long time to get over it. She's not going to be happy when she hears my news."

Marnie desperately hoped Mary would refuse to let Kitty go.

Kitty rolled over. "Tell me what's it like - at the brothel?" she whispered.

Marnie spoke candidly. "You don't want to know, it's not for the likes of your innocent ears."

"But I'm interested, do you have to go with a man, or can you refuse?"

"If you refuse, you'd get your face and other parts blackened. You do what you're told, and you can either choose to make the most of it, or live a very sullen, depressed existence."

"It is nice wearing satins and laces?"

"Sure, it's nice to have nice things but having your bits exposed for men to lust over isn't. It's easier not to feel, not to think, just act the part, and give them what they want, it's the only way to survive."

"I'm sorry Marnie." Kitty found Marnie's shoulder and gave it a small squeeze.

Grace snuffled and turned in her sleep.

There was a moments silence then Kitty propped herself up on her elbow. "Why do you love Jack?" she asked, curious.

"Because he loves me, the real me. I see it in his eyes."

"And you? Do you love him?"

"I wouldn't be here otherwise." Marnie changed the subject. "Dan told me Yankee holds a candle for Meg, but she loves Mr Burns. Is that true?"

"Mr Burns was in love with Annie, and he came to Long Gully to ask for her hand. We had to tell him that Annie had passed away."

Marnie was wistful. Annie would always remain immortal, beautiful and timeless in death. "It's so tragic."

"Yes," agreed Kitty. "And Meg is but a poor substitute." She turned and faced the wall.

Marnie frowned, surprised by the sting in Kitty's words. The room was quiet apart from the crackling flames.

Marnie whispered, "Does Meg love Mr Burns?"

But there was no reply other than a loud snore.

Eyelids heavy with the drag of sleep, Marnie realised it was the first time in a long time, no one was demanding anything of her body. She shut her eyes and slept.

Mary got ready for bed without a word. Her angry silence made the air feel brittle. Jim knew better to attempt a kiss or cuddle when Mary was in a mood, so he pretended to be asleep. The bed dipped slightly as Mary got in.

"I know you're awake, James Healey," she said, through tightly-gritted teeth. She prodded him in the kidneys with the tip of her finger. "Don't pretend otherwise."

"No," he replied, his eyes closed. "I'm definitely asleep."

She swatted him with her pillow. "What's the meaning of letting that young strumpet in my house?"

Pushing the pillow aside, Jim wearily sat up. "All right, I'm not asleep. And if you really want to know, I snuck that young beauty in here to have my wicked way with her under your very nose," he said fractiously.

Mary belted him again.

"All right, all right," he said, holding his hands up in surrender. "Dan brought her up here at Jack's request, and she was standing in the kitchen afore I knew a thing about it. She's here now. Obviously, she can't go back without being beaten to a pulp, so I guess we're stuck with her. We're just going to have to make the best of a bad situation." Jim tucked the offending pillow behind his head and lay down. "I've told you all I know, now, may I go to sleep?"

"That's my pillow," Mary said, tugging it out from under him. "I don't know how you can sleep at a time like this."

"It's easy, and if you'll stop hitting me, I will show you just how easy. Goodnight Mary me love," Jim rolled over and faced the wall. God, he'd have another battle tomorrow when she heard Kitty's news. Dear God in Heaven, there would be hell to pay. He might as well move back into the stables now to save her the trouble of sending him there tomorrow.

Chapter 4   Deception

Pat was happy to be back in his old stomping ground. But God damn it, he missed Tiny. He shook his head trying to shake away the plaguing sadness he felt whenever Tiny, or Annie, came to mind. Cooped up under his mother's watchful gaze Pat had had to behave himself, and out of respect for his father's new stance on sobriety he made every effort not to get too carried away with the grog. But here, here on The Arrow, the sudden rush of freedom was exhilarating. He was a free man and had a bag of gold on his person that was itching to be spent.

He wondered if that old whore, Bull Pup Bridie, still haunted these parts, or if she'd gone to the new rushes. A dirty banshee with lank black hair, she was as foulmouthed as the demons in hell. The type of woman you would expect to be riddled with diseases. And worse still, she had a score to settle with him. He wouldn't put it past her to slash him with a knife, or gouge his eyeballs out given the chance. Now his fortunes had changed, he had the gold he owed her, but he was reluctant to part with it for such inferior merchandise.

He would start at The Royal and work his way up Buckingham Street, visit the dancing halls and billiard salons, and then finally move on to the Chinese settlement. He pushed open the door to The Royal and greeted the barman by name.

"Why if it's not Pat Healey," Ned, the hospitable barman, said. Ducking under the counter, he reappeared and placed an unstopped bottle of ale on the bar.

"Thank you kindly," Pat grinned. Raising the bottle to his lips he took a swig, and another, and another.

Ned generously replenished Pat's drinks and with an unquenchable thirst, Pat drank every drop. The drink was taking effect and loosening his tongue. Boasting, Pat raised his bottle in a mock salute, calling out, that a life spent on the river was harsh but not without its rewards. Patting the money bag hanging from his belt, Pat cried, "Here's to good fortune boys," and took another swig of liquid cheer.

"Steady on," warned a middle-aged man with a bowler hat and a large handle bar moustache. "There's roughnecks about who would dearly like to relieve you of your gold faster than you can spend it, lad."

But Pat took no heed and continued to boast. The man shook his head, grunted and moved to a quieter corner to drink in peace.

Pat doffed his hat to the barman and walked ungainly through the swinging doors out into the bustling street. The street lanterns had been lit, casting a golden circular glow, they looked like small moons set on poles. It was bone chilling cold but the liquor had warmed his gizzard and he noticed the cold less than he should have. The billiard rooms and dancing halls were in full swing and doing a roaring trade. He'd heard the Buckingham's theatrical troupe was worth watching, and Rosie Buckingham a pleasure both to the eyes and the ears, but tonight he sought a different kind of pleasure.

The shop's wooden veranda post supported him while he wrestled his pipe from his trouser pocket and found the tin of tobacco in the other pocket. Fumbling, he placed a fresh plug of tobacco in his clay pipe, and pressed it down with a nicotine-stained finger. He lit the pipe, drew on it, and coughed twice. Cocky, and puffing like a steam engine, Pat swaggered up the street towards the New Orleans where he downed another couple of drinks before heading to the Chinese settlement to feed the demon.

Pat had to duck to enter Wei Nam's smoky stone-walled hut. He was welcomed by the Chinaman who bowed politely to his customer. Wei Nam was small and as wrinkled as a raisin. Slightly built he had a long thin pointed beard that hung from his chin like a dog's mangy tail. Under his silk hat, he wore a long grey plait which swung like a pendulum when he walked. Having given Pat credit in the past and been burnt, Wei Nam asked for bank notes or gold up front, before he'd hand over the precious opium Pat craved. Pat parted with a small nugget. Wei Nam bit it to check it was solid and not just painted lead. Satisfied it was the real thing, Wei Nam shuffled to the back of his hut where he crouched on his haunches and unwrapped some sacking. He placed a measured amount of opium in a piece of newspaper folded and rolled it, twisting the ends.

Bowing, with hands pressed together as if in prayer, Wei Nam thanked Pat for his custom, and handed him the twisted roll. But Pat did not wish to leave, he wanted company, so he sat cross-legged on the damp mud floor and asked Wei Nam to bring out his pipe. Resigned, Wei Nam gave Pat the pipe and crouched on his hindquarters patiently waiting. Pat plugged the pipe with powder, inhaled, and let the effects take hold.

Snow flurries surrounded them, the going was rough and steep. At the summit, there was an unbroken field of soft snow as far as the eye could see. They could barely find the markers; they were covered that deep. They were dog-tired and up to their knees in snow. They weren't the only ones lost on Old Man but they became separated in the howling blizzard that stung their eyes and threatened to blow them clear off the mountain. Some succumbed to the force of the lashing wind, and the biting cold that ate through the flesh and into the soul. Many lay dead where they fell.

They were going in circles. A few steps ahead, Pat reached Old Man rock first. Stopping to catch his breath, he saw the valleys below were white and the face of the glacier as smooth as glass. Pat turned to see his father disappear over the edge, his hand outstretched, begging him to save him. Pat thrust out his hand but all he felt was air. It was too late, Da was gone. Pat woke with a start as his father's cries echoed hollowly in his ears.

He came to in the arms of a native girl. He could hear himself sobbing. He felt remote, like he was out of his body watching himself from above. She was stroking his cheek and muttering something in her own language in his ear. Tears trickled down his fuzzy red beard and onto the pillow. She was young. He didn't know her name but she seemed kind, it didn't really matter he just wanted to numb the pain. And for now, she was a comforting tonic as any.

"Miss them sometimes, you know," he said, his voice trembling. "I saved others but couldn't save me best mate from drowning. Couldn't save me good sister neither," he sniffed, and wiped a finger under his nose.

"Hush, hush hoa taunekune, they are with the ancestors now," she replied, smoothing his ruffled hair.

Jim considered himself a brave man, but Mary in a temper was something to strike fear into the heart of the devil. He slunk away at first light, and headed to the river for peace and quiet, and to do a good morning's prospecting. He hoped a few gold nuggets would help sweeten Mary's mood, and maybe even put a smile on her thunderous face.

The wedding was only weeks away, and Meg and her betrothed had arranged to meet the priest at the hotel to go over the prerequisites before the big day. With Marnie arriving so sudden like, Jim thought it likely Mary would've forgotten that this afternoon she would be hosting not only the priest, but Meg and Burns as well. It was probably good that Pat had gone to Arrow for a couple of days, for to have him in the mix, would most likely send Mary to the asylum.

Jim dipped his pan and swirled the water around, his ever-watchful eyes searching for gold. He'd be forever in Father Whooley's debt. He was by no means cured, but without the curse of liquor in his veins his life had been transformed, and now his wife, still hot-headed by nature, was soft and pliable in his arms. It wasn't easy; some days he craved the drink so badly his skin cracked with desire, but one sip and he'd slip back into hell. Since sobriety he'd been blessed, The Redemption was a remarkable claim and he thanked God for the miracle of finding it. Now, he was able to provide for his family and had the chance to make up for some of the wasted years. Back then he'd felt so worthless, such an utter failure he thought it was better for everyone if he just disappeared. Initially, Pat was so angry at his betrayal that he thought he'd lost him for good. He feared his eldest son would never forgive him, but little by little, Pat was softening. Father Whooley said he couldn't change the past, but he had a chance to change the future. And God willing, he would earn his family's trust in time.

Jim worked separating the gravel until there were only a few flecks of gold sitting in the base of the pan. Gathering it, Jim smiled to himself, Mary would be a touch happier by the afternoon if he had anything to do with it. But how best to bring up the subject of Kitty? After arguing it from all four points of the compass, he decided it would be best to announce it when everyone was present, and pick up the pieces later. Mary wouldn't be able to get too riled up with Burns and the priest there. He shook his head, she was a prickly wee beastie but he loved her dearly, fiery red hair, temper and all.

Mary cursed her way around the kitchen. Sleeves rolled up, her arms deep in the sink, Mary scrubbed the pots in an absolute fury. Eager to leave and get away from Mary's foul temper, Dan tiptoed into the larder. He put a wedge of cheese and a loaf of bread in a flour bag and tied a knot in the top.

"Taking to thieving have ye?" Mary came up behind him. She shook her head. "You'll have to be quieter than that to slip past me."

"Sorry, Ma." Dan hung his head. "Didn't want to disturb you is all."

"Take more than that, you're a bag of bones, just look at you, your clothes are fair hanging off you," she scolded, putting some sliced cooked mutton, and two loaves of bread plus a jar of pickles in another flour bag, she tied it tight and handed it to him, then went back to the sink.

"Thanks Ma." Dan kissed her cheek. "Give me regards to me brother, and my love to Da and the girls, won't you."

A pan crashed down on the bench. She turned on him. "You are not going already?" she bellowed. "You bring that girl here to this hotel, knowing how much it would upset me, and then just up and disappear. You're a no-good lousy coward, Daniel Healey!" Mary cried, her green eyes sparking.

"That I am," Dan admitted. "But for all that, I love you dearly and I will come and visit soon. Maybe when the dust has settled, or I'll see you at Meg's wedding, whichever comes first." He nipped out the door and bolted across the lawn to the stables.

Fuming, Mary threw the dishcloth at the door. "Coward!"

Marnie slept through most of the commotion, but her eyes opened when she heard a baby cry. She blinked in confusion, then it all came back to her in a horrible rush. She had run away. She was at Jack's parents' hotel. Kitty was planning on leaving and then she would be on her own with the notorious, Mary Healey. Marnie sat up, her ribs grabbing as she did. A spear of light split the curtains in two. Dressed in her nightgown, Kitty stood next to Grace's crib, looking like an angel sent straight from heaven. Grace bounced on her chubby legs, begging to be picked up.

"Poor little love, you've a very wet bottom," Kitty tutted as she lifted Grace out of the crib. "Come on, let's get you changed." Kitty turned and saw Marnie watching her like one studies a curiosity.

"Good morning," Kitty smiled. "Sorry if I kept you awake last night; I've been told I snore like a bush pig. Ma says, it's something to do with having small nasal passages."

Marnie grinned, for a petite girl, Kitty had a ripper of a snore but it hadn't bothered her in the slightest, she had endured worse. "Don't be, I slept well enough. But who's that making such a damned awful racket?"

"Ah, that would be, Ma, and when mother's in a temper, nothing's safe. Come on, you better get up. I will change Grace then we better set to burning your clothes before there's more trouble."

Kitty wrestled the baby out of her wet napkin and into a fresh one. Marnie wrinkled her nose as the stink of ammonia assaulted her nostrils.

Marnie pushed back the bedcovers and holding her ribs she got up. Troubled, she asked, "But what will I wear?"

"My other day dress," Kitty said matter-of-factly.

Marnie stared at her in disbelief. "But...won't you...need it?"

"It is all right, I don't mind, I've got two, and I can make another. I will get Ma to order a bolt of material next time Dusty comes. I'm a dab hand with a needle." She smiled.

"Can keep my corsets and bloomers?"

"Of course," Kitty grinned. "You can keep anything Ma can't see." Kitty threw Marnie's petticoats to her. "Keep your petticoats. And I expect you'll need more than one set of drawers," she said, laying a pair of her own on the bed for Marnie. "I'll be back in a minute," Kitty said. She bundled up the wet napkin. "I'll just deposit this in the washhouse. Watch Grace for me." She disappeared, leaving Marnie no choice.

Marnie tentatively reached out a hand and touched Grace's hair. Grace's hair stood at attention like dark sticks of straw but it was soft, light and fuzzy to the touch. Kneeling, Marnie pulled faces and made funny noises to keep Grace entertained. Sucking her thumb, Grace frowned uncertainly up at the newcomer. Kitty came back and placed a tin of wooden peg dolls on the floor. Squealing with delight, Grace banged the peg dolls against the tin and scattered them around the room.

Taking a day dress out of the wardrobe Kitty gave it a good shake to rid it of wrinkles. "Here try this on," she said to Marnie, "it won't fit right but it will keep Ma from shitting turnips."
Surprised by Kitty's bad language, Marnie laughed, then winced as her ribs bit.

Kitty helped Marnie do up all the tiny buttons at the back of her day dress, some buttons were false, just hooks and eyes, but Marnie couldn't manage those on her own. Marnie buttoned the neck of the plain frock. Kitty stepped back and studied Marnie with a critical eye.

"It doesn't sit right on you," she frowned gathering in the sides. "I must be bigger in the bust."

"I don't know how it's too big on me, you're only little yourself," Marnie replied, plucking at the extra fabric.

"I'll tack it," Kitty decided. "We can alter it proper later."

Kitty clinched the waist with some plain grey ribbon and tacked a few stitches in the chest to serve as darts. She took another look, she wasn't satisfied, but it would have to do for now.

Marnie sat on the edge of the bed, pulled on her stockings and garters, and buckled her boots while Kitty got changed. Intrigued, she watched as Kitty rummaged around in the hope chest looking for the pinking shears, then picking up Marnie's discarded dress Kitty cut the lace flounces off the sleeves and neckline, and a couple of feet of fabric from the front panel.

"One day I'll make something nice for you," Kitty promised. Hiding the scarlet satin at the bottom of the hope chest, she closed the lid. No matter how beaten Marnie was, she was still sure to draw the eye. To make her as inconspicuous as possible her long fair hair would have to be covered. "You could wear a couple of sacks sewn together and still look pretty, black eye to boot," said Kitty, feeling a pinch of jealousy.

Ma reckoned women were still such a rarity on the goldfields that it didn't matter if the woman had the body of an elephant and the face of a sheep she'd be married within a week.

Marnie stared at the mirror. It was like looking at a stranger. Her right eye was black and swollen shut, her face was devoid of colour, and her hair was braided into a single loose plait. She looked unkempt and dowdy. She gently touched her lip with her fingertip; it was crusting nicely.

"Sit here," Kitty commanded, patting the three-legged stool. With the aid of the brush and a few pins, allowing only a wisp of fair hair to curl at the nape, Kitty secured Marnie's hair into a tidy bun. Kitty handed Marnie a cap to put on. Marnie donned the cap, and once again looked at the stranger in the mirror. Apart from the black eye and thick lip, she decided she looked like an ordinary respectable servant girl, just one that had been badly beaten.

"Gather your things and take them out back to the old drum. I'll meet you there it's near the outhouse," Kitty instructed. Gathering Grace in her arms, Kitty said, "I'll be there in two shakes of a lamb's tail, I'll just give the little one to Ma to mind." And she disappeared into the hallway.

Marnie tucked her mutilated dress under her arm and carried it outside. She followed Kitty's instructions and found the old drum not far from the rear of the building. She shivered, it was cold out and wisps of steam curled from her mouth like ghostly snakes. Marnie clutched her dress tightly to her chest to keep herself warm. She wished she'd thought to ask for a shawl.

Kitty came striding across the lawn, a peek of white petticoat showing now and then as she walked, she carried a kerosene tin in one hand and a matchbox in the other.

Kitty misread the look on Marnie's face. "Don't fret, I'll make something nice for you to wear, I promise."

Marnie threw the dress into the rusty drum. It had no hold on her, she wanted to say goodbye to that life anyway, and burning her clothes seemed like a good way to do it.

Telling Marnie to stand well back, Kitty doused the dress with kerosene. She lit a match and threw it inside the drum, the clothing went up in a sudden terrifying whoosh. The searing heat forced them to cover their eyes as bright red, orange and blue flames licked at the cloth, then decreased in size, burning steadily for a few minutes until the whole lot was nothing but a smelly, charcoal mess.

The dew wet the hem of her skirts as Mary walked towards them with Grace on her hip. Without a word to either girl, she walked past, her head held high.

Kitty whispered to Marnie, "It'll be all right, you'll see."

Marnie hoped Kitty was right, Madame was tough, but Mary Healey appeared tougher.

Mary put Grace in the highchair. Skimming the cream from the milk pail, she sploshed some on each bowl of porridge. Excited by the prospect of food, Grace squealed and banged her spoon on the highchair's wooden tray.

Mary frowned at the child. "Patience little one," she growled. "It's too hot." She plunked the bowls on the dining table, and hollered, "Breakfast!"

Kitty arrived in the kitchen with Marnie trailing behind. Feeling awkward, Marnie waited to be told where to sit. Kitty patted the stool beside her, relieved Marnie took it.

Mary sat at the head of the table. "It's just us for breakfast," she said in clipped tones. "Your father, God rot him," she said sarcastically, "is in hiding, and your brother, deserted long before you were out of bed."

Grace squealed and banged her spoon. Mary scowled at the child; Grace stopped. Kitty sprinkled a good helping of sugar on her porridge and passed the sugar bowl to Marnie.

Marnie lavishly coated her porridge with sugar, and was about to take her first mouthful when Mary eyed her and pointedly said, "We'll say grace first."

Marnie's face coloured, she put down her spoon and solemnly bowed her head. Unable to find anything to be grateful for, Mary allocated the task to Kitty.

Kitty squeezed Marnie's hand. "Our Father which art in Heaven hallowed be thy name, thy kingdom come, thy will be done on Earth as it is in Heaven. Give us this day our daily bread and forgive us our trespasses as we forgive others that trespass against us, lead us not into temptation but deliver us from evil, for thine is the Kingdom, the power and the glory, forever and ever, amen."

"Yes, deliver us from evil," Mary echoed, narrowing her gaze at Marnie.

Marnie mumbled amen, she kept her head lowered and waited until Kitty ate before dipping her own spoon. Tasting the sweet, thick creamy porridge she closed her eyes and savoured each mouthful - it was delicious.

The girls ate quietly while Mary fed Grace and ate her own breakfast in stony silence. Then Kitty happened to mention to Marnie, that Mr Burns, Meg and Father Whooley were arriving later this afternoon to discuss the up-coming nuptials.

Mary paled; in all the kerfuffle she had plain forgotten. God in heaven, a prostitute and a priest under the same roof!

After breakfast, Mary handed Kitty the tea towel, and instructed the girls to do the dishes. Standing over Marnie, Mary criticized her every move. Shaking her head in disgust, she put a couple of dishes back in the sink.

"Do them again and properly this time," Mary snapped.

Nervous, Marnie carefully checked each one before placing them in the dish rack. Kitty quickly dried them before Mary could find fault. When they had finished the dishes, Kitty took the tablecloth outside to give it a good shake and Marnie was told to wipe down the table.

"Put some elbow grease into it, girl," Mary said tersely, leaning over her.

After everything was put away and in order, Marnie was given the task of stripping and remaking the beds while Mary supervised.

Mary pulled the covers back off the bed. "Do it again, and this time tuck the corners in properly."

Marnie's heart sank, she knew how to please men but how on earth was she ever going to satisfy this fastidious picky woman? She was impossible.

Kitty sailed past the open window her arms laden with wood. "And as luck would have it, you arrived in time to help us with washing day," she said cheerfully.

When Dan arrived back at Moonlight, he could hear the familiar noise of the pick and shovel, and Harry singing above the sound of the mighty rushing river. Harry had a beautiful powerful voice that carried on the wind. A voice that could make the angels cry. Dan wished he had such a gift; he couldn't carry a tune in a bucket. Tu tore towards Dan, his white-tipped tail waving like a flag. Dan rewarded the collie with a pat and a quick scratch behind the ears. Tu ran ahead to announce Dan's arrival. Dan tied his horse to the hitching post before skidding down the steep shingle bank to the river's edge. He waved his hat at his mates.

Up to his calves in water, Yankee stopped shovelling. Straightening, he shaded his eyes from the sun and called, "How did it go then?"

"About as well as expected," Dan yelled. He ran his hand through his messy dark hair before jamming his hat back on.

Harry waded out of the river, sat on a large rock and plugged his pipe with tobacco, he liked a good story. Tu lay contentedly at his master's feet.

"Not only that," Dan said, "Da is about to give Ma the news that Kitty wants to go to Dunedin to work as an apprentice dressmaker."

Harry squinted up at him. "Your Ma won't allow it, will she?"

"Poor Da, I reckon we'll probably hear the gunshot from here," Dan said with a dry laugh.

Harry's chuckle was low and soft. He blew out his cheeks. "Aye your poor Da might as well be dead as the poor bugger's life won't be worth living."

Yankee put his shovel down and wandered towards his mates. Harry thought it best to let them be, they had some unfinished business. He'd tactfully give them time to sort out their differences.

"You two get the fire lit and the pan heated and I'll make breakfast," Harry offered.

"There's food on the table from Ma," Dan told him.

Harry happily rubbed his belly. "Kai," he grinned. He clambered up the bank and headed to the hut.

"Good," Yankee said, pleased. "It will make a nice change from Weka."

"Thought you liked Maori Hen," Dan joked.

"Get sick of the same thing night after night, it's a wonder I haven't come down with the bleedin' scurvy." Yankee stirred the ashes of the campfire back into life. He threw some brush on it and sparks flew around them like fireflies.

They sat on the rocks positioned around the fire and stared at the flickering fire.

"I'm sorry mate," Dan began, "I didn't mean to offend you, it's not like...it's just, well you know...," he hesitated, unsure how to phrase it.

"I know, I know, you didn't want me to see Meg again," Yankee finished for him. "It's okay, mate," he said, not meeting Dan's eye. "I know you're trying to save me from making an even bigger fool of myself than I already am." He let out a low sigh. "Meg's made herself clear. Seems I was wrong in my assumption that she felt anything for the likes of me."

"I'm sorry," Dan muttered to the smooth round stones lying at his feet. He picked up a stone and sent it skipping across the water. It was killing him not knowing how to protect one from hurting the other. He patted his mate on the back and offered his hip flask to him. "It's for the best, mate," he said, shifting his gaze to the river.

"Aye, for the best," Yankee agreed, taking a swig of whisky.

Harry yelled from the door of the hut, "How's the fire coming along?"

Nudging Dan with his boot, Yankee lightened the mood by saying, "Do you think Harry's got a sister that's passable then?"

Snorting with laughter, Dan shook his head. "Love-struck or not mate, either way yer a blame fool."

Jim checked the position of the sun, it was getting on, regardless if he was welcome home or not, he was hungry. He gathered his tools; he couldn't stay away much longer no matter how tempted. No, he'd best head back and face whatever new catastrophe awaited him. He patted the leather pouch dangling from his belt, aye, the little lady should be happy. He stumped back up the track his head busy with assumptions. It was like preparing for a prize fight, move to the left and she'd move to the right. He came over the rise to see Marnie battling the mangle and Kitty carrying the heavy wicker basket to the clothesline.

Approaching Kitty, Jim whispered in her ear, "Is it safe?'

Kitty secured a flapping napkin to the line. "No, Da. Ma's in a frightful temper and I'm afraid Marnie is bearing the brunt of it. Ma's hissing like a spitting tomcat. How's she going to be when she hears my news? She may well burst her boiler." Kitty picked up another napkin shook it, and pegged it onto the line.

Jim scratched his head. "This apprenticeship, are you quite sure? Is your heart truly set on it?"

Kitty's eyes were soft and pleading. "We can afford it, can't we, Da?"

"Aye, affording it's not the problem child. It's that your mother isn't ready to be rid of you just yet, and I reckon I'm going to have a hard job of convincing her that she is."

Jim squared his shoulders. He would put up a courageous fight and to hell with the consequences. "Never mind lass, I'll talk to your Ma. It will be all right, you'll see."

Father Whooley arrived early in the afternoon. Clean shaven, with cropped blonde hair and kind blue eyes, he was as tall and lean as a string bean. The priest was well regarded in the district, and despite his tender years, he had a reputation for being a wise soul.

Father Whooley slid from his pony and grasped Jim firmly by the hand, "Good to see you, Jim. How have you been?" Jim was pleased to see him; the pair shared a special bond that went deeper than words.

"Mighty fine," Jim replied with a lopsided grin. "But I warn you my wee wifey isn't at all happy."

A frown creased the young man's forehead, "What's the matter? Is it the wedding preparations?" he asked, concerned.

"Not that one but the next," Jim answered cryptically.

Kitty arrived in their midst. Taking the pony by the reins, she said, "I'll take care of him for you Father."

Father Whooley smiled warmly. "Bless you my child."

As Kitty and the stalwart little pony moved off towards the stables, Father Whooley said loud enough for Kitty to hear, "She's a good girl that one, bless her."

Aye, I'm going to miss her, Jim thought. "Right, best you meet our new guest before the future bride and groom arrive," Jim said, shepherding Father Whooley inside.

Marnie was dusting the mantelpiece when the two men came into the small living room. Unsure what to do, and unable to hide herself in time, she hid the duster behind her back.

"Marnie," Jim said with a sweep of his long arm, "meet Father Whooley."

Marnie went white to the lips but nodded, and with a slight curtsey said, "Father," with just the right amount of reverence.

Father Whooley was surprised to find one of Queenstown's gaudy vice in Mary Healey's living room, and his face showed it. He took a moment to recover. "I've seen you about town but I don't believe we have ever met." He inclined his head. "Good day to you...Miss...Marnie."

Mary bustled in. "Oh, Father, I see you've already met - Marnie."

"Aye, just now," Father Whooley nodded, looking puzzled.

Mary noticed the duster hidden behind Marnie's back. "I don't want you dusting that mantelpiece," she barked. "Everywhere but there, understand?"

Marnie nodded.

"And, you are supposed to stay out of sight; no one is to know you are here," Mary hissed.

Marnie was about to ask whether she should leave when there was the sound of horses' hooves and a jangle of harnesses as a gig pulled up outside the hotel.

Mary peeked out the window. "Oh no, they're early," she said flustered. She hurried to the door to let the young couple in.

Jim grinned, "I'd say their timing's perfect." He gestured to Marnie to stay put.

117

Meg sailed into the room pulling off her kid gloves as she walked. She stopped abruptly. She hadn't expected to see a lost soul with a black eye standing in the living room. Looking like she might burst into tears, the girl was hiding something behind her back.

Removing his hat, Burns nodded politely to the stranger, "Hello Miss..." he paused waiting, but when no one had the decency to introduce the girl, he bowed, "Mr William Burns, at your service, Miss."

Marnie shrank into the wall.

"Are you a friend of Kitty's?" Meg asked.

"Jack's," Mary answered, her voice flat.

"She's mine too," Kitty corrected, coming in the side door.

Meg's mouth fell open, she stared at the girl, "You must be..."

"Marnie," Mary said, losing patience.

Father Whooley could tell by the faces of those present now was not the time to ask questions, but a lot could be gleaned by listening. Fascinated, he stood beside Marnie and watched the interaction between the family as enthralled as if he was at the theatre.

"Marnie staying here is a secret and is to remain so, do I make myself clear?" Mary told them.

There was a murmur of assent.

Kitty nudged her father.

Jim shuffled his feet. There was no good time so now would be as good as any. He took a deep breath and began. "Ah, I'm glad we're all gathered here, there's something that needs to be said, and Mary my love this includes you. Best you take a seat," he said, taking her arm.

She shook him off. "Has the sun fried your brain you great galoot?" Mary cried. "The priest is here to go over things with the bridal couple, not us."

Ignoring her protests, Jim steered Mary towards the rocker. "I know that my dear but Kitty has something to tell us."

"Kitty has?" Mary sat. Puzzled, she gazed up at her youngest daughter.

Kitty flushed. All eyes rested on her. She cleared her throat. "Ah, Ma, the letter I received is ... well it's an offer of a placement as an apprentice dressmaker," she paused, taking a deep breath, the rest came out in a rush, "for a boutique fashion house in Dunedin."

"What!" Mary cried, leaping out of the chair.

Kitty hurriedly added, "Da said we could afford lodgings."

Fists balling by her side, Mary rounded on Jim, "You knew about this?" she accused.

"Only last night, my dear," Jim replied. "You were that upset already I didn't have the heart to tell you or you'd have not slept a wink."

Hoping to stop a lengthy tirade before it started, Kitty interrupted, "Marnie's here she'll help. It's only three months, Ma. They want to see I'm good enough, and if I'll like it. Please, Ma, please," Kitty implored.

"Truly?" Meg stared at her sister, shocked. Kitty had never managed to keep a secret in her life, and she couldn't believe Kitty could have kept something like this from her.

Kitty nodded, her eyes starting to fill with tears.

"But not until after my wedding?" Meg's brows knitted.
Kitty chewed her lip.

"Sorry Meg, if I'm allowed to go it would mean I'd have to leave more-or-less immediately."

Meg cried, "No, Kitty! You have to be my bridesmaid!" Meg rushed at her and threw her arms about Kitty's neck. "Oh Kitty. You can't. I'd miss you so much. If it's about the gown, I love it. I'm so sorry I didn't make a big enough fuss."

Kitty's throat tightened. "It's not about the gown."

Meg stepped back. "It's not?"

Burns came to Kitty's defence. "Kitty does have a talent for dressmaking. To become an apprentice in a fashion house in Dunedin would be an excellent opportunity for her."
Mary gave him a look that should have nailed him to the door by his ears. There was a long drawn out silence as emotions threatened to overwhelm the room.

Meg sighed reluctantly agreeing. "William's right, Ma. Kitty does have a rare talent, and she is wasted here mending trousers and fixing hems."

Desperate, Kitty begged. "Please, Ma, please. Mr Burns has business in Dunedin next week." She turned to her father, "And he could escort me, couldn't he, Da?"

Mary's hands flew to her hips. "Hold it right there!" Struggling to control her temper, she spluttered, "The cart's got way ahead of the horse. I haven't said she can go." She froze Jim with an icy stare. "Have you forgotten the child is only fourteen?"

Jim hardened his resolve. "Father Whooley has come to have a chat with William and Meg, so you three go and do that." He

120

opened the door to the sitting room for them. Then he turned to the younger girls. "And Kitty and Marnie please organize afternoon tea. And, Mary, me darlin'," he said in his best wheedling voice, slipping his arm in hers. "How about coming for a wee stroll with me so we can discuss the situation, in private like?"

Mary shook herself free. "James Healey, you lying snake in the grass!" she spluttered, pushing him. "If you are planning to charm me with your forked tongue you can forget it!"

Jim didn't bat an eyelid but calmly said, "Please carry on with your plans, Father. Mary and I will just go for a wee doddle up the track." He held the side door open for her and waited.

Furious, Mary debated whether to go or stay. In the end to save face she flew out the door like sailcloth caught in the wind.

They walked up the track towards Deep Creek. Mary walked briskly, her arms swinging at her sides as stiffly as a solider but long limbed and lithe, Jim easily kept pace. When they had walked far enough away from the hotel so their voices would not travel, Mary stopped abruptly. She stamped her foot and called down all manner of curses bruising the air with her words. Jim waited patiently until she ran out of steam.

"Now darlin'," he said calmly, "you make the demons in hell tremble when you behave so. You're going to have to confess your sins, and spend a month of Sundays on your knees to make up for that torrent of poisonous venom you just spewed."

Mary glared up at him. "Don't you go using religion on me James Healey!" she said jabbing a bony finger at him. "Not when you're as treacherous as Judas Iscariot himself!"

"Now, now, darling, I'm not the enemy. I'd dearly love our wee Kitty to stay put, but be reasonable Mary we can't keep her here forever. She's fourteen and old enough. The time for letting go has got to happen sometime, seems it's going to be sooner rather than later."

Mary lifted her chin irritably. "I need her."

Jim nodded. "I know you do dear heart. And I know you'll miss her something fierce but come now, it's only three months, and who knows, maybe she'll not like it, or maybe they'll not like her."

"Of course, she'll love it and they'll love her, she's a good girl and a grand little seamstress. What's not to like?" And as quickly as Mary's temper had flared now it dissipated, and she felt spent. "Kitty's my baby, Jim. I'm not ready to let go of her, not yet."

Gathering her in his arms, Jim kissed the top of her head. "I know little darlin' but on the bright side you still have me."

Placing her palms on his chest, Mary pushed him away. "I want Kitty here, with us. She belongs here."

Jim sighed. "The trouble is, Mary," he paused as if considering whether to continue or not, "Kitty is smitten, and it kills her to see her sister about to marry the man she loves."

Mary thought he was joking but the look on his face told her he was not. "What! Are you sure? Did Kitty say as much?" she asked, shocked.

"Not in as many words no, but yes, I'm sure. Kitty hangs on William's every word; don't you see the besotted way she looks at him?"

Mary had been too busy with the hotel, the baby, and all the chores to notice, but now that Jim mentioned it, it made sense.

Perhaps that was why Kitty had been belligerent lately and did not actively engage in conversation about Meg's wedding. Even though Kitty had made Meg's dress and detailed it beautifully, her heart didn't seem to be in it.

Jim stooped, picked up a pebble threw it in the air and caught it again while he watched Mary waiting for his words to sink in. He could see various thoughts scurry across her mind like mice in a haybarn. She was weakening.

He tucked a wayward curl behind her ear. "My dear, you have to agree it is a wonderful opportunity for Kitty."

Mary didn't respond.

He continued, "This opportunity will give her a chance to showcase her talent to people who can pay high prices for such luxury. And, it will also give her the distance she'll need so she can get over her infatuation." He hurried on. "Plus, we can afford to buy her an apprenticeship."

"But... she's my baby, Jim," Mary said feebly, all the puff and wind gone out of her.

"Aye, we will all miss her, Mary, but she needs this, besides we'll have Marnie here for a little while yet."

"Huh!" Mary snorted. "The girl is useless. She can barely boil a billy."

"You're a woman of many talents, I'm sure you can teach her how to cook, clean and sew, my dear." Jim tossed the stone and caught it one handed. He lowered his voice, "Be fair, Mary, the child has not had to do that before so you can't expect her to know how."

Mary looked dubious. "I'd have as much luck training a donkey to keep house."

"And we can afford to get someone to help you. Put out your hand."

Mary wrinkled her nose at him. "Why, so you can give me a stone?"

Jim let the stone fall to the ground, it landed in the dust with a soft poof. Taking the pouch off his belt, he poured some grains of gold into Mary's open palm.

"Some river stones for my lady." He smiled, bowing gallantly. Mary's eyes gleamed at the sight of the gold.

"See, the claim is yielding more than enough colour to get you a domestic."

"That's if we can find one," Mary muttered sceptically.

Knowing he was making headway, Jim continued, "What's more, William can escort Kitty to Dunedin."

"If what you say is true," Mary replied tartly, her hand closing about the gold, "he should be the last one to escort her. Don't you think?"

"Aye, you're right of course," Jim conceded. "But there's nothing else for it, no one else can go. And maybe, just maybe time spent with him it will help her get over her infatuation."

"You're a terrible optimist."

"And you're a tremendous pessimist," Jim returned.

"I reckon the tea will be well and truly brewed by now." Mary started walking back.

"Aye, it'll probably be so strong it'll taste like it's been strained through one of my socks," Jim joked, trying to lighten the mood.

Ignoring him, Mary kept walking at a brisk pace. Jim chased after her. He'd done his best; what happened from here on was in God's hands.

The lace tablecloth and the special china adorned the table. Mary gave Kitty a quick nod of approval, and while Marnie's back was turned, she reached for the tea caddy on the mantelpiece and deposited the gold within.

Jim whispered in Kitty's ear, "I've done my best darlin'. The Almighty himself couldn't have been more convincing."

Kitty anxiously studied her mother's face, but Mary wasn't giving anything away.

Kitty said, "The tea and cakes are ready, Ma, but the others are still in the sitting room, talking."

"Go and tell them that I said afternoon tea is ready."

It was a tense time filled with polite conversation in a confined space. Everyone except the good Father and Burns seemed to have lost their appetites. Father Whooley was the first to excuse himself from the table, saying he had a sermon to prepare, so he'd retire while the light was still good. Keen to get away from the tension, Jim asked Burns if he'd like to join him for a walk.

Placing the dishes on the bench, Mary told Marnie to wash, and Meg to dry, while she had a word in private with Kitty out on the veranda.

Like a condemned man about to climb the gallows, Kitty followed her mother outside.

As the door closed, Marnie asked, "Do you think Kitty will be all right?"

Meg nodded. "Don't fret, Ma's soft on Kitty, always has been."

Marnie strained her ears for any sounds that meant Kitty was being beaten but there were no raised voices or any signs of a scuffle that she could hear.

Meanwhile Meg was summing Marnie up. Although Kitty's dress hung limply on Marnie's slight frame, and the thick lip and a black eye marred her good looks, Meg could see why Jack had fallen for the girl. Marnie was pretty, a light dusting of freckles dotted the bridge of her small turned up nose, she was petite, but her brilliant blue eyes reflected a deep sadness. What did she see in Jack? Jack was only a lad, barely shaving, hardly a catch for any woman.

They were nearing the last dish when Meg finally asked the question that had been plaguing her. "Marnie, can I ask you something?"

Marnie dried her hands. Cocking her head to one side, she whispered, "Is it about your wedding night? Do you want to know what to expect?" She nudged Meg, "I fancy the priest couldn't tell you that."

Meg flushed scarlet. Why did everyone feel the need to tell her what to expect. "No, no," she hastily replied. "No, actually, well I was wondering," she paused, "I'm curious, I don't mean to sound rude but - you are an attractive girl, and there are men far better looking and richer than Jack, so why him? Why my brother?"

"Ah," Marnie said cheerily, "Everyone else has always wanted something from me, he don't. He wants to give me a better life. Others want me to please them somehow, be something I'm not. And I'm good at that, I'm real good at pretending, I give them what they want, tell them what they want to hear, that's how I have survived. Sure, I know Jack is taken with my packaging and don't want no old sow for a wife, but its more than that, Jack sees me, the little girl that sits in the dark and cries, and he loves me regardless." Face clouding with emotion, Marnie said softly, "I haven't felt that in a long time, not since my mother passed."

"But how do you know Jack is the right decision?" Meg persisted.

Marnie sighed wistfully. "I don't. I have to hope to God I have made the right decision, and not been hoodwinked by him. But no matter what happens I can't go back; they would kill me." She shuddered.

Meg bit her lip. She didn't know what to say. She didn't have to live with the fear of someone trying to kill her.

Marnie tried to lighten the mood. "Mind you, your mother scares me half to death, if Jack doesn't come for me soon, I might die of fright."

Meg grinned. "Don't worry, Ma's got a hiss like a snake but there's goodness beneath, one day you'll find it. Besides, if Jack said, he's coming for you, nothing will stop him."

Unless someone or something prevents him, Marnie thought, fear pulsing through her veins. What if Madame or Bill had hurt him so badly he could not travel? He'd risked his life to save hers, it was wrong of her to doubt him. She was pleased that she wasn't alone, she would have gone crazy with worry if she didn't have people around, and in a way, Mary Healey was doing her a favour by keeping her too busy to dwell on things. Marnie watched Meg speculatively as Meg gave the last teaspoon a polish before placing it in the cutlery drawer.

Marnie leant against the bench and grinned. "But you'll know that feeling, right? That feeling of being special, otherwise you'd not be marrying Mr Burns?"

"Yes, of course," Meg replied, hanging the tea-towel up to dry.

"Sit," Mary commanded.

Kitty obeyed, taking a seat beside her mother on the settle.

Mary asked, "Why? Tell me why Dunedin, why this place, and why now?"

Kitty had rehearsed the answer in her head. "I love sewing, and I want to be the best, this fashion house will give me the opportunity to become that."

Mary scrutinised her youngest child's face looking for any tell-tale signs that she was lying.

Kitty knotted her fingers in her dress. "It's what I want to do, Ma. I love sewing."

"But Dunedin is so far away. Are you running away from something? Or someone?" Mary asked pointedly. "Is it me?"

Kitty gazed into the distance. "No," she said quietly, her brow furrowed.

Mary believed in being direct. "Your father says you have feelings for, William. Is that true?"

Kitty's head jerked up in surprise. After a moment's hesitation, she nodded.

"I see." Mary blew out her cheeks. She was silent while she sought the right words to say, finally she said, "If that's your reason for going I don't think it's good enough."

Kitty argued, "I don't want to be around them, Ma. I can't bear it. Besides, I do want to be the best dressmaker."

"Does Meg know?"

"About William? I don't think so. I haven't told a living soul."

"Ah," Mary nodded sagely. "Well, it seems that your father has better eyes than most, and Meg's are as blind as mine." She patted Kitty's knee. "It is an infatuation, Kitty. Running away isn't the answer. It won't make the pain go away, but I promise it will ease over time. And before you know it you will find someone nearer your own age and you will love them more than you ever could have dreamed possible."

Kitty desperately wanted to believe that. "I hope you are right, Ma, but for now, I don't want to witness their affection for one another. It hurts too much."

They fell silent.

Minutes later, Kitty raised her head. "Can I go?" she asked meekly.

Mary wasn't about to be swayed by a few choice words. "I don't like the underhand way you went about things young lady. Furthermore, I don't like the idea of you going anywhere, certainly not going to Dunedin by yourself. Nor do I like the idea of having to pay them to keep you. In fact, Katherine Healey, there is not a lot I do like."

Kitty grasped Mary's hand. "Please, Ma, please," she implored. "It would mean the world to me. They can teach me new things, more than Granny McNab can, and then I can be recognized as a proper seamstress, and perhaps one day have my very own shop." Mary smiled, she admired ambition.

Kitty pounced on the chance. "William said he'll escort me, and Da said we can afford it."

Determined not to show any sign of weakening, Mary stood. "I'm not saying yes, and I'm not saying no, Katherine Healey. What I am saying is I'll sleep on it." Perhaps it was because Kitty was the youngest, perhaps it was because being so strict on the others had worn her down over time, but she knew Kitty had a way of getting around her the others did not.

Kitty threw her arms about her mother's neck and cried, "Thank you, Ma!"

"I haven't said yes," Mary gently reminded. "Come on, we best get back inside, God only knows what the stupid girl has done now."

Kitty winced. "For Jack's sake, Ma, please be nice to Marnie."

The men walked along the track smoking their pipes in companionable silence. Jim thought if it wasn't for Marnie's unannounced arrival, and Kitty's impending departure, he would be a happy man. The sun was shining, there was good gold in his claim and Meg was marrying a man with a good business head. Jim wondered if Burns knew what he was letting himself in for. Meg could be fiercely determined. His middle daughter was a tricky bundle, and he'd learn that soon enough for himself. She would argue black was white till she was blue in the face. Say no to her, and she'd want it all the more. Lost in thought, he puffed away on his pipe. He wanted to warn Burns that Kitty had feelings for him, and he should tread gently and not destroy her dignity should Kitty make those feelings known, but he said nothing.

Instead, he said, "Thank you for offering to accompany Kitty on the journey, William, it eases our minds to know you'll be with her."

"More than happy to oblige," Burns assured Jim. "Has it been decided then?"

Jim released smoke slowly from his lungs so that it drifted in lazy circles above his head. "Not exactly," he admitted, "but I'm certain it will be. Mary just needs a little time to get her head around it. It won't be easy for her; she'll feel like she's losing two daughters at once."

"But she is gaining a son-in-law," countered Burns.

The easy banter made Jim relax. "Aye, that she is, and a daughter-in-law too if Jack has his way," Jim replied, amused.

Astonished, Burns stopped in his tracks. Scandalized, he said, "But that girl is a..." He couldn't bring himself to say *whore*, so he let the inference speak for itself, "is she not?"

"Aye and I'm a liar and a drunkard, and been a deserter to boot so who are we to judge, right son?"

Burns had chosen to overlook these things and he didn't want to be reminded of them now.

Jim clapped a hand on Burns shoulder. "Come on lad, best we head back. The women will be waiting."

Mary packaged up a pound of butter, a block of cheese, and a pot of blackberry jam as a gift for the Asterlys. Meg put on her gloves and tied her bonnet, then they all went outside to see the young couple off. Marnie stayed in the shadows near the stables, careful to not be seen. Meg gave the basket to William to put in the gig and went back to speak to Marnie. She couldn't help

131

thinking that despite knowing what Marnie was, she quite liked the girl.

"Jack told us how lovely you were and it's a pleasure to have finally met you, Marnie," Meg said with a warm smile.

Marnie wished there was something she could do to repay Meg's kindness, and it suddenly occurred to her, she had something to give.

Grasping Meg's hand in hers, Marnie said, "I would very much like it if..." she broke off, embarrassed.

"Go on," Meg encouraged.

"I know you probably have everything for your wedding but I was hoping... well, would you like to use my parasol? It's white, lace, and almost new."

Touched, Meg said, "Oh Marnie, that's very sweet."

Marnie smiled, feeling sheepish she said, "You know it's the only thing I brought with me, perhaps it was meant for you."

"Thank you for your kind offer. If it's all right with you, I will get it next time I visit." She whispered, "Wouldn't want Ma to see it."

Delighted, Marnie smiled and the crust on her lip pulled taut.

Mary beckoned, calling out, "Meg, hurry up."

"Coming," Meg replied.

Mary grasped Meg by the arm and said, "Don't get close to her, you have a lot to lose," she said casting an eye in Burns direction.

"But Ma... I only..."

Mary didn't wait for Meg to finish. "You have a habit of caring too much and it will only come back to haunt you," she warned.

Father Whooley ventured out of his hut to say goodbye. And while Jim and Burns were in deep conversation, he seized the chance to have a quick word with Meg. Taking her aside, he said, "It's good to know Yankee has someone else to concentrate his affections on now, isn't it?"

Meg's eyes widened. "Has he, Father?"

The young priest frowned. "I was under the impression he told you."

Meg nodded. "Yes, yes, he did," she said softly, remembering Yankee saying he would take a wife.

"I told him when he had another to focus his affections on, the pain will ease."

"Did you, Father? And he took your advice then?" Intrigued, Meg wanted to know more.

"Yes, he has... and he's chosen a fine young..."
William interrupted their conversation before the priest could finish.

"Come, my dear, we must be on our way," Burns said, taking her arm.

He assisted her onto the gig then clambered aboard the driver's seat, with the quick flick of the reins and a cheery wave they were off.

Meg held tightly to the side while the gig jolted its way along the treacherous track. Her thoughts were swirling like eddies in a river. Yankee Brown was telling the truth he was taking a wife!

They were nearing Gooseberry Gully when William said, "You're very quiet." He glanced across at her. "Is everything all right?"

"Tired, is all," she replied, dismissing his concern.

"Are you thinking about that girl? And about Kitty wanting to go to Dunedin?"

"Yes, it has been a day full of surprises."

William slanted his hat in an attempt to block out the sun's blinding rays. "Your mother appears as shocked as we."

"A lot has happened in a short time," agreed Meg.

"Jack's lady friend," he paused, considering how best to phrase it, "I gather you realize the woman is a prostitute."

Meg nodded. "So I believe."

"She is. I've seen her flaunting herself on the wharf. I want you to know Margaret despite what people may say about your brother's choices, I'm still prepared to marry you. However, I am pleased that their wedding, if they are to marry, will be a secret one, and they plan to leave the district. It wouldn't do to have our good name and reputation sullied by their relationship."

Meg looked at him sharply. He sounded so magnanimous. It never occurred to her he would alter his decision based on her brother's choice. Was he serious? Ma was right, William was affected by the appearance of evil, and to him, the harlot, Marnie, paved the road to hell.

He patted Meg's gloved hand as if to reassure her. "It seems like you will have to find a new bridesmaid my dear."

"Yes, so it would seem," Meg replied. She was annoyed by his condescending tone but before they reached Pleasant Beach her anger had subsided. She supposed she should be grateful that William would not let public opinion sway him. And happy, that he supported Kitty in choosing to do what she loved most. Well-dressed, bowler hat, carefully manicured moustache and goatee beard, he was every inch the gentleman. He would make a fine husband. She should be relieved by the news Yankee was going to wed. Well, if nothing else she was certainly curious. Who had Yankee chosen to marry?

Mary clapped her hands, "Right, hop to it, there's work to do, and plenty of it."

Kitty smiled sweetly. "What would you like us to do, Ma?" Her eyes flickered to Marnie's face. Marnie appeared to be wilting from fatigue.

"There's chickens to pluck," Mary answered. "Your father killed two this morning. Then there's a pile of ironing the size of a haystack."

Kitty grimaced, she didn't mind ironing but hated plucking chickens.

The girls were kept busy until Mary opened the tavern that night, then they were sent away and told to keep out of sight. Kitty was allowed to sit by the fire with Jim but Marnie was sent to the bedroom. Marnie didn't mind, she felt safer there, away from Mary. Grace sat on the rag mat happily playing with her wooden blocks, Marnie smiled wistfully at the babe thinking perhaps one day she might have a child of her own. So far, the cap and sponge seemed to have done the job and she hadn't gotten pregnant, other girls had, and their babies had been punched or kicked out. The babies that survived the gruelling beatings and made it to life were given to the Nuns. Removing her boots, she rubbed her aching feet and thought how young and handsome Meg and Mr Burns looked together. She envied them. Everyone was happy for them. No one would be happy to see her wed Jack, that is, if Mary Healey allowed them to wed. Jack would need his parents' permission to marry and while Jim might give his, Marnie very much doubted Mary would give hers.

Kitty bounced into the bedroom wearing a smile from ear to ear. Marnie watched as Kitty changed Grace, gave her a warm bottle, and settled the babe for the night. Worn out, Marnie could hardly string two words together, let alone ask Kitty why she was so cheerful. Exhausted she fell asleep only to dream troubled dreams. But brimming with excitement and wide-awake, Kitty stared at the rafters, Glory be! Ma had said yes!

Chapter 5   Difficulty

Marnie was coming back from her morning trip to the outhouse when she noticed Father Whooley sitting on the old stump, his hands pressed together in prayer. Not wanting to disturb him, she tiptoed past.

He opened his eyes. "Come and sit with me a while child," he entreated, patting the space beside him. Marnie thought the term child was ironic since he was not much older than her, three or four years at the most. She hesitated.

"Come," he beckoned. "I'd like to talk to you."

Worried, she excused herself by saying, "Ah, I don't think Mrs Healey would like it, I'm to do the sweeping."

He wouldn't take no for an answer. "She'll be perfectly fine. Come."

Reluctantly, Marnie sat beside him, curling a finger nervously in her hair she waited for the priest to speak. Was he going to condemn her to hell?

"Would you like to take confession child?" He looked at her with his intense blue eyes and Marnie felt her soul was laid bare.

Startled, Marnie stared at him in horror. Confession? Where would she begin? And what was her fault and what wasn't? Did the lines blur between the two sometimes? The stump was an odd place for a confessional. Didn't such things have to be done in a church?

"Ah," she faltered, "I'm not of the faith, Father."

"You're not?" He seemed surprised. A moment passed before he said, "Well, would you like to be? Confirmed and baptized?"

Marnie tried to collect her thoughts. She dug the tip of her boot into the dewy grass. "Ah, I don't rightly think God would want the likes of me, Father."

"That's where you're wrong, I believe he does," he argued.

She hung her head and quietly said, "But I'm not worthy."

"Aye well, you are right there," Father Whooley acknowledged. "None are, for the scriptures say, all have fallen short of the glory of God, but if we confess our sins, he is faithful and just to forgive us our sins. Sin is sin, anger, bitterness and pride are also sins and most have experienced them."

Marnie shook her head. "I know you mean well Father, but I still don't think the good Lord would want the likes of me. I have done a lot of bad things."

"And why not?" he asked briskly, his brow furrowing. "Did you know that one of our Lord's most faithful followers was a harlot named Mary Magdalene?"

Avoiding the scrutiny of his intense blue eyes and direct manner, Marnie kept her voice soft and her head down. "I've heard stories Father," she admitted, "but I'm not sure of the truth of them. Some folks call us the Magdalens."

But Father Whooley had not finished. "If Mary Magdalene who was delivered of seven demons was good enough to be a disciple of our Lord, do you think he'd deny you to come to him child?" It was a thrust of a question as sharp as any dagger.

Uncertain, Marnie replied, "I don't rightly know, I've not thought about it afore." And indeed she hadn't, she'd survived her childhood by not thinking too much, otherwise she would have felt robbed and would have been angry at God and bitter in spirit. If she didn't expect much then she couldn't be disappointed.

"Promise me you'll consider becoming part of the faith," Father Whooley said. "For all may come to him. Our Lord turns no repentant sinner away."

Unable to find her voice, Marnie dug the toe of her boot further into the ground and nodded.

"Next time I visit, you and I can talk some more. Think about turning your life over to God. He came to seek and save the lost and he cares for you, Marnie."

It was too much for Marnie to think that the Almighty might care for her but she could see that Father Whooley was waiting for a response.

"I promise I'll think on it, Father."

He smiled. "Good. Let us pray." He bowed his head. "May the God of hope fill you with all joy and peace as you trust in him, so that you may overflow with hope by the power of the Holy Spirit. May the peace of the Lord Jesus Christ be with you always, may his face shine upon you and may he make himself known to you." He intoned the words, "In the name of the Father, the Son and the Holy Ghost, amen."

Marnie clumsily copied the father's hand gestures as he made the sign of the cross.

She left him sitting on the old stump, and went into the hotel through the back door thinking about the woman called Mary Magdalene. She knew nothing other than the name, for she had no remembrance of religion in her violent upbringing. All she knew was the pious, righteous men who looked down on her with condescending eyes by day, were the same ones who visited her at night.

Father Whooley packed his travelling case and set out to find Jim. He had helped Jim find the strength to face a life of sobriety, and in return Jim had given him the gift of friendship. Last winter they worked tirelessly to help save those trapped, cut off or injured in the Big Flood. It was a lonely life being a priest; though revered by most, he was used to peoples' guilty consciences keeping him at a distance, so he was grateful Jim didn't treat him differently than any other man.

Hearing whistling coming from the stables, he followed the sound and found Jim hard at work. It was gloomy inside the stables but the open door shed light where it was needed. The place smelt of damp hay and horse manure. Jim was dubbing and polishing the saddles, the muscles in his arms strong and sinewy from years of hard work.

The priest said, "Thank you for your hospitality my friend but it's time for me to visit my fledging flock up at The Branches."

"It is me that's indebted to you, Father." Jim grinned. "Reckon just by being here you have saved me skin." Putting the dubbin tin and cloth aside, he said, "Here, you put the bridle on and I'll saddle your pony for you." Jim put the saddle around the small chestnut pony's girth and buckled it. "I'm mighty tempted to come with you Father, the hotel is not an overly pleasant place to be at present."

Father Whooley's pony willingly took the bit. The priest ran a hand over his faithful pony's neck. "Ah, I guessed as much. You'll be in my prayers."

"Well, now Father," Jim thoughtfully stroked his beard, "the good Lord is testing me almost beyond my endurance. My wife wants to wring Jack's neck for sending Marnie here, and she wants to wring my neck for daring to say I would allow Kitty to go to Dunedin. It's enough to make me want to crawl inside the bottom of a whisky barrel and stay there."

Alarm flashed in the Father's eyes.

Jim hastily added, "Don't worry, Father, for as much as it's called me, I haven't succumbed to the terrible temptation just yet."

"Ah yes, these are challenging times," Father Whooley agreed. "But the good Lord is looking after you Jim. Don't forget to thank him for his kindnesses."

Jim roared with laughter. "Father me wife wants to kill me and not kindly either. In fact, I think she wants to string me up by my entrails, no come to think of it Mary would like to string me up by..." Jim pointed to his nether regions. "And the way she feels about me at the moment I won't be using them, so it won't matter anyways."

A tickle of a smile teased Father Whooley's mouth. "Makes me glad I've chosen celibacy," he confessed. He grew serious. "Jim, I have a favour to ask?"

Surprised, Jim was eager to please, after all, Father Whooley had been there for him in his darkest hours. "Gladly, what can I do for you?"

"I want you to be part of the church committee. I need a good group of men to help organize the building of a school, and as an esteemed member of our congregation I hope you can assist."

"Me!" Jim spluttered. "When have I ever been an esteemed anything?"

Father Whooley clapped a hand on Jim's shoulder. "You've changed since you've given up drinking, Jim. Folks in these parts like and respect you," he paused, adding hopefully, "will you consider it then?"

"Member of the congregation," Jim snorted. "Why, I've never even set foot in your parish."

The pony turned its head. Father Whooley patted the restless pony's neck. "True, as I have brought the gospel to you, as much as it's a fine sanctuary surely you can see we need a school and a hall. And you are just the kind of man I want on the committee. What do you say?"

Jim opened his mouth and closed it again. How could he have gone from being a no-good drunk to an esteemed member of the community in such a short space of time? Why only a year ago he was lying in a ditch as pickled as an onion.

Father Whooley lifted his hand, halting further protest. "No, don't give me an answer yet, think on it. I'll be praying for you Jim, for wisdom and divine guidance." He led his pony out of the stables and placed his foot in the stirrups.

"And while you're at it if you could pray for patience and forbearance for Mary, I'd appreciate that also Father."
Jim followed man and beast outside.

Father Whooley mounted and pressed his heels in his pony's side. Suppressing a smile, he said, "The Lord bless, and keep you, and your family Jim."

Jack wiped his slick forehead, leaving a smudge of soot. There was still work to do, but tired and hungry, he decided to call it quits. Bennett had spent the better part of the afternoon convincing him that to leave too soon would only add to their suspicion, and they'd come looking for him. He reckoned best wait until the dust settled and they could come up with a better plan. Bennett went home, promising he'd think on it that night. His parting instructions were those of warning. He told Jack to stay put, keep his head down, lock the door, and camp the night at the forge.

One by one, Jack put the tools away, hung the lanterns on their hooks, and let the fire die down. He sat on the upturned barrel and eased the muscles in his aching neck and shoulders. He needed a wash, he felt grimy to the core but what he wanted most was food. It didn't matter what, but he needed something in his empty belly. Bennett had forgotten to get Jack something before he left, and Jack hadn't liked to ask.

Bill had spent the day on the other side of the road, watching and waiting to see if there was any sign of Marnie. Hoping the coast was clear, Jack opened the forge door's iron slot and checked the surroundings. There was no sign of Bill. It was a risk, but there was nothing to eat in the shop but some oats for the horse, and he didn't fancy those. He should have thought to ask the stable boy at the livery next door to get him a bun or two, now it was too late, the boy had gone home. He'd have to risk it, or his growling belly wouldn't let him to sleep tonight. He shrugged on his jacket and knotted his necktie; it was warm in the forge but it would be cool outside.

He opened the door a crack. Darkness was falling quickly and the street lamps were being lit. There was some carousing coming from the hotels and dance halls across the road but no sign of Bill. He must have given up and returned to the brothel. Jack tore down the side alleyway, past a few drunks with bottles of comfort in their hands, and nipped down the lane towards the sweet-smelling bakery. The sign on the door read CLOSED, but he hammered on it regardless.

A gruff Scot's voice answered, "Canna ye nae read mon, I'm closed." But Jack beat on the door like a man possessed, until frustrated and angry, the baker opened the door. For a man with a deep voice, he was short and rotund, with a full beard and moustache, a bald head and a quick temper.

"What do ye want?" he demanded, bristling like a snarling dog. "I'm closed. Come back in the mornin'."

"I need something to eat, anything will do. I've coin and I'll pay double," Jack offered.

The canny Scotsman cocked his head and lifted a bushy eyebrow.

"Leftovers will do." Jack held out two shiny coins. The baker opened the door, his chubby hand snaked out and took the coin from Jack's open palm. For his persistence, Jack was rewarded with a crusty sugar loaf, a plain loaf and a cold mutton pie. Thanking him, and anxious to get back to the forge, Jack picked up the flour bag and ran down the side alley. The forge door was in sight when a sudden stitch grabbed at his side forcing him to slow down and catch his breath.

Out of the shadows stepped a hulking figure. Jack's flesh prickled. Heavy hobnailed boots came up behind him. Tripping over his feet, Jack pushed on and made it to the forge's large red wooden door. He searched desperately in his breeches pocket for the padlock key but fumbled.

"Oi!" called a voice he recognised.
Jack spun around and pressed himself hard against the door.

Smiling nastily, Bill tapped a wooden batten into his open palm. "Where are you keeping her then?" He took a menacing step towards Jack.
The noise of the dancing halls and salons across the road were escalating, it would drown his screams. Could he make a break for it? A drunk staggered past them with unseeing eyes.

Jack feigned bravery. "I don't know what you are talking about." A bead of cold sweat trickled down the back of his neck. Bill bore down on him, suffocating him. He could see the whites of the man's eyes and feel his stale breath on his face. There was no hope of escape, he'd have to take the beating like a man. He prayed Bill didn't damage his bad leg further, he had only just rid himself of the limp.
A woman's high pitch laugh carried above the noise coming from the rowdy dancing hall.

Jack swallowed. "I haven't seen her. If she's chosen to run away it's nought to do with me," he argued. Fear curdled his gut, turning his legs turning to jelly.
No one seemed interested in what was happening in the shadows.

Bill grabbed Jack by the necktie, pulled him away from the door and pushed him hard against the plastered brick. "Yer lying."

Again, Jack said, "It's the truth, she's not with me."

Bill put the batten against Jack's throat, and pressed, crushing his windpipe. Jack's hold on the flour bag slackened, it dropped to the ground, and the pie rolled out onto the dusty, wheel-rutted road. Black spots danced before Jack's eyes.

Bill sneered, "If you are lying, I'll cut yer filthy tongue out."

He let go. Jack's hand flew to his throat as he breathed in great, choking, gasps of air. Pulling his arm back, Bill took a swing with the batten and struck Jack hard in the stomach, winding him. Jack doubled over and fell headlong in the dirt, wheezing. He tried to get up on his hands and knees, but Bill put the boot in, kicking him twice in the ribs. As Jack collapsed Bill stomped on his head for good measure. Everything went black.

Whistling, and twirling his batten like he was in some sort of parade, Bill walked away. Madame would be pleased with him for giving the lad a good beating but she'd want the girl. He must find her, or Madame would blame him for her escape. He had been waiting outside the forge for nigh on two whole days and not a whiff of her. He was sure Healey knew where she was, but wasn't letting on. A few more beatings and he'd wear the lad down to the point he would either talk, or be brain-damaged. He stepped inside the Ladies of the Lake and was greeted by the rowdy piano music. The girls were saucily displaying their wares to inebriated customers. He smiled nastily - soon Marnie would be back where she belonged.

Coming to, Jack groaned. He had no notion of how long he'd lain prostrate in the road. Out of the corner of his eye he spied a filthy rat gorging itself on the remains of his pie. His fingers searched for a stone, finding one, he hurled it at the rodent and missed. The rat hissed, picked up the last scrap and scurried away. Jack got unsteadily to his feet. His ribs grabbed and he inhaled sharply. He felt like he'd been run over by a wagon.

He carefully bent down to pick up the flour bag. The bread appeared unharmed. He tore off a piece, and tried to poke it in the corner of his mouth without hurting his throat but it was impossible. Jack swallowed. A moment later he retched and threw up the little that was in his stomach. Wiping his mouth with the back of his hand, he leaned against the forge door waiting for the dizziness to pass. Finally, he found the key in his trouser pocket and unlocked the padlock. Pushing open the heavy door, he stumbled in and lurched sideways. His legs collapsing under him, he slid down the wall. Slumped like a sack of coal, the flour bag forgotten, Jack cradled his battered head in his hands, and passed out.

In the morning, Bennett found Jack in a frightful state. The forge door was unlocked and the battered, bloodied boy lay curled up on the floor. Bennett carefully lifted the lad's chin with his finger and checked him over. Jack opened a slit of an eye and muttered incoherent babble.

"Did ye not heed my advice yer silly young fool?" Bennett grumbled without heat. "I take it you ventured out, or did the blackguard dare to beat you senseless in my shop?"

Jack tried to stand then thought better of it. Sick and dizzy, he was finding it difficult to think.

"I was hungry," he murmured, his head lolling to the side. Bennett pushed the three-legged stool hard up against the wall. Placing his arm under Jack's elbow Bennett hauled Jack to his feet. He grunted.

"You should have said, I would have brought you something."

Bennett helped Jack by supporting him as he sat down. A flash of worry crossed Bennett's ruddy face. He went out the back to the pump and filled a bucket with water. He came back with the bucket and a rag, and kneeling in front of Jack he gently sponged his wounds. Jack groaned under Bennett's careful ministrations.

When Bennett had finished, he threw the bloodied rag aside. "Damnation!" he said irritably. He wiped his hands on the back of his moleskins and began to pace. "They are likely to burn the shop down as retribution, with you and I in it."

Jack hung his head. "Aye, you're right," he mumbled. "I didn't mean to put you in any danger. I'm sorry for the trouble I've caused."

Bennett was solemn. He passed Jack a bottle of ale and watched as Jack tried to drink, some dribbled from the corner of Jack's mouth and spilled onto his shirt.

"Guess I best leave today," Jack handed the bottle back to Bennett and attempted to stand, but Bennett placed a firm hand on the young man's shoulder.

"Sit there for a bit and think. You got to use your head boy, and by the look of you it's not in much shape for thinking. You walk out of here today, they will follow you and find her, and it will be all for nothing. Besides, you aren't capable of going far now."

"I had hoped," Jack began, trying to string his words together, "I had hoped to make enough money to be able to get far away from here, but I realize that was foolish now. I'll go and not cause you any more trouble."

Bennett pulled up the other three-legged stool and sat opposite Jack. "I will be sorry to lose you, son, you're a good tidy worker and given time you'd be a great smithy. For your sake, I hope she's worth all the trouble she's caused."

"She is to me," Jack replied wistfully, squinting at Bennett through his blackened eye.

"Well then," Bennett lowered his voice, "I've been thinking long and hard about it, and if you want to protect yourself and the lass, this is what I suggest..." he stopped short, went over and closed the heavy wooden door.

Chapter 6   Advance

Coach passengers were allowed two items of luggage each. Kitty packed her case several times, and still it bulged. Meg sat on it while Marnie and Kitty strapped it shut for her.

Marnie giggled. "You'll need to leave some behind or you won't be able to close your case unless Mr Burns sits on it for you."

"Marnie's right," Meg agreed. "And you won't be able to lift it without William's help."

Clingy, Grace kept getting underfoot. Meg picked Grace up and held her while Kitty hauled her clothes out onto the bed and started again. Both girls offered advice on what she should take and what to leave. Finally, Kitty was happy with both the contents, and the weight.

Kitty glanced at the clock. She'd been so excited she hadn't had time to think, now it struck her she was leaving the people she loved behind. Overwhelmed with emotion, she took Grace from Meg's arms and held her close.

She ran her fingers across the top of Grace's fine wispy hair. "Now little one," she said, her voice cracking. "You have to be a good girl for Granny, and look after Aunty Meg and Aunty Marnie for me. They've promised me they will take good care of you." Grace frowned.

"Love you." Kitty kissed Grace's forehead. Grace burrowed into Kitty's shoulder; her arms tight around Kitty's neck Grace clung on like a drowning man to a life raft.

Meg stretched her arms wide and hugged them both. "I'm going to miss you so much." She stepped back and dabbed her eyes with her handkerchief. "And now I have no bridesmaid."

Kitty whispered, "I know someone who would like to be."

Meg gave a nervous laugh. "You think Ma would allow that?" Mary entered the bedroom followed closely by Jim. The air was heavy.

"It's time," Mary announced, prying Grace from Kitty's arms. Grace squirmed and reached for Kitty, but Mary held her fast. "See you outside," she said taking Grace with her.

Jim solemnly lifted Kitty's case off the bed and carried it out. Meg plucked Kitty's hat box from the bed and followed after him, drying her eyes.

"Oh," Kitty said, "I almost forgot." She opened the bottom drawer. "You were asking about Mary Magdalene," Kitty handed the black gold-leaf edged book to Marnie. "Here, I want you to have it. Read the gospels and you'll find Mary Magdalene's story."

Marnie stared in awe at it, and traced the gold lettering with her fingertip. She looked up at Kitty stunned. "But...I..."

"And here," Kitty continued. "This was Annie's prayer book I'm sure she would have liked you to have it."

"I can't read," Marnie hung her head, ashamed.

"Oh," Kitty said, surprised. Brightening, she said, "Then get Meg to read it to you when Ma's not around. Better yet get Meg to teach you to read. Quick, hide the books so Ma doesn't see them." Her brow wrinkled. "Oh yes, and if you are looking for your parasol, I've hidden it in the back of the wardrobe."

"You are kindness itself," Marnie said. Reverently she returned the books to their hiding place and closed the drawer.

Kitty's tears spilled down her cheeks. Marnie gave her a bolstering hug. Thanking her, Kitty blew her nose and dried her eyes. She donned bonnet, and pulled on her white gloves, took a deep shuddering breath and walked outside. Marnie followed behind; her head bent like a drooping daffodil.

Jim was busy giving William last-minute instructions, telling him where the miners said the latest slips lay.

"Don't worry, Kitty will be safe with me," William assured him. "I'll see she comes to no harm," he promised. Turning to Meg, he put his arm around her shoulder. "Don't worry, my dear, I'll take good care of your sister, and I'll be back within the fortnight." And he dared to kiss Meg's cheek in front of her parents.

Mary jiggled Grace on her hip. She was finding the long-drawn-out goodbyes excruciating. She wanted them gone before she changed her mind entirely, and refused to let Kitty go.

Sensing Mary's misgivings, Jim hurried things along. "Right then, you'd best be off," he said checking Kitty's bag and hat box were strapped securely.

"I'm only sorry Pat's not here to say goodbye to," Kitty said sadly. "Give him my love, won't you?"

Mary promised she would.

Kitty hugged everyone twice before kissing her father goodbye. As solemn-faced as a standing stone, Jim helped his youngest daughter onto the gig. Pretending to mop his brow, he wiped his eyes, and put away his handkerchief.

Mary looked up at Kitty, her green eyes glistening. "Write."

"I will, Ma. Love you all," she cried, blowing kisses.

Burns flicked the reins the gig moved off. Kitty waved until she could no longer see them, but her mind was swirling like a pannikin of water, gravel and washdirt. What had she done?

William was quiet. He carefully guided the horse along the track thinking about the conversation he had with Asterly yesterday. He had brought up the possibility of working with Yin Xiaoxu, dredging the river. Asterly refused to contemplate the idea of entering into a partnership with him, saying Chinamen were not to be trusted. William believed what Asterly really meant was, he didn't trust him. Regardless of what Asterly thought, he would visit Yin, the man was a successful merchant and his fellow countrymen liked and respected him.

Aware Kitty was deathly quiet, he glanced sideways at her. He guessed she had never been parted from her mother before. If he dared to ask her how she fared, she might well burst into hysterics, so he decided best to leave well enough alone, and have a quiet trip into Queenstown.

Kitty hadn't seen Queenstown for well over a year and became excited when they could see the valley below. She held on tightly to the side of the gig as they made the descent into Arthurs. They passed a variety of hotels and grog shanties on the way. She was overwhelmed by the sights, sounds and smells. She twisted first this way then that to get a better look at the picturesque mountain peaks and the icy blue lake. The surrounding mountains hemmed in a bustling ramshackle town. White canvas tents dotted the area like mushrooms in a muddy field, but larger wooden and brick-and-plaster buildings had sprung up since she had last seen the place.

The roads were busy with foot traffic as anxious bearded men with wheelbarrows scurried here and there, sidestepping horse manure and ruts in the road. Sailboats, paddle steamers and rowboats crossed the lake's shores in such an unruly fashion they looked like paper boats on a pond. Everything, and everyone, seemed to be in a hurry.

Kitty noticed a symphony of colour as ladies standing on street corners solicited trade. She tried not to stare but she was fascinated by their scandalous short clothing, hairstyles, and heavily made-up faces. A compassionate soul, Kitty's heart went out to them and she wondered if any of them knew Marnie. Maybe one of them was Marnie's friend Daisy. Perhaps the women thought Marnie had been murdered, and her body disposed of in some deep mine shaft, or she'd been thrown in a river and left to drown. She wondered if they cared.

Pat enjoyed the solitude as he walked back to the hotel by way of the Dan O'Connell track. Fit, he did not find it hard going. The sun was warm on his face, and a gentle breeze tickled the air. Mountain daises sprigged through the earth colouring the track like a dusting of fine powder. He loved this time of year, the weather was settled and the days long. Hat set low over his eyes, he carried his blanket and a small swag across his back. His money bag, now empty, hung limply from his belt but he was cheered by the fact he still had some tobacco left.

He couldn't remember all he had done these past three days, it was a black hole in his memory, a fathomless well in which one throws a pebble and hopes to eventually hit something that resonates, but nothing did. He decided it was better that way, you can't feel guilty about something you can't remember. He sported a few bruises here and there from his drinking spree, but otherwise was unharmed.

But for all its fun, life on The Arrow wasn't the same without his best mate. It didn't seem right that Tiny, a man with a heart big enough to match his body was taken while he who had nothing good to offer the world, remained. He slashed his hand across the tops of the rust-coloured mountain grasses, life was unfair and God unjust. If his mother heard him moaning, she'd glibly say, life is not fair so put some dark treacle on it and be done with it.

He was surprised to discover he was looking forward to getting back to Long Gully. At times, Ma watched him as carefully as a fox watches chickens and it stifled him and made him long for freedom. Sometimes he would have loved to walk away just as his father had done, but something, or someone always stopped him. Maybe it was the richness of the claim that kept him loyal, for it was good to have coin in his pocket, food in his belly and a bed to sleep in. He didn't believe it was his Ma, strong woman that she was, nor was it her good cooking that kept him there, no he believed it was more than that. He and Da had unfinished business, even if both of them wanted to avoid it like one avoids a terrible sickness.

When they arrived in New Zealand, back in '61, they left the rest of the family in Dunedin, and together, he and Da set off to stake a claim at Gabriel's Gully. Initially they found gold, and it was easily won, but the problem at Gabriel's had been getting water. They needed water to wash the paydirt. Shysters set up water races for their own claims and charged others extortionately for the use of them. Stores were in short supply, and scurvy and starvation killed many. Flour was sold at a premium and dished out equally, one pannikin at a time with a rifle at the ready in case starving miners rushed the wagon.

Once the gold in their claim had been worked out, they moved on seeking better pickings. News of a rush at the Dunstan broke where two men, Hartley and Riley, had struck gold so they stumped their way there, only to find the best claims already gone. Then there were stories of a wily old fox, William Fox, striking it rich further afield. Fox had tried to keep his find a secret, but they patiently followed him whenever he'd ventured out for stores, once or twice he'd given them the slip, but finally the smoke from his campfire gave him away, and then the rush to The Arrow was on.

So much had changed since then. Pat realized of all the changes that had occurred since last year, the most profound was his Da. Pat sighed. He preferred the old Da, they were on an even keel, and understood each other. But drink had overcome Da to the point he thought his family were better off without him, and he'd abandoned them. Pat thought if he had children, he'd never abandon them, he'd never want a child of his to feel that pain. It was probably best if he never had any, at least then he couldn't disappoint them.

Da may have returned from the dead and was trying to restore some of the wasted years but Annie and Tiny were gone forever, and a terrible blackness had settled in his soul, a heaviness that he couldn't seem to shake. It seemed to Pat that everyone he loved, he lost. It was best not to love, it hurt too much when the loved ones were gone. He felt like he wore an invisible cloak of sadness that weighed heavy on his heart.

The curse of Da's new found sobriety was Da wanted him to give up the drink as well. He wasn't ready for that kind of carry on just yet. No sir, he needed a drink to get through each day, and more than one if the truth be told.

"I'll be in the stillroom if you need me," Mary said, depositing the wicker basket at Marnie's feet.

Marnie rolled up her sleeves, hoisted the basket onto to her hip and carried it out to the washhouse. Her ribs weren't hurting nearly as much and this morning, and the swelling had gone down so that she could open her right eye properly. Mary had taken great pains to remind Marnie that it didn't matter how respectable she looked, she was to keep well out of sight. No one was to know that she was staying at the hotel. Marnie wasn't sure if that was for her own protection, or the sake of Mary's respectability.

It took several trips to the pump to fill the tin tub with cold water, more trips to the pump to fill the copper, then light and feed the fire beneath. At the brothel, the washing, cooking and cleaning was done by a dim-witted deformed mute, who as soon as her chores were finished disappeared from sight so her ugliness didn't scare customers away. Marnie knew the girl's name, nothing else as Madame didn't permit the girls to speak to her. She felt sorry for Gladys, all the work the girl did for no other thanks than food and shelter. Now, she, like Gladys, was hidden from sight, working her fingers to the bone, and looking as ugly as sin.

She picked up the long-handled paddle. Washing day was a trial - the tubs were in the washhouse, and the copper outside because the fire had to be lit to heat the water, and if the copper was inside, the washerwoman would end up like a cured ham in a matter of minutes. That meant some washing in cold water in the washhouse, some in hot outside, and going back and forth between the two. Marnie wondered if it was part of Mary's plan to make her regret her decision to become a housewife. Perhaps Mary planned to make life so unbearable that she would desert them and return to the brothel. But Marnie knew that wasn't an option - she could never go back. Here might mean drudgery, but there meant death.

A wicked thought came to her, she could steal the gold from the tea caddy, and make a run for it. But where could she run to? There was nowhere to go. No, Mary Healey would expect her to do that. In fact, she probably wouldn't mind losing a bit of gold if she kept her precious son safe from the snares of a wicked harlot.

Back bent over the scrubbing board, shirt in one hand and soap in the other, Marnie was pondering this, when she happened to glance over her shoulder to see Pat strolling across the lawn as cocksure as a prize rooster. Marnie recognized his familiar swagger long before she saw his freckled, red-bearded face.

At first glance Pat thought it was Kitty in the washhouse and deviated from his path to speak to her, then realized it wasn't Kitty. Leaning against the washhouse door, he stroked his wiry red beard, and gave Marnie the once over.

"Why hello Marnie," he said, cheerfully. "This is indeed surprise. What happened to your pretty face?"

"I'm right enough thank you, just a small altercation with someone's fist. And how's yourself Master Pat?" Worried that Mary might think she was shirking, she turned her attention back to the shirt and scrubbed it across the board.

"As right as I'll ever be," Pat replied, lowering his gaze. "But I must admit," he said admiring the way Marnie's bottom jiggled as she soaped and scrubbed, "I'm mighty surprised to find you here." He hooked a finger in his braces and gave them a tug. "Why are you here?"

Marnie wiped her sudsy hand across her forehead, pushing a loose strand of fair hair away from her perspiring face. "Dan brought me here at Jack's request. Jack's coming soon."

Pat moved closer. "Well, well," he mocked, "has my little brother rescued you from that sort of life only to have you enslaved here in the canyon as a domestic drudge?"

Marnie flinched; he'd struck a nerve. She raised her chin. "Jack and I are to be married," she said indignantly. "And he's taking me far away from here." Ignoring him, she plunged the shirt into the cold water.

He snorted derisively. "Married! Marnie, my sweet little petal," Pat drawled, closing in, his arms circling her waist. "Why ever would you want to do a silly thing like that?" He breathed into her ear "That kind of carry on is for fools." He dropped his hands to her buttocks and squeezed.

"Don't!" Marnie jerked away. The shirt sank to the bottom of the tub as she turned to face him. Pat lunged, and grappling with her skirts tried to push them up, as he ardently kissed her.

159

He grinned. "Now, now, my pretty little petal, are you playing coy?" He stuck his leg between her thighs.

She pushed him away, her hands leaving wet imprints on his shirt. "Pat no! I'm... to be your brother's."

He looked at her finger. "I see no ring." He pulled her to him. "Come on, little darling," he coaxed. "I've been starved for entertainment in these parts, and you're a sight for sore eyes." He pressed his lips to hers.

Despairing, Marnie thought men were always going to see her as a whore, something to use when their prick felt desire. She had been stupid to think anyone would ever see her as anything else. She fought to free herself from his grasp "Don't, please don't!"

He lost his hat in the scuffle, and cursed. "What the devil are you playing at?"

"I'm to be married, Pat," she said. "To your brother no less, you ought to be ashamed." That was if Mary Healey allowed the marriage, she thought miserably.

"Ah little darlin', there's no need to be like that," he said, bending down and picking up his hat. Dusting it off, he put it back on his head. "You and me have been acquainted in the past, you and me been friendly like." And in his best wheedling voice, he said, "Just one for old time's sake. Jack needn't know. I've got gold, good gold." He touched the empty leather pouch on his belt. "Well, I can get some, and you'll be needing that if you're to set up house." He lunged.

Marnie stepped aside and his leg banged against the tub, some water spilt onto the dirt floor.

He cursed, his ardour quickly turning to anger. "What the … you think you are too good for me?" he flared. "I think not."

Intent on his prize, Pat didn't see or hear his assailant approaching, nor did he manage to dodge the blow that struck his ear.

"Oww!" Clutching his reddened ear, Pat turned to face his attacker. Mary's eyes burned like hot coals. She was a small woman but she had a powerful right and she'd cuffed him good and proper.

Horrified, Pat and Marnie stared at her, their mouths gaping. Mary stood between them, her hands on her hips and her face livid.

Mary fixed Pat with a hard stare. "Leave now," she commanded her voice tightly controlled.

"What? Do you mean for good?" Pat mumbled.

"For now," Mary said, her voice like ice. "And don't let me see your heathen face again until sundown."

Pat bent down to pick up his hat. Cursing, he stalked across the lawn and up the track, his swagger less self-assured and his step quicker. Taking deep breaths, Mary strove to get her temper under control. She waited until Pat disappeared from view, then turned to face Marnie, who had edged her way into the far corner. Marnie collapsed in a heap. Weeping, her placed her hands protectively in front of her face waiting for the beating she was sure was coming. Nothing would change. Men saw her as prey. Once a whore, always a whore, she thought despondently.

"I'm sorry, I didn't mean to… cause trouble, I'll go," she babbled, tears streaking her face. Go? Go where?

"I heard it all, and I know you didn't encourage him."

Confused, Marnie looked up in disbelief.

"I'm ashamed of the dirty rake!" Mary said vehemently. "Ashamed to call him my son, and I'll tell him so good and proper, when I calm down enough to do it without wringing his flamin', scrawny, no good, neck." Mary took another breath.

Sniffling, Marnie got to her feet.

Mary said, "Don't you worry he won't bother you again and if he does, you tell me?"

Marnie wiped her eyes.

Mary continued, "I know I haven't been easy on you girl, but I hope you realize it's for your own good. Now, we won't mention this episode again, not to anyone and especially not to Jack. Understood?"

Marnie nodded.

"Good," Mary said. "Get on with it then, these clothes won't wash themselves." Then she was gone.

Marnie's legs buckled, she sank down and pressed herself against the wall. Mary Healey had shown her kindness, and sided with her when she'd least expected it. God be praised! Miracles do happen, and she'd just witnessed one.

Jim wasn't surprised when his son turned up at the claim reeking of alcohol, he didn't need to ask where he'd been, he knew. He'd been lucky enough to have reasons to change, a wife and a family, and the support of the priest, Pat had none of these.

Pat was in no mood for talking so Jim let him be. They spent the afternoon in the river, washing, panning and sifting for colour, and had good gold to show for their labour.

Downing tools, Jim said, "Come on, son, let's head home."

Pat grunted, chucked his tools in the wheelbarrow, and dried his hands on the back of his moleskins.

Jim started to push for home. "Oh," Jim said, as if suddenly remembering, "There's been an arrival while you were away."

"I know," Pat said, his tone bitter. "We've met."

Jim wondered if perhaps Marnie had something to do with Pat's dark mood. Maybe Pat had fancied his chances with the girl. Or perhaps Mary had told him Kitty was gone. Whatever was bothering him, he was more tight-lipped than a clam.

Pat's long-legged gait easily matched Jim's own.

"So," Jim drawled, "if you have already called in to see your Ma, you'll know that Kitty's gone."

"What!" Pat cried, stopping in his tracks.

Ignoring him, Jim pushed on. Pat caught up. "What do you mean - gone?" he asked, incredulous. He'd been away for three days. How could have so much had happened in three days?

"Son, I've been knee deep, in more shite than you can find in an outhouse, since you left," Jim told him.

Pat shook his head trying to clear it. "Stop talking in riddles, Da, and tell me what's going on."

By the time they reached the hotel Pat was reeling like he was punch drunk.

Supper was a subdued affair full of uneasy silences. Even baby Grace was somber. Everyone missed Kitty's frivolous chatter. Marnie sat between Jim and Mary, studying the tablecloth. Pat ate in glowering silence.

"When did Kitty leave?" he finally asked.

"Only this morning son," Jim answered. "She'll be staying in The Camp tonight." Jim dug his fork into a piece of warm pie crust and raising it to his mouth said, "Burns is escorting her to Dunedin."

"That's mighty good of him," Pat muttered darkly.

"He had business in Dunedin so it worked out well," Mary said, wondering if Pat doubted William's motives.

Pat regarded Marnie with bloodshot eyes.

Feeling uneasy, Marnie picked at a burr in the tablecloth. Seeking escape, she asked. "May I be excused?"

"No, you may not. You haven't eaten enough to feed a sparrow," Mary replied tartly.

Marnie sagged, defeated.

Mary relented. "Have another slice of pie then you may."

Marnie cut a delicate sliver of pie and put it on her plate.

"Right then," Jim said putting down his fork. "Anybody want to tell me who died? A funeral would be more cheerful than this dinner table tonight."

"We all miss Kitty, Jim," Mary said accusingly, like it was his fault.

Jim gently placed his hand on Mary's. "She's not gone forever, love."

Mary sighed. "I hope you are right, but my gut tells me different."

Jim withdrew his hand. "Well far be it from me to argue with your gut," he snapped.

Burns informed Kitty he was going to call on a business acquaintance and asked if she would she like to visit her brother during his absence. Kitty was delighted to have the opportunity to see Jack and asked the hotelier for directions to Bennett's Forge. The hotelier told her the forge was only a stone's throw away, it was a brick and roughcast building with large red-painted wooden doors, she couldn't miss it. She found it easily enough. The double wooden doors were open to the street, and the searing heat of the fire came out to greet her. She was relieved to see Jack's long thin frame bent over the anvil hammering the blazes out of a wagon wheel. She stood in the doorway, cupped her hands, and called his name.

Jack raised his head. "Kitty!" He threw down the hammer and came quickly towards her, removing his gloves. "What are you doing here? Is everything all right?" he asked, anxiously.

"Oh Jack!" she cried, staring in horror at his damaged face. "What happened?"

Shying away, he said, "Don't fuss now, it's nothing. A horse kicked me while I was trying to shoe it. Lucky I'm a hard-headed Irishman, hey." He untied his leather apron and hung it on the nearest hook. Hugging Kitty into his good shoulder, he whispered in her ear, "Is she all right?"

"Grand," Kitty assured him. Keeping her own voice low for fear of reprisals, she said meaningfully, "Everyone is grand." Even if her brother thought her naïve, she was not that stupid that she didn't think someone might think Jack may have something to do with Marnie's disappearance. Jack had obviously had a taste of someone's idea of revenge.

He breathed again. "Then what are you doing here?"

165

"I'm on my way to Dunedin," Kitty answered, a smile lighting her eyes.

"What! Why?" Confounded, Jack waited for her to explain.

"I'm going to study as an apprentice dressmaker," she told him proudly.

Disturbed by this news, Jack asked question after question, and some she couldn't answer.

"Be careful, Kitty," he warned. "I hear they use girls for a year's free labour and once they are done with learning, they get rid of them rather than pay wages, then they get another child to work for free."

Kitty neglected to tell him that after three months, should she be accepted and stay on, their parents would be paying for the privilege of her tutorage. She lifted her chin. "I am not a child, I'm fourteen," she reminded him.

"You may be fourteen, but you're still my little sister so it's my job to look after you," he argued.

Looking pointedly at his damaged face, she replied, "And mine to worry about you."

He took her arm. "Come, let's not quarrel. Let's sit outside while there's still a slip of sun to enjoy." Jack was relieved not to see Bill standing on the other side of the road, waiting.

They sat on the small stone wall outside and chatted amiably. Kitty told him all the local gossip. Careful not to mention Marnie by name, Kitty kept reassuring Jack by referring to Marnie as her or she, so that anyone overhearing their conversation would not guess they were speaking of Marnie, the runaway whore. The air was beginning to cool as nightfall approached.

Curious, Kitty asked, "Does Mr Bennett pay you wages, or does he just give you food and lodgings while you learn your trade?"

Jack shook his head, "He pays me, I'm skilful enough to be useful to him. I have a hut of sorts, at the rear of his cottage to doss down in. He's a bachelor, and not one for cooking, so I cook my own food over a campfire. It's not much of a life, but it's good enough for me."

"Is he a good man, this Mr Bennett?"

Jack thought back. When he'd first met Bennett, he'd worried that the bachelor might like boys, but he was relieved to find Bennett was only interested in his forge, and the bottle.

"Aye, he's a bit of a drinker but he does no harm to anyone but himself. He's a quiet man, not one for a lot of words." Jack stretched and yawned. "Unlike you," he added with a wry grin.

"Oh, you're horrid!" Kitty gave him a playful shove. She smiled "Don't you think it's marvellous, how Da has managed to sweeten Ma's bad temper just by staying sober?"

"Aye," Jack laughed, "There's two miracles right there, Da sober and Ma in a better temper."

Kitty's face fell. "I'm going to miss them all dearly, especially little Grace."

"Aye, they will miss you and all," Jack agreed wistfully. He paused and said softly, ""I'll miss you."

Kitty bit her lip. Jack's raw honesty was unusual. Close in age, the siblings playfully baited each other. Worried about him, Kitty couldn't settle into their usual easy banter. It was as if he thought they may never see each other again, like this was goodbye.

167

Not wanting their time together to end, Kitty said, "Come back to the hotel with me, and have supper with us."

"Us?" Jack frowned.

"William and I."

He raised his eyebrows. "Oh, William, now is it?" he said mimicking her.

"He's going to be my brother-in-law in a couple of weeks so I think I am entitled to call him by his Christian name," she replied airily.

"Listen to you sounding like a real lady, and not some lowly apprentice." He nudged her.

She gave him with a withering glance.

"Please?" Kitty implored.

He shook his head. "I can't."

"Why?"

"I've a job to finish."

"But you have to eat," she argued.

"Tell you what, I'll walk you back. You shouldn't be walking the street unescorted anyways, shame on Burns for letting you come alone. And I will visit the bakery on the way. It's just down the alleyway. Will that satisfy your ladyship?

"It's a start," she agreed.

Fascinated by the bustling throng, Kitty held on tightly to her brother's arm as they threaded their way through the busy laneway to the bakery where he bought a pie and a stick of toffee. Kitty noticed while they walked to the hotel, Jack kept checking over his shoulder like he was afraid of his shadow.

They stopped outside the hotel. "Please, come in and say good day to William."

Jack shook his head. "I'll see him at the wedding."

"When I write home, I'll tell them you're brave and will be visiting soon," she promised.

Jack held the door open for her. The entrance to the hotel lobby was small and ill-lit, but had high ceilings giving it a spacious look that it did not really possess. Burns was seated in the lobby reading *The Observer*.

Burns folded the paper and tucked it under his arm. "Jack!" he cried, alarmed. "What happened?"

"A horse kicked me while I was trying to shoe it, don't worry I'm as hard-headed as any nail."

"I met..."

Kitty put a warning finger to her lips.

Frowning at her, Burns finished his sentence. "I met with Mr Thompson today. He's considering my business proposal," he told them proudly. He told them he had been busy during Kitty's absence. The horse was settled in the stables and he'd organized their rooms and managed to get some other business done in town.

Kitty stifled a yawn.

"Either I'm boring you or you are exhausted, either way you are forgiven," Burns smiled at her indulgently. "Your bags are in your room. Would you like me to show you the way? It's first on the right at the top of the stairs."

"Thank you, if you give me the key, I'm sure I can find the door. I'd appreciate it, if you would walk Jack back to Mr Bennett's house. Jack needs the company and you probably could do with some air." Burns raised his eyebrows, he was not used to being treated like some lackey.

Jack protested. "No, no, don't trouble yourself."

"Please," Kitty implored, looking at Burns with her big green eyes.

Burns shrugged. "Let's amuse her shall we, or we may never hear the end of it."
Jack kissed his baby sister goodbye and she held him tight.

"If I ever get to Dunedin, I'll visit," he promised. Kitty knew it was a hollow promise, and a deep sadness washed over her.

"We will have supper when I return," Burns said, following Jack out into the busy street.

"Splendid," Kitty said, turning away to hide her tears.
Although Jack was embarrassed by Kitty cajoling Burns into walking him home, Jack felt more confident with him there. He didn't think Bill would risk taking on the two of them. No, Bill was the kind of coward that made sure he got his prey alone. He stopped to glance over his shoulder. No sign of the brute.

Burns stopped abruptly. His face serious, he said, "I want you to know, Jack, that despite your reckless behaviour, I still intend to marry your sister."

"Despite my reckless behaviour?" echoed Jack.

Burns straightened his hat and levelled his gaze. "You realize the shame you have caused your family by wanting to make this woman your wife?"

"I have shamed my family because I love her, and am willing to risk my life for her?" Jack was furious. How dare Burns look down at him. How dare he!

Undaunted, Burns continued, "You must know she is a stain on the respectability of your family name, and others will not take it kindly. You may be shunned, and those associated with you may be shunned. Did you consider your family before you made such a rash decision?"

"I suggest you quit talking before I punch you in the nose," Jack said, his fists at his sides, ready.

Burns held up his hands in an effort to pacify Jack. "Calm yourself man, I'm only telling you how others will see it."

"Well, it doesn't matter how they see it. I don't intend to be staying in the area anyway. Don't worry, folks won't have to endure seeing the likes of us. My relationship should not taint your reputation."

"It shouldn't, but it will," Burns said emphatically.

Jack gritted his teeth. "You may go now, tell my sister that you walked me to Bennett's cottage, she'll be none the wiser. I won't suffer your judgmental attitude a minute longer."

"I promised your sister I would see you to your door, and God help me I will."

They walked on in silence, Jack seething with rage and Burns feeling more affable since speaking his mind.

As they reached Mr Bennett's cottage, Jack mumbled gruffly. "Take good care of both my sisters, won't you?"

"I will," Burns said. "Take better care of yourself," he said, eying Jack's battered face. "Maybe you should rethink your choice."

"And maybe Meg should rethink hers. If you weren't my sister's fiancé I would knock you down where you stand. Goodbye Burns," Jack said, ducking inside his hut. Angry, he wanted to slam his fist into the wall but thought better of it. Marnie's past would always haunt them. He had to take her somewhere where she would be treated like a lady and not with contempt, even if it meant taking her to the end of the world.

Chapter 7   Devils Staircase

Kitty sat on the seat in the hallway, her toe impatiently tapping the hall runner. Bonnet tied, gloves on, and bags packed, she was ready. She was pleased the girls had made her pack less for she managed to get the case closed, and could carry it, if need be. Last night, during supper William was quiet and introspective. Afterwards, he spent time downstairs in the smoking room at the card tables while she stayed in her room, alone, until such time she thought it a decent time to retire.

Kitty fiddled with the ribbons on her bonnet tying them, and untying them. She couldn't stop worrying. What if she had made the wrong decision? What if she hated it at the dressmakers? Even if she did, she couldn't return, her pride wouldn't allow it. Besides she couldn't face seeing Meg happily married to the man she loved. It would be like a knife to the heart. Anxiety threatened to overwhelm her. She missed her family, her heart felt heavy with loneliness, there wasn't anyone she could confide in, she was on her own now. And, she couldn't stop worrying about Jack, what chance did he and Marnie stand?

William finally appeared with his bag in hand. "Good morning Miss Kitty." He greeted her cheerfully. "I trust you slept well?"

"Good morning," she returned. "I don't think I slept a wink."

He grinned broadly. "All set for your big adventure then?"

His patronising tone irritated her. "I'm ready, are you?" she answered, picking up her hat box.

The large landlady came barrelling towards them barking orders. "Come, come, the coach is ready to leave," she flapped her arms excitedly, shooing them down the stairs as if they were chickens.

"May I assist you with your luggage Miss Kitty?" he graciously offered.

Kitty inclined her head. "Thank you, Mr Burns, you may," she said primly.

"At your disposal, Miss," he bowed. Surprised, he exclaimed, "Goodness, are you carrying the escort's gold in here?"

Kitty knew he was only teasing, but she felt piqued. "I'm expecting to be gone a long time."

"Oh, I'm sorry to hear that, I hoped you'd hate Dunedin and come back to Long Gully immediately."
She stared at him, amazed, wondering if he meant it?

A smile curled the edges of his mouth. "Margaret is not happy you are going to miss our wedding," he qualified. "She said your brothers would make very ugly bridesmaids. She told me, I was to take you to Dunedin and bring you straight back."

Kitty felt it like a dart. "I'm afraid it can't be helped," she mumbled.
William staggered down the stairs with the bags. Carrying her hatbox, her chin set a little higher, Kitty followed him downstairs.

They walked out of the hotel lobby into the still, dark street. Dawn was about to split the fresh sky in two. They met the small knot of passengers gathered outside, and introduced themselves, their breath curling around them like ghostly whispers.

"We're in luck!" Burns told Kitty excitedly. "Our whip is the infamous Carmichael. He tells the best stories this side of the black stump."

Kitty raised her eyebrows as if only mildly interested.

They were travelling with Mr and Mrs Rossbotham, and Mr and Mrs Featherson, and a young digger who skulked in the shadows and didn't offer his name. The digger was about Kitty's age or thereabouts while the rest were middle-aged. The young digger would be travelling up top. He was roughly dressed, his clothes worn and tattered, a bed roll was tied across his thin bony shoulders, and he smelt. He held a clay pipe in his hand and had a hungry look about him that suggested it had been a long time since he'd seen proper food.

Kitty was so excited she wanted to clap for joy when six dapple greys were led around, the name Cobb & Co proudly displayed in gold lettering on the coach doors, but refrained, reminding herself that well-mannered young ladies did not behave in such a frivolous manner.

"Are you feeling well, Miss Kitty?" Burns asked, frowning at Kitty.

"Quite thank you." Kitty fiddled nervously with her buttons.

"I'll ride up front on the box seat with Carmichael. I love the freedom of fresh air, and find the compartments stifling and rather taxing on my ears."

Kitty thought he meant she was taxing on his ears. Everyone told her she was a chatterbox.

"Besides Carmichael has the ability to tell a great yarn," he added, with a cheeky grin.

Kitty was disappointed, she had been looking forward to sharing the stage with William but he'd chosen to sit up on the box seat with the driver. With a sinking heart she sedately accepted the coachman's assistance, stepped onto the velvet footstool, up and into the coach. The coach's plush crimson seats looked luxurious but were hard. Having woken early, her travelling companions were in a sombre, sleepy state, and in no mood for conversation, which suited her fine as she didn't know how to converse with these middle-aged strangers.

They set off with a lurch, and once clear of the town Carmichael cracked the whip and urged the horses on. Fascinated, Kitty watched the scenery pass in blurring rush of blue, green and gold. Tears pricked her eyes. She felt homesick. Too young to understand, Grace, the poor lamb would be wandering all over the hotel calling her name, she thought miserably.

And, she missed Meg. She wondered how could you love someone and yet be jealous of them at the same time? She wanted everything Meg had, especially William. This was her last opportunity to spend time with him before he became her brother-in-law yet he seemed to be doing everything to avoid her. Perhaps he found being lumbered with her unbearable. There were so many things she wanted to say to him, but the words dried up in her mouth and felt like chalk dust clogging her throat so that nothing came out. It was probably just as well. It would be wrong to jeopardize her sister's happiness. No, it was better for everyone if she was the only one who was truly miserable. Perhaps Ma was right, and one day she'd love another, and then maybe she'd be able to put these raw feelings behind her, and come back home with a liberated heart. Dear God, she hoped so.

The coach swayed alarmingly, but the constant jarring rhythm combined with lack of sleep made Kitty drowsy and she dozed on and off, her head lolling with the motion. Once or twice, they came to a sudden stop and Kitty woke with a start. She hoped she hadn't dribbled, or worse, snored. Her sisters used to tease her mercilessly about her snoring. It was very hard to appear ladylike when you sounded like an old sow in your sleep.

As it grew lighter, Mr Rossbotham read aloud an account from *The Otago Witness*, saying bushrangers were known to be in the Mackenzie basin.

Kitty gasped in horror.

Mrs Featherson shuddered. Placing a hand on her ample bosom, she said, "Oh, we live in such perilous times. The gold has bought all the ruffians and the world's outcasts into our midst."

Her husband, a small bespectacled man, gave her a sharp, reproving look. "It has also brought great wealth to the province, of which, you are enjoying some of the benefits, my dear," he reminded her.

Mrs Featherson huffed and turned her head.

"Take no notice of my husband, he's just trying to frighten us," Mrs Rossbotham whispered behind the safety of her gloved hand. "He sensationalizes everything. He does it on purpose, he craves attention."

At the mid-morning mark, they pulled up outside a shanty in Cromwell. The place wasn't much, but it was a chance to get out and stretch the legs while the horses were changed. The passengers disembarked, and the boy came down from up top, pale and sickly looking.

"The outhouse is down the path at the back of the building," called Carmichael. The term 'Building' was too grandiose a term for what resembled a rough-sawn lean-to. Kitty had been warned Mr Carmichael was prone to exaggeration she could see now that was true. The ladies hurried to relieve themselves but they needn't have worried they had plenty of time. Mrs Featherson and Mrs Rossbotham seemed content to chat over a cup of tea, leaving Kitty feeling ostracised. Burns bought her a glass of lemonade and some egg sandwiches.

Kitty asked for some newspaper and wrapped one of the sandwiches inside the paper.

"Saving it for later?" Burns asked, lifting a curious eyebrow.

"Yes, I'm sure to be hungry later," she said, putting it in her drawstring bag.

With a chuckle he told Kitty, "Carmichael told his winter passengers, he was such a good driver he could drive all the way with a glass of beer and not spill a drop," he laughed. "But little did they know, the beer was frozen before they started and stayed that way until they reached their destination."

The young digger scratched around outside; he accepted a glass of water before stoically climbing back up on his perch.

Kitty was first to the coach. She banged on the side to get the lad's attention. He leaned over the edge gazing at her with large questioning eyes. She passed the parcel up to him. Peeking inside he smiled gratefully, and resumed his post, steeling himself against the biting wind. Kitty climbed aboard and sat near the window. The others, except William, joined her. Carmichael did a quick head count before he hopped up on the box seat, and they were off.

The coach negotiated steep hills and low valleys, streams and rough ground. Tired of the long bumpy journey, Kitty was becoming impatient for the next rest stop. She couldn't wait to spend the night at the two-storeyed Beaumont Hotel in Lawrence. She had heard it was grand. Being on the coach reminded her of being on the ocean. She was only a tiddler when her family left Ireland, her mother told Kitty she wasn't seasick, but Ma had been ill for weeks. When they landed in New Zealand, Ma emphatically said she'd never ever set foot on another ship again. She told her children she would have to sprout wings and fly if she was ever to see her family in Ireland again.

Kitty remembered losing her baby brother on the long voyage out. Weighted in sailcloth he was cast over the side, a tiny bundle bobbing twice before disappearing beneath the choppy waves. Thinking of him made Kitty feel sad, and she thought about Grace again. Grace would be having a bottle and an afternoon sleep about now. The coach lumbered through the muddy scarred hole of Tuapeka, the diggers swarming like ants on a dung heap, turning over the soil as they searched for precious colour. Finally, the beautiful newly built Beaumont Hotel was in sight. Delighted to see it, the grateful passengers disembarked, stretched their legs and made their way inside.

Kitty watched the lad scramble down and disappear into the stables. The horses were stabled and the hotel passengers fed and their thirst slaked. Kitty saved a drumstick for the lad, she wrapped it in her napkin and hid it in her pocket, it was too much of a risk to venture out to the stables tonight, she resolved to slip it to the young digger in the morning. It had been a trying day, and no one wanted to linger long in the dining room, so one by one they made their apologies and disappeared to their rooms. Tomorrow, God willing, they would arrive in the new Edinburgh - Dunedin.

On Sunday, along with the stores, and local gossip, Dusty delivered a sealed letter addressed to The Healey Family. The hand-writing was unfamiliar and the penmanship good. Because Dusty loved to embellish a good story to make it a better one, Mary couldn't wait to get rid of him. She certainly didn't want him getting wind of Marnie being there. If he did, it wouldn't be long before the whole district knew where the girl was hiding. She took the envelope from him and went inside abruptly closing the door. Leaving Dusty to wander up the track to his next stop without so much as an inkling as to what was in it.

When Jim arrived home, Mary told Marnie to change Grace, just to get her out of the way. As soon as Marnie left the room, Mary tore open the letter. She gasped.

Jim peered over her shoulder. "What's wrong?"

"Nothing's wrong, it's just unexpected, is all."

Mary read, "*Dear Mr and Mrs Healey & family,*

You, and your family, are cordially invited to attend the wedding of Miss Niamh Boyle and Mr Joseph Brown to be held at St Mary's Catholic Church in Church Street, Queenstown on the 21st day of January at 1pm. Please join us to celebrate this happy occasion. A wedding breakfast will follow the ceremony.

Yours sincerely, Miss Niamh Boyle and Mr Joseph Brown."

"Can't get used to calling it Queenstown. It was always Rees station, I don't know why the bloody Queen has to stamp her name on everything," grumbled Jim. He paused, processing. "Does Meg know?" he asked.

"I reckon she would have mentioned it if she did."

Meg walked in, surprising them. She was early.

"Does Meg know what?" she asked.

Jim and Mary exchanged worried glances.

When they didn't answer immediately, she panicked. "What's wrong? Is it William? Kitty? Are they all right?"

Mary handed her the letter and let her read it for herself.

"Oh, how marvellous," Meg said, with a flickering smile. "Of course, you'll go, and I'll come with you."

"Are you sure that's wise?" Jim asked, treading carefully.

"Of course," Meg brushed aside his concern. "I'm only happy to know he's found someone. It eases my conscience somewhat."

Mary's eyebrows arched "Is that so? You don't seem overly surprised. Did you know about this then?"

Meg nodded. "Father Whooley hinted as much."

"Really?" Mary looked at her, incredulous. "And you didn't think to mention it?"

Meg shrugged. "Why would I?"

Marnie came back carrying Grace. Seeing Meg, Grace squealed with delight. Marnie put the little one down and Grace ran to her aunt and wrapped herself around Meg's skirts. Meg scooped her up and kissed Grace's chubby cheeks. Grace ripped the letter from Meg's hand and chewed one end. Mary rescued the invitation and put it on the mantle.

Meg put Grace down. "Hello Marnie, I trust you are well."

"Well, thank you, Meg." Distracted, Marnie wondered what was in that letter? Fearing the worse she waited anxiously, hoping someone would explain.

Meg could feel her mother's eyes burning her. "All right, all right," Meg conceded holding her hands up in surrender. "I'll admit I want to go because I'm curious. I want to see what the bride looks like. Is that a crime?"

Relieved, Marnie let out the breath she'd been holding. The letter was nothing to do with her.

"We could tell you," Mary replied, thwarting Meg's reason.

Meg said, "I can give Jack a message from Marnie."

Marnie felt a surge of hope. She wanted to scream, tell him to come get me - now.

"We can do that," Jim argued.

Undaunted, Meg continued, "It's been donkey's ages since I've been to Queenstown, and, it's perfect timing since the wedding is on the weekend."

Mary's face showed she wasn't convinced.

"Right," Meg said, "What time do we leave on Saturday?"

Jim and Mary talked until the wee hours. Mary did not want to leave the hotel to go to Yankee's wedding, but she didn't want Jim to go to Rees without her either. The fear of abandonment raised its ugly head, and although she didn't say it, she was worried if he was out of sight, he might drink.

"I'd rather have me wife by my side than me daughter," he argued, "so you'd best come with us."

Mary shook her head. "What's the girl thinking? I swear it will only lead to trouble."

"Come with us so you can keep an eye on both of us."

She still looked uncertain.

He sighed, "I swear to God, Mary Healey, you drive a man to drink. There is no pleasing you."

The more she thought on it the worse she felt. She hadn't left the hotel since she accompanied Annie to Dunedin. She didn't like leaving Pat in charge, he'd most likely drink the profits, or if feeling generous shout the bar, but she liked the idea of letting Jim go alone, albeit with Meg to Rees, even less.

"I'm going whether you are or no," Jim told her emphatically. "Sooner or later, you have to learn to trust me."

He was right, and she knew it, but it didn't make it any easier.

Heaving a sigh, she said, "All right, I'll come."

Jim exhaled slowly. It was going to be a long week till Saturday with Mary stewing about leaving the hotel in Pat's hands and worrying about Meg. "Good, now that's settled, go to sleep, it will be morning before we know it."

Chapter 8   Hells Gate

Kitty clapped her gloved hands and stamped her feet to get the blood circulating. It promised to be a fine day when the cloud lifted. No new passengers joined them for this leg of the journey. Everyone was heading towards the goldfields, rather than away from them. They waited for the coach to be brought around, and while no one was watching, Kitty slipped the young digger the drumstick she'd saved for him. He thanked her by smiling at her with his haunted brown eyes. Burns told her he would ride up front again. After hearing one of Carmichael's yarns, she had to agree the man could tell a good story, and if she wasn't trying to act so grown up, she would have laughed out loud.

Fitted with fresh horses the coach was a majestic sight. The young digger resumed his perch up top, swag in front of him like a shield to ward off the cold. Carmichael gallantly assisted the woman passengers onto the stage and left the men to climb up and take their places. They set off through the township of Lawrence, the coach rattling along the rough roads towards Lake Waihola. As it got lighter, the men hid behind their newspapers, and Mrs Rossbotham and Mrs Featherson chatted about the rigours of life in the new country.

Alone with her dark thoughts, Kitty wondered if she would hate Dunedin? When she'd left Dunedin as a twelve-year-old girl, it had been a cesspool of mud, and little more than shanty town. She'd heard the gold won on the Otago fields had improved the quality of the buildings and Dunedin was now enjoying a boost in population. She hoped so, for when she was last there her family lived in a draughty canvas tent, and the sanitation was terrible.

She glanced out the window at the watery sky. Trees hid fields and farmland, but now and then, she noticed a glint of blue through the scrubby trees. Lake Waihola! Her Da told her when he and Pat were heading to the goldfields there was a ferry on the lake but the ferryman charged like a wounded bull, so those who couldn't afford the quick crossing walked. She wondered if the ferryman was still enjoying a busy trade now the rush was on to the West.

There weren't many souls on the road. She had only seen two men walking the tracks with their tools in hand and swags on their backs. Kitty wished the horrible jarring and rattling would stop. She wouldn't want to sit for a week. How much further until they arrived in Dunedin? What would Grace be doing now?

Carmichael shouted, "Whoa!"

The horses pulled up, their traces jangling as the coach rumbled to a stop, and the brake was applied. The passengers eyed one another warily. Kitty cast a glance out the window wondering if they had reached a rest stop. It did not appear to be a populated area, nor did there seem to be any sort of watering hole nearby. It was a tree-lined enclave with scrubby bush of Flax and Toi-Toi on either side of its banks. Odd, she thought, for the coach to stop here in this lonely stretch of road.

Burns tapped on the passenger window. Mr Featherson opened the window and peered short-sightedly at him.

"What's wrong?" he asked, alarmed.

"Nothing to worry about," Burns reassured Kitty. He turned his attention back to the men. "A fallen tree is blocking the road. It's a large one, we'll need help to move it."

Keen to be of service, the two older men offered to assist. Welcoming the rest, the women got out to stretch their legs and relieve their aching posteriors. Looking stiff, but a better colour, the boy jumped down and put his shoulder to the tree. Mr Rossbotham handed his hat and coat to his wife and rolled up his shirt sleeves.

"Heave!" Carmichael commanded. The men strained. The tree moved a little way. Carmichael suggested they unhitch the horses and use them, but the others assured him together they were strong enough to complete the task without tiring the horses further. The women watched while the men combined their strength, they pushed and groaned under the weight, but dragged the tree away from the track.

Mr Rossbotham scratched his bald spot "I think this tree was cut."

There was the thunderous noise of horses' hooves rapidly approaching. Bloodcurdling cries rent the air. Out of the corner of her eye, Kitty saw the young digger scarper up the coach ladder, and grab his swag. He jumped off the roof, tumbling as he landed on the other side, then hopped up and disappeared into the scrub. In a flurry of skirts and coat tails, the other passengers scattered into the bush and hid amongst the flax.

Panicked, Kitty froze. Burns grasped Kitty's hand and dragged her down the overgrown bank. Pushing her into one flax bush, he threw himself in another and motioned to her, to stay down and stay quiet. Three masked mounted men rode into the clearing. Brandishing revolvers they rode in circles around the coach, their guns held high.

Peeking at her through the sword-shaped flax, Burns warned Kitty, to be quiet and stay hidden.

The largest man shouted from atop his horse, "Come out, or we'll shoot." He waited. No one moved. "To kill," the large man added, sneering. He lowered his gun and aimed his pistol at the spot where Kitty lay hidden.

Her heart stopped. Trembling, she squeezed her eyes closed waiting for the bullet.

"Don't shoot," Burns cried. Scrambling to his feet, he stuck his hands in the air. He walked bravely towards them, but his hands shook.

The large robber glared menacingly from under the brim of his black slouch hat. Snarling he said, "I won't shoot you if the rest of them buggers come out of the bushes." He paused, "But if they don't," he aimed his gun at Burns chest. "I will shoot you first, then the horses, then find every one of them and kill them dead."

Kitty clamped her hand tightly across her mouth, and buried herself deeper in the dirt.

The large man leaned forward in his saddle, crying out, "If you want this man to live come out with your hands up!"

No one moved.

"Don't think much of you, do they?" With his gun trained on Burns, he shouted orders to his men. "Get in there and flush the buggers out!"

The other two men dismounted. One man swished a machete through the long grass while the smaller of the two, manhandled Burns. With a gun at his back Burns was marched to the tall trees.

"Take what you want but don't harm us," Burns said.

The ringleader shouted, "I'm not interested in taking any lives unless it's absolutely necessary. Pray it won't be," he said, his revolver fixed on Burns chest.

"It may be," the other replied squinting up at the boss. After tying up Burns, the smaller robber searched his pockets, and took his fob watch and wallet. He weighed the gold fob in his hand. "Nice, but if this is all there is…." he drew his finger across his throat.

The robber with the machete continued to wade his way and slash through cutty-grass and Toi-Toi. He was getting closer to Kitty's hiding place. Instinctively she clutched her rosary beads, *Holy Mary, Mother of God, keep us safe,* she silently prayed. She could see the Feathersons and knew it wouldn't be long before the robbers found them.

Drawing their fire, Carmichael raised his hands. "Don't shoot!" he cried, getting to his feet. "I'm the seat. I don't carry gold, there's no strongbox on the stage." He waded through the long grass his hands held high in surrender. Carmichael struggled up the bank towards the head gunman. "All the gold is on the escort. I only carry passengers."

The leader stared maliciously down at him. "We know that, you silly old fool," he said, dismounting. "Now get the rest of yer passengers out here or we shoot to kill." Pointing his revolver at Carmichael, he said, "You first then him."

Kitty bit her lip, and prayed harder.

The robber with the machete stopped whistling. He waited a full minute before kicking Mr Featherson sharply in his side.

"Stand up you cowardly weasel," he said gruffly, pulling the small man to his feet.

"Kill any of us and you'll hang, you'll burn in hell," Mr Featherson replied, his fear suddenly making him reckless.

The man with the machete laughed. "I'm going to hell anyway; I don't see how I could make it any worse by taking yer sorry carcass with me. Of course, you could save yer foolish skin by giving me whatever gold you do have."

The robber motioned for Mrs Featherson to get up. Mrs Featherson stood but looked like she was going to faint.

"We raised money for charity, it's for the orphans," Mr Featherson said in a high-pitched voice.

The large robber nudged his horse and moved towards the Feathersons. "That's very charitable of you mister," he remarked, as he put his gun on the banker's forehead. "As luck would have it, I'm an orphan, so save your own skin, and hand it over."

Mrs Featherson shrieked. "No! Take whatever you want. Please, don't harm us!"

"We tell you what to do, not the other way around," replied the smaller thief. He prodded her with the gun and forced the pair to walk to the trees.

"Save the ropes and tie them back-to-back," the main man instructed.

The smaller man nodded, and tied them up.

Mr and Mrs Rossbotham were found hiding behind some Toi-Toi bushes. They were flushed out like pheasants. The small robber pushed the muzzle of his revolver into the small of his victims' backs, and marched them towards the trees. Dishevelled, with bits of twig and Toi-Toi in her hair, and mud smeared on her face, Mrs Rossbotham whimpered as she was forcibly tied to the tree. Her husband, tied on the other side, was unable to console her.

Hobnailed boots stopped in front of Kitty. Their owner, bent down and looked at her with keen eyes.

Cocking his head, he said, "Pretty one here, boss." He touched the curve of Kitty's cheek. Repulsed, she shrank from his touch. He grabbed Kitty under the arm and hauled her to her feet. She cried out as he twisted her arm behind her back.

"Don't hurt her," Burns warned, struggling against his bonds.

"Or what? What you going to do about it, hey?" he jeered. "Is this your pretty one?" He draped an arm around Kitty's shoulder and pretended to kiss her.

Kitty felt bile rising in her throat. She swallowed it down.

The ringleader turned on his accomplice. "Leave her," he barked. "We haven't got time for that kind of carry on."

Disgruntled, the man with the machete, pushed Kitty into the smaller robber's arms.

The smaller man marched Kitty to the trees. "Take off your gloves," he ordered. Trembling, Kitty did as she was told. The smaller man's ice grey eyes lit up when he saw the signet ring on her finger.

"No, please, my father gave it to me."

His voice was hard. "Give it to me."

190

Kitty twisted, and pulled, but the ring was stuck fast. "I can't," she said, now in tears.

"Spit on it and try again," he growled, losing patience. "You don't want me to have to cut off your finger."

Kitty blanched. She tugged until her finger was hot, red and swollen, but she managed to wrest the ring off and pass it to the man. He wrapped in a grubby handkerchief and put it in his waistcoat pocket. Then he tied her, back-to-back with Carmichael. The ringleader impatiently strode between his prisoners, his hobnailed boots heavy on the ground while the smaller man checked the prisoners to make sure their bonds were secure.

The one with the machete went to the coach, he appeared to be checking the horses. The small one climbed on top of the stage, he threw the luggage down to the other man, then the pair ransacked the bags looking for valuables. Kitty was pleased her mother had the forethought to sew money inside a secret pocket in the hem of her petticoat. She prayed the robbers wouldn't think to search her person and her money would remain safely hidden.

The main man stopped pacing between his prisoners, standing in front of Carmichael, he asked, "Is this all?"
Carmichael glared at the large man, his eyes full of hate, and nodded.

But the ringleader wasn't convinced. "Liar," he accused, punching Carmichael in the stomach. "Where's the lad?" he demanded.

Carmichael buckled, slumped against the ropes that held him. Kitty gasped as the ropes tightened around her waist. Carmichael wheezed.

Fists ready, the ringleader's eyes narrowed, "The little golden boy? Where's he? Don't lie, we saw him riding up top."

Suddenly there was a movement in the long grass as the lad sprang up, and made a break for it. A shot rang out, it whistled past the boy's ear. Spooked, the coach horses bolted. They sped off with their traces trailing behind them. The coach lurched forward and hit the ground with a thump. They had removed the kingpin. The horses were gone.

A second shot rang out. Defeated, the boy stopped, dropped his swag, turned and raised his hands in surrender.

"Got him," the smaller robber said triumphantly. He waded through the scrub to the boy and picked up the lad's swag. Holding the machete to the boy's neck, he forced him to march to the gang's leader. Shoved roughly against the tree that held Burns, the robber tied him up. Convinced they now had all the stage passengers, the bushrangers enjoyed tormenting the lad. The smaller robber pulled out a dagger and nicked a button off the boy's tattered coat. The boy flinched, and shut his eyes as if he expected death to come swiftly.

Tired of the sport, the boss man picked up the boy's swag and emptied it. A large gold nugget the size of a man's fist fell to the ground. He picked up the nugget and grinned, "Thank you kindly sir, I'm going to enjoy spending this." He waved it under the boy's nose.

The lad fought hard to keep his tears at bay.

"Best keep yer mouth shut hey boyo, liquor loosens the lips, it's not wise to go around bragging about yer rich find when there's the likes of us about, who want gold without doing any of the back-breaking work."

The one with the machete said, "Yeah, and even more stupid to tell folks you were planning to catch the next stage to stake your claim."

Kitty watched the robbers searching the bags for money and jewels. Her pearl hatpin and ivory hairbrush were stolen. They upturned Mr Featherson's bag and his clothing was strewn about. They found money secreted inside the lining and held it up, triumphant. Mrs Featherson cried as her cameo broach was plucked off her starched collar, her pearl earbobs removed, and her rings stripped from her fingers.

"Thank you kindly, Madam, I know a little lady who will like those." The small robber mocked while the boss man stuffed the loot into his saddlebags.

Burns caught Kitty's eye and he mouthed to her, 'Keep calm.' Kitty blinked to show she understood.

"If you promise not to scream, we won't gag you," the boss man said, swaggering amongst his prisoners, his pistol at the ready.

"There's water for the ladies," he lifted his flask and poured some water down Kitty's throat. She coughed, spluttering as some water spilt down her front. The robber with the machete leered at her breasts.

The boss man strode between the trees, offering them water. He searched coat pockets for tobacco, finding some in Burn's pocket, he lit his pipe and blew smoke in Burns eyes.

Patting Burns shoulder, he said in a patronizing tone, "Don't fret sir, we have decided to let you live, the next stage will be along shortly - tomorrow perhaps."

Burns glared at the man, his eyes full of hate, but he didn't respond. The boss man laughed and signalled to the other robbers to mount their steeds.

Turning his horse, the ringleader bent low and said to the boy, "Easy pickings son, easy pickings." And with a cry that rent the air, the robbers rode away.

The prisoners were silent until the sound of the horses' hooves became more distant, and they could no longer hear them.

"Kitty! Are you all right?" Burns called, twisting his hands he struggled against the bonds.

"Y-yes," Kitty stammered. She couldn't stop shaking.

Burns could feel the boy's wrists moving as he tried to free his hands.

"Keep trying," Burns commanded.

Mrs Rossbotham had wet herself and was sobbing. Her husband was trying to comfort her, telling her help would come, but she was inconsolable.

Carmichael kept repeating, "They got what they wanted, they won't be back. Don't fret, another stage will come and we'll be rescued."

Mrs Featherson berated her husband, saying it was his fault they were in this predicament. She had had a premonition and had wanted to delay their journey another day.

Insisting the lad not give up but keep working on getting his hands free, Burns felt a spark of hope as the ropes that burned into his flesh slackened.

Calling out he said, "I think I might be able to get free. Carmichael, is there a knife somewhere?"

"Aye, there is," Carmichael replied. "Under the box seat there's a toolbox, and it's not locked. Let's hope the blackguards didn't take the tools as well."

The boy dropped to the ground, and pushed away the last of the ropes before nimbly scrambling to his feet.
Burns rubbed his tingling hands trying to get the feeling back.

"Go and untie the others," Burns told the lad. The lad sped off. Burns ran to the stage and found the toolbox under the box seat, unlocked. Inside the tin box he found a small pocket knife. He ran back to the others and began sawing through the ropes that bound Kitty and Carmichael together.

Carmichael sighed with relief when the ropes fell away. "Well done Burns," he praised. "Here, give me that," he said, taking the knife. "You look after the girl."
Holding Kitty's hands in his, Burns rubbed her wrists to get the blood flowing again. "It's all right, you're all right," he repeated over and over again as if he wished it were true.

Trembling, Kitty stared at the dent on her finger where here signet ring should be. "They took it," she said bitterly. "My father had it made especially for me." Her eyes large, like green lamps, she looked up at him anxiously. "They won't come back, will they?"

"They won't," Burns assured her. "They'll be going like the clappers as far away from here as they can."

Kitty threw her arms around his neck, and clung to him. She could hear herself crying, but the sound seemed distant, like she was in some terrible dream.

Patting her back gently, he said, "It's all right, you're safe now." Kitty reached up and kissed him.

Shocked, Burns detached himself. He took a step back. "I am engaged to be married to your sister in a little over two weeks' time." He frowned at her like he thought she'd lost her mind.

"I'm sorry," Kitty said penitently, her face flaming red, her eyes downcast with regret.

"I'll go help the others." He turned and walked away.

Kitty sat on the grass, head in her hands, and wept. She was joined by Mrs Featherson, and Mrs Rossbotham who huddled beside her. Mrs Rossbotham stank of urine.

Carmichael came to check on them. "Don't worry ladies, they won't return. Sit here and don't move while Burns and I go look for the horses. I'm hoping they haven't gone too far. Mr Rossbotham and Mr Featherson will stand guard."

Too frightened to speak, the woman merely nodded.

"Pray the horses haven't gone far," Burns said, his eyes not meeting Kitty's.

Mr Rossbotham suggested to his wife that she might like to use the stagecoach to change. She nodded miserably, and wiped her eyes. Finding her carpet bag, she gathered her things, climbed inside the coach and pulled the blinds.

The horses were found grazing in a nearby clearing, their damaged traces tangled. Carmichael led his team back to the stage and refastened the king pin, stressing the importance of getting to

Dunedin quickly to report the robbery, he urged his frightened passengers to get back on the stage. Burns made the lad, who told them his name was, Joe, sit up front on the box seat with them, so they could question him.

The stage rattled and shook as Carmichael drove the horses on. Overwhelmed, the passengers barely spoke; they may have lost their possessions but they were grateful to still be alive. Kitty couldn't stop shaking. The rest of the journey seemed interminable as she replayed the robbery over, and over in her mind, and the moment of insanity when she kissed William! She couldn't forget the shocked look in his eyes. Pressed hard up against the padded wall, Kitty stared out the coach window, ashamed. She had made a dreadful mistake. William wasn't hers to love, and she had betrayed Meg's trust. How could she have done such a detestable thing?

At last, they reached the outskirts of Dunedin. Kitty could not believe the change in the place. Permanent buildings, large stone edifices testified of the prosperity gold had brought to the town. Instead of pulling into the Wains Hotel stables, Carmichael reined in his team alongside the Police Barracks. He asked the passengers to go next door to the tearooms and order refreshments on the Cobb and Co account, while he and Burns reported the robbery.

As the rest of the passengers headed for the tearooms, Carmichael collared Joe. "You'll come with us," he told him.

The constable was studying a broadsheet and looked only mildly interested in their appearance. He wrinkled his nose as they approached.

Carmichael banged his fist on the counter. "We were robbed," he declared, his frayed nerves making him angry.

"What?" The Constable straightened up, instantly attentive. Another figure, an older, much taller man appeared from the back room and headed towards them, his footsteps heavy on the wooden floor.

"Bushrangers attacked us just before Lake Waihola," Carmichael told the constable shortly. "They were lying in wait. They tied us to trees, and robbed us. This lad, in particular," he put his hand on Joe's bony shoulder, "lost a lot of gold."

"I'm the Sergeant here," the tall man introduced himself, giving the lad a curious glance. He focused his attention back on Carmichael. "Please continue."

"Fortunately, we were able to free ourselves," Burns chimed in, eager to give his account of the ordeal. "Thank God nobody was harmed, but the ruffians must be stopped before they strike again."

Carmichael interjected. "Not only had they taken off with all my winnings from the gaming tables but they stole my father's gold fob watch. But it's the boy who lost the most," he said, his chest heaving with fresh indignation. "And it's he, who nearly got us all killed." He scowled at Joe.

Forlorn, Joe looked down at his worn-out boots.

The Constable picked up his pen, his eyes noted the rope burn on their wrists. "Did you get a good look at them?" he asked as he began writing notes. "Would you recognize them if you saw them again?"

"By God I would," Carmichael assured him. "They wore hats and masks, but you could see the evil buggers' eyes and a brood of uglier vipers yer'd be hard pressed to meet."

The sergeant pushed the broadsheet across the counter. "Is this them?" he asked pointing at the sketches.

"Aye," Carmichael nodded. "That's them."

"That's them all right," Burns agreed.

"It's the Sullivan gang." The sergeant told them. "Sullivan is the big one in the centre, the one on the left is Crowle, and the small one is Butcher." He peered out the window at the coach. "I'm afraid I'll have to get statements from all of the passengers," he told them.

"It's been a harrowing ordeal; can the ladies not go and freshen up first?" Burns asked.

"No." The sergeant was firm. "Best when fresh."

Burns was disturbed by the thought of Kitty having to relive the nightmare all over again. She was fragile. He'd failed to protect her. There was no telling what she might do.

Carmichael blustered, "Instead of bothering the ladies, shouldn't you be out there catching these villains!"

"Sir, you will not raise your voice at me again," the sergeant said, commanding respect. "You are upset but you must calm down." He turned to Burns. "Be kind enough to ask the other passengers to come in so we can take their statements." He gave his constable a nod signalling him to continue taking notes.

"Right then, Mr Carmichael, can you start at the beginning."

Burns went next door and asked the other passengers to make their way to the barracks when they had finished their refreshments. When he returned Carmichael was seated on a long bench seat, still muttering under his breath. Burns had asked for three mugs of tea and some mutton sandwiches to be delivered next door, one for him, one for Carmichael, and one for the lad. After he'd given his statement, Carmichael went out into the street and asked a passer-by to notify Cobb and Co of their arrival, and to send someone to collect the stage.

Carmichael stayed while the sergeant made the weary travellers relive their nightmare while the constable listed the items stolen. Presently a groomsman arrived and retrieved the stagecoach. When all the statements were taken, the passengers were free to go, and collect their luggage.

"Are you all right Kitty?" Burns asked, as they walked up the hill toward the Wains Hotel. She was deathly pale and very quiet, and the freckles across the bridge of her nose stood out. She looked very young and vulnerable.

Kitty nodded. "Yes, thank you," she murmured.

Struggling with the bags, and the steepness of the hill, he began to puff. "Would you like me to send a telegram to your parents?"

"No, no," she assured him. "They'd only worry."

He was pleased she had spoken, she'd barely said a word. "You were very brave."

Kitty bit her bottom lip. "I'm grateful no one was hurt."

"We were lucky to get away as quickly as we did, it could have been a long cold miserable night."

"Yes, I'm thankful."

He paused to catch his breath. "I'm sorry you lost your ring."

"Yes, it was very special," Kitty said sadly. "Best not say anything, it will only upset Da."

Like a beacon in the darkening sky the canopy of the Wain's Hotel came into view. The place was a welcome sight for sore eyes. The hotel was grand and luxurious, and Kitty wished she had the heart to enjoy it. Burns held the hotel door for Kitty and ushered her inside. Kitty wanted to cry, but she studied the glittering chandelier that graced the foyer to keep herself in check.

Embarrassed by her dishevelled appearance, Kitty stood quietly to one side while Burns spoke to the hotel clerk. The attendant gave her a curious glance then took their bags. They followed him up the sweeping staircase to the landing. The attendant deposited her bags in her room and gave her the key, then turned and unlocked the room directly opposite and handed Burns his key, with a respectful nod, he left.

"I will be just across the hall should you need me," Burns said. "I pray you sleep well." He closed the door.

Then she was alone. Wrapping her arms tightly about herself she stared out the window in a trance. A building was going up on the other side of the road, the stonework stood like a great gloomy fortress with columns like something from ancient Roman times. Kitty wanted a bath, but she would have to make do with a wash, most of all she wanted to forget about the horrors of the day.

Exhausted, she slid between the starched sheets realizing she never felt as alive as when she thought she might die. The adrenaline which had pumped through her body has dissipated and she felt like a hollow shell. Was it fear that made her behave so irrationally? She had kissed William and he had spurned her affection. He had been politely distant ever since. Would he tell Meg? She wondered. Dear God, she hoped not! Meg would never forgive her. Then not only would she have lost her ring, but her sister as well.

Chapter 9   Shifting Sands

"Morning Miss Kitty." Burns knocked, his voice muffled by the heavy wooden door. "Are you ready?"

Kitty opened the door. "Yes," she said, pointing at her bags.

"Leave your bags here, I'll send the doorman up for them. We will have breakfast in the dining room, then when the bank is open, I will go and withdraw funds to pay our accounts."

"I can settle them." Kitty lowered her voice, "They didn't get my money. Ma made me sew pounds into a hidden pocket in my petticoats."

"She is a very clever resourceful woman," Burns said, his voice full of admiration.

Burns left their bags in the care of the hotel doorman while they breakfasted in the dining room. It was a hearty meal of scrambled eggs and bacon. Kitty thought the coffee terribly bitter so she added three sugars to make it more palatable. Still mortified, by her rash behaviour she could not meet his eyes.

Burns seemed reluctant to engage in any conservation other than the weather.

"Did you sleep?" he asked, concerned.

"Yes," she replied but the dark circles under her eyes betrayed her.

The waiter brought the bill to the table and laid it in front of William.

When the waiter had retreated, Kitty whispered, "I'll pay."

"I cannot allow that," he protested.

"My mother and father would want me to, to thank you for all your kindnesses," she told him firmly placing a bank note in the folder. "No one needs to know."

When they exited the hotel, they saw stonemasons as busy and as industrious as ants in a nest crawling over the building opposite Wains. It was noisy. Dust rose in great plumes like smoke and dirt settled over everything like a blanket. They walked carefully up the street as there were building works all around the main centre of town and they were in danger of falling into a hole. Kitty was relieved when at last they reached the fashion boutique. Burns offered to wait outside with her bags while Kitty went in and introduced herself. He stood stiffly against the backdrop of dust and noise, and waited for her to return.

Madame Juliette le Roux welcomed Kitty in her charming French accent, asking if she would like to look around the shop before they showed her to the boarding house.

Kitty let out the breath she'd been holding, it was going to be all right, they seemed nice. "Thank you so much, my brother-in-law kindly accompanied me on my journey he's just outside with my bags." She motioned to him to come across. Burns picked up her luggage and carried it inside while Kitty held the door open for him.

He deposited Kitty's bags, and with a polite bow said, "Good morning ladies." They nodded and smiled at him.

"Please excuse us," Kitty said to the ladies, "I'll just take a moment to say goodbye." She followed him out into the street.

They stood awkwardly, like strangers, as people intent on their business hurried past.

"Thank you, for everything," Kitty mumbled to her feet, her emotions teetering on the edge of the abyss.

"I'm sorry you had to endure such a terrible ordeal, Miss Kitty. I failed in my duty to protect you as I promised your sister and parents I would." He shifted from foot to foot.

Kitty wasn't used to seeing him so ill at ease, he was normally so self-possessed. "I'm here, and still alive."

"Thank God." William looked at the stylish sign above shop, and swiftly changed the subject. "They look like good people."

"Yes," Kitty agreed. "They seem very nice."

He grinned. "If they are not, one word and I'm sure your mother will come immediately, deal to them and drag you home by your ear."

Kitty gave him a wobbly smile.

Burns glanced nervously about. "Well, I'd best be off," he said. "I've got business to attend to. And a meeting with the shareholders before heading back."

Kitty's eyes grew moist. "Give my love to everyone back home."

"I will," he promised.

"Especially Grace."

He nodded. "Especially Grace."

Feeling breathless, Kitty tried to keep calm. "I hope you and Meg have a wonderful wedding, and a very happy marriage."

"Thank you," he replied, shuffling his feet. "Well, I'd best be going."

"Forgive me." Throwing her arms around his neck Kitty hugged him tightly, then let go. Hurrying across the street she disappeared inside the shop.

Troubled, Burns shook his head. Even as he entered the Chinese merchant's shop, he could still feel the warmth of Kitty's embrace. She was only a child. He felt responsible for her, nothing more. Her erratic behaviour was disturbing. He was relieved to have delivered her to the dressmaker's shop, and relieved to leave her there. Somewhere along the way she'd developed feelings for him. It was best forgotten. To mention the kiss to Meg may cause a rift, and he didn't want that. God only knew how she would react. He pressed a thumb to the knot in the base of his skull. He had the makings of a fine headache. He couldn't wait to get home, but first he had some business to attend to.

His anger abated, Carmichael felt sorry for Joe, and invited him to stay the night at his house. Having nowhere else to go and no money, Joe readily accepted. Motherly, and with all her children grown and gone, Mrs Carmichael was horrified by the state of the boy. She gave him supper, and insisted he bathed, while she washed the rags he called clothes. It was midmorning when Burns knocked on the Carmichaels' door. The door was opened by Mrs Carmichael who looked at him suspiciously through dark hooded lids. She was used to collectors calling for Carmichael was a gambler, sometimes he'd win but more often than not, he'd lose.

Joe was seated by the fire, wearing one of Carmichael's shirts which looked like a tent on the boy's small frame.

Burns removed his hat and bowed politely. "Hello Mrs Carmichael, I was wondering if I could have a word with..."

206

"My husband is out," she interrupted, and tried to close the door.

Burns put his foot in the way. "Actually, it wasn't him I came to see. I would like a quick word with Joe, if I may."

"Joe?" Mrs Carmichael looked dubious, and glanced at the lad to gauge his reaction. "Why?"

"It's all right Ma'am," Joe nodded. "I know this gentleman, I met him on the stage."

She opened the door and allowed him to pass. "Take a seat Mr...?"

"Burns, it's William Burns," he smiled. "Your husband may have mentioned me."

"Ah yes, now I recall. Would you like some tea?"

"No, thank you," he assured her.

"Well, Mr Burns. I will just be out back getting the washing off the line if you need me," she told them. "There's been a good wind blowing and they have dried in no time."

Thanking her, Burns took a seat by the fire. He waited till she left the room before he began. Leaning forward, he said, "I've been thinking lad..." he paused, eyeing Joe speculatively, "about your claim."

Joe stiffened. "It's mine." He folded his arms and moved back deeper into the chair.

Burns waited a moment, sitting back he crossed his legs, then said, "Not if you can't register it. Not if you can't pay the miner's right, it's not."

Joe looked alarmed. "I have to get back to Macetown and get more gold so I can register my claim."

"It's a long walk," Burns reminded him.

Joe turned his head and looked at the flames dancing in the grate. They looked like dancing devils.

"That's where I may be able to help," Burns said with an encouraging smile.

Eyes full of distrust, Joe scowled. "Why, why would you want to help me?"

Burns didn't answer but looked at the lad the way a cat watches a mouse.

"Oh, I get it, you want my claim in return? Well, you'll not have it. And I'll not tell you where it is. You can't force me."

Burns uncrossed his legs and leaned forward. "I don't want your claim son, only a very small percentage of it. And in return I will buy you a new set of clothes, pay the miner's right, and your passage back to Macetown."

Joe was silent while he digested the proposal.

"Think about it, it's a very good offer," he paused, adding, "remember, it's a very long walk."

He studied Burns. "How much?"

"Say ten percent. That's very low, and reasonable, don't you think?"

Joe squinted, his eyes small like slits. "How do I know I can trust you?"

"You have my word as a gentleman."

Joe snorted, unconvinced.

"If you are agreeable, I will draw up a contract at my solicitor's tomorrow, which we will both sign. That legally binds me to fulfil my part of the bargain."

Keeping his guard up, Joe said, "Can't read, so how will I know what it says?"

"I will get my solicitor to read it to you in full before you make your mark. And to assure you I mean to fulfil my bargain, to show good faith before you sign, I will buy you new clothes, pay the miner's right and register it in your name. And, I'll pay your stage fare back to the fields, all before you sign the contract."

"I need new boots."

"And new boots."

Joe rubbed his chin thoughtfully. "I need a tent, a pick and shovel."

"Think about it. By the time you get back to your claim someone else could beat you to registering it. And if you have to walk all the way back with no food in your empty belly and holes in your boots it will take you a long time to get there. It's the only sensible decision, lad."

"I want a tent and a pick and shovel," Joe repeated. "And some tucker."

Burns smiled. "You drive a hard bargain, Joe." He pondered the proposition before agreeing, "All right, twenty per cent and they are yours."

"You said ten percent."

"Ah, but you added things of value. Besides, twenty percent is nothing." Burns relaxed but watched Joe shrewdly. Joe was weakening. "Eighty percent is yours to do with as you like."

Mrs Carmichael bought the washing in. She folded Joe's torn patched trousers and his threadbare waistcoat, and handed them to the lad in a nice neat parcel.

Joe looked at the raggedy clothes on his lap then up at Burns. "Deal," he said sticking out his hand.

Chapter 10   Crossings

Meg didn't say why she was going to Queenstown, just that she was, and would be back Sunday. A no nonsense man, Charles Asterly normally demanded an explanation for any deviation from the usual plan, but to Meg's surprise, he didn't bother to ask. Meg left Skippers as soon as lessons were finished on Friday. She was pleased with the children's progress; they were doing well. It was a hot, dusty eight-mile walk. The grey mountain dust clung to everything coating it in a layer of chalky powder. Wearing her best hat, Meg carried a leather satchel and her travelling cloak over her arm. The temperature dropped sharply at night and it was best to be prepared. Summer days were long and warm, but when winter arrived they would be snowed in at Asterlys Terrace, the track would become impassable, so they had to make the best of the weather while it lasted.

Meg walked over the Saddle and down the hill. She would have loved to visit the library at Maori Point but there wasn't time. She wondered how William and Kitty were getting on. She missed Kitty already. The hotel would feel empty without her. Life was changing as quickly as a river in flood, nothing would ever be the same. She hoped Kitty would be happy. She couldn't bear to think of her little sister being miserable so far away.

Annie's death had taught Meg that family was to be valued. She couldn't understand how her own mother and father could have left their parents on the other side of the world. She knew very little about her grandparents, only snippets here and there when Ma let her guard down and said, my old mother did such and such then she'd clam up again as morbid as a crow. It was a shame; she expected her grandparents would have liked to have seen her well married.

When Meg arrived at the hotel, she went round the back and found Marnie in the vegetable patch spreading chicken manure. Grace was toddling behind her, playing with the trowel, more hindrance than help. Seeing Meg, Grace squealed in delight and tottered towards her aunt, her arms outstretched. Meg picked Grace up and carried her inside, and Marnie followed, carrying a bunch of silver-beet in her arms. Setting the silver-beet down on the bench Marnie quickly washed her hands in the bucket and dried them on the towel.

Meg wiped Grace's hands and face with a cloth. "Where's Ma?" Meg asked.

"Here." Mary came out of the larder, a smudge of flour on her cheek.

Mary glanced at the silver-beet on the kitchen bench. "Have you finished?" she asked Marnie.

"Yes," replied Marnie.

"Good," Mary nodded curtly and went back to her breadmaking.

Marnie followed Meg and Grace down the hallway to the bedroom "Did you come to get the..." she stopped herself in time, she glanced over her shoulder and whispered, "parasol."

"Not yet," Meg replied. She put Grace on the bed and hung her cape in the wardrobe. "I'm staying the night. I'm heading down to Queenstown with my parents in the morning."

Happy to have company, Marnie sat on the edge of the bed and swung her leg. She missed Daisy and the other girls' mindless chatter. They could talk for hours about nothing in particular. "To Yankee Brown's wedding?"

"Yes."

Marnie looked at Meg wide- eyed. "Didn't he once hold a candle for you?"

"Yes, but seems he's found another to focus his attentions on."

"How are your wedding preparations going?"

Meg shrugged, "There's not a lot to tell, there's just posies left to pick on the day."

"Oh, when you need it, the parasol is in there. At the back." Marnie pointed to the wardrobe. "Kitty hid it there."

"Thanks Marnie, that's very kind of you."

Marnie pulled Grace onto her lap and rested her chin on to the top of Grace's head. "So where will you live?"

"William has a cottage not far from the schoolhouse."

"He's a handsome man, you must be very excited," Marnie enthused.

"Yes, and intelligent too," Meg agreed. "He's meeting with the shareholders talking about the possibility of a dredging partnership." Meg tucked her bag under the bed.

Marnie cocked her head to one side. "Do you miss him?"

"I do," she admitted. "But he's generally at the mine, and I'm busy with the school and my charges. We don't get to spend a lot of time together."

"I expect that will change once you are married," Marnie said.

"Yes, I expect so." Meg turned. "Your face has healed well."

Marnie gingerly touched her eye. "Aye, barely hurts a bit now. Would Mr Burns and Kitty have reached their destination yet?"

"Yes, and all going well William should be back on Saturday."

Marnie's face clouded with concern. "Do you think Kitty will like it there?"

Marnie asked questions that were too close to the bone, and they made Meg squirm. "I hope so. I can't bear to think of her as miserable. I better go give Ma a hand with dinner," Meg said, leaving the room.

Grace scrambled off Marnie's lap and hurried after her aunt.

Marnie was disappointed. She had hoped Meg would share gossip and they could prattle away for ages, laughing about nothing but Meg was quieter, more reserved than Kitty. Meg seemed guarded, like she was hiding something. With a huge sigh, Marnie headed to the kitchen, women's work was never done.

Mary bustled about, rattling pots and pans. "Hop to it," she told them. "Meg, fetch a pail of water, there's potatoes to peel. Wash the silver-beet thoroughly, we don't want to eat crawlers." She cast a furtive glance at the clock. "Marnie, see to it that you grind that meat properly, I don't want no gristle in it, understand? Come on, move!" She clapped her hands.

Over dinner, the men talked about the changes in the river, they worried that when the rains came, some of the claim would be underwater, and slips would cut off the road. There had been another slip up at Blue Slip and it had taken days to clear. Preoccupied with the time, Mary hastily ate dinner while reprimanding Grace for being a greedy wee mouse.

Meg felt like a remote observer. Meals at the Asterly homestead were quiet civilized affairs. Well-mannered, the girls waited politely, ate delicately, and only spoke when spoken to. Horrified, Meg watched Pat attack his food with the ferocity of a wild beast. Marnie barely said a word throughout dinner. Strange, Meg thought, she was chatty enough before dinner, now she sat as silent as a stone. She noticed Pat and Marnie didn't interact, and seemed reluctant to engage each other in conversation, she couldn't help wondering why.

Pat raised his head. "So," he eyed Meg speculatively as he dug his fork into a potato, "Why you are going to Yankee's wedding?"

Meg narrowed her eyes at her brother. "Yankee's a family friend, I'm going to celebrate his special day."

Pat bored his finger into his temple. "You think we are as green as we are cabbage looking."

"All right, I'm curious. Are you satisfied?" Meg snapped. "I want to see the bride."

"Want to compare yourself, you mean." Pat said, knowing he'd struck a nerve.

"I do not," Meg retorted. "I want to see what her dress is like."

Pat was smug. "Long way to go and a lot of trouble to go to when someone else can tell you what it looked like."

He was deliberately goading her and she could feel her temper rising. Annoyed, Meg finished her last bite and pushed her plate aside. "While I'm in Queenstown I will see Jack, and I'll give him your love, Marnie," she promised.

Marnie's eyes lit with hope, she wanted to say, tell him to come quickly, but couldn't in front of Mary.

215

Jim cut across the conversation. "Can't get used to calling it bloody Queenstown," he muttered. "It will always be Rees or The Camp to me."

"Ma could do that," Pat countered, ignoring Jim. He stabbed another hunk of potato and stuffed it into his mouth making his cheeks bulge.

Meg glared at him. "I want to go. I need to order a new dress."

"I reckon yer jealous and can't bring yerself to admit it," Pat drawled with a sly grin. He winked, incensing Meg further.

Meg rose, gathered up the dirty dishes and they clattered noisily as she dumped them on the bench.

Mary glared reprovingly at her.

Pointing his fork at her, Pat laughed. "You are jealous, admit it."

Exasperated, Meg rounded on him. "No, I'm not, I'm curious. Curiosity is not a sin!"

Jim who had kept out of it until then elbowed Pat sharply in the ribs. He hissed "Unless you want your sister to throw the plates at you, for heaven's sake shut yer gob, son."

Mary reluctantly agreed to leave Marnie in charge of the household chores. She reminded her to keep out of sight, telling her the fewer people who knew she was there, the better for all concerned. Jim offered Pat the chance to go to Rees with them, but Pat said he'd rather be boiled in oil than see a good man like Yankee wed. Besides, he added, the claim would need working and the bar tending. That made Mary nervous. Grimly, she reminded Pat that Smiley was in charge of the bar. The toothless old digger known as Smiley, had been a parson in the old country, and folks joked he

216

was more reliable than God himself. She'd been anxious about leaving Marnie and Pat together but they seemed to have come to some sort of uneasy truce. Now he'd been warned, Mary hoped Pat would keep a respectful distance and his hands to himself.

Jack shrugged the jacket over his own, buttoned it and pulled Bennett's hat low over his eyes.

"Will have to do," the blacksmith muttered, shaking his head. "Let's hope our plan works and the simpleton thinks you are me, lad."

There was a catch in Jack's voice as he said, "I can never thank you enough for your kindness, Mr Bennett, but I'll remember it to the end of my days."

"Aye, that's if you live that long, you've rather a reckless streak my lad. Ah well, if you get there safe and sound, you can send me clothes back with the packer, that'll be a start." He held out a leather purse.

Humbled by the gesture, Jack said, "Ye don't have to give me wages as well, Mr Bennett, I'm only sorry to bring you so much trouble."

"No, I'll pay ye what yer due lad, and a wee bit besides. You've been a good worker and a quick learner, and I'm damned sorry to lose you."

Jack turned his head to hide his emotion. Mr Bennett was an odd soul, he'd never so much as engaged him in conversation which wasn't about work, and now here he was risking his own neck, and to think to begin with he thought badly of the man.

"Now, now, don't you go thinking I'm being generous. Keeping you here is a danger to me as I'm worried those despicable blackguards might torch the forge, you're worth more to me away," Bennett said, handing Jack the purse. He checked the time on his fob watch. "Right lad, it's the time I usually go, off you go, and don't look back. Go to my digs. By the back door there's a sack with some bread and cheese and a flask of water to help you on the way, make sure you make good use of them. Head straight for the canyon and don't come back." Bennett grasped Jack's hand. "God be with you son, you're a fine young man, and a credit to your mother."

Jack opened his mouth to speak but Bennett raised his hand to silence him. "Just remember me in your prayers as I'll remember you. Now be off with you son. I'm a creature of habit if you don't leave now, you'll ruin our plans."

Swallowing hard, Jack nodded.

He went out the side door like Bennett usually did at precisely 5:00pm. He spotted Bill across the road, leaning against the hotel veranda post, puffing away on his clay pipe. Jack's heart raced but he tried to imitate Bennett's casual bandy-legged walk. Jack went up the side lane and turned down the alley. Resisting the urge to look over his shoulder, he kept walking, head down, hat low over his eyes. Bennett's coat was large on his thin frame if he wasn't wearing two coats it would swim on him. When he got to Bennett's stone cottage he went around back, relieved to have made it so far, he sank to his knees. The sack was where Bennett said it would be, on top of the coal bin tied tight with string to stop rodents getting

218

in. Jack slung the sack over his shoulder, gathered his courage and made tracks. In a few hours he'd be with Marnie.

A hulking figure appeared in the open doorway casting a long shadow across the wooden barrel that served as Bennett's card table.

Bennett, wearing only his holey old singlet and moleskins, looked up from the game of poker he was playing with Sergeant Mackie and scowled.

"Come in, come in," he said impatiently, waving an arm at the intruder.

Bill didn't budge. He frowned at the pair. He hadn't seen Mackie enter the building.

"What can I do for ye?" Bennett asked gruffly. "Can't you see you're interrupting a good game, man?"

Bill glanced about, unsure. He hunched his shoulders then lumbered towards them.

"Can't you see I'm busy man, make it quick and spit it out," Bennett snapped, holding his cards close to his chest.

Bill's slippery eyes darted about the forge. "Er, I thought...," he hesitated, "I was looking for..." he faltered, "Jack Healey?"

"Aye and I'm looking for the scoundrel as well, and so is the Law." Bennett slapped his cards down on the table. "The ungrateful beggar stole me best hat and coat, and some of me hard earned dough to boot. Just up and disappeared he did without so much as a by your leave!" Bennett jerked his head at the sergeant. "Sergeant Mackie here was just taking my statement over a friendly game of cards. He's about to set off to look for the thief, aren't you Mac?"

"Aye, that's right." The sergeant put down his cards. He got up and walked deliberately over to Bill. The same height he looked Bill in the eye and narrowed his gaze, "What's he to you?"

Flummoxed, Bill could hardly say he wanted to bash Healey, the weasel, into smithereens for stealing away a good little earner. Forced to stump up with a reason the cogs in his brain turned slowly. They stared at him, waiting for him to reply.

"Ah, it's nothing, just a small job the lady wants doing. She wants a new fireguard but I can see you're busy, I'll come back tomorrow."

Bennett shook his fist. "Well, if you see that no good lousy cur...," he swore, "you can tell him I'm looking for him and so is the Law. Mackie will hunt him down like the dog he is, he won't get away with stealing from me, no sir."

"Aye, that's right," Sergeant Mackie agreed. "A bit of time in the lockup will make him sorry for his sins."

Bill grunted. "Aye, I'll let you know if I see him." He tipped his hat. "Good day to you gentlemen." Bill stepped outside into the glaring sun.

With a sinking feeling, Bill realized he'd been hoodwinked. Healey must have disguised himself and escaped under the tip of his nose. Now with the Law chasing Healey's tail he couldn't hunt him down and execute his own form of rough justice. He'd waited days outside the forge hoping to catch a glimpse of Marnie, or the pair of them together, and now the slippery eel had wriggled free from his grasp and skulked away in broad daylight. Madame would be furious. She'd take it out on him and maybe even take away his privileges. Cursing his bad luck, he kicked a stone with the toe of his boot.

"Bastard," Bill muttered, shoving his clenched fists deep inside his trouser pockets. "He'll keep."

The pub was in full swing. Billiard balls clacked, boots stamped in time to the fiddle, glasses were raised, cards played, and fortunes won and lost. Mary gaily served her patrons, enjoying the noisy familiarity and the friendly banter of good honest hardworking men. She was resplendent, like a buttercup in a field full of daisies.

McDougall wore his full Scottish regalia, sporran, dirk and all. He was in fine fettle tonight, with a belly full of whisky under his belt he sang at the top of his lungs. A good eighteen stone and as delicate on his feet as any ballet dancer, he entertained the diggers by dancing jigs and reels the whole night. Mary's ribs ached from laughing.

Alone in the kitchen, Jim sat feet up by a crackling fire half-heartedly reading a week-old paper. His wooden pipe had long since gone out but he kept it clenched between his teeth by force of habit. Tomorrow they would head down to Rees where Father Whooley would be waiting for his answer. Of course, he'd accept, he was overawed by the honour. And, he couldn't wait to get that special present for Mary. He'd been scheming for some time and here was an opportunity to get a ring just like the one she'd pawned. She told him it was to pay for Annie's fare, clothing and upkeep in Dunedin, but he knew the hotel made enough that she wouldn't have had to sell the ring. She sold it because she thought him gone for good.

He wanted to make a statement by giving her another with the same inscription 'love remains', he wanted to make her feel secure, to show her he didn't plan on going anywhere. He'd keep it a secret until just the right moment and then surprise her with it. He smiled to himself, trying to guess her reaction. The warmth of the fire made him feel drowsy. Jim's head began to droop, his pipe dropped on his lap as he began to snore.

Meg thought it was ironic that they were whispering so as not to disturb the baby when there was such a tremendous racket coming from the tavern. Marnie bolted the bedroom door and the girls changed into their night things, Meg brushed out her hair and braided it into a single long plait while Marnie chose to leave her hair loose, she was too tired to bother to brush it. When they climbed into the double bed, a spring squeaked in protest, they held their breath, Grace stirred but didn't wake. Marnie sighed, every muscle in her body ached and she was weary to the bone. She blew out the candle.

Meg whispered in the darkness, "How is Ma treating you?"

"Better than before, and better than I dared to hope," Marnie replied, yawning. "But it is lonely without Kitty."

"I wish she was here too; it makes my heart bleed to know she won't be at my wedding," Meg sighed wistfully. She turned over and propped herself up on her elbow. "Have you and Pat had some sort of argument?"

Marnie thought for a moment before replying. "Don't reckon he's that happy that I'm marrying your brother.

"Why not?"

"Not good enough."

Meg snorted. "He's got no right to judge."

"And your Mr Burns, is he happy about the likes of me marrying into your family?"

Meg murmured something that was incoherent.

Marnie said, "What about you, Meg, are you happy?"

"Of course, I am, if you and Jack are happy, I'm happy."

"No, I meant with your choice. Do you think you will be happy with Mr Burns?"

Meg was quick to reply, "William's a good man and a good businessman, he'll make a fine husband." She was silent for a moment. "Why do you ask?"

"I was just wondering, it's just that you don't talk about him overly much," remarked Marnie.

"Don't I?" Meg asked, surprised.

Marnie pulled the covers up a little higher. "Oh, you talk about him, what he's doing and what not, but not about how much you care for him, or any other sort of endearments, you don't say nothing like that. Are you marrying him for money?"

"Don't be silly," Meg said dismissively. Rolling over to face the wall she lay in the darkness, contemplating Marnie's words. Did she really say nothing endearing about William? Marnie was being ridiculous. She just didn't fuss or fawn like other women did over their men. It didn't mean anything, did it?

Jack trod the familiar path that thousands of diggers marched before him. Looking like just another digger on the trail no one gave him a second glance. He got a brief nod from one or two men heading down for stores, but they seemed in no mood to stop and chew the cud which suited him fine. Each step meant he was one step closer to the Welcome Home Hotel and another step further away from being discovered. He decided it was best to take the lower track which was closer to the river and only had room for two abreast. More folks used the wider trial above but he wanted to lie low until he was safely away from anyone who may recognize him, and report his whereabouts back to the Madame.

He'd walked for hours wearing two jackets and was perspiring badly, he wiped the sweat from his brow and took a swig of water from his flask. Believing he was far enough away he decided it was safe to remove his outer layer. He took off Bennett's jacket and tucked it into his swag. Jack checked the position of the sun; summer made the days feel endless but sunset was not far off. He'd best get off the trail and find a place to bed down in for the night. He'd have a bite of cheese and a hunk of bread before dossing down, the extra jacket could act as a blanket and the sacking as a mattress. Marnie was safe, and he was alive, everything was going to be all right.

Having worked all day, and walked for several miles, Jack felt spent. He flattened some tussock, put the sacking beneath him to stop the dampness of the ground chilling his bones. Grateful for the extra warmth of Bennett's jacket, he lay down and pulled it up around his shoulders. Curling up, he closed his eyes and whispered a prayer to Saint Christopher for travelling mercies. Tomorrow he would see Marnie and all the trouble he'd been through would be worthwhile. Soon they would be married. He'd feel whole again. He might not be the richest man but he felt like the luckiest.

Chapter 11   Wedding

They set off at dawn, taking the high road, single file. Jim, rode in front on Nugget, Mary behind on docile old Magpie, and Meg brought up the rear on little Thistle. The mountain grasses were a glorious carpet of green, rust and gold. The river snaked its way through the canyon chiselling a path between the chasms. Towering stone edifices loomed out of the mountain as testaments of strength. The ponies' steady rhythm, nodding heads and swishing tails were comforting and dependable in an ever-changing landscape. The three riders stopped a moment to take in the panoramic view of the township nestled in the valley below, before they made their descent.

When they arrived in Rees, they went straight to the livery to stable the horses, then made their way to Church Street. There was barely a minute to spare, certainly not enough time to visit Jack. They would need to hurry as half the population would probably want to watch the young couple wed and the church would be packed with well-wishers. Mary consoled herself with the fact she'd have an opportunity to give the boy a good piece of her mind at the wedding.

Jim slapped his forehead with an open palm. "I've just got a wee errand to take care of first. You two go ahead, I'll be along shortly."

Suspicious, Mary asked, "What kind of errand?"

"It's a secret." He tapped a finger to his nose.

She narrowed her gaze.

"It's not that kind of errand, Mary. I'll only be a few minutes," he promised.

"Don't be late," Mary warned, she took Meg's arm, and the pair hurried along the alleyway towards St Mary's.

There was a good crowd gathering outside the parish. Dressed in his Sunday best, Dan was outside, greeting the guests.

Surprised to see Meg he cocked an eyebrow. "Hello dear sister, it was kind of you to come."

"Daniel," she said coolly, annoyed by his pointed sarcasm.

Dan kissed his mother's cheek. "I'm pleased you have managed to tear yourself away from the hotel Ma, at least long enough to see Yankee wed."

"Can't promise we'll stay for the festivities afterwards, but Yankee's as good as family so we had to come, didn't we, Meg."
Meg inclined her head ever so slightly.

"Where's Da?" Dan peered over their shoulders. "Oh, here he comes now."
Red-faced and breathless, Jim hurried towards them.

Mary frowned. What had he been up to? Where had he been? It wasn't like him to be so secretive. Not since he'd been dry, and she didn't like it one little bit.

Jim was puffing like the wind as he hastened to Mary's side. Mary's grip tightened on Jim's arm, her fingers digging in. "Where have you been?" she hissed. She sniffed, smelling his breath for any tell-tale signs, nothing.

"Can't a man have a secret or two?" He grinned, looking like he'd eaten the last bun.

"Da," Dan interrupted, shaking his father's hand.

"Son," Jim said, breathing hard. He pumped Dan's hand firmly. "How – are – you - holding up? It's a terrible responsibility you have."

"Aye, it is in all," Dan agreed, wiping a hand across his clammy brow. "I've been that worried about losing the ring, I've barely slept. Yankee says Niamh's a spirited woman. I wouldn't want to have to explain losing her ring." Dan fumbled in his waistcoat pocket. "See, Yankee had it made out of gold from our own claim." He held it out for them to see.

Jim let out a low whistle. "It's a fine piece of jewellery, so it is."

"Yes, very nice," Meg agreed.

"Aye, so it is," Mary said, briefly glancing at the ring resting in Dan's palm. Distracted, she scanned the crowd for Jack. "Is Jack about?"

Dan shook his head. "Haven't seen hide or hair of him. Reckon he'll be here shortly; expect he's got jobs to do first. The bridegroom's not arrived either, probably needs a shot of Dutch courage to steady his nerves knowing his bachelor days are over." Dan tucked the ring back in his pocket and patted it for luck. "And I could do with one and all," he muttered.

"Daniel Healey, you exaggerate," Mary chided.

"Not at all, Ma, see my hands are shaking."

Mary shook her head.

"The bride is at Father Whooley's place getting ready," Dan told them.

Meg's expression changed.

Dan noticed, and whispered in her ear. "She's not as pretty as you, Meg."

Meg gave him a waxy smile.

With a deep bow and a sweep of his arm, Dan ushered his family inside. "Sit up front where you'll be noticed. Yankee would want you to," he told them.

The Stations of the Cross were nailed around the wooden church. The pews were nicely spaced on either side of a wide aisle, in case the bride wore a crinoline.

Yankee's mother died when he was a nipper, and his whaling father remarried, a native woman, not long after her death. His father had now passed, and although Yankee had a number of half-caste brothers and sisters, none had made the long trek to celebrate his wedding, not that anyone expected them too; it was a long way. So as not to appear presumptuous, the Healeys chose the second row. Meg purposely sat on the aisle so she could get a better view.

Meg suddenly came over all queer. She opened her drawstring bag, took out her fan and vehemently beat the air with it.

Father Whooley entered the building and greeted the guests as he made his way to the pulpit. Pleased to see the Healeys amongst the congregation, Father Whooley stopped, shook Jim's hand and smiled warmly at Mary.

"Mary, you are a picture to behold."

Mary laughed easily, "Is flattery not a sin Father?"

He chuckled. "It's not flattery when it's the truth, now is it?"

To Meg, he said, "Not long now till we'll be celebrating your wedding day, my dear. And such a lovely bride you will be."

"Thank you," Meg replied, blushing. She couldn't help thinking Father Whooley would have made someone a fine husband.

Jim leaned across, his face serious and quietly said, "Father, I've thought about what you said, about joining the church committee, and I'd be delighted."

"I'm that glad to hear it," Father Whooley beamed.

"You're right Father it's not fitting for the church to have a scrap of canvas as a school hall, no the good Lord deserves better," Jim said.

Elated, Father Whooley said, "I'll come and see you after the nuptials and we'll discuss it further."

More folks filed into the church and found their seats. A few stood near the back. Harry entered the building, removed his hat, smiled and nodded warmly at the growing crowd, showing a flash of white teeth. He made his way to the front. He looked fearsome with his Tribal facial tattoos, dark skin, long black hair and powerful shoulders that threatened to rip the stitching on the seams of his rough woollen jacket. Harry sat in the front row. He believed he had every right to be there; he and Yankee were like brothers. He caught sight of Meg and his eyes widened in surprise.

Recovering, he politely inclined his head. "Miss Margaret."

"Haerakia." Meg hadn't seen Harry since the Big Flood. Then he had seen her at her worst, standing dishevelled and barefoot in their hut proclaiming her innocence. She fanned her face. Damn, it was hot.

Jim shook Harry's hand. They chatted briefly about the price of gold, and typically decrepitated how well their claims were doing. They mentioned the fact that miners were leaving the area in droves for the new rushes on the West Coast. That kind of talk made Mary nervous., eager to change the subject, she expressed her hope that Dan was behaving himself.

Harry chuckled. His deep voice, soft and rich, "You've no worries there, Ma'am, Dan's better behaved than the Pope himself."

Mary smiled. Of all her children, Dan was the easiest. He was no bother, no fuss. Unlike Jack, whom she'd happily box his ears if only she could find him. That boy was going to send her to an early grave. She twisted to get a better look at the growing crowd. Yankee was a popular figure about town and everyone liked a good gathering. Folks had turned out to see him wed. Apart from the front row which convention dictated was kept for family, it was standing room only. Still no sign of Jack.

Mary frowned, leaning across she squeezed Jim's knee. "I can't see Jack," she whispered.

He gently patted her hand. "Don't worry love, I'm sure he's not far off."

Meg couldn't concentrate, the chatter sounded like bees buzzing in her ears. She heard her father telling Harry about Kitty going to Dunedin, and Harry said something in return, but finding it hard to breathe, she couldn't quite make head nor tail of it. Her eyes on the pulpit, Meg didn't see Yankee enter the house of worship but she felt him pass by. So close, he almost brushed her sleeve.

Dressed in dark trousers, white shirt and a black waistcoat, Yankee looked tall, handsome, and respectable. Hatless, his wavy blonde hair was slicked back, and his beard neatly trimmed. He stood at the altar with his back to the congregation waiting for his bride. Absently picking at a thread on her skirt, Meg took a deep breath she kept telling herself, she had made the right decision, William was the right decision.

Fidgety, Dan kept rechecking his waistcoat pocket. He tried to ease the tension by ribbing his mate telling him he still had time to run. Yankee took the teasing good-naturedly on the chin. Suddenly a long drawn out hum came from an old wheeze of a piano accordion signalling the bride's arrival. Meg snapped her fan shut and stood for the bridal march. Yankee waited to watch his bride make her procession. He caught sight of Meg, his eyes widened in recognition and surprise, then he looked away.

Polly the bridesmaid, a plain wisp girl of about thirteen, came first, shy, she ducked her head as if bowing to royalty. She was smartly dressed in sky blue silk and carrying a small posy of white flowers. She was followed by the bride. Niamh's light brown hair was coiled in a French roll and a thin gauze veil covered her face. She was small in stature and wore a simple, long white dress with a wide light blue sash tied above the waist, and carried a cascading bouquet of flowers.

Niamh looked straight ahead as she took slow halting steps up the aisle. She had a nice trim figure but what Meg could see beneath the veil she thought Niamh had a rather homely face. Perhaps being a good cook and housekeeper was enough for Mr Yankee Brown, but she doubted it. Guilt cut her like a knife, and she chastised herself for being so uncharitable. She would have to go to confession and repent for entertaining such mean thoughts.

Tugging at his waistcoat, Yankee smiled determinedly at Niamh as she made her way towards him. The wedding march finished abruptly. The piano-accordionist slipped the straps off his shoulders and solemnly laid the instrument at his feet. Yankee stepped forward and lifted the veil of Niamh's face, and stepped away again. Together they turned, and solemnly faced the priest.

"You may be seated," Father Whooley told the congregation.

There was a general shuffling as those who had seats, took them. Meg edged forward on her seat to get a better view. Father Whooley began by saying the Mass. There was a murmur from the spectators as they echoed the responses. Meg couldn't focus, the Father's words blurred inside her brain like water gurgling over rocks in a mountain stream. She felt dizzy, alone in a sea of people. When the Mass was over Father Whooley cleared his throat and in his holy sing-song voice began the marriage ceremony.

"Dearly beloved we are gathered here today in the sight of God to witness this man and this woman being joined in the holy bands of matrimony..." the Father intoned.
Meg felt nauseous, the air felt too close. She thought she may faint. She needed air.

Father Whooley uttered the words, "If anyone here knows why these two shouldn't be joined in holy matrimony, speak now or forever hold your peace."

Meg rose. She had meant to bolt for the door but her legs wouldn't move. She froze. Her heart beating fast, she heard herself say, "I do."

Father Whooley was astonished. There was a loud gasp as everyone, turned, and stared at Meg.
Niamh whirled around. She glowered, her eyes sparking dangerously.

Mary tugged Meg's sleeve. "Unless you mean to make it right, for God's sake sit down," she hissed.

Shocked, the congregation waited.

Yankee looked at Niamh, then at Meg, then back to the priest.

Father Whooley found his voice. "On what grounds?" he asked.

"I love him," Meg replied weakly. The words were out. Her confession of the truth at last, now when it was too late. It seemed suddenly important that before he married Niamh, he should know the truth.

Shrinking in her seat, Mary covered her eyes. What a scandal! There would be no end of gossip. It would probably be in all the newspapers tomorrow. God forbid William would hear it from someone on the street, or worse read it in the paper.

Yankee smiled softly, he looked at Meg like they were the only two people in the room, his blue eyes shining brightly, he said, "And I you."

Niamh slapped him, her fingernails drawing blood. "How dare you!" she cried.

Yankee grabbed her hand before she swung again. "Niamh can we talk about this, somewhere in private."

"In private!" Niamh shrieked. "What's the point of privacy when I've been publicly humiliated?" she demanded.

Yankee tried to apologise but was drowned out by Tu who began to bark furiously. Harry shouted in his native tongue and the barking stopped.

Niamh tore down the aisle towards Meg. "How dare you! How dare you ruin my wedding," she cried, throwing her bouquet at Meg's feet.

"I'm sorry," Meg mumbled. "I didn't mean to..."

"Yes you did or you wouldn't have come." Niamh fled the church in tears.

Trembling, Polly ran after her, she did not fancy standing up in front of all those people making a spectacle of herself. A pious needle-nosed woman dressed in widows' weeds got up, and left, to show her disapproval. But only a recent arrival, Niamh hadn't had time to establish friendships, and besides, everyone wanted to see what happened next.

"It's as good as the theatre," one old digger said to his mate.

Yankee slowly walked over to Meg. Her big brown eyes were filling with tears. Meg stared at the scratches on Yankee's face, a thin trail of blood trickled slowly into his beard.
The congregation held their breath, waiting for Yankee to speak.

"I'm sorry," she murmured, a tear fell from her lashes and tracked down her face. "If you love her you should go after her."

Yankee got down on bended knee, and picked up the discarded bouquet of flowers that lay at Meg's feet and held them up to her. "I love you, always have." He took a deep breath. "Margaret, will you marry me?"

Mary's jaw dropped. She grabbed Jim's knee and squeezed hard. She whispered in his ear, "Holy Mother of God, I was afraid this would happen. She was never sure."

Jim muttered, "Let's hope she knows her mind now."
Meg bit her lip and nodded. Another glistening teardrop made its way down her face as she accepted the bouquet.

"Is that a yes?" Yankee asked hopefully, his voice sounding strangled.

Wiping the blood away about to drip from his chin with her finger, she nodded. "Yes," she answered softly. "Yes."

Yankee closed his eyes briefly as if silently thanking God. Leaping to his feet he threw his arms around Meg and passionately kissed her. The congregation cheered and stomped their feet.

"Be a waste of a perfectly good wedding not to get married now, don't you think?" he grinned. "Besides, if we don't do this now, I'm scared you'll change your mind."

"We couldn't, could we?" she looked at him uncertainly. "It wouldn't be seemly."

"Let's ask the man of God." He crooked his arm.
Holding the damaged bouquet in one hand, Meg hooked her arm in his, and together they walked to the altar.

Yankee said, "Ah Father, I know things haven't quite gone to plan, but can you look past that and start where you left off?"

Troubled, Father Whooley looked undecided he rubbed his clean-shaven chin, wondering what to do next. There was the legality of things to consider, the bans hadn't been called for the proper length of time.

"Go on, Father," Yankee urged. "It's God's will."
When the priest looked doubtful, Yankee quickly took him aside and negotiated. "You know, Father," he began slowly, "we both have had the instruction albeit not with each other but we've received it." He continued, "And, we both had have the bans called for the proper length of time, just not with each other, but no one has come forward with any reason either of us cannot enter matrimony. It's God's will, I'm sure of it."

Raising his eyes to the heavens, Father Whooley offered a few quick prayers asking for forgiveness and made the sign of the cross.

Taking a deep breath, he began again, "if anyone knows why this man and this woman should not be married, speak now or forever hold your peace." No one uttered a sound.

Smiling through her salty tears, Meg could barely comprehend what Father Whooley was saying, but she responded in the right places. Reaching over, she wiped away a spot of blood that was about to drip onto Yankee's starched collar.

Managing to catch his sister's eye, Dan looped his finger around his ear and mouthed, 'Crazy girl,' at her, but she could tell he wasn't angry. Meg glanced over her shoulder at the front row, Harry's grin was as wide as the ocean, whereas her parents' faces were set like granite. Oh God, what had she done? She was going to break William's heart. Meg shifted her focus back to Yankee, who smiled lovingly at her, his clear blue eyes never leaving her face. She had made the right choice; Yankee was the right choice. She loved him and he loved her. Why had it taken her so long to see the truth? Her eyes swam with tears.

Everything felt surreal. Meg tried to concentrate as the priest spoke, she heard the congregation respond. Father Whooley was saying something about the sanctity of marriage and bringing their children up in the faith. Her mind was racing. How was she going to explain this, to William, and the Asterlys? The school inspector was due to visit soon. What could she possibly say to justify her behaviour? There was nothing logical about it, it was as if an eclipse of the heart had taken place and suddenly nothing and no one else mattered, being with Yankee was the only thing that truly mattered.

Father Whooley called for the ring. Dan stepped forward, his face grave as he handed Yankee the ring. Meg hastily removed her gloves and gave them to Dan who tucked them into his coat pocket. Feeling guilty, she removed William's engagement ring and put that on her other hand.

"With this ring, I, Joseph John Brown take thee Margaret..." he paused, uncertain.

"Theresa," Meg told him.

"Margaret Theresa Healey, to..."

"Have and to hold," Father Whooley chimed.

Yankee repeated the words.

Placing the ring on Meg's finger, he said after Father Whooley, "With this ring I thee wed."

Everything felt surreal. Meg stared at the filigree gold band on her finger. Yankee's hand was warm while hers was cold. There were now three rings on her hand. The signet ring from her father, this one, meant for another, slightly too big, and her engagement ring; William's ring on the wrong hand. Meg repeated the vows in parrot fashion, and squeezed Yankee's hand as she said the words, "I do, and I will."

Dan's shoulders relaxed, and he gave his sister a wink.

To the delight of those present, Father Whooley triumphantly said, "I now pronounce you man and wife. Joseph, you may kiss your bride."

Yankee took Meg in his arms, he kissed her tenderly, then more passionately to hoots and hollers from the crowd.

Yankee squeezed Meg into his shoulder. "I'm that happy I could bust my stitching."

Father Whooley was candid. "I can't say I'm entirely happy about the situation, but I suppose I should be grateful that I still have a housekeeper."

Yankee's face fell. "I'm not sure how to make amends, Father, I'll need your guidance there."

Butting in, Harry said, "I'll wager she'll have fifty proposals by the end of the week."

"There will be no gambling in the house of God." Mary reprimanded him tapping him on the shoulder.

"Ah, we'll need another witness for the bride," Father Whooley said, checking the congregation for a likely candidate.

Harry volunteered. "It'd be my pleasure."

"Are you agreeable?" Father Whooley asked Meg.

Amused, that her bridesmaid should not be some demure maid but a burly warrior instead, Meg readily agreed. "Delighted," she assured the father.

Meg signed her name inside the space marked bride, and Harry drew his facial tattoo then signed, *Haerakia Takatimu* beside it. Meg blinked, surprised.

"Mission school," he explained, chuckling softly. "Only useful things I learned were reading, writing and 'rithmetic." He glanced at Father Whooley. "They were such a miserable lot you would swear someone ate their relatives." He nudged her and with a grin said, "There wasn't enough space for my whole name so I shortened it so yours would fit."

Meg bit back a laugh. Harry loved to tease; he couldn't help himself.

Yankee signed the marriage license; his penmanship was shaky but his hand firm.

When Dan signed, he placed the pen back in the inkpot and patted Yankee's shoulder. "Now you've gone and done it, boyo."

"Aye, there's no getting rid of me now, I'm family," Yankee grinned.

Meg was a jumble of nerves. She had broken up a wedding, married the man she wasn't engaged to, and made a spectacle of herself in front of the entire district. There would be no end of tongue wagging. The thought of breaking the news to William, the Asterlys and the school was overwhelming and she felt her knees beginning to buckle. Seeking comfort, she moved closer to Yankee for support. Yankee tucked her under his shoulder and kissed her cheek. She had gone about things the wrong way but she knew now she loved him and didn't want to be without him. Whatever happened they would face the future together.

Father Whooley coughed and cleared his throat. He blessed their union, saying, "May the Lord bless you and keep you, the Lord make his face shine upon you and be gracious to you; may the Lord lift his countenance upon you and give you peace, Amen."

The ceremony over, everyone was free to chat amongst themselves. After what seemed to be endless months of misery, Dan was rapt to see Yankee and Meg looking happy. He felt a measure of sympathy for the abandoned bride, but Harry was right she would be quickly suited, every eligible bachelor was bound to be knocking on her door. It was Burns he felt badly for, he was a decent bloke, his heart and his pride was going to be crushed like a quartz in a battery stamper.

Father Whooley and Jim moved aside to discuss the date of the committee meeting while well-wishers surrounded and congratulated the newlyweds.

Her gut curdling with worry, Mary seized the opportunity to speak to Dan. She said in a hushed whisper, "Where the hell is Jack? Maybe somethings happened to him."

Dan shrugged. "Don't rightly know, Ma. He knew the wedding was today. I was sure he'd be here."

Yankee found them whispering in the corner. "What you doing hiding back here?" he asked. Taking Mary by the arm he steered her in the direction of the marquee, "There's food, music and dancing to be had. Come, let's celebrate, I'm part of the family now!" He slapped Dan's back, his blue eyes full of mischief.

Dan tried hard to look disgruntled but his cheeky smile betrayed him. "Aye, can't seem to get rid of you, you stick like death to a dead volunteer, you do."

A worried look clouded Yankee's face. "Niamh would have made a good wife. I'm sorry for hurting her but I love your sister, always have, promise I always will."

Dan shrugged. "She will be all right, don't worry, the good father will look after her."

"But I should make amends all the same, I must make a peace offering and I will need your help," Yankee told Dan, his face grave.

Mary interrupted their conversation, "We would love to stay but I'm afraid we must be on our way."

241

But Yankee wouldn't hear of it, and insisted they stay for the wedding feast. After a token protest, Mary agreed. Yankee had bought a few geese from a farmer and his Chinese station cook had prepared hearty fare for the guests. The warm air was ripe, full of the smell of roast goose which made the mouth water in anticipation; after existing on bacon or mutton, goose was a welcome change in diet. Jim and Mary helped themselves to a generous portion each, topped with roast potatoes and smothered in gravy. Dan delivered a halting speech toasting the health and happiness of the bride and groom, and everyone raised their glasses in salute.

"Here's to love, long life and happiness," Jim raised his tankard of water. He squeezed his wife's shoulder and whispered, "Love endures."

Mary lifted an eyebrow and looked quizzically at him. "Those words have a double meaning, Jim Healey," she replied.

Jim chuckled. "Oh, so you prefer love remains then."

With the toasts over, and the dancing about to commence, Father Whooley excused himself. "I'd love to stay and celebrate with you but I fear my housekeeper needs consoling, and Polly would have had to return home by now, so I'd best be going."

Meg bit her lip. "I'm truly sorry, Father."

"I'm sorry too, honestly Father," Yankee said looking contrite.

"You join the guests while I escort Father Whooley out," Meg told Yankee.

"My wife is bossing me about already," Yankee quipped. "Night, Father." He returned to the party.

Outside the tent, Meg whispered discreetly in the Father's ear, "Please keep your appointment at the Welcome Home next week. There will still be a wedding."

Puzzled, he frowned. "William isn't going to marry Niamh, is he?"

"No Father, I'm very sorry for what's happened but it's not Niamh I'm asking for. I'm not sure what will happen yet, but please come prepared with a marriage license. Say you will?"

Against his better judgment, Father Whooley assented.

Mary interrupted. "We must be going and all." She turned to the priest. "Have you heard from Jack?"

"No, sorry, Mary, I haven't." A flash of concern crossed the Father's face.

"Don't fret, I'll get word to him Ma," Meg promised.

Mary thanked the bridegroom for his hospitality, and kissed her daughter's pink cheeks. Mary grew serious as she said, "We'll not say a word to anyone, it's your place to tell them, not ours."

Meg nodded. "Thank you, Ma, I appreciate that."

"I hope you will be very happy," Mary smiled.

Meg's eyes shone brightly. "Thank you, Ma, it's nice to know we have your blessing."

Mary shook her head and sighed. "It's a crying shame you didn't' get to wear that lovely dress Kitty made you. She'll be that disappointed."

"Don't you worry about the dress Ma, I'm sure someone will get to enjoy it," Meg replied, a knowing smile curled the corners of her mouth.

"I'll pay the stable hand to keep Thistle until you come for her," Jim told Meg as he hugged his daughter goodbye.

"Pay him till Sunday Da. I'll be back Sunday," Meg told him.

Yankee frowned. "Isn't this something we should discuss Mrs Brown?"

Alarmed, Meg replied, "I have to go back. I told the Asterlys I would be home on Sunday, and I must tell William, and the Asterlys. I can't just up and disappear, can I?"

Mary flinched — three years ago Jim had done exactly that, just up and disappeared.

Yankee grudgingly agreed. "Promise not to desert I'll let you go but it will not be willingly. I don't want to lose you, not when I've only just staked my claim."

Meg kissed his cheek. "You won't, I promise." Turning back to Mary she said, "Don't worry about Jack, Ma, I'm sure he's fine."

Mary hooked her arm in Jim's, they shouted and waved goodbyes to Dan and Harry who were looking relaxed with ale in hand, their toes tapping in time to the music. Tu had crept into the tent and was hiding beneath the table, Harry turned a blind eye and pretended not to notice him, and no one seemed to mind.

The feasting was over and done, the picked over platters were carted away in handcarts to be washed elsewhere. Dan and Harry had made room in the middle of the tent to act as a dance floor and sawdust was liberally scattered about so that it didn't become a quagmire. Punch was freely available for the thirsty. The accordionist had been joined by a squat stocky man with a fiddle and together the pair played rollicking tunes that guaranteed to get the feet stomping and the blood pumping. Hearts beating fast, the guests danced reels till late in the evening when their wobbly legs could no longer hold them. It was a fine party, with everything anyone could wish for, all the drama of a play, the food of kings and a dance to rival any held in the district. Everyone agreed, Yankee Brown was well and truly wed.

Mary was convinced something was wrong. It was unlike Jack not to participate in a celebration, especially not that of a close family friend without sending some sort of apology. She hoped the people Marnie had run from hadn't hurt... no, it didn't bear thinking about, she refused to believe the worst.

"Hurry," she called to Jim, ducking down the side alley.

"I've got blisters on me backside from sitting on a horse half the day and you expect me to run woman," Jim griped, following her.

"I want to see if Jack is all right," she called back over her shoulder.

Jim shook his head. "Ah well, I daren't argue with your bones, your gut or your water woman."

They entered the forge and found a lad about twelve sitting on a stool whittling a piece of wood. He jumped up to greet them.

"What can I do fer you?" he called congenially.

Jim cast his eye around the place and was impressed by the tidiness of the shop. Everything was in its proper place being a smithy himself he appreciated order and well-kept tools. "Is Jack Healey about?" he asked.

The lad shook his head. "Nah," he answered his tone suddenly serious. "The rascal stole from Mr Bennett and up and scarpered, he did."

"What!" Mary exclaimed. She scowled at the boy. Jack would never steal unless he had to. "What? What did he steal?"

"Mr Bennett's best hat, and coat, and money too, no doubt. Reckon he'd hang for less in the old country." The boy was enjoying telling his tale.

Wary, Jim lifted a sardonic eyebrow. "And who are you?"

"Why I'm 'is replacement. Tom's me name. I used to be the stable boy next door but Mr Bennett saw potential and honesty in me he did, so offered me the job. What can I do for you?" He cockily tucked his fingers into his braces and gave them a tug. Suddenly aware he may have given away too much, he looked at them suspiciously. "Here, who are you, and what you want with Jack then, eh?"

Deadpan, and as quick as wink, Mary answered, "I came to see him about the money he owes me."

Puffed up with importance, the boy said, "I'd head off down to see the constable if I were you. That Jack Healey, he's a black-hearted devil, that one. He had us fooled right proper, he did."

"Aye, thanks son, reckon we'll do just that." Jim took Mary by the arm. They walked in the direction of the police camp but as soon as they thought they were out of sight they slipped down the side alley and double-backed to the livery to collect their horses.

"What do you make of that then?" Mary panted, as she stopped to catch her breath.

Jim could not hide his concern. "I don't rightly know, but I hope the lad is making his way home so we will be able to ask him first-hand. If he's said he was returning for Marnie then here's hoping

246

that's where he is headed, and trouble hasn't found him along the way."

"Come on," Mary urged, holding her hat, she lifted the corner of her skirts and ran.

Exhausted, after a fretful night with barely a lick of sleep, Jack finally fell asleep near dawn and then slept late into the day. He woke when the sun was low in the sky, it was approaching dusk. He was stiff and sore, his head muzzy and his skin prickly. But it was better to travel later close on dusk he'd be less recognisable that way, it had to be safer. Dear God he hoped so. He eased his shoulders and rubbed at the crick in his neck. He ate the last of the cheese and drank the remaining water, throwing his swag over his shoulder, he set off again. Long Gully was less than a couple of miles walk. Soon he'd be in Marnie's arms.

When the Welcome Home's whispering chimney stacks came into view Jack's heart lifted. Now that he'd made it this far, he was convinced all would be well. He stood for a moment breathing in the sweet smell of wild thyme. Ah, home, he thought almost overcome with relief. But they were not out of danger yet so he must not be blasé now. The last thing he needed was for Madame to get wind of their whereabouts. He wouldn't rest easy until he got them safely away from Lake County. He went around the back and tried the door. It was locked. He knocked and waited.

Marnie timidly crept to the door. Mary gave her strict orders not to open it but Marnie reasoned, only family used the back door. "Who's there," she whispered.

"Marnie!" Jack cried. "It's me, Jack!"

"Jack?!" Marnie's fingers quickly undid the bolt. She flung the door wide and threw her arms about his neck kissing him. "Jack! Oh Jack!"

Jack breathed in the smell of her hair. "You're a sight for sore eyes an' all," he smiled.

"Oh Jack, I've been that worried," she told him. She stepped back her eyes drinking in the damage done to his face. Her brow creased with concern. "Did Bill do that?" Marnie put her finger to his blackened eye but he shied away from her touch.

"Don't you worry, I gave as good as I got. I'll mend." He held her at arms' length. "Look at you all respectable looking, I barely recognize you," he laughed.

"Do you think me plain?" she asked, disappointed.

"No matter how respectable you are you are still my little pixie," he said tweaking her upturned nose.

Fears blown away like chaff in the wind, Marnie knew he loved her.

"May I come in or do you expect me to tell all me tales standing on the stoop?"

Marnie let him in and closed and bolted the door behind him. She followed him down the passageway into the parlour.

"Where's Da?" Jack asked, staring at the empty chair by the fireplace.

Marnie lifted her shoulders. "Expect they are on their way back from Yankee Brown's wedding."

Jack smacked his forehead. "Yankee invited me but I plain forgot all about it." He paused, reasoning, "But I couldn't hang about any longer, it was becoming too dangerous."

Marnie trembled.

"They?" Jack frowned. "Did you say they? Did Ma go?"

"Yes, and Meg too."

"Well, well, wonders never cease," he shook his mop of red hair.

Jack lowered himself into the armchair, put his feet up on the tatty stool and began to unlace his boots. "Aww me boots aren't half killing me, think they have grown clean into me skin." He tugged them off and put them to one side.

"Your mother would have your guts for garters for not cleaning your boots on the scraper before traipsing into her house," Marnie scolded. She picked up his boots and placed them neatly on the hearth and with the shovel and brush tidied away the mess.

"Please don't be cross little one." Jack rubbed his aching leg. "Me ribs pinch and gammy leg pains me bad. I walked me feet clean off I did coming here to see you and for what, a good scolding?"

Marnie turned to face him, her big blue eyes glistening. "I thought you might never come."

Jack knew what abandonment felt like, and he'd never do that to her. "Never," he said tenderly reaching for her hand and kissing it.

The fire crackled in the grate and the room was warm in the soft glow of buttery candlelight.

"Do you need a drink? Are you hungry?" she asked, eager to please.

"I could eat my own arm," Jack confessed. "What's to eat?"

"Greedy Pat's gobbled up most of supper but I'll see if there are any leftovers." She went to go but Jack grabbed her by the hand.

"Where's Pat?"

"Tending the bar."

"Glory be," Jack breathed. "Does Ma know?"

Marnie nodded.

"Forget supper, come here and sit on me knee," he grinned. "I've missed you darlin'."

Giggling, Marnie curled up on his knee and put her arms around his neck and kissed him. "Thought your leg was hurtin' you."

He pinched her small turned up nose. "Not all of me is damaged. Besides you weigh next to nothing. Has Ma not been feeding you? Did she ban you to the chook house and feed you on the scraps?"

"She fed me," Marnie said, her face clouding.

Jack shook his head. "I can't believe Ma left the hotel to go to Yankee's wedding. And to put Pat in charge, now there's folly."

"There's a man called Smiley helping to keep Pat honest."

Jack blew out his cheeks. "And did you say Meg went?"

"Yes, she said she was curious to see what Yankee's bride looked like."

"Well, my bride is still beautiful even in this drab rigout," Jack murmured. He removed her cap and his fingers twisted the wisps of hair that curled at the base of her neck. A lock of her hair came loose from its pins and curled lovingly around her cheek. He rubbed her gently, hair between his fingertips, and sighed, a happy and contented man.

Then the door that led to the tavern opened.

"And just what the bloody hell do you think you're doing?" Mary demanded her face as sour as a pickled lemon. Marnie jumped off Jack's lap. Tucking her hair back under her cap, she stood shamefaced before them.

Jack groaned and clutched his ribs as he raised himself slowly out of the chair. He met his mother's fearsome gaze.

"I will not have that kind of carry on in my hotel," Mary snapped.

"I was only kissing my fiancé," Jack replied immediately defensive. "We are to be married Ma." He reached for Marnie's hand but found only air, he reached again and found her hand.

"I don't remember anyone asking me if you could marry. You're only fifteen. Too young to marry without permission," Mary told him.

"But Ma I will be sixteen soon," he argued.

"Don't Ma me," Mary advanced pointing a bony finger. "And just look at yer face. Who did that to you?"

"It's nothing, horse kicked me when I was trying to shoe it," Jack lied.

Mary refused to be side-tracked. "This is all because of her!"

"Now Mary," Jim interrupted.

Mary swung round. "Don't you dare tell me to calm down! He's too young to marry, he's not known her long enough, she's the first girl he's met." She took a breath. "If he really wants to marry her, he can wait till he's old enough."

"I can't," Jack argued.

"And why the hell not?" Mary thundered.

Jack tried reason. "Because I need to get Marnie away from here. She's not safe in these parts. Do you really want her to be just my common-law wife?"

Mary vigorously shook her head. "I don't want a common anything! You're too young to know your own mind. You are far too young to know what you're doing." In jerky movements she removed her riding cloak, untied the ribbons on her bonnet and flung it at the peg. She put her apron on and rolled up her sleeves, all the while glaring at Jack.

Jim put a green log on the fire; it hissed and spat. "I think it's better to discuss this tomorrow darlin'. We are tired, it's been a long day, and you might do or say things you might not necessarily mean."

"Oh, I'll mean them all right," Mary countered.

Marnie sought escape but Jack kept a firm grip on her hand.

"And don't think you will be sharing a bed with her," Mary told Jack, jabbing a finger at him.

Jack gritted his teeth and said, "Ma, we have already lain together."

"Well, that won't be happening under my roof. And to make sure of it, you will sleep in Pat's room, and your father will sleep on a stool outside Marnie's room with his rifle, primed and ready. If you take one step towards her bedroom door, he'll shoot."

"Mary," Jim reproved.

Ignoring him, Mary said, "Now if you'll excuse me, my tavern needs attending to. I expect everyone to go to their own bed and stay there, understand?" Her anger giving her newfound energy she flounced out the room.

Pat arrived in the kitchen soon after. He'd had a fair skin full and was feeling gregarious with it.

"Jack me lad," he slurred grinning sheepishly at his youngest brother. "Hear you are bunking in with me tonight." He belched. "Ma has kicked me out of the bar telling me I'd drunk my fill."

Jack grunted.

Ignoring Pat, Jim said to Jack, "I'll try to reason with her son but for tonight there's not an ounce of reason to be had. Let's all get some sleep, and I'll try to talk to your mother in the morning. Best we all humour her for now, or there'll be hell to pay."

Pat leaned on the mantle for support.

"Off you go," Jim shooed them.

"But Da..." Jack began.

Jim held up his hand. "Be on your way, son, we will talk about it in the morning."

Disgruntled, Jack picked up his boots and bade Marnie goodnight. His eyes told her what he couldn't say.

As Jack opened the hallway door for Pat, Jim said, "I'll be there with my shotgun at the ready so don't even think about it."

Jack was furious. This was not the homecoming he'd envisaged.

Pat staggered up the passageway. He fell against the wall and stayed there for a moment or two before struggling on like a sailor on a heaving sea. Pat's room was the last room, tacked onto the very end of the building. Jack pulled the curtains on the lone sash window to and placed the lantern on the sideboard. Not bothering to undress, Pat flopped on his bed as limp and boneless as a rag doll.

Jack removed his moleskins, coat and shirt, and trimmed the wick. The lantern went out leaving the room in darkness. Pat was already snoring. The springs creaked as Jack sunk on to the bed with a weary sigh. His empty belly was growling. He hadn't expected his Ma to make things easy, but why did she insist on making life so flaming difficult?

Marnie heard a chair scrape outside her room and someone sit heavily upon it. Obviously, Jim was obeying his wife's instructions and camping outside her room. She hoped Jack wouldn't try and defy his mother and attempt to visit her under the cover of darkness. She didn't think Jim would shoot his own son but she was certain Mary would tell him to aim close enough to give Jack a hell of a fright if he dared try. If there was one thing she'd learnt, it was that Mary Healey meant what she said.

Marnie stripped off, donned her nightgown and got into bed. She had been so relieved to see Jack. Now she was worried that Mary wouldn't allow them to be together, and terrified that Jack might defy his mother. They could run away but with no money, nowhere to go, and no one to help them, how would they survive? They could steal the tea caddy and make a run for it, but that would be wrong. Marnie sunk into depression. She had been naïve to believe that she could get away from her life at the brothel and start fresh with Jack. He had filled her head with pipe dreams and she had believed them because she so desperately wanted to. There was no new life for a prostitute. Her past would always be there to haunt her.

It suddenly struck Marnie, that Meg hadn't returned with her parents. That was odd. Surely it was too dark for Meg to venture up to Asterlys Terrace alone. Why wasn't she at the hotel? With Mary carrying on like a bellowing bull Meg's absence had been overlooked. Unable to come up with a reasonable explanation, Marnie was determined she would ask come morning.

Rifle tucked under his arm, head on his chest, Jim was asleep in the chair.

Mary shook him gently.

Startled, he blinked in confusion.

"Reckon you can sleep in your own bed now," Mary said in a low whisper.

Jim stretched and yawned. "Is it safe or do I need my shotgun?"

Mary snorted. She held the kerosene lantern up and lit the way to their bedroom. "Come on, you blame fool, I doubt you'd have the energy to even raise an eyebrow tonight, so I reckon I'm safe unless you plan to shoot me with that there shotgun."

"Don't tempt me woman," Jim grumbled, rubbing at the crick in his neck.

The newlyweds seized their chance and escaped.

Yankee whispered, "Follow me," as he took Meg by the arm. They quietly slipped away from the crowd of revellers and walked to the hotel under a moonlit sky. Meg was apprehensive as they climbed the tight staircase to the upper room. Yankee turned the key in the lock and opened the door for his bride. Meg stood timidly on doorstep feeling unsure. This room was where Yankee had planned his wedding night with Niamh. That poor girl was probably sobbing into her pillow this very moment. Meg tried to chase that thought away. She didn't want to think about Niamh, not now.

She squealed with surprise as Yankee swept her off her feet, and carried her over the threshold. Yankee kissed her before gently putting her down. The curtains were drawn and a fire warmed the room. Small, the room was frugal in its furnishing. She couldn't help feeling disappointed; she'd expected something more - lavish.

Meg stared nervously at the bed. "I didn't bring any nightclothes with me," she told Yankee. "I ... my clothes are..."

Taking her in his arms, he kissed her. "Darlin', you are not going to need them."

Meg gave him a wobbly smile. "I never meant to..."

"What?" He pulled away. "Marry me? Do you regret it already?"

She shook her head but somehow his teasing made her relax. "Not yet, so don't make me."

She grew quiet. "I feel bad for Niamh, I feel like I've stolen her life."

He shook his head. "Niamh would have made me a fine wife but you are the woman I love, always have, always will." He rested his chin on the top of her head and held her in his arms. She could hear the beat of his heart.

He drew back. "But can you cook?"

She gave him a playful shove. The man was incorrigible. Laughing, she said, "You looked so handsome in your finery that I couldn't let you go, well, not without a fight."

"Ah, a compliment, I've been waiting a long time for that." He sat on the bed and stared adoringly up at her.
Not knowing what to do she stood uncertainly in the middle of the room.

"Come darlin', sit," he patted the covers.
Meg walked stiffly towards him and slowly lowered herself to the bed.

Nuzzling her ear, he said, "You're not still scared of me, are you?"

"A little," Meg admitted. "I don't know how you did it, but somehow you managed to cast a spell on me."

"My captive bride," he murmured softly kissing her neck. She closed her eyes and let him caress her.

Suddenly she broke free. "I'll have to go back."

Startled, Yankee frowned, "What? Now?"

Her tinkling laugh eased the tension. "No silly, tomorrow. Alone."

"I don't think that's a good idea," he said taking her hand in his, he kissed her palm. "I will come with you."

"No," Meg answered. "William deserves to hear the truth from me."

"Yes, but I will be there if things get..." he broke off unsure of how to phrase it without causing alarm.

Meg's jaw was set determinedly. "I can do it by myself."

"Oh, I don't doubt it my dear, but now you are my wife and as such it is my sworn duty to protect you. I can't have you gallivanting all over the countryside alone, can I? How can I protect you if I don't know where you are?"

"Wife," Meg repeated, the word it sounded strange and didn't roll off the tongue easily. "I'll be fine really," she said, insistent.

"Darlin', you forget I'm just as stubborn as you are. I'm coming with you. Now, let's agree not to fight on our wedding night. I think we should get reacquainted as you obviously don't know me well."

"All right," Meg conceded, "I will allow you to accompany me but you have to let me tell William and the Asterlys by myself. Promise?"

There was a long pause as Yankee thought over the proposition. "I'm not happy about it, but all right if it means I get my own way tonight then so be it," he agreed.

Meg wrung her hands. "I can't abandon my pupils without a replacement teacher so it may take some time."

He rolled his eyes. "Now you tell me there are a thousand conditions I have to agree to. It's not fair to negotiate after the fact. You are not playing fair. The moment we are wed you start making demands."

Meg's face crumbled.

"Darlin' I can wait," Yankee assured her. "I've waited a long time already."

He pulled her on to his lap and they sat for a while, cuddling.

Yankee's arm slid from her shoulder and rested on her hip. "Darlin' may I help you undress?" he asked hopefully.

Meg nodded shyly. Yankee removed the pins from her hair and the long dark tresses cascaded down her back. He ran his fingers through her soft silky hair, then sweeping it aside he gently kissed the hollow of her neck. His touch was soft and tender. She closed her eyes, and shivered, as her body tingled at his touch as if some strange electricity ran through it.

"Hush, don't talk, just feel," he instructed. He continued to gently kiss her neck and shoulders. He nimbly undid the tiny buttons on her dress, and threaded his fingers through the long laces loosening the stays on her corset. She slid off his knee, stood up, turned to face him, and let her dress, corset and all fall in a puddle of fabric. She undid the ribbon on her bloomers and they fell to her ankles, stepping out of them she stood before him, naked.

He stood up, and putting his arms around her pulled her close. They stood skin to skin, moulding into each other's flesh.

Her eyes widened in surprise.

His fingers ran the length of her spine and traced the outline of her curves.

"Don't be frightened dear," he said lowering her to the bed. "It may hurt the first time but after that it won't. I'll be gentle, I promise," he said. his voice husky. "I want you to desire me as much as I do you. I'd never hurt you, surely you know that?" His feather like touch on her bare arms made her shiver. "Your skin is so soft," he murmured.

She closed her eyes and allowed her body to respond to his touch. Arching her back, her hips rising to meet his she wrapped her legs about his torso, drew him close and the two become one flesh.

Later, feeling loved, and a little tender, Meg rested her head on Yankee's chest. Her finger stroked the fine dusting of hair that disappeared into his belly button.

"I love you," she whispered, afraid of the power of the words.

Kissing her forehead, Yankee replied, "Always have, always will."

Feeling blessed, he leaned across and blew out the guttering candle, and together they fell into a blissful, contented sleep.

Chapter 12   Lost Love

Burns caught the 5:30am stage. A newspaper boy offered him a fresh paper but he declined, reading in a swaying coach made him feel ill. Besides, he did not wish to read another account about the Sullivan Gang; it was a nightmare he desperately wanted to forget. He didn't recognize the whip, a big man, stout and sober in his manner. Besides there was a chill wind blowing so he chose to ride inside. After the initial polite introductions, and passing remarks about the weather, the other passengers settled under the sleepy blanket of early morning fog, leaving him be, which suited him fine, for it gave him time to think.

The expedition had been unpleasant but not entirely unsuccessful. The bankers and shareholders were not prepared to invest in his idea for setting up a dredge with a Chinaman. Especially since he did not have the support of his main business partner, Charles Asterly. And when he said he would be prepared to buy Asterly out, they argued the point, saying Asterly was a man of sound business principles, and they respected his judgment. William was convinced it was because they didn't trust the Celestials. He'd heard the term Yellow Peril bandied about, and though they tried to disguise their contempt they didn't succeed. Convinced that a partnership could work, he was frustrated.

The coach swayed and rocked, Burns held his stomach, hoping the motion sickness would pass. The light lifted and infiltrated the coach windows; the other passengers began to stir. Burns kept his eyes closed so they would think him asleep, but he listened as they talked amongst themselves. He couldn't wait to get home. It had been a hellish time, the only light in his dark week had been purchasing a share of Joe's claim. He made up his mind after the wedding, as soon as he could, he would sell his shares in the sluicing operation and try his luck on the West Coast.

He couldn't stop thinking about Kitty. Kitty had been entrusted into his care, he'd promised to protect her, and he'd failed. Kitty had kissed him, and in public too. She was only a child. Fourteen, a mere slip of a girl yet she had dared to kiss him not as a close relative does, but passionately, on the lips, like a lover. He'd done nothing to encourage her and yet somehow, she'd developed feelings for him. He had handled things badly but his response was such that he thought she wouldn't dare try to kiss him again. God, what would Margaret say if she knew? Would she accuse him of infidelity?

He could feel curious eyes watching him. Burns opened his eyes, he raised an eyebrow waiting for the question he was sure was coming.

Mr Twist, a man with sharp eyes and grizzled hair, shuffled forward in his seat. "I hear you were robbed at gunpoint, Mr Burns."

Mrs Twist, a thin wisp of a woman, gasped and covered her mouth with her gloved hand. "Really?" she squeaked.

William scrutinized Mr Twist's face and decided he was more concerned than nosy. He chose his words carefully in the hope to alleviate some of Mrs Twist's fear.

"Yes, however I'm certain if the blackguards have any sense they would have fled to the West Coast. Rest easy, Mrs Twist, they won't be bothering us."

"I sincerely hope you are right Mr Burns," Mrs Twist said, her fingers anxiously fiddling with the string of ebony beads she wore.

They fell silent again while Burns relived the events in his mind. He still could feel the burn marks on his wrists from the ropes. His pride was damaged and he was ashamed to admit he'd been frightened.

The coach rattled to a stop outside the Victoria Hotel where they were to stay the night. Usually, a personable man who enjoyed the company of others, Burns felt disinclined to socialize. He had a drink at the bar and ate in the restaurant with Mr and Mrs Twist, and Mr Brody. After making initial small talk, he declined the invitation to join the men in the smoking room for a cigar and a glass of porter. Instead, he went upstairs to his room, undressed, and fell into bed only to relive the robbery in his dreams.

The next thing he knew the hotelier was banging on his door. Dressing quickly, he headed downstairs, and found the others out front ready to embark on what would be for most of them, the final leg of the journey. The trip from Lawrence to Cromwell was tiresomely long but thankfully uneventful. Although logic told him the bushrangers would have escaped as far away as possible until the heat died down, he was feeling anxious.

At the Junction, while the horses were changed, they got out, stretched their legs and wet the back of their throats. With his hand around a comforting glass of ale, Mr Brody decided to ask Burns to tell him about life in the Golden Canyon.

Burns told them he believed it to be the richest river in the world. But Brody, a bull of a man, dared to contradict him, saying he'd heard incredible stories of the new rushes on the West Coast.

"Aye, I've heard amazing reports too, but I've yet to see for myself," Burns acknowledged, hoping he wasn't leaving his run too late.

The horses were changed, the velvet footstool proudly put in place, and the bell rang. Mrs Twist required assistance so he obliged by lending her his arm. She took her seat by the window. Once all were aboard the door closed with a bang, the coachman climbed up on the box seat and with a quick crack of the whip, they were off.

"You're not from these parts?" Mr Brody said, his head swaying with the motion.

Burns lifted a sardonic eyebrow, "Unless you are a native New Zealander most are from somewhere else. Very few are born here," he said in a condescending tone that he instantly regretted. He coughed. "No, I'm from mother England, been here a little over two years now."

Mr Brody didn't appear to have taken offence, and asked, "Burns? Isn't that a Scots name?"

"Yes. After my parents died, I went to London to live with my mother's uncle who sent me to a boarding school in Cambridge. I think that's why my accent may appear confused."

Mrs Twist asked him if he was married.

"Not yet," Burns replied, smiling.

Mrs Twist interrupted before he could explain, "So many bachelors in this part of the world, we should send shiploads of girls to help populate the nation."

"I believe that's what's happening," Mr Brody chipped in. "Boat loads of girls being shipped in." He winked at Burns.

"I'm to be married next Saturday," Burns quickly told them worried Mrs Twist may have an eligible niece she'd like to introduce.

"Is she...?" Mrs Twist asked, her bland face awakened with excitement.

"From here? No, Miss Healey's family are Irish, they spent a few years on the Ballarat goldfields before coming to Central Otago. My fiancé is the school ma'am at Skippers."

Mr Twist laughed good-naturedly, "My, my, you'll have to watch your p's and q's then, my boy."

Burns humoured him. "Her family tolerate me because I'm Scottish rather than being English born and because I was brought up Catholic, otherwise I think they would have chased me away with clubs and spears."

"Ah, one must always beware of the fighting Irish," Mr Brody said ironically since he was Irish.

At Mrs Twist's insistence, Burns told them a little more about himself. He told them he was twenty-three and had travelled extensively. His parents died when he was eleven. First, his father was carried off by the scarlet fever, then his mother. After their deaths, he had been placed in the guardianship of an aged uncle who provided for his education by sending him to boarding school. When he turned twenty his uncle died, and passed on a tidy sum of money to his nephew, who used it to be adventurous and travel to the other side of the world. He had come to the goldfields to seek his fortune, and during that time he had the good luck to meet the Healey family and fall in love with not one, but two of their daughters. Unfortunately, he told them, the elder Miss Healey died but there was a light in the darkness and he was soon to marry her younger sister. Having been an only child, then an orphan, family was important and he was looking forward to becoming a part of theirs.

It grew quiet. Mrs Twist appeared to be remembering something, perhaps the Healey name was familiar. "Would you like the paper to read, my husband has read it," Mrs Twist offered.

Burns declined, saying, "Thank you kindly but attempting to read with the constant motion makes me ill."

"Later?"

"Perhaps."

"Full of gossip anyways," Mr Brody quipped.

Mrs Twist leaned forward. "There's a terrible scandal about a wedding in Queenstown."

Mr Twist scowled at his wife. "Mr Burns is a businessman and not interested in such trifles. I'm sure he doesn't waste his time reading the society pages."

Piqued, Mrs Twist turned her attention to the others, trying to get them to tell her more about themselves to alleviate the tediousness of the long bumpy journey.

The stage was waylaid at the next watering hole while the horses were changed for fresh ones and two men joined their travelling party. The new members of the group, Mr Stokes and Mr McLennan, were seasoned travellers, and going to Queenstown to set up a tobacconist shop. Proud of his collection, Mr Brody discussed snuff and snuff boxes at length, his favourite being one made of tortoiseshell rumoured to have once belonged to Prince

Albert. The coach arrived in Queenstown before sundown. Tired, Burns chose to stay the night at the Queens Arms.

He knew out of politeness he should drop by the forge to see Jack and try to make amends but he was too annoyed with Jack to pretend otherwise. He ate a light supper and then went straight to his room. As the sun was sinking, he stood on the hotel balcony, looking across the lake's icy blue waters, and sighed. It was a grandiose view and it did the soul good to see it but the West Coast sounded more and more appealing. He must go before all the good claims were gone.

When morning dawned, a sharp spear of light pierced the gap between the heavy velvet curtains. Meg blinked, yawned and stretched like a cat. Yankee was still sleeping. She smiled fondly remembering the intimacy they had shared. Trying not to disturb him, she slid off the bed and found the chamber pot. Trying to be as discreet as possible, she tiptoed behind the screen.

Yankee opened his eye a crack. "You pee like a mare," he said with a soft chuckle.

Red faced, Meg appeared from behind the screen and used the cold water in the pitcher to wash her hands. "And you don't need to pee at all so it seems, your bladder must be fit to burst."

"Now that you mention it," Yankee said slipping past her and ducking behind the screen.

When he reappeared, he found Meg attempting to cover herself with her abandoned clothes.

"For goodness' sakes," he cried. "Don't think we are getting up yet, it's barely daylight and we are on our honeymoon."

Feeling self-conscious, Meg hopped back into bed and pulled the sheets up to her chin.

"Feeling shy, are we?" Yankee asked, amused.

"Cold," she lied.

Admiring his body, she watched as Yankee stirred life into the glowing embers and banked the fire. He climbed in bed beside her and cuddled her close. Meg put her head on his chest, listening to the steady thump of his beating heart.

"I'm sorry," she lifted her chin to look at him.

"What for?" He frowned. "For marrying me?"

"No, for stealing you."

"You didn't force me to do anything I didn't want to do." He ran his finger lightly down her arm. "Now let's leave that be. We will try to make restitution where we can, but for now let me enjoy being here, next to you."

"Do you always have to have the last word?"

"Yes."

She smiled. "You know," Meg drawled, her finger lazily tracing a circle around his nipple, tickling the hairs on his chest. "I rather think I like making love, and I believe we will both improve with practise."

Chuckling, Yankee kissed her. "My blushing bride," he laughed. Pulling her on top said, "Aye, come on darlin' let's practise."

The rooster crowed. Rolling over, Mary cursed. She groaned. Rubbing her eyes, she said, "That bloody rooster is going in the pot."

Jim propped himself up on his elbow. "Well darlin'," he said, "a lot happened yesterday and I've got a feeling a lot more will today." His fingers tickled the back of her knee.

Opening a gimlet eye, Mary said, "Are you trying to butter me up?"

"Is it working?" he asked hopefully.

"No, you'll have to try harder than that."

"I try to please," Jim said, gathering her in his arms.

They made love and when Mary lay back languid, her passion sated, Jim gently said, "Now darlin' can I talk to you without fear of you trying to attack me with a weapon of sorts?"

"Depends what it is you want to say, so think carefully before you speak," she said placing a warning finger to his lips.

He gently moved her hand. "You're a thrifty woman, Mary, and there's a perfectly good wedding planned for next week that's going to waste. There's a priest booked, a cake, and a wedding gown made, it seems a crying shame not to use them." Meg had planted the seed in his head and had begged him to try and convince Mary it was a good idea, her idea.

Mary sat up. She looked at him, incredulous. "Are you saying what I think you are saying?"

"Think about it my dear, Jack's as hard headed as..." he almost said, 'you' but corrected himself in time, "a nail," he took a breath, "and if you say no, he'll only run away with the girl putting both their lives in danger. And, they'll have no money to set up elsewhere. You don't want your son to suffer hardship on account of you being unhappy with his choice, now do you?" He smoothed her hair away from her face so he could see what she was thinking.

"We can help them. We have enough gold to help them set up a Smithy somewhere far enough away that folks won't know Marnie, somewhere she can remain respectable, untainted by the gossip mongers."

Mary was unnaturally quiet. She got up and wrapped her shawl around her shoulders.

"Where are you going?" Jim frowned.

"Outside to think," Mary replied, her hand reaching for the doorknob.

Jack woke to the cacophony of Pat snoring. He snorted, thinking he'd have been better off sleeping with the pigs. He sat on the edge of the bed, and ran his fingers through his hair. He was pretty sure he could count on his father's support but be wasn't sure where Pat's allegiances lay. Pat could hardly look down his nose, or complain about his choice of wife when he had been the one to introduce him to Marnie in the first place. Back then, Pat warned him to be careful not to get to close to Marnie, he'd said, that little lady was everyone's sweetheart. Well, he wanted Marnie to be his and his alone. No one would ever pay for the privilege of Marnie's attentions again.

He left Pat sleeping and went to visit the outhouse. He met his mother on her way back from there. She came across the dewy grass towards him, still dressed in her night things.

She stopped. "We will discuss the situation after breakfast," she told him coolly then walked on, stiff-backed, her head high.

Jack's heart sank. To convince his cantankerous mother to allow him to marry Marnie would be the battle of a lifetime.

When Jack opened the door to the kitchen, he found Marnie stirring the porridge with Grace comfortably tucked into her hip. The pleasant domestic scene warmed his heart. God willing she'd be a mother one day. A niggle of worry formed in his mind as he wondered if she could have children. As far as he knew she'd not been pregnant.

Marnie turned, her cornflower blue eyes lighting at the sight of him. "I'm glad you're up. Breakfast is ready. I'd appreciate it if you could put the wee one in the highchair, she's fair breaking my arm."

"Be my pleasure," Jack beamed, stealing a kiss. He took Grace from her; Grace went stiff as a board when Jack tried to deposit her in the highchair so that he had to tickle her to get her to bend.

"There you are little one," he said, ruffling Grace's hair, "breakfast is on its way."

"Sleep well?" Marnie asked lifting an inquisitive eyebrow.

"Sleeping in the same bed as my brother is not my idea of a fine homecoming."

Marnie grinned. "I suppose not."

Marnie tensed when Mary entered the kitchen closely followed by Jim.

"Where's your brother? Mary asked.

"Still sleeping off his rotten head." Jack replied with a shrug. "Don't reckon he'll be bothering with breakfast anytime soon.

Mary set spoons, milk and sugar on the table. "Bring the porridge to the table, Marnie," she instructed, not looking at the girl.

Marnie quickly did as she was told.

Mary took her seat. "We'll have breakfast first then we'll discuss," she paused, "the situation."

Jack and Marnie glanced at one another nervously.

"Aye, we will have a discussion," Jim agreed, taking his seat. "But that will be after I finish the last bite of breakfast because I don't want to ruin my appetite by hearing a lot of hot-headed nonsense - from anyone."

Glowering, Jack dipped his spoon in his bowl.

Mary rapped the back of his hand. "We'll say grace first."

Shamefaced, Jack put down his spoon and bowed his head. Jim thanked the Lord for the food on their plates and their family.

Breakfast was eaten in silence. The tension was thick as fog.

"Right," Mary said putting her bowl aside. "There's things that need to be said and it's time."

Marnie began gathering the dishes.

"Leave them," Mary commanded.

Marnie stopped, sat back down, lowered her head and studied the tablecloth. Jack sought her hand under the table and gave it a reassuring squeeze.

"Firstly, you are too young to marry without our permission," Mary told Jack.

"But Ma..."

"Don't but Ma me, just listen."

"I thought it was going to be a discussion?" Jack said, prickling.

"Don't be smart," Mary retorted. "Especially not if you want my permission."

Jack sucked in his breath.

271

"Secondly, I don't' think you are right for each other. And thirdly, given Marnie's profession and the number of men she's had she's likely to be riddled with diseases and unlikely to be able to bear you any children. Have you thought about that?"

Jack's chin jutted forward in defiance. "I don't care. I love her."

"You say that now, my boy, but marriage takes work, it's just not a bunch of lovely words. Where are you going to live? Have you thought about that, have you? You'll need to go far enough away that Marnie won't be recognized, or captured by the people she fled from. And, what will you do for money? Is Marnie going to take in washing to help you survive?"

Jack's face clouded; he had expected a fight but he hadn't expected to have to defend himself in front of Marnie. He let go of Marnie's hand and inched forward on his seat. "I can work. I'm a good blacksmith. And you'll be surprised to know that I have thought about it Ma, and I believe the small town where Yankee hailed from is far enough away for a fresh start."

Mary wasn't impressed.

Jack hurried on, "Everyone is heading to the West Coast, no one will expect us to go South. Riverton is small, no one will expect us to go there, and we'll be far away from anyone who may want to do us harm. They'll need blacksmiths. It used to be a whaling station, now it has a flax and timber mill, and transports cargo to and from Australia. I'll get work."

"But what about now?" Mary countered giving him a hard stare. "What money do you have now?" She glanced at Marnie.

When Jack didn't answer, Mary continued, "And how you going to get there without putting yourselves in danger? You'll have to go back through Rees to get there."

Jack threw up his hands in despair. "Are you saying you are not going to give your blessing, that we are on our own? You won't help us?"

"What I am saying," Mary folded her arms across her chest, "is you haven't thought anything through. In fact, I'm certain you haven't got a scrap of common sense in your thick Irish head."

"How can you say it's a discussion when you have already made up your mind?" Jack argued. "All you do is tell, not talk. Is this discussion over? Can we go now?" Pushing his hands on the table top Jack went to stand up.

But with the table acting as a buffer between them, Jim leaned across it. "Sit!" he commanded.

Surprised by the sharpness of his father's tone, Jack sat down.

Jim's face was grim as he said, "The discussion is not over by a long shot. No son, it's only just beginning."

After a long drawn out pause, Mary said, "I've decided…"

"Oh, you have, have you?" Jim lifted an ironic eyebrow.

Meg insisted Yankee settle the account before she could be persuaded to venture downstairs. As soon as he returned from paying the bill, she donned her cloak and hat, and swept down the stairs, past the woman on the counter, and out into the bustling street.

Catching up, Yankee tucked her arm in his. Meg kept her head down and tried not to make eye contact with anyone. If Yankee noticed people's curious stares, he didn't show it.

He whispered, "Are you embarrassed you are no longer a virgin and they'll know it?"

She blushed. "I'm embarrassed that I'm the talk of the town for ruining your wedding."

"You didn't ruin it, love," he patted her arm affectionately. "I couldn't be happier. However, I do think I'll have to make some atonement for my sins."

Meg wondered what he meant, but couldn't bring herself to ask.

Yankee collected his horse from the stables, then together they walked to Sanders livery where docile little Thistle waited patiently for Meg.

The pock-marked stable hand doffed his hat to Meg and smiled. "The wee mare has been fed and watered and is all set to go, jest give me a minute to saddle her Miss."

"It's Mrs," Yankee corrected.

"Mrs," the boy ducked his head in apology.

"Mrs Brown," Yankee told him proudly.

Meg tugged Yankee's sleeve, "I'm hungry," she whispered.

Not used to eating before ten it hadn't occurred to Yankee that she might be hungry. "Are you telling me you can't live on love, my dear?"

"No, I believe I'm going to need my strength." She gave him a meaningful look.

274

He snorted with laughter. "I beg your pardon, my dear, I can't believe I'm neglecting my husbandly duties already. Shall I stop at the bakery first, or would my lady prefer a hotel breakfast?"

"The bakery is fine," she replied. She was anxious to get home. Meg glanced nervously out the large double doors, was that Niamh hiding in the shadows, ready to pounce and rip her hair out by its roots?

"As you wish my lady." Yankee kissed her kid-gloved hand.

The groom brought Thistle out and handed Meg the reins. "There you go Mrs Brown," he said politely. She thanked the groom, patted Thistle's neck then mounted.

They went to a bakery where Yankee bought her an iced bun, relishing the sticky sweetness she ate hastily.

"Do you wish to call in and see Jack?" he asked.

"Yes," Meg answered turning Thistle's head. "I must tell him that everything is all right at Long Gully."

But when they alighted at the forge, they were told by a young lad that Jack Healey no longer worked there, and a bit more besides. Horrified by the boy's torrid tale, Meg went pale. Yankee whispered in her ear, not to worry, he was sure Jack would have headed for home. Yankee thanked the lad, turned his steed and they set off for the canyon.

As they began the ascent, Meg's thoughts raced ahead, she tried to anticipate how everyone was going to react. Would they condemn her rash behaviour? She'd never intended to hurt poor William. This was going to be a cruel blow for him. William was a proud man, if he felt humiliated, he might... it suddenly occurred to her she had no idea how he would react. She was pleased

275

Yankee had accompanied her; she would need his support. Meg looked at her husband sitting straight-backed in the saddle, tall and handsome. She had made the right decision. She loved him, and it occurred to her she had never felt more content. And much to her surprise, she enjoyed making love. To think all this time, she had been dreading it, instead she found the intimacy between two people who genuinely loved each other beautiful, honest, and real. She wished they could stay in that cocoon of love forever.

They picked their way along the packer's trail, their horses' heads nodding, tails swishing as they slowly made their way to the hotel. Every now and then she caught Yankee gazing lovingly at her and she smiled back, but as they got nearer to the hotel Meg's anxiety increased and her breathing became shallow, she hoped they didn't run into anyone they knew on the way, especially Dusty.

They arrived at the hotel and Meg waited on the veranda settle while Yankee stabled the horses. She shivered, it was uncommonly cold for late January, the air had a nasty bite to it, she drew her cloak close.

Marnie flung the door open. "Meg! Where have you been? Why are you sitting out here in the cold? Quick, come in!"

Meg smiled faintly. Tired, she hoped to avoid Marnie's endless questions. "I'm fine Marnie. How are you?"

Marnie beamed, her eyes dancing with excitement. "Jack's here!"

"That's a relief." Meg sighed.

"The men are up at the claim but they will be back soon for lunch. Mrs Healey is making a pot of potato soup. Come in, come in, before I'm scolded. I shouldn't be opening the door but I spied you sitting there through the window. Quick, we are letting the draught in."

"Has Ma been keeping you in the broom closet?" Meg teased.

Marnie grinned. "I think she'd like to, but Mr Healey won't let her."

"Someone else is here." Meg pointed to the figure coming out of the stables. Hat set low on his ears, Yankee strolled across the lawn, a cocky jaunt to his step.

Marnie squinted short-sightedly at the man coming towards them. "Who is it?"

"It's Yankee," Meg replied, watching Marnie closely.

Marnie frowned, her fingers gripping the back of the settle. "Will you... are you, all right?" she whispered, worried.

Meg laughed lightly. "Yes," she smiled. "It's fine, Marnie, Mr Brown and I are on speaking terms."

Marnie's face showed a myriad of emotions. "Oh, but from what ... I thought..." she paused. "Never mind what I thought, it's great to see you." Marnie whistled through her teeth. "But I'm warning you now, your Ma has been like a bear with a sore head, it wouldn't do to get her riled up again."

Yankee doffed his hat as he came up the steps. "Good to see you safe, Miss Marnie, and your face nicely healed and all."

"Mr Brown," Marnie returned, puzzled. "Where is Mrs Brown?"

Yankee tapped his finger to the bridge of his nose. "That would be telling."

Frustrated by his reply, Marnie took Meg's arm and left Yankee to follow in their wake.

"Ma!" Meg called, coming into the kitchen.

Mary looked up from stirring the soup pot and smiled. "How are you me darlin' girl?" draping the tea-towel over her shoulder, she wiped her hands and went to greet them.

"Well Ma, well," Meg assured her kissing her mother's hot cheek.

Mary drew back and gazed questioningly into her daughter's eyes. "Happy?"

"Yes." Meg blushed. "And before you ask, fine."

"I'm fine too, thanks for asking," Yankee chimed in. "I have no complaints, but then my wife hasn't so much as boiled me an egg yet so I'm not sure if I'll be a happy man or not."

Mary flicked the tea-towel at him. "Yankee Brown, you have more cheek than an organ grinder's monkey. I'm not sure what Mrs Brown can do to cure you of it but if I were her, I'd wrap you in vinegar and brown paper for starters."

Yankee chuckled. "I'm fair shaking in me boots."

"And you have an uncanny knack of turning up whenever food is about. I may have to add a potato or two to the pot, but don't worry we'll have enough."

Marnie offered to take Meg's hat and cloak. Meg handed them to Marnie but kept her gloves on insisting her fingers were cold. Marnie frowned.

"Don't worry, Marnie, I won't die of the frostbite."

"Why don't you two warm yourselves by the fire," Mary suggested. She went back to seasoning her soup. "Marnie, peel some more potatoes."

278

Marnie peeled the potatoes but every now and then she peeked over her shoulder, she watched Meg take a seat by the fire, and Yankee Brown sit next to her. Marnie felt indignant on Meg's behalf. Meg was engaged, Yankee should respect her choice and stop flirting with her, it wasn't right. She might not have learned many morals in her life, but she believed flirting with a woman who was engaged to be married was wrong.

Marnie set a place for two more at the table. "Did you two meet on the road?" she asked unable to hide her curiosity.

"Marnie!" Mary reproved. "Stop asking questions. Do you want to ruin their appetites? In all my born days I have never known anyone as nosy as you. You'll give the pair of them indigestion."

Pat was enjoying his youngest brother's company, working alongside Jack was easy. He was nothing like Dan. Dan was always looking down his nose on anyone who didn't share his high moral standards. Then again, Jack couldn't act all high and mighty when he planned to marry Marnie. Their marriage would always be a thorn in Pat's flesh - not that Jack would ever know but Marnie had held a special place in Pat's heart, and if he'd known he could buy her, he would have. He'd promised Ma he'd behave, so even if it killed him, he would stick by his promise.

Da generously told Jack whatever gold he found that day he could keep. Jack beavered away but at noon their grumbling stomachs told them it was time to head back to the hotel for lunch. As luck would have it, they arrived just as the potato broth was brought to the boil.

The men crowded the small room with their presence. Meg and Yankee stood to greet them.

"Jack me lad, it's good to see you," Yankee cried, clapping a hand on Jack's back. "When you didn't make me wedding, I thought you must be dead. By the look of you, you weren't far off."

"Almost was," Jack said, "but I'm hard to kill."

Marnie went as white as a flour bag.

Pat congratulated Yankee on purchasing a fine parcel of land.

"Oh," Yankee chuckled. "Mrs Brown is a fine purchase; she's cost me dearly in loss of sleep."

"Good choice, then," Pat laughed.

Jim shook his head.

Mary scowled.

"I meant Riverstones Station," Pat said, looking apologetically at his Ma.

"Where is Mrs Brown?" Jack asked, looking past him.

There was silence.

"May I?" Yankee glanced at Meg.

Meg inclined her head.

"Folks, I would like to introduce you to my wife, Mrs Brown," Yankee said, hugging Meg into his shoulder.

"What!" Jack spluttered.

Pat sat heavily on the closest stool. "Well, I'll be darned," he said, slapping his knee.

"You... you're... married?" Marnie stammered her blue eyes wide. "But what about...?"

"Niamh?"

"Who? Oh, yes her, but I meant Mr Burns?" Marnie replied.

280

Pat gripped Yankee's hand. "I have always liked you better than that stuck up hatter anyways," he said dryly. "You're proper family now boyo."

Before Pat could get too free with his opinions, Mary wisely interrupted. "Soup's ready." She poured a swirl of cream on top of each one. "Take your places. Yankee can tell you all about it while you eat. I don't want a good meal going cold."

"Heed your mother, that's sensible advice," Jim said, taking his seat.

Leaving Thistle at the Welcome Home where she belonged, Yankee led his horse as he and Meg walked along the track.

"A year ago, I delivered you up here to meet your new employers."

"Yes, and you teased me mercilessly all the way."

"If I remember rightly you were tearful and I offered you my shoulder to cry on," he said with a grin.

The corners of Meg's mouth twitched into a smile.

"You are very quiet, my dear," Yankee said putting his arm about her shoulder. "I've been told that if a woman's quiet something's wrong."

"I'm worried," Meg said, she couldn't stop fretting. She was about to hurt and humiliate a good man, something she'd never intended to do, and she had to tell the Asterlys about her marriage.

"I know, but I'm here, right beside you."

This morning they had discussed Meg would stay until a suitable teacher could be found. Yankee said he did not mind delaying going to live at Riverstones; the station manager and farmhands could take care of things for him. In the meantime, he'd work with Dan and Harry at the Jewellers Shop.

Meg felt guilty. Yankee had made so many concessions for her but to be uprooted so suddenly would be too difficult; however, she knew she could hardly stay in the same area as William. The injured look on his face would be unbearable and if she had to see it every day it would destroy her. Meg wished the blow had already been dealt.

As if reading her mind, Yankee said, "Burns will not be happy. On the other hand," he said stealing a kiss, "I am delighted."

"Stop it, people might see," she replied primly, pushing him away.

He frowned., indignant. "I'm allowed to kiss my own wife."

"Not in public you're not," Meg remonstrated.

"More conditions," he sighed, sounding disheartened.

The trail was empty, but set well below the track, Maori Point was a bustling community - there was a police outpost, the bank of New Zealand, the bakery, the butchers and the library. Droves of diggers were working the riverbed, industrious as bees making honey; they did not stop to look up.

Yankee tried to alleviate her fears. "I'm not going to let anyone harm you, you can count on that," he said.

Meg smiled, "You know, initially I had my doubts about you, but I think you may make a good husband after all."

Chapter 13   Penance

Dan wasn't looking forward to this, he always got the tough jobs. Somehow it fell on his shoulders to make things right, and smooth the way when there was no way. He resented being given the task but he'd promised Yankee he would do it. He squeezed the pouch, patted the letter in his breast pocket for luck, steeled himself, knocked and waited.

Niamh opened the door. Recognising him, she tried to close it again but Dan put his foot in the way.

He noticed her sandy hair was hidden under a cap, her figure trim and neat. She looked smaller than he remembered, less confident, like she had shrunk inside herself.

"The Father's not in," she scowled. Her eyes were red-rimmed from crying.

He swallowed. "It's not him I came to see, it's you."

Her pride made her as stiff as a poker. "What for," she demanded. "So you can laugh?"

"Can I come in?" he asked. "What I have to say is not for everyone's ears."

She looked dubious.

"I have something for you," he said quietly.

Reluctantly, she opened the door and let him in. Dan loosened his kerchief, straightened his vest, and followed her to the sitting room.

"Well?"

He shifted uneasily. Dan held out the pouch which was packed with banknotes and gold. "Yankee asked me to give you this."

She stared at it, "What is it? Thirty pieces of silver?"

"Something like that. Call it penance if you like."

"I don't need his money, and I sure as hell don't need your sympathy." She crossed the floor and held the door open for him. "I've been publicly humiliated; money can't fix that."

He admired the way she carried herself, upright, full of indignation.

Dan bowed. "I'll leave this here." He placed the bag on the small side table.

"You can return to him if you like but I promised I would give it to you." He paused and took a breath. "And he asked me to tell you, that he's dreadfully sorry for what happened. There's a letter too, and he's not that good with his letters so I had to write it for him." Dan placed the letter on the side table. Surmising she might not read the letter, he said, "He's sorry for what he put you through, and knows it's too much to ask, no, to beg your forgiveness, but he hopes in time you can find it in your heart to forgive him."

"Forgive him?" Niamh cried. "I never want to see his heathen face again. He promised me a good life, instead he's made me look a fool in the eyes of the district."

"It was my sister's fault. Yankee would have honoured his promise to you if she hadn't..." Dan drifted off uncertain how to phrase things.

"Your sister, your sister, she was engaged." Niamh's jaw tightened. "How could she do such a thing?"

Dan shuffled his feet and shrugged. "Love, I guess. I'm given to understand it's not logical."

"A promise is a promise," Niamh said, through gritted teeth.

"There are so many bachelors in these parts desperate for a wife it will not be long before one will be asking for your hand."

Niamh's eyes became as sharp as knives. "Am I a cattle beast to be haggled over? Am I to count my lucky stars when any old digger asks for my hand? Do I get a choice?"

Dan took a step back. "Yankee thought some money may help buy you whatever you want, or need. He told me to tell you, if you need more, to let him know."

"Get out!" she shrieked.

Dan tipped his hat and gently closed the door, as he walked away, he heard the jangle of coins being thrown against it.

Burns spent the better part of the morning in Queenstown. He went to the milliners to be measured for a new top hat, his was beginning to look tatty. He bought a small vial of lavender oil as a present for Mary, and a pouch of tobacco for Jim. He couldn't decide between the lace handkerchiefs for Margaret, so he bought three. Satisfied, he picked up the horse and gig and set off for the canyon. The weather was good, and the ride pleasant, which helped elevate his dark mood. He planned to call in on the Healeys on his way home but he was dreading telling them about the robbery. He feared they would blame him. He hoped Margaret would be visiting them, seeing her would bring some cheer to his heavy heart.

His heaviness lifted when he caught sight of the Long Gully pub's three smoking chimneys. And, if Margaret wasn't there, he knew it was only a further eight miles until he would see his betrothed again. As soon as he was married, he'd sell his shares and move to greener pastures. He'd be damned if Charles Asterly was going to dictate to him. Assuming, Jim, would be at the mine, Burns thought he'd best unhitch the horse and return the gig to its rightful place. He watered his horse before going inside.

Burns did not wait to be invited but feeling at home, knocked and entered.

Calling, "Afternoon!" he removed his hat and coat and hung them on the peg.

"Burns!" Jim said, clenching his cold pipe in his teeth. Ashen, Jim turned to Mary and said, "The wanderer returns."

Mary shot him a warning look. Her face carefully expressionless, she said, "William, it is good to see you back safe and sound."

"It is great to be here," he said, meaning it. "I must say it's a surprise to find you at home," Burns said, shaking Jim's hand. "Thought you'd be up at the mine."

"Aye, well Jack's helping Pat on the claim."

Burns stiffened. "Jack's here?"

Jim continued, "The pair of them told me I was neither use nor ornament, reckoned I was best out of the way. Besides, since they believe I'm nearly as old as Methuselah, and its Sunday they told me to rest."

"I'm pleased to see you, but I have to admit, I was rather hoping Margaret might be visiting. It seems an eternity since I've seen her. She normally visits on a Sunday, doesn't she?"

Jim frowned grimly at the clock. "She came and went early today."

"My fault," Burns stifled a yawn. "I stayed in Queenstown later than I planned. Which reminds me." He went over to his coat and extracted the vial of lavender oil and tobacco from his coat pocket. "I bought presents."

Unwrapping the tissue paper, Mary cried, "Oh, how kind, thank you." She placed the bottle on the sideboard and refolded the tissue.

"Aye, you'd no need to be doing that but I'm mighty glad you did," Jim said, sniffing the packet of tobacco. "This looks far superior to the dandelion weed I've been smoking, and I'd run out, so I've been smoking a cold pipe just for the taste of it."

Mary picked up the kettle and weighed it in her hand. "Cup of tea, and something to eat?" Not waiting for him to reply, she put the kettle on.

"Lovely." Burns nodded.

"I've made a jam roll." Mary bought out a cake tin. "Say you'll have some."

Jim whispered in her ear, "Is that wise?"

"We have to stall him," Mary hissed. She reached for the crockery.

"Sounds wonderful. I've eaten nothing but dust for days," Burns grinned. He took a seat at the table and stretched his long legs out in front of him.

"I'm sure you've had more in your belly than just dust," Mary said with a wry grin. "An ale or two perhaps to help wash the dirt down?"

"Not nearly enough," he laughed, at ease.

"Would you like one?" Jim asked, wishing he could have one himself.

Burns shook his head. "No, if I start, I won't want to stop, and I may fall off my horse before I reach home."

Jim let his hand fall limply by his side. He floundered for a moment wondering what to say. "Ah, I take it the roads are no better then."

Burns shook his head. "They are worse. Thank goodness it's been a dry summer or we could have been bogged for days."
Jim wiped his sweaty palms on the back of his trousers, he'd have much rather been with the boys up at the claim.

Jerking her head at him, Mary said, "Jim, lend me a hand, will you?" When she handed him the tea tray she whispered, "Try to act naturally."

"You're making me nervous," Jim grumbled. Steadying himself, he carefully carried the crockery to the table, "Seems I've been made the serving girl now," he quipped.

"Oh, where's Marnie?" Burns glanced about. "Has she gone?" he asked hopefully.

"She's out the back feeding the chickens," Mary answered. She scooped four large teaspoons of fresh leaves into the teapot. "One for each of us and one for the pot," she said with a smile. She poured the water over the tea leaves and brought the pot to the table. "So, William, tell us all about it. How was the journey?"

"Yes, how was Kitty when you left her?" Jim asked, placing the cake in the centre of the table.
Mary fired questions like she was shooting birds.

As difficult as it was, Burns knew he had to tell them the truth. He spread his hands wide. "I promise I'll tell you all when I've got a nice cup of tea to unclog my parched throat." He swallowed. "I'm afraid there's rather a lot to tell."

Mary looked up sharply. She turned the teapot three times to the right and once to the left. Stroking his goatee, Burns watched her, fascinated, it was ritual that never failed to amaze him, it was like watching a fortune-teller at a country fair, he half expected a spirit to come out of the pot. Mary poured his tea first, then Jim's, picking up the knife she cut several generous slices of cake.
Jim took a careful sip of his piping hot tea and waited for Burns to speak.

Stalling, Burns asked a question more out of politeness than interest. "So how was the wedding?"
Jim choked and almost spilt his tea, he put his cup down.

Startled, Mary said, "Oh, you've heard?"

"Are you all right?" Burns asked, pounding Jim on the back.
Wiping away his tears, Jim nodded.

Satisfied, Jim was in no in immediate danger, Burns continued, "I was told Mr Brown was marrying the good Father's housekeeper. The wedding was on Friday in Queenstown, was it not? Were you invited?" He arched an expectant eyebrow.

Mary faltered. "We were..." she began hesitantly.

"Did you go?" William interrupted.

Jim waded in. "Yes, but we didn't stay long. Mary was anxious to get back to the hotel, and you know me, a wedding is a wedding, and without a drink in my hand it's as hard to endure as a dry argument," he said with a shrug.

Amused, Burns snorted. "I hope you find our wedding more tolerable then."

Jim and Mary exchanged worried glances.

"Cake?" Mary asked. Not waiting for an answer, she handed Burns a slice.

Burns took a bite. "Mmm delicious," he praised, and took another bite. "I hope your daughter can bake like this, it's divine."

Flattered, Mary dimpled. "I taught my daughters everything I know," she said, "but if they listened - that's another thing entirely." She added two spoons of sugar into her cup and gave it a good stir.

Jim reached for a slice of cake, reasoning if he kept his mouth full perhaps it would stop him from accidentally saying things he shouldn't.

Mary eyed Burns over the rim of her cup. "Please tell us all about your trip. We are dying to know how Kitty is, and if she's settled. How was she when you left her?"

"I think she's going to like it there, but I'm afraid we ran into a spot of bother on our journey." Burns' face grew serious. "It was not the weather, nor the roads that troubled us."

Mary could tell it was more than just a loose wagon wheel. She put down her cup. "What happened?"

"Our stage was held up."

Mary's mouth dropped open. "No!"

Jim's hand shook and tea slopped into his saucer.

Burns hurried to reassure them. "No one was hurt, but we were robbed at gunpoint by three masked men. The police believe it was the Sullivan gang."

Mary's hand flew to her throat. "Oh, my poor, poor, baby!"

"Kitty was shaken but very brave. You should be proud of her. She told me to tell you her money was safe, but," he paused and looked forlornly at Jim. "But I'm afraid her signet ring was stolen."

"The blackguards!" Jim spat.

As he feared, Burns had to retell the whole awful tale again from start to finish. When it was done, and all the questions exhausted, he fell back leaning against his chair. He felt terrible. Would they ever forgive him for failing them?

Jim reached across the table and squeezed Mary's hand. "Thank the Lord nobody was hurt," he said. "And thank you William, we are forever in your debt."

"Yes," Mary agreed, "truly."

Burns hung his head. "I'm only sorry Kitty had to endure such a terrible ordeal. The robbers will have fled to the West Coast for news of the robbery but sketches of them will be in every paper in the Country."

Mary guessed Burns hadn't read any papers on his journey home or he might have read other newsworthy items such as the sensational marriage of Mr Joseph Brown, of Moonlight, to Miss Margaret Healey, of Skippers Canyon.

"I believe they will be planning to terrorize wealthy prospectors or rob the odd bank clerk riding alone, no doubt." Burns was thoughtful a moment before adding, "I don't think they would have killed us, but you never know, I wouldn't have liked to press them."

"Aye, that would have been foolish against armed men," Jim agreed.

291

"Do you think the Law will catch them?" Mary asked. But even as she said it, she thought of Charlie Butler. Thus far he had evaded capture, and these villains might well evade the Law too. How many other poor souls might be attacked in the meantime? Mary shuddered, it made you afraid of your own shadow. Her baby had been robbed and almost been killed. Kitty in peril, it didn't bear thinking about, she couldn't bear the loss of another child.

"I sincerely hope so," Burns said, his voice bitter. "I hope to God they hang."

"Did you encounter any problems on your way home?" Mary asked. She was taut as a string on a bow.

"No, not so much as a horse throwing a shoe," Burns replied.

Marnie came inside, she carried a basket of eggs which she almost dropped when she saw William Burns sitting at the dining table. "Mr Burns!" she cried.

"Frighten you, did I?" Burns asked, amused by the shock on Marnie's face.

Mary clucked her tongue. "You'll never make a proper housewife, not when the slightest thing makes you jump girl."

Marnie blushed and put the eggs on the bench. "Sorry," she mumbled.

"Marnie," Jim said, addressing her, "William, was just telling us that their stagecoach was robbed. Kitty's all right but they have been through a hellish time."

Marnie uttered an expletive and quickly clapped a hand over her mouth. "What happened?" She hurried to the table and took a seat next to Burns.

He shifted down. No matter how respectable she looked, Marnie was a whore, and he did not want his reputation sullied.

"Have a slice of cake, you need fattening. Your just skin and bone girl, and I'll not have my son thinking I've been starving you while you've been here," Mary told her.

Marnie ate cake and listened intently as Burns recounted the events again. Drained, he swallowed his last gulp of tea. Mary asked Marnie to clear the table. Marnie bobbed her head and gathered the plates, stacking them neatly in the sink.

Burns placed his hands on his thighs and made to get up. "Right, I must be off, I'm desperate to see Margaret. I'll just visit the little house and be on my way."

Mary and Jim glanced at each other, each reading the other's thoughts. All hell was about to break loose and there was nothing they could do to stop it.

Chapter 14   Rebuffed

Burns decided to go home first to freshen up. He wanted to look his best before calling on Margaret. When he came by the cemetery, he saw a horse by the gate, and two people standing by Annie's grave, heads bent close together talking. He recognized Margaret's bonnet but he couldn't quite make out the other figure, though it was a man. Instinctively he knew something was wrong. He slipped off his horse, tethered it, and silently opened the wrought-iron gate, closing it gently before crossing the lumpy ground.

"Margaret?"

"William!" Meg turned, her dark eyes wide with fright. "You're back!"

Burns voice was gruff. "What's he doing here?"

"We came to visit Annie," Yankee said, stepping forward.

"I wasn't speaking to you," Burns growled.

Meg took a deep breath and prayed for strength. "William, we need to talk."

There was something in her tone that unnerved him. A confident man, he was not used to feeling insecure, and it bothered him.

"And I have rather a lot to tell you too, my dear," he replied, scowling at Yankee he added, "in private."
Yankee folded his arms and gave Burns a menacing look.

Meg spoke to Yankee, her brown eyes soft and pleading. "Can you give us a moment, please?"

"I'm here if you need me," Yankee said stiffly, glaring at Burns.

Meg beckoned Burns to follow her. This was not the homecoming he'd envisaged. He didn't know what was going on, but he didn't like it. Astonished, he followed, catching up with her in a few long-legged strides. "Is something amiss?" he asked.

She didn't reply. Instead, she walked to the far end of the graveyard then stopped. Meg felt she had been deceitful long enough. There were no choice words that would soften the blow. Reaching for the gold chain hidden under her high neckline, she pulled it up, undid the clasp, and slid off the ring.

Looking him in the eye, she said, "I'm sorry William, I can't marry you." She held out his ring.

He stared at the ring resting in her palm but didn't move to take it. "You don't mean it. It's just your nerves talking, Margaret."

She shook her head. "No William, I'm afraid it's not. I can't marry you," she said, her voice stronger now. Placing the ring in his hand she closed his fingers around it.

Confused, he spluttered. "What are you playing at Margaret? What kind of nonsense is this? I don't understand."

"I can't marry you William because," she paused, "I am married."

A muscle twitched in Burns' cheek. He laughed nervously. "I've known you for nigh on a year and you have never mentioned being married before. "
Yankee watched them warily from the other side of the graveyard.

Meg closed her eyes and opened them very slowly. "I got married on Saturday."

"You what!" William thundered. For a moment he was speechless, then the cogs slowly clicked into place. "Are you telling me that you married that... that..." he pointed wildly at Yankee, lost for words, the muscles in his jaw taut and twitching.

Waves of guilt crashing over her, Meg said very quietly, "Yes. I'm sorry William."

"God Almighty!" Burns cursed, his face turning puce.

"Please believe me, I had no intention of hurting you, William. But I always had my doubts. I believe you thought you loved me because I reminded you of Annie," she said, hoping he'd see reason. "To be fair, I thought that if I cared enough for you that love would grow given time, but when I saw Yankee about to wed another, I knew caring wasn't enough."

Burns' nostrils flared. He smacked a hand to his forehead knocking his hat clean off. "I cannot believe my ears!" he thundered.

Meg hurried on, "Don't get me wrong, I'm very fond of you. I respect and admire you greatly but that's not enough. You're a good man and will make someone a fine husband but you were not meant for me." There, she'd said it, she should feel better but knowing the pain she was inflicting, she felt worse.

His words were sharp. "I can't believe you have the audacity to ... this it is preposterous, outrageous, it's unbelievable!"

Meg stood her ground, she knew any sign she was being intimidated, Yankee would quickly come to her defence, and then should the two rivals come to blows she would not know how to stop them.

There was a sting in his words as he said, "I thought you were a woman of honour. I can see now that I was wrong about you Margaret." His voice was thick with contempt. He blinked several times as if expecting to awaken from a bad dream. "I called in to see your family on the way here and they didn't even so much as warn me. They let me talk about how much I was looking forward to our wedding. Ours," he emphasized. "I've a good mind to go back and punch your father in the nose."

Despairing, Meg said, "You have every reason to be upset William, but it's not my parents' fault, they didn't deceive you, they just thought... well they thought it would be better coming from me."

"Better? Better!" he snorted. Arms flailing, he cried, "Were they party to this? Did they put you up to it?"

"No, no, they had nothing to do with it at all," Meg said feebly. "I am sorry."

His voice dropped, quiet now, he said, "If the marriage hasn't been consummated it can be annulled." He was grasping at straws, like a drowning man clutching a twig.

"It has been," she said quietly.

The brutal truth made him reel in horror. "Dear God in Heaven!" he exclaimed, throwing his hands in the air. "I can't listen to another word. You have played me for a fool, Margaret. I'll be the laughing stock of the district. I'll have to leave Lake County."

Meg grasped his arm. "No, no, don't go, I'm going to leave. I've only come back to tell you, and the Asterlys, and to teach until a replacement teacher can be found." Her voice sounded desperate to her own ears.

He shook her off. "You planned this," he accused. "You planned this entire thing!" He longed to fling words at her like daggers but he suddenly realized there was nothing he could say or do that could change the situation. "And as for that, that...idiot..." he faltered, his voice reaching fever pitch.

Yankee's fists balled at his sides as he strode towards them.

Longing to reason with William, Meg tried to keep calm. "I wanted to tell you myself, before the Asterlys or anyone else for that matter. I thought that was the right thing to do."

"Am I to be thankful for small mercies?" he shrieked.

Yankee walked towards them. "The lady has made her choice."

Burns turned and snarled, "A bad one, and one she'll live to regret, I'll wager."

Still trying to appease, Meg said, "I'm sorry there's nothing I can say that can make it right but to marry you and love another would have been wrong, wouldn't it?"

"If I hadn't gone," he panted, finding it hard to breathe. "If I hadn't escorted your sister to Dunedin, none of this would have happened and you would be marrying me this Saturday as planned."

"You should go now," Yankee said. "It would be the gentlemanly thing to do."

"Who the hell are you to remind me of manners!" Burns shouted. Turning his back on Yankee, he said to Meg, "Do you know we were set upon and robbed? Do you even care?"

Meg's face blanched. "Is..."

"Is Kitty all right?" he finished lamely, his voice dropping in defeat. "She's fine." Burns lifted his chin. "She kissed me, you know," he said in an effort to hurt her.

Meg didn't respond.

Yankee repeated, "You should go now."

Burns went to walk away, thought better of it, turned and punched Yankee on the nose. Yankee felt a white lightning strike of pain and heard the sickening crunch of bone breaking. Blood squirted everywhere. He went down, but came up swinging. Yankee hit Burns on the jaw, knocking him to the ground. Yankee threw himself on top of Burns, they wrestled, tumbling until Yankee managed to pin Burns down. He pummelled Burns with his fists.

"Stop! Stop! Please stop," Meg cried, tugging on Yankee's arm.

Panting, Yankee got off, and allowed his opponent to get to his feet. "You're lucky the lady is here," Yankee told him, his voice coming in ragged gasps. He spat and wiped the blood from his face with his bruised knuckles.

Eyes full of malice, Burns spat on the ground and wiped his bloodied mouth. His collar was torn and hanging by a thread. His jacket and trousers were covered in dirt, and his hat trodden on. He left it where it lay.

Burns cried, "You're mad! Your whole family is mad." He turned to Yankee shook his fist. "Damn you Brown, rot in hell!" Charged with adrenalin, Burns walked out of the gate slamming it loudly in his wake. He mounted his horse and rode away.

Blood streamed from Yankee's nose and ran into his beard. "Set me nose," he muttered, his mouth full of the coppery taste of blood.

Meg removed her gloves, rolled up her sleeves, and commanded him to sit. Yankee did. Kneeling in front of him, Meg gripped the bone and thrust it back in place.

His eyes swelling black, he flinched but didn't cry out. "Now me good looks are ruined," he gurgled.

Meg looked at him worried, he had cat scratches on his face from Niamh, now a broken nose courtesy of William. Poor Yankee, it had been a tumultuous couple of days.

Meg sighed. "I don't want to take you to meet my employers looking the way you do."

Yankee grunted. "He came off worse," he said with grim satisfaction.

Meg handed him her handkerchief. "Best you stay at the Otago until I've had a talk with the Asterlys."

She noticed William's engagement ring glinting in the grass, he must have dropped it during the fight.

Yankee lightly touched her shoulder. "Give it to someone to give back to him."

"He'd only throw it in the river," Meg told him sadly. "I know," she said. Carrying it gently in her palm she carried it across the graveyard like a golden chalice. When she reached Annie's grave, she dug a small hole under the rosebush and planted the ring, covering it again she patted the soil in place. She turned to Yankee and said, "His heart belonged to Annie, she should have his ring."

Burns did not go to his cottage but rode down to the mine instead. He stormed into the tin shed where Asterly sat at his desk going over the ledgers.

Asterly put down his pen, and leapt to his feet. "Good God man! What happened" Were you robbed?"

"As a matter of fact, I was," Burns replied, his tone crisp.

"Do you need medical attention?" Asterly asked looking around for the mine manager. "There are a couple of men with medical knowledge nearby, I'll summon them."

Ignoring the offer, Burns told him in a condensing tone, "I've come to tell you I'm selling my shares and giving you first option to purchase. If you cannot raise the capital, I will offer them to the other shareholders."

Taken aback, Asterly wheezed, "What?"

"You heard me."

Asterly puffed with pride. "I will have no trouble raising capital but what price are you talking? When do you want to sell?"

"Immediately." Burns went over to the desk and picked up the pen, he scrawled numbers on the top of the ledger. "This is the amount. A bargain I'd say. You can sort it out with my solicitor's office in Dunedin. You have the details."

Asterly stared at the figure in amazement. It was indeed a bargain. He raised his head and nodded, wondering if Burns was of sound mind. "You're being a little hasty, aren't you?"

"Not soon enough," William replied. "I am leaving tomorrow. In the meantime, the cottage can remain empty. I will send someone to take care of my affairs." Then he was gone.

"Well, I never!" Asterly sat heavily on his chair

Meg arrived back at the Asterly homestead at her usual time. The little girls were in the garden chasing butterflies, they waved, and she waved back. She was going to miss them. Her heart heavy she climbed the veranda steps. She found Lady Asterly upstairs in the nursery playing with little Henry.

"I'm happy to see you," Lady Asterly said with a sunny smile. "Henry is cutting teeth." She jiggled Henry on her hip and handed him a rattle to chew. Dribble ran down the baby's chin wetting his bib. "And the girls want my attention. There just isn't enough of me to go around, I don't know what I'd do without you."

Meg prayed for wisdom. "May I speak to you and Lord Asterly in private? It's important."

The seriousness of Meg's tone made Lady Asterly stem her usual rush of words. "Is it about the wedding?"

Meg bit her lip. "Yes."

Lady Asterly wiped Henry's chin. "Can it wait until after dinner?"

Meg sighed "Of course," she said, her stomach churning. She wished she could get it over and done with quickly, drawing things out was excruciating.

"Good. Take Henry for me please," Lady Asterly said passing Henry.

Meg ate very little. After dinner, she got the girls ready for bed while Lady Asterly fed and settled little Henry down for the night. While Lottie went about her chores as quietly as a shadow, Meg washed the girls' hands, scrubbed their feet and knees before helping them dress for bed. Propped up with down pillows behind their heads the two girls listened intently to the story of little Red Riding Hood.

"Does the big bad wolf live around here? Does he live in the outhouse after dark?" Mabel asked, hiding under the covers.

"No, there are no wolves in our canyon," Meg assured them. "No wolves in this country at all."

Amelia looked doubtful. "Can we say our prayers? she asked.

The little girls said their prayers, they asked the Lord to bless and keep them, then they snuggled beneath the covers, their clean cheeks were kissed, and the pretty porcelain lamps extinguished.

Downstairs, Lady Asterly ushered her husband into the sitting room telling him that Margaret needed to speak to them before they retired for the night. Lady Asterly sat on the ottoman and Asterly sat in his favourite armchair. Meg closed the double doors. Asterly steepled his fingers and looked expectantly at Meg.

Meg wondered how to begin. "Have you seen William?" she fished.

"Briefly," Lord Asterly replied shortly. "He plans to sell his shares and leave the area immediately. I take it that you called this meeting to tell us that you are leaving us."

"You're leaving us?!" Lady Asterly blinked like a startled owl. "No! Say it's not true!"

"Did he say why?" Meg asked, ignoring Lady Asterly's outburst.

"No," Lord Asterly said coldly. "He didn't have the manners or good grace to behave in any sort of rational manner."

"Did he say anything at all?" Meg pursued.

"No. In fact, I am not used to being spoken to like that, and told him I would be pleased to buy him out."

"But the wedding?" Lady Asterly said bleakly, her soft grey eyes filling with tears.

"Is off," Margaret replied.

"Off?" They echoed in unison.

"I'm afraid so," Meg admitted.

"Well, that explains his rash behaviour this afternoon," Lord Asterly muttered. He gazed up at Meg with something that almost looked like admiration. "Given his behaviour of late, I think that's the most sensible thing to do." Lord Asterly grunted. "The man is an impatient railroader who won't listen to an ounce of reason. And a Celestial lover to boot."

"But why?" Lady Asterly cried, now on the edge of her seat. "What happened?"

Meg mumbled to the floorboards. "I told William I didn't love him enough to marry him. He's very upset."

Lord Asterly was pragmatic. He shrugged. "Better to know that now than live with regret."

Meg wrung her hands; she took a steadying breath. "Ah, and there's something else."

"Something else," Lady Asterly squeaked, looking as if she might faint.

Meg took a deep breath. "Mr Joseph Brown and I were married on Saturday."

"What!" Lady Asterly cried.

Asterly turned to his wife. "No wonder Burns is upset."

It took a while to tell the tale because Lady Asterly kept interrupting. Meg patiently explained all that had happened since leaving them on Friday. She told them she didn't want to leave their service but she didn't want to live without Yankee either, reiterating that she loved him, and it had been a mistake to accept William's proposal in the first place. However, if they insisted, she leave immediately she'd respect their wishes and go.

Lady Asterly shook her head throughout Meg's story while Lord Asterly listened thoughtfully stroking his goatee beard. Meg stopped and waited for them to respond.

"So, you're leaving us, and the school, which we have helped fund, to go and live on a sheep station with your husband," Lord Asterly summarized.

"Yes, I'm afraid so, but I've spoken to Yan... Joseph and told him I couldn't just abandon you, or the schoolchildren for that matter. If you still want me, I said I would like to wait for end of term for a replacement to be found. Isla Sutton is almost fourteen and she'd make a fine teacher. And it will give you time to find a new governess."

"Well, that's jolly decent of you," Lord Asterly said his voice rich with sarcasm. He got up to light his pipe, decided against it and picked up his snuff box, taking a pinch he inhaled, then shook his head to clear it. "Do your parents know? Do they approve?"

"Yes," Meg said quietly. "Joseph is a family friend."

"And where is your husband now?"

"He's staying at the Otago Hotel. If I'm not welcome anymore, I will go."

"No!" Lady Asterly gasped.

His tone condescending, Asterly said, "Were you planning on leaving tonight?"

"No, but in the light of what's happened I wasn't sure if you would want me here. I asked Joseph to stay there, at the Otago until I had a chance to speak to you."

Asterly smirked, the corner of his mouth lifting, "Did Burns and he have a stoush then? Is that why Burns arrived at the mine all bloodied?"

Meg lowered her eyes. "Yes, I'm afraid so."

305

He slapped his knee. "I think I would rather like to shake the man's hand."

"Charles!" Lady Asterly remonstrated. "Oh Margaret, really! I don't know what to think." She put her hand to her head. "I feel a migraine coming on."

Meg was close to tears. "I know this is difficult for you to accept, but I would like you to be happy for me."

Lady Asterly blanched. "Quite frankly, Margaret, I'm shocked. I have to be truthful, and say I'm disappointed. I have decorated the cake and organized the picnic and everything, all for nothing."

Meg took a step. "There is to be another wedding," she said. "All your work need not be wasted."

Lady Asterly frowned. "Whose?" she asked.

"My brother Jack is engaged. And If it's all right with you, can Jack and Marnie have the picnic you had planned for me?" Meg asked hopefully.

Lord Asterly spluttered in indignation. "You have a nerve!"

"Charles!" Lady Asterly reprimanded. Rising, she stood with her back to the fireplace. Asterly said to Meg, "Lady Catherine and I have a lot to discuss. Leave us now."

Head bowed; Meg left the room. Closing the door, she leant against it, praying their answer would be, yes.

Eliza Jones was surprised when young Yankee Brown asked for a room. He was normally a frequenter of Mary Healey's pub down at Long Gully, and didn't usually venture this far afield. But a patron was a patron, and she happily gave him a room for the night.

"It maybe one night, maybe more," Yankee drawled as Eliza scrawled his name in the book. "And I may have company."

"You can stay as little or as long as you like, and if there's two you'll pay for two," Eliza returned with a grin. "Horse kick you?" she asked, squinting at his blackened face.

"Something like that," he said with a lopsided grin. He gently touched the bridge of his nose, it smarted. He hoped there would not be a bump in his beak to mar his good looks. Still, the pain was worth the pleasure of laying into that pompous ass Burns.

If Meg arrived within the first few hours then things would have gone badly with her employers, they might dismiss her and ask her to leave immediately. Not that he minded, but she would. If that happened, he thought they would spend some time with her family at Long Gully and then he'd take his wife to her new home at Riverstones. Wife, the word still seemed foreign but he was a happy man there was no denying it. He just wished he didn't feel so guilty about Niamh. He knew money wasn't going soothe Niamh's hurt pride but at least it was something, a token penance for the pain he'd inflicted. He didn't expect her to understand, or forgive him, but he had warned Niamh when he proposed, that he was in love with Meg, and his heart still belonged to her. He hoped Dan had paved the way to restitution.

He played a game of billiards with a young Swedish digger but was so distracted he kept constantly checking the door for any sign of Meg that he lost the game. The penalty for losing was to shout the bar but he didn't mind in the least; in fact, he was only too happy to oblige. As the hour grew late Yankee realised his wife wouldn't be coming and he should retire. He surmised things must have gone well with the Asterlys, he was pleased for Meg's sake, but disappointed she wasn't going to be sharing his bed. Thanking Eliza for her custom, he put down his glass of ale and with a touch of his hat, he gave her a nod, and although he was a happily married man, he went to bed alone.

Chapter 15   Whisperings

Yankee tapped the window pane and waited for Meg to notice him. Catching a glimpse of him out of the corner of her eye, Meg put down her chalk.

"Excuse me, children," she said, her cheeks suddenly hot. "Continue on with your work. I won't be long."

Meg stepped around the corner of the school building away from the children's prying eyes.

"Hello wife," Yankee grinned, kissing her cheek. "I missed you last night." He breathed in the soft silkiness of her hair.

She checked his bruised face. His black eyes. "Sorry, I couldn't leave. They were very upset but didn't throw me out."

"They wouldn't have dared," he said, feeling protective.

"Fortunately, Lord Asterly was angrier with William than myself. Unfortunately, Lady Asterly is sympathizing with William, she feels he's been hard done by. But she's a lovely person and doesn't stay cross for long, once she meets you, I'm sure she will like you. I just wish you didn't look so disreputable."

Yankee looked pained. "I'm a fine upstanding citizen and done you a favour my lady." He paused, and looked sad. "Does that mean you won't be returning with me, that I have to wait?"

Meg nodded. "I'm afraid so," she sighed. "I offered to stay until they can find a replacement and a new governess."

"Can I at least be introduced to folks around here as your husband?"

"I can't see why not since the *Wakatip Mail,* and *The Observer* are full of the news of our sensational marriage."

He brightened. "Are they? Are we famous?"

"Darling, we are Infamous."

He grinned. "So now that it's official and the whole world knows, you can stay with me at the Otago tonight all respectable like?"

"I'll try," she whispered. "Perhaps I can persuade the Asterlys to let you stay with me, however I wouldn't like to push It just yet. No, I'll either send word, or come myself."

Molly, with her lovely jumble of golden curls came outside. She stood cross-legged, one hand raised, the other clutching the front of her pinafore.

"What is it, Molly?" Meg asked.

"Excuse me, Miss, I need to go to the outhouse."

"Off you go," Meg replied with a sigh.

"Thank you, Miss." Molly ran towards the outhouse.

"The child has the weakest bladder I've ever seen," Meg said, frowning. Mindful of the time, Meg turned to Yankee. "Now run along, I've got to get back to my class." If she didn't get back inside soon Norman would seize the opportunity to tie Lorna's hair to her chair.

"Run along," he snorted. "Ma'am I'm prepared to get my backside smacked for tardiness by the prettiest teacher in the district. In fact, I think I'd rather enjoy it."

Meg blushed. "I'll see you later," she promised, quickly kissing his cheek. She headed back into the schoolroom.

"Don't worry about me," he said, amused. "I'll find myself something to keep me occupied in the meantime."

Itching to know what happened, Mary couldn't stand it a moment longer. To put herself out of her misery, she thought, the best thing to do was to go up to Asterlys Terrace and find out for herself. Leaving Marnie minding Grace, Mary walked the track to Skippers. It was cool when she started out but after a brisk walk she soon warmed up. Hard at work, diggers toiled away, and she heard the occasional blast of gelignite and saw plumes of smoke in the distance. Even though the land was grey and desolate in places, scarred by the hand of man, the canyon was still beautiful with its azure river threading through the canyon, and tufts of golden tussock and mountain daisies dotting the trails.

Mary did not often allow herself the luxury of having time to think. Time on your hands was a dangerous thing, thinking only made you miss your homeland. She always felt melancholy when she thought of her Ma and Da, hot-tempered and energetic, left behind to rot in the Emerald Isle. To escape poverty, her brothers and sisters scattered to the four winds to seek their fortune leaving their parents behind, because stubborn to the marrow, they refused to leave. Although she regretted her parents' choice, she had to admit, Jim, had made the right choice for their family. They were successful hoteliers and owned a profitable claim; none of that would have been possible if they had stayed in Ireland.

And now Jim was given the honour of helping plan and build the first Catholic school in Queenstown. It meant he was recognized as a decent citizen, and a leader among men. She couldn't help feeling more than a little proud. He still struggled with the call of the drink but so far, as far as she knew he'd managed to keep his promise and not to let a drop pass his lips. And that wasn't easy when he lived in a hotel with plenty of good grog ripe for the picking.

Mary reached the Saddle; it was 3000 feet above sea level. She stopped for a moment to catch her breath and survey the grim surroundings before continuing on. It was hard to believe that a poor Irish farm girl like her had come so far, and achieved so much. Her parents would be proud, she had carved a good life here. Occasionally, she came across fellow countrymen who gave them news, and promised to send some home in return. Family, and keeping them close was important to Mary because her own were so far away.

Right now, two of her children were her chief concern. She was dying to know what happened when the Asterlys, and William, heard the news that Meg was married and was planning to live on a sheep station on the other side of the lake. And, if that wasn't enough to worry about, Jack wanted to marry his whore which meant travelling to the pimple on the bottom of the world to get away from everyone, particularly those who wanted to kill them.

By all the saints, her children would send her to an early grave. Not Dan, fortunately, he gave her no trouble. And since Pat had a stern talking to, she thought he'd behave himself, Heaven help him if he didn't. She'd still not heard from Kitty, she hoped Kitty's silence was for no other reason than because she was too busy to put pen to paper. It occurred to Mary, that Kitty probably would never have mentioned the robbery, if William hadn't told them. Kitty wouldn't have wanted them to worry. Mary would worry regardless; it was part and parcel of being a mother. But any more worry and she might be carted off to the Asylum.

Mary crossed by the lower bridge and then climbed the hill to Asterly Terrace. Her friendship with Catherine was borne out of loneliness and isolation. Female company was a rarity in these parts and to have someone to talk to was a blessing to be cherished, regardless of age, race or religion. It was an unspoken rule that neither would try and convert the other. Mary was still brooding on the twists and turns of life when she reached the Asterlys door. It felt wrong to be entering a Protestant's house. Felt like she was betraying her religion, her Country, and her class when she walked over the threshold. She crossed herself for protection, knocked, and waited for the servant to let her in.

Lottie showed Mary into the sitting room. Seating herself on the ottoman, Mary surveyed the room with open admiration. Everything was clean, tidy and in its proper place. Catherine was nothing like Mary first imagined, Mary had imagined a genteel English rose but although Catherine was a dainty wee thing, she was a hard worker. And when grief left its mark on her soul, she wore it like a badge of honour, strong, noble, unbreakable, it was a quality they both shared.

"Mary!" Catherine breezed in the sitting room; her face ashen. "Oh, my dear! How are you? I can't believe what's happened!" She clasped Mary's hands in hers and squeezed them tight. "What a terrible scandal, you must be beside yourself!" Without waiting for an answer, Catherine dropped Mary's hands and gathering her skirts, sat down beside her.

Overwhelmed by Catherine's rush of words, Mary quietly asked, "Is Meg here?"

"Margaret's not back from the schoolhouse yet but while she's out you and I will have a chance to talk." Catherine inched closer, searching Mary's face for signs of distress.

"I could barely sleep for wondering so I thought I'd best come and see for myself," Mary confessed.

"You have not just come to see Margaret, have you?" Catherine looked stricken. "I've so much to tell you. I've asked Lottie to make us some tea and bring out the ginger biscuits. Say you will stay, won't you?"

Mary grinned. "Could hardly pass up a good ginger biscuit, now could I?"

Catherine sighed, relieved. She stared at Mary, waiting. "Well?"

"I was rather hoping you could tell me. What happened?"

Lady Asterly put a hand to her bosom. "I must say I was shocked."

"Aye, it was a shock to us all, but Jim reckons if Meg's happy the world will be a better place to live in."

"I'm so upset that Margaret will be leaving us. The girls adore her and the pupils at the school will be devastated. But it is William I feel for most," Lady Asterly sighed. "My husband doesn't share my sympathy for him, but he still doesn't think what Margaret did was right either."

Mary nodded. "I absolutely agree, but what's done can't be undone."

"If you believe this man, Joseph, is good for her then I can try to be happy for Margaret. But if she wasn't sure of her feelings it would have been kinder to tell William before now."

"And I agree with you there and all," Mary nodded. Feeling protective, Mary sought to defend Meg. "Meg tried to tell me she was unsure, but I dismissed her feelings telling her she had a dose of cold feet. Turned out I was wrong; she didn't love William enough to marry him. She was in love with Yankee."

"I have to admit Margaret did mention feeling unsure to me, but I didn't take a lot of notice thinking it to be just a case of nerves," Catherine murmured.

"Love is a strange creature, is it not? It does weird and wonderful things to normally sane people. Take me and Jim for example, I have no idea why I love him, just do," Mary shrugged.

Lottie came into the room pushing a trolley laden with china teapot, cups and saucers and a plate of ginger biscuits. The room felt suddenly chill. Mary shuddered.

"Thank you, Lottie, I'll pour," Lady Asterly said, dismissing the girl. The women waited until Lottie left the room before continuing the conversation.

"Have you seen William? How is he?" Mary asked, genuinely concerned.

"Distraught," Catherine replied. Picking up the teapot she poured two cups of tea. "I didn't get to say goodbye but I know he took it very badly indeed. He sold his shares in the mine and left." Catherine shook her head sadly. "I don't know if he abandoned his cottage or if he plans to sell it."

Mary frowned. "I'm sorry to hear that. William was good to our family, and it pains me to know he's hurting."

Catherine passed the biscuits and Mary took one.

"My husband is of the opinion that William was trying to develop the mining company too fast, too soon, and although adventurous in nature Charles is cautious when it comes to business. He prefers to do business with," she hesitated, "people of the same race. Milk?"

"No thanks." Mary took the cup and stirred a spoonful of sugar in. They sat for a moment in silence.

"It's a terrible shame Margaret didn't get to wear the gown Kitty made."

"Now about that," Mary said, putting her cup and saucer down on the side table. "I've been thinking there's no reason to waste perfectly good wedding preparations when there's another bride and groom who wish to tie the knot."

Catherine put down her cup. "Really?" she said, diplomatically neglecting to tell her that Meg had already broached the subject, and Lord Asterly had flatly refused.

Marnie felt a tap her on the shoulder. Her head still muzzy with sleep, she blinked up at Mary in confusion. It took her a moment to remember where she was. She was in the Healeys sitting room and she was supposed to be minding the child.

"Oh," Marnie jumped. "I only sat down for a moment, I must have fallen asleep," she said, flustered. "I'll go check on Grace".

"She's still asleep in her crib," Mary said, her face expressionless.
Marnie breathed a sigh.

"You let the fire die down," Mary accused, putting a couple of pieces of wood on the fire.

"Sorry," Marnie mumbled. She could never do anything right. "Are the men still up at the claim?"

"Best place for them," Mary replied. "For it's you I wish to speak to - alone."

Fully expecting Mary to berate her, telling her how she wasn't fit to be a wife or a mother when she couldn't stay awake for a few hours to look after an infant, or keep the fire going, Marnie fiddled with the lace trim on the cushion.

Mary cocked her head to one side as if studying Marnie then handed her a parcel. "Meg asked me to give this to you." Dumbfounded, Marnie stared at the brown paper tied with string.

"Well, open it." Mary turned her back and added some wood to the fire. "It's a gift," she said.

Marnie untied the string, parting the tissue paper she gasped.

"Does this mean...?" she asked, her voice strangled.

"Wear it well." With her back still to Marnie, Mary calmly said, "I'm a thrifty woman and I don't want to see a beautiful dress and a good celebration go to waste." Mary dusted off her hands. "It's going to be too big and too long, I'm not Kitty but I'm not a bad hand with a needle and thread so I can alter it for you."

"But... but what about the priest?"

"You are Catholic, aren't you?"

"I - I don't rightly remember," Marnie admitted. "My Da wasn't a praying man."

"You are either Catholic or you're about to turn," Mary informed her. "Whether you are or not you will tell Father Whooley you're a Catholic; it will make things simpler."

Marnie couldn't believe her ears. "What about Jack?"

317

"He's definitely Catholic."

"No, I mean what does he think about all this?"

Mary waved a dismissive hand. "He said he wants to marry you. He'll be told what's happening and that's that. But the moment you're wed, you're to leave here, understand? Jack's right, it's too dangerous here for you."

"And Mr Healey?"

"Reckon he's no obstacle," Mary replied. "Best you go try on that dress."

Her heart threatening to burst, Marnie headed for the door to the passage carrying the parcel in her arms

"And Marnie?" Mary called.

She turned, "Yes, Mrs Healey?"

"Don't make me regret my decision, for as God is my witness should you hurt my son, or make his life a misery, I'll come back from the dead and haunt you, understand?"

"Perfectly, Mrs Healey."

Marnie made her way to the bedroom where she fell back on the bed, flabbergasted, "It's a bleedin' miracle!" she exclaimed, waking Grace.

Chapter 16　　　Folly

It was stuffy in the sewing room, and Kitty longed for the smell of sweet grass and fresh mountain air. It had been a tiring day spent hemming, and her neck and shoulders ached. She yawned. Mrs Fitzgerald kindly gave her the nod signalling that she was finished for the day. Her teachers were strict expecting her to be precise in her handiwork, for it was their reputation that would be damaged should the work not be up to standard. Kitty was fortunate, they had recognized her ability early and did not make her do such menial tasks as picking up pins, or running errands. She was in awe of Mademoiselle le Roux who had worked in the best fashion houses in Paris, she wore ostrich feathers in her hats, and her clothes were stylishly cut in the latest fashion. Kitty longed to be just like her.

She felt guilty that she hadn't penned a letter home, but by the end of a twelve-hour day she went back to the boarding house, ate her dinner cold, and fell into bed only to rise early and complete the process again. She found keeping busy helped dull the hurt. William would be married by now and the loss she felt threatened to break her heart. If she didn't write home soon, Ma would be suspicious and come to Dunedin to find out why. She was surprised she hadn't received a letter from Ma or Meg telling her all about the wedding, but as yet no word had arrived. Perhaps they thought it would upset her greatly and things were better left alone, unsaid, or perhaps they were just too busy.

It was warm and the summer evenings long. Thankful that she would be able to enjoy the last few shreds of sunlight, Kitty gathered up her things, packed away her pincushion, scissors and threads into her sewing basket and stacked it neatly on the shelf. Bidding Mrs Fitzgerald goodnight, she stepped outside. The sky looked like a patchwork of silk, glowing orange and pink hues. The dressmaker's shop was becoming dwarfed by the new businesses springing up. Huge architectural buildings were being erected all around the town centre. Dunedin was becoming magnificent and she felt proud of its transformation.

Kitty stopped dead in her tracks. She gasped as she recognized the rider of the black gelding on the other side of the road. Delighted and forgetting the embarrassment of their last meeting, she raced across the road crying, "William! William!" Breathless, she panted, "William!"

"Miss Healey," he returned coldly, and made to move on.

Kitty frowned at the formal use of her name and grasped hold of bridle. "Wait. Tell me, how are my family?"
The look of outrage upon his face shocked and bewildered Kitty. Frightened, she let go the horse's bridle.

"How would I know? Ask Brown," he spat. "I hope I never see them again, Miss Healey."

Mortified, Kitty's jaw dropped. "But why?"

"Don't you think being made a complete fool of, is not enough?" he cried. He stopped and checked himself. He could tell by the puzzled look on Kitty's face she didn't know what he was talking about. "Has word not reached you here yet while all Lake County knows that while I was escorting you here, your sister ran off and married that rogue Brown."

Kitty staggered back, his words hitting her like hammer. "No, no, I didn't," she said softly.

"I cannot bear to show my face in the area. I've sold my shares in the mine, and I never want to see or hear from your family again. Good day to you Miss Healey." Burns urged his horse into a trot. Horse and rider disappeared around the first corner they came to, and were gone.

Kitty stood in the middle of the road staring after him in sheer disbelief. After what they had suffered together, she couldn't believe he the audacity to speak to her so callously. Meg had married Yankee! What she had longed for had come true, but now William hated her whole family and she would never see or hear from him again, he was more lost to her than before. A moment's hope followed by crushing despair. Life was so unfair. Dodging carts and people, Kitty hurried up the road towards the boarding house, she must write home at once.

The diggers didn't usually frequent the hotel in the morning, but to ensure there were no unwanted visitors, a closed sign was placed on the tavern door while the lounge was hurriedly converted into a chapel. Mary kept this room for formal occasions. The wedding was a family affair, the only other guests being the Asterlys, and the room was only just big enough to accommodate them all. So as not to favour one brother over the other, Jack wisely chose Yankee to be his best man. By default, Meg was Marnie's matron of honour.

Father Whooley reverently opened his travelling case. He placed the crucifix in the centre of the mantelpiece with the chalice and tray on either side. The marriage licence, ink pot and pen, were positioned on a small side table in front of one of the carved armchairs. He assumed his position by the fireplace, put his robes, hat and stole on, and began to intone prayers under his breath. Mary lit the candles, and together with the stained-glass kerosene lampshades, they gave a soft romantic glow to the room. There were only two carved chairs and a maroon ottoman with cream embroidered cushions and a small round side table in the room. Since there were not enough chairs to go around, the ladies sat, and the men stood behind them, waiting for the bride.

Mary thought Jack looked shabby. She had hastily put together some of Jim's best clothes for him to wear but to her critical eye he looked underdressed. Jack said he wasn't worried about looking like a dandy. He didn't need a top hat and tails to impress Marnie. With a cheeky smile he said his bride appreciated him in nothing more than his birthday suit.

Mary huffed, and went to check on the girls.

Jack shook Father Whooley's hand. "Thank ye Father, it's so good of you to do this for us, you're an angel in human form."

The good father smiled, amused. "Circumstances have led me to conduct this hasty union rather than divine guidance, however, I believe it to be a fortuitous match. Your bride has a repentant heart, and she will be a fine servant of Christ."

Marnie hadn't been able to bring herself to lie to the priest so she had been hastily baptized and confirmed earlier that morning.

Lady Asterly sat on the ottoman, baby Henry secured on her lap and the little girls on either side of her. Lord Asterly stood as stiff as a flagstaff behind her.

"Charles," Lady Asterly tugged on her husband's sleeve. He bent his head so she could whisper in his ear. "There is no need to look like you have been forced to drink vinegar."

He hissed, "I'm here against my will, and my better judgment to endure a Catholic ceremony. I never promised to enjoy myself and I refuse to pretend I am," he retaliated. Squaring his shoulders, he shoved his hands deep inside his trouser pockets and glared angrily at the rug. Pretending not to notice her husband's obvious displeasure, Lady Asterly smiled serenely.

Pat looked on the scene as if he was being strangled by his own necktie. Did Jack know what he was getting himself into? The silly young cockerel was mad. He had to flee his position, leave his family and a place he'd come to know as home, all for a piece of skirt. A piece of skirt I'm particularly fond of, Pat thought sadly. He was going to miss Marnie's charms, if he'd only known she wanted to be a wife.

Wearing her best dress, Grace cuddled into her uncle Dan's shoulder, wrapping her pudgy arms around his neck she babbled away. He grinned. It would be nice to have children one day but there was such a scarcity of respectable young ladies on the goldfields that he'd be hard pushed to find a suitable one. Niamh sprung to mind, he pushed the thought away, it was highly unlikely she'd want to see his ugly face again, let alone consider him as a prospect. It wasn't his fault Yankee married his sister, but Niamh blamed him for delivering guilt money, and disliked him just because he was a Healey. He wondered if Jack's union would be successful. Could the likes of Marnie live the life of an honest hardworking housewife? He glanced across at Yankee who only had eyes for Meg. Despite the odds, those two seemed to be well suited, so who was he to judge matters of the heart when he'd yet to experience love himself. Seemed to him, that the head had nothing to do with love. People in love seemed to lose all reason.

Meg tied the satin bow in place, stepped back and smiled. "Take a look in the mirror," she instructed.

Marnie stared at her reflection in the long oval mirror. The bruising was gone. A couple of golden ringlets curled becomingly around her heart-shaped face while the rest of her hair was swept up in a bun, adorned by a mother of pearl comb that Mary had given her as a wedding present. She felt resplendent in Meg's gown, with its high collar and tiny rosebuds embroidered on the bodice. A trail of tiny pearl buttons ran the length of her spine and a satin sash nipped in the waist. She looked every inch a lady. Tears pricked her eyes.

Marnie had never believed this would be possible - her married, respectable. Hadn't Father Whooley told her, though her sins were red as scarlet they could be washed as white as snow, and here she stood like a virgin bride, all dressed in white. Perhaps God answered her prayers, for Mary Healey was allowing a soiled dove to marry her son, and that truly was a miracle.

Mary entered the bedroom with a bouquet of red roses tied with white ribbon. "They are from Annie's grave," she said. "That way it's like Annie's at the wedding," she told Marnie, handing the bouquet to her.

Heart flooding with gratitude, Marnie accepted the flowers.

Meg kissed her mother's cheek. "That's special, Ma."

Her eyes misting with tears, Mary abruptly left the room.

"She wishes Annie was here," Meg said sadly. "We all do."

Marnie took a final look in the mirror. She blinked. It was like a dream. A stream of sunshine fell on her through the open window, she looked angelic.

Meg covered Marnie's face with the veil. "Ready?" Meg asked, her hand resting lightly on the doorknob.

Marnie took a shaky breath and nodded. Meg opened the door a crack and they could hear shuffling and murmuring. Mary gave the signal and Yankee took his harmonica out of his coat pocket and played a few bars.

Enchanted, the guests watched as Marnie made her way to the fireplace where her groom waited for her, his face shining with delight.

"Oh," Lady Asterly breathed. "What a beautiful gown."

Mary swallowed back her tears. It would not do for others to see her cry.

Jack gave Marnie's hand a small reassuring squeeze. "You look gorgeous," he told her, his face full of pride. Jack's hand in hers had a calming effect, and she stopped trembling.

Father Whooley smiled at them and began the proceedings starting with Mass before moving onto the wedding ceremony.

Suddenly realising there was no father of the bride, his eyes darted to Jim. "Who gives this woman to this man?" he asked.

"I do," Jim stepped forward then back.

Yankee bent his head and whispered in Meg's ear, "You would have looked beautiful in that dress but then you know, I think you look best in nothing at all."

"Hush or someone will overhear," Meg reprimanded, her face blushing crimson.

Father Whooley enjoyed being with a family he dearly loved and it showed in the way he conducted the service. After mass, he began the wedding ceremony, half expecting Mary to object, he paused when he asked if anyone knew why these two should not be joined in holy matrimony, but to his relief no one uttered a word.

"Do you, Jack Thomas Healey, take this woman, Marnie Eliza Livingstone, to be your lawfully wedded wife, do you solemnly swear to have and to hold for better, for worse, in poverty or riches, in sickness and in health and forsaking all others be faithful only to her, till death do you part?"

"I do," Jack said grinning confidently.

"Do you, Marnie Eliza Livingstone, take Jack Thomas Healey, to be your lawful wedded husband, do you solemnly swear to love him, to honour and obey him, to be faithful only to him, till death do you part?"

Marnie smiled. "I do."

"By the powers vested in me by the church, and under God, I now pronounce you man and wife." Father Whooley patted Jack's shoulder. "Jack, you may kiss your bride." Jack lifted Marnie's veil, took Marnie in his arms and kissed her soundly.
Mary coughed loudly. Breaking away, Jack winked cheekily at his mother.

When it came time to sign the register Marnie was embarrassed that she could only manage an X in the space which was pointed out to her to make her mark.

326

Jack whispered, "Don't worry my love, I'll teach you."

After the witnesses had signed, the small congregation followed the bride and groom down the passageway and out the back door into the dazzling sunshine. Marnie felt like a princess in her beautiful gown. She had decided not to use her parasol. The parasol belonged to a life she wanted to forget, and she did not want to sully her beautiful dress with bad memories.

Lady Asterly leaned in and said to Mary, "Such an elegant young lady, wherever did they meet?"

"The Camp, I believe," Mary answered and swiftly changed the subject. "Let's get cracking with the picnic, shall we?"

The little girls played happily in the long grass, and carted Grace around like she was a doll while baby Henry sat on the edge of the picnic rug plucking daisies with his chubby fingers. Now that the ceremony was over Lord Asterly became more amenable. He seemed a lot happier outside in the open air where it was neither Catholic or Protestant dominion but they were one under God's blue sky and a part of His Kingdom. He even spoke to the priest, not about anything in particular, just the weather, but it was enough to thaw the frostiness between two religions.

Yankee strutted over and introduced himself to Asterly. He began by apologizing, saying he was sorry if he'd made a bad impression.

With a hoot of laughter, Asterly shook Yankee's hand. "I wish I'd had the pleasure of punching Burns myself. I only came today to meet the man that did."

Yankee grinned and with a sweeping bow, said, "At your service, sir."

"Looks like he did some damage to your nose," Asterly remarked.

"Aye, I'm not as pretty as I was, but I think you'll agree, he came off worse."

Asterly tossed his head and laughed.

Jim introduced himself to Asterly. Meg had told him that Asterly didn't drink. Delighted to find a teetotaller in his midst, Jim offered Lord Asterly a plug of tobacco from his pouch. Lord Asterly accepted and together they went and sat on the log, and smoked their pipes as they discussed tunnelling, sluicing, and life on the fields.

Yankee took the opportunity to speak to Lady Asterly. He knelt on the picnic rug and apologized profusely for not coming to see her to introduce himself properly. "I'm sorry we haven't met sooner my lady, but my good wife thought I looked way too disreputable with my broken nose for you to take a liking to me."

"I am very angry with you, young man." Lady Asterly spoke to him like he was a miscreant child. "We will miss Margaret dearly, and my daughters will be devastated, they have grown so close."

"Aye, but it's your duty Ma'am, it is for the good of the Country. Meg has promised to educate me farm hands, those who couldn't read and write. And from what I've heard she's such a fine educator she can teach the sheep."

"Please excuse my husband." Meg said rolling her eyes. "He's always jesting, he belongs in the circus."

Yankee made an elaborate bow.

Ignoring him, Meg complimented Lady Asterly on the cake. "Iced beautifully," she enthused. "And it tasted divine."

"Aye, and with a good dose of brandy to boot," laughed Yankee.

When everyone had eaten their full, Mary began packing things away. She was reasonably happy, as much as one could be when their son married a whore, but all in all the day had gone well. She was rather proud of herself that she'd managed to deflect all Catherine's questions on Marnie's background with cunning and expertise.

Jack suddenly appeared by her elbow. "Thanks Ma," he said kissing her cheek.

She nodded. "Don't make me regret my decision to allow this marriage, will you?"

"I won't Ma," he promised. He dug the toe of his boot into the soil. "So, tonight Ma," he used his best wheedling voice, "may I sleep in the same bed as my wife?"

Mary laughed. "If you're sleeping, you're not the man I thought you were." She left Jack staring after her open-mouthed.

Jack sought out his bride and saw her seated with Meg and Lady Asterly. Yankee was entertaining them retelling some of his favourite tall-tales. Seizing the opportunity, Jack wandered over and interrupted. "Excuse me, Lady Asterly, Mrs Brown, and Mrs Healey," he bowed.

Marnie smiled radiantly at the use of her new name.

"May I steal this gentleman away for a few minutes? I want to bend his ear."

"Excuse us ladies," Yankee bowed. "Looks like young Jack needs some marital advice." He winked at Meg.

Blushing profusely, Meg gave him a warning look he chose to ignore.

As soon as they were out of earshot, Jack's freckled face grew serious. "Tell me about Riverton. Do you think Marnie and me could make a go of it there? Do you think it's far enough away for us to be safe?"

"Aye, it used to be a thriving whaling station but nowadays it's more trade and shipping than anything, flax mills, timber mills and the like, but there's rumours there may be a little gold in Roundhills." Yankee shrugged. "There's always the chance some sailor or other might recognize Marnie, but I reckon it would be far enough away for the brothel keeper not to bother coming after her."

"Reckon there would be work there for me?"

Yankee stroked his beard. "I reckon so. Aye, I reckon there would be plenty of work for a young blacksmith thereabouts."

Jack exhaled "The sooner I get Marnie away from here the better."

"Aye, folks will expect you to go West so it would be wise to go South. No one will think to look there."

Yankee took his pipe out of his trouser pocket, plugged it with tobacco and struck a match. "It's a long way mind." He lit his pipe then blew out the flame. "There's a railway being built but they are only beginning to lay tracks." He drew deeply on his pipe while he waited for Jack's answer. A circle of smoke encased his head like a lazy grey halo.

"Are there drays or wagons at the Kingston end of the lake that we could catch?" Jack asked hopefully.

"Yes, and bullock trains that will cut through the middle from Five Rivers if you can't find any other transport, but any way you choose it's going to be a long journey."

Jack gazed into the distance. Everything was a risk. "How many days' journey d' you reckon?"

"Depends on your mode of transport, whether it's foot, horse, dray or bullock, but well over a week maybe two."

Jack rubbed his chin as he mulled it over. "Twenty miles a day by horse, you reckon?"

Yankee nodded. "Reckon so. The Captain owns and runs the town. He was a good friend of my fathers; God rest his soul. I'll ask Meg to write a letter of introduction that you can give to the Captain," Yankee offered. "I'm sure he'll see you right."

As they walked back to join the others, Yankee said, "Now the Captain, there's a man that married well, married a Maori princess he did and all her land came with her."

"Reckon we cut a raw deal?" Jack laughed.

Yankee chuckled. "Reckon so."

Sandflies were biting at any bit of unprotected flesh they could find, sick of fighting the hungry beggars, Mary decided it was time to head indoors. Lord Asterly loaded his girls in the cart. Catherine held baby Henry firmly on her lap as her husband took the reins. Mary waved them away with a sigh of relief. All in all, the wedding had been a success. Catherine was none the wiser, Jim and Asterly seemed to get on well enough, and Asterly seemed to have accepted Yankee without much hoo-ha. And, none of the children fought. She had been worried Dan and Pat would come to blows. Even the good Father seemed content. The hardest part was yet to come, saying goodbye to Jack would tear her heart in two, and who knew if she'd ever see her darling boy again.

When Mary opened the pub that night no one knew there had been a celebration earlier that day. Mary told Jack to keep his bride well out of sight, hidden away from any prying eyes for fear that someone might recognize her and give them away. Jack was happy to oblige, he wanted his wife to himself. Swooping Marnie off her feet, he carried her over the threshold into Pat's room and kicked the bedroom door closed.

In a benevolent mood, Mary happily poured drinks for the rowdy patrons who stomped their feet in time to the music. A good old fashioned 'knees up' was just the ticket to take her mind of the sadness that was sure to follow. Dan and Pat had been told they would be sleeping rough in the stables as the recently married couples were occupying the other bedrooms, and the rest of the hotel was full. Pat muttered a token protest about being turfed out of his bed, but he was all puff and wind, he didn't really mind, as long as he could drink, he was a happy man. Dan, on the other hand, knew his best bet was to get some shut-eye well before Pat turned in for the night, otherwise his brother's raucous snores would be bound to keep him awake and he might smother his brother out of sheer frustration.

Dan insisted Yankee join him in the bar for a couple of celebratory drinks before retiring. Meg told him to go ahead and enjoy himself, she would sit by the fire and keep her father, and Father Whooley, company.

The boys leaned on the bar determined to whet their whistle, a glass each in their hands.

A concerned look flashed across Yankee's face. "How did it go with Niamh?" he asked Dan. "Did you give her the money?"

"Aye, not well, I'm afraid," Dan confessed. "Best you not visit church for a while."

Yankee sighed and took another sip of his ale. He really did not know what to do to ease his conscience.

Dan jogged his mate's elbow. "I'm glad you're going to keep working on the claim with us. Harry and I would miss yer ugly mug."

Yankee raised his glass in salute. "Aye, and I'd miss yours in all. Besides nothing would get done if I wasn't there to oversee things."

Dan laughed and slapped Yankee's back. "Yankee Brown, you are incorrigible."

"Aye, so I've been told, come on, that's what you like about me, go on admit it," Yankee said, the old twinkle back in his eye.

"Well, I'm happy to see you no longer looking like you wish you were dead. You were more depressing to be around than a three-day-old corpse."

"Aye, I'm a happy man," he chinked bottles with Pat and Dan. "Let's drink to Jack's health and happiness."

Pat chugged back his drink.

Father Whooley, Meg, and Jim sat by the fire long into the night. Jim stretched his long legs and sighed. He looked longingly at the wedding cake but Lady Asterly had laced it with lashings of brandy. He had another piece of shortbread and washed it down with a cup of tea. Jack had married his girl and Mary hadn't lost her temper. All in all, it had been a good day

Father Whooley was pleased Mary hadn't interrupted the ceremony and the young couple were now in a holy union. He was impressed by Marnie's hunger to know more about the scriptures, and the holy sacraments – he was sure she was going to make a fine disciple of Christ.

Meg was happy that Lady Asterly was speaking to her again, and Lord Asterly seemed to have accepted Yankee without fuss. Her one regret was knowing, William, was still smarting. She hoped he'd fall in love again, soon. She wanted him to be happy.

The three companions enjoyed the easiness of the company until their heads began to nod with sleep and they excused themselves and drifted off to their beds.

Grace's crib had been moved into Jim and Mary's room and placed at the foot of their bed. Disorientated, she took a long time to settle but eventually gave up the fight, and was now curled up cat-like in the bottom of the crib with her thumb in her mouth. Jim lay in his bed and watched as Mary pulled the pins from her hair. She picked up her silver hairbrush and impatiently attacked her unruly curls.

"Father Whooley has asked me to return with him to Rees on Monday," Jim casually remarked.

Mary put down the brush. Jim hadn't left the canyon since the day he'd been hit over the head and left for dead.

"What for?" she demanded.

He rolled his eyes. "For the committee meeting, have you forgotten?"

"No, I haven't," she said climbing in beside him and pulling up the covers, "but I've got a bad feeling about it I don't think you should go."

"You don't trust me, admit it," he said crossly. "You think the moment I'm out of your sight, I'll drink."

It was so close to the truth that she didn't dare answer.

"I'm with the priest for God's sake!" he said exasperated.

Mary snapped, "I'm telling you I'm not happy about it, I've a bad feeling in my gut but go if you must." She trimmed the lamp. But there was the unease of words left unsaid.

Jim went to touch her but Mary pulled away.

He softened his voice and patiently explained, "I'm going to a meeting about building a church school hall and I'll be with the priest. What could go wrong?"

She did not reply.

Jim sighed. "You're not happy your youngest son married a whore but there's no reason to let that colour your view on everything."

"I'm not," Mary said crossly.

They were both quiet, aware of each other's breathing, knowing the other wasn't asleep.

"Jack has decided to take his bride South to Riverton, he's leaving the day after tomorrow," Jim told her.

Even though she knew it was coming, the knowledge hit her like the blow from a knife. Jack was going. She was losing her baby boy. She did not reply.

Jim continued, dipping one toe in the water at a time. "All right woman, would you be happier if the good father and I accompany the newlyweds to Rees?" He paused letting the words sink in. "They can catch the steamer across the Lake and make their way South from there. Whoever's after Marnie won't expect her to be in a travelling party, there's safety in numbers." He waited for a response.

It was a long time coming, but finally Mary sighed. "I'll think on it," she promised, relaxing a little.

"Am I not lord and master in my own home?" he grumbled. He didn't need the lamp lit to know she had burnt him with her eyes. Clearly, he was not.

Mary tossed so much she woke Jim.

"Now what's wrong? For Heaven's sake are you still mad about me going to The Camp? It means a lot to me ye know, it's an honour to be asked, but if you're that worked up about it, then I won't go."

"It's not that," Mary replied.

"Then what the blazes is it?" Jim asked impatiently.

"It's knowing that... they are making love in my house."

"Well, it's their wedding night, is it not? Wasn't that what you were doing on yours?"

"It was too long ago to remember."

"Then let me remind you," Jim said his fingers playfully running the length of her thigh. "It will distract you," he reasoned.

"Hush you'll wake the babe."

"Having a babe in the room never worried you before, besides, Grace, can sleep through anything, she'll be fine."

"You're impossible!" Mary pushed his hand away.

"Aye, it's one of my finer qualities. Come here my pretty wee flower and stop wriggling away."

Chapter 17   Blue Moon Rising

Dan left at first light. He was anxious to get back for Harry's sake. Anything could happen, an accident and a man left lying for a couple of days could quickly die of frostbite, or a scratch could easily turn to blood poisoning. Besides, he didn't want to be part of the longwinded goodbyes. It felt too raw. Best remember his brother as he was, not all het up about leaving, and wondering if they would ever see each other again.

Dan rode through the sleepy mountain fog. Blankets of mist hid treacherous chasms and slips that the unfortunate traveller might not realize were there till it was too late, one wrong footfall and they could end up dead at the bottom of a cliff. But Dan knew the tracks like old friends, and he respected the mountain's fickle nature.

Grateful for the solitude, he rode down to Moonlight. After a busy time of family festivity, it was pleasant to hear himself think again. Since Annie's passing it always felt like someone was missing. He felt guilty whenever he thought of Annie. He had been angry with her before she died, and because he didn't get to tell her he was sorry, he prayed for her departed soul, and spoilt Grace as penance.

Things were changing as swiftly as the depth of the river. Meg was married, Kitty in Dunedin, and Jack now married and about to leave for Jacob's River. He sighed. That only left Pat, and they had never been close. Always having wanted a brother he could look up to, Dan felt cheated by Pat's inability to play anything other than the drunken fool. For a little while longer he'd have Yankee's company at the Jewellers shop. With Yankee and Harry by his side, at least one part of his life felt solid, and like family. What if Harry should choose to leave, or worse marry? Change was inevitable, but lately change felt as uncontrollable and devastating as a slip, and Dan didn't like it one little bit. No matter how hard he tried, nothing was ever going to be the same. He might have to start looking to his own future and find a suitable wife. Trouble was, women were scare and good ones even rarer. He chuckled to himself as he remembered Yankee saying, he wondered if Harry had a sister that was passable.

Mary took the priest's breakfast out to his hut. Thanking her for her kindness he told her, he would return later in the day. Mary wished him a safe journey and headed back inside. She couldn't bring herself to call the newlyweds to breakfast.

Soon a tantalizing smell of fried bacon filled the small kitchen. Pat arrived looking worse for wear with purple hollows under his eyes and sunken cheeks. He sat at the table and rested his chin in his hands as if to prop up his sorry head. "I take it Dan's gone."

"Aye, he's like a scared rabbit around goodbyes." Mary deposited a plate of bacon and eggs in front of Pat and went back to the stove. "Eat up before it gets cold, heaven knows when the others will rouse themselves."

Rubbing sleep from his eyes, Pat said, "Yankee's going to stay on at the Jewellers shop until Meg can join him at the station."

Mary shrugged. "Makes sense," she said, wiping her hands on her apron. She glanced at the passage door wishing the others would hurry up. Five more minutes and breakfast would be ruined. She'd get Jim to knock on the door.

Pat picked up his fork and toyed with his bacon. "Reckon I might go over to Fox's for a couple of days."

"You'll be staying put until your father returns from Rees," Mary said bluntly. "Your father, God bless him, has decided to accompany your brother and Marnie to Rees, then they will catch the steamer and go South. Your Da plans to stay for the church committee meeting then return home, you can stay put until then."

Pat frowned. "Why have I got to stay put?" he pouted.

"Because I said so," Mary said, pushing at stray curl with the back of her hand.

Pat's voice softened. "Are you worried, Ma? That he won't come back?" When Mary didn't answer he said, "He's a changed man, there's a different spirit in him these days."
Aye, but the old fear was ever present. She didn't reply.

He understood that fear, it was like rocks in the pit of your stomach. Resigned, Pat shrugged. "All right, if it will make you happy, I'll wait."

Mary put her hand on his shoulder. "It may be the last time you see your brother, make today count."
Pat nodded soberly knowing it likely to be the last time he saw either Jack or Marnie.

Jim arrived at the table. "You mother has agreed to let me out of her sight for a day, I can hardly contain my joy. I can almost smell freedom," he teased.

Mary glared at him. "It's bacon you can smell."

"Aye, I know how you feel," Pat grumbled.

Mary could stand it no longer. "Jim, go and get..."

The hallway door opened.

"Nice of you to finally present yourselves," Mary said as the newlyweds straggled into the room. Jack and Yankee sheepishly joined the men at the table. The girls offered to help but Mary tersely told them, they were too late, she'd done everything already. Looking repentant, they each took a seat as a plate was pushed in front of them.

Yankee received the most generous portion of bacon.

Pat winked at Yankee. "Ma must think you need your strength."

Ignoring him, Mary said, "Pat tells me you're staying on at the Jewellers shop at least for now?"

Yankee grinned. "Yes, that way I can see my wife on the weekends here, at the Welcome Home." Realizing he was being presumptuous, he glanced at Mary and quickly added, "That is, if you don't mind, of course."

"We'd be delighted, wouldn't we, Mary?" Jim smiled.

You're not the one changing the sheets, Mary thought, giving him the gimlet eye.

It was a subdued breakfast. Marnie and Jack were thinking about the journey ahead of them. Yankee and Meg were sad knowing they would have to separate until she was able to join him. Mary's heart was heavy with the knowledge she might never see her youngest son again. And she was worried about Jim going to Rees without her. Could she trust him?

A heavy silence blanketed the room.

"It's like the last supper," Mary said looking at Jim. "Hope there is no Judas in our midst."

Marnie thought the arrow was aimed at her.

Father Whooley returned from visiting his flock up at The Branches to discover not only would he have the pleasure of Jim's company, but the newlyweds as well. They agreed to leave the following morning at dawn. After a light meal Father Whooley retired to his hut to rest. Having dozed off he was startled by the knock.

Sitting on the edge of his cot, he yawned and scrubbed his face. "Come in," he called, expecting to see Jim.

Marnie poked her head in the doorway, surprising him.

He rose and came to the door. "Mrs Healey," he addressed her cordially. "How can I assist?" He thought it wise to step outside. It would not do for anyone to get the wrong impression.

Marnie smiled at the unfamiliarity of her new name. It felt odd but like a new beginning. "May I speak to you, Father?"

"Certainly. Come, let's sit on the old log and have a chat," he said, leading the way. Marnie followed. Once they were seated, she began. "Father, I'm afraid," she confessed.

"Go on," Father Whooley patiently encouraged.

"I'm worried when we get, if we get, to where we are going, that I won't fit in, and that Mrs Healey will be proved right, I won't be an upstanding wife."

"Have you a rosary?" Father Whooley asked.

"Yes." Marnie showed him the rosary Jack had given her. "Jack gave me these."

"It is a precious gift indeed. Each bead represents a prayer. Would you like me to teach you the prayers?"

Marnie stared at the string of beads. "Yes Father," she breathed in wonder.

"Praying is talking to God," he told her.

"I wouldn't know what to say," Marnie said staring at the crucifix in the palm of her hand.

"You can talk to him like you are talking to me but I'll teach you some prayers to keep you safe on your journey."

Tears welled in Marnie's eyes. "Thank you, Father, you're too kind."

"And if you can't remember the prayers, just speak from your heart. The Lord will hear you."

"Kitty gave me some books but I can't read. Please tell me more about Mary Magdalene, Father?"

Father smiled, "Of course." He told Marnie stories from the New Testament, and then said, "Your past is washed away Marnie and all things are made new but it's important for you to learn the ways of Christ. When you get where you are going, there should be a church of sorts where you can worship, and meet with other believers. And, no matter what anyone says, or thinks, God loves you, Marnie, you are precious in his sight."

"Thank you, Father. I'll never forget you."

Chapter 18   Muddy Rivers

Everyone was up at dawn, they stood awkwardly in a small cluster outside the hotel. When Mary wasn't looking, Marnie slipped the Bible and prayer book in Jack's swag, he looked at her surprised.

"So you can teach me to read," she whispered.

Signalling it was time to go, Father Whooley mounted his pony.

Knowing it would be a long time before he saw his family again, if ever, Jack looked as if he was trying to swallow an egg, shell and all. His Adams apple bobbed. "Thank you for everything Ma. We'll do our best to make you proud." Jack kissed his mother's cheek. Mary embraced him, squeezed him tightly before letting go.

"The wedding gown is covered and hanging in the wardrobe," Marnie told Mary.

"Good," Mary nodded. "Kitty will wear it when it's her turn." Mary shrugged off her cloak. "Swap cloaks," she told Marnie, "yours is too easily recognisable." Marnie mumbled her thanks. They exchanged cloaks, then Mary surprised Marnie further by handing her a carpet bag.

"I've packed some things you may need on your journey." Marnie was lost for words. She didn't know how she was ever going to convince Mary of her devotion to Jack, but somehow, someday she'd find a way. She would try to be the best wife she could.

Yankee shook Jack's hand and wished him well. "Use that letter to introduce yourself to the good Captain," Yankee advised, "he'll see you right." Meg threw her arms around Jack and Marnie hugging them in a crushing embrace. Stepping back, she promised once the railway was built, she would visit and bring Kitty with her.

She dabbed her eyes with her handkerchief. Yankee placed a hand on his wife's shoulder and held her close.

He told them he would see his wife safely back to the Asterly homestead. Waving goodbye, they walked up the track their shoulders stooped with sorrow.

Mary kissed Jack's cheek, hugging him tight, she whispered in his ear, "Your father has something for you, see you get it now, won't you."

"As soon as we are settled, we will send word," Jack assured her.

Only too aware of the dangers they faced, Mary said, "Just make sure you get on the boat."

Jim cuddled Grace then handed her back to Mary.

He mounted his horse and blew Mary a kiss. "Don't worry love, I'll be home tonight, or tomorrow. You know how longwinded church meetings and preachers can be."

Used to Jim's teasing, Father Whooley grinned, and flicking the reins he nudged his little chestnut pony on. Jim's horse, Nugget followed, and Jack and Marnie rode Thistle.

Pat and Mary watched until the riders disappeared from sight. Pat put his arm around his mother. "Don't worry Ma, everything's going to be all right, you'll see."

She patted his hand. "I wish I could share your confidence, son," Mary said forlornly as the little travelling party disappeared from view. Kissing the top of Grace's soft, downy head Mary muttered, "All I seem to do lately is say goodbye."

The closer they got to Queenstown the more anxious Marnie became. She kept her head covered, her eyes lowered, and silently recited prayers. Jack was nervous too, but he tried not to show it. When they reached town, they went directly to the wharf. Jack tied Thistle to the nearby hitching post and helped Marnie down. Father Whooley and Jim also dismounted. Jim thanked the good Father and told him he'd see the children on their way and join him at the committee meeting presently. Father Whooley blessed the young couple and wished them god speed, then leading his tired pony he branched off in the direction of the Church.

Jack tipped his hat over his eyes and pulled his coat collar up around his chin, his knuckles were white and tense. Marnie clutched the carpet bag to her chest as they walked to the ticket office. There were so many people on the wharf they were jostled along with a tide of people. They could have easily been pickpocketed and not notice a thing. Row boats and steamers were criss-crossing the lake in an unruly fashion. The wind skimmed the waters causing white peaks.

Marnie caught sight of Daisy strolling along the end pier her hips swinging enticingly, she was wearing her bright red dress with its black lace flounces and lace up stays, the wind lifted and stirred the hem of Daisy's dress showing her fine stockings and buckled boots. Marnie knew Bill would be somewhere close by, keeping watch. She longed to run to Daisy embrace her and say goodbye but could not. Wrapping herself tightly in Mary's cloak, she turned away.

Jim checked the sailing times with the whiskery old sea dog who sat inside the booth smoking a large whalebone pipe. They were in luck; The Royal Mail steamer was about to leave for Kingston.

"Two for Kingston please," Jim said to the man. He took Jim's bank notes and exchanged them for tickets. Jack sagged with relief when Jim handed him the tickets.

"Put out your other hand," Jim told Jack. Jim placed a folded handkerchief in Jack's hand. "A wee wedding present from the tea caddy to help you on your way. Use it wisely and it should go far."

Jack tucked the gold in his trouser pocket. Unable to find the words to thank his Da properly, he hugged him.

Jim sniffed, and muttered something about having an infernal cold. "Don't forget to use the letter Yankee gave you." He rubbed a finger under his nose.

Jack nodded. "Aye, it's a fine letter."

"Do us proud, son," Jim clapped a hand on Jack's shoulder.

"Bill!" Marnie fingers bit into Jack's arm. "We must go now," she hissed.

Jack hooked Marnie's arm in his and together they walked down the gangplank. "Try to act naturally," he whispered, his own pace quickening with each step. After handing the purser the tickets, they went below. Taut as a wire, Marnie sat stiffly, staring straight ahead. The whistle blew three times, and the water churned as the boat pulled away from the wharf. Marnie let out the breath she had been holding, and buried her head into Jack's shoulder, her big blue eyes swimming with tears. For now, they were safe.

Oblivious to the unsavoury man standing behind him, Jim watched the Royal Mail Steamer puffing proudly across the lake sending clouds of thick grey plume into the brilliant meridian sky. The knowledge they were going to have a hard time of it, weighed heavy on his heart. He'd done his best, how they fared from here on in was in God's hands.

He didn't notice the heavyset man follow him to the livery. Jim stabled the horses, removed the hat and jacket from inside the saddlebags and went next door to Bennett's forge. Ducking inside he called out Bennett's name.

The clanging of hammer against anvil stopped. "Aye, I'm Bennett." He regarded Jim suspiciously. The blacksmith ambled towards him. "What can I do for you?" he asked squinting up at him.

Jim stretched forth his hand and shook Bennett's. "Name's Healey. Pleased to make your acquaintance. I believe this belongs to you, Sir," he said giving Bennett his hat and coat. "I owe you a debt of gratitude, thank you kindly for what you did for my son."

"Ah," Bennett said at last, his puffy face brightening. "The lad is safe then. I'm that glad to hear it. I was worried ye know, he was a good lad and it was a crying shame to lose him."

"Aye, he's safe." Jim replied. "They caught the steamer this morning. I'm only sorry for any trouble he's caused you. God bless you for your kindness, I hope someday I can repay the favour."

"Nothing any Christian wouldn't have done," Bennett said.

Jim tipped his hat. "I must be off, got an errand to run and a meeting to attend."

Bennett nodded. "Mind how you go."

Jim hurried down the end of the street to the jewellers. The bell tinkled announcing his arrival. Delighted, the eager jeweller looked up, and welcomed him. On display in the glass cabinet were many trinkets to feast the eyes on, small silver snuff boxes, revolvers, ivory blades, jewellery of many descriptions.

"Name's Healey," Jim said, approaching the counter. "There's an order. Should be waiting for me.'

"Ah yes, Mr Healey, I remember." The jeweller smiled politely. His head bobbed out of view, as he bent down and opened a drawer. "I'm sure you will find it to your satisfaction." The jeweller held the ring gently between his forefinger and thumb and dropped it into Jim's open palm. Jim lifted it to the light to check the engraving. *Love remains.* Yes, it was a replica of the one Mary had pawned for Annie's keep. Back then, she thought he was never returning. He wanted this ring to be special, a reminder that he loved her, and wasn't going anywhere.

"Perfect," he said, reaching for his wallet.

"Bank notes or gold?"

Jim counted out bank notes and placed them on the counter. "That's what I was told it would cost, and that's how much I'm prepared to pay."

Swooping on the notes, the jeweller hid them in a locked drawer. He put the ring inside a small black velvet pouch and drew the strings together. Bowing slightly, he said, "Pleasure doing business with you sir," and handed Jim the pouch.

Jim glanced at the grandfather clock gracing the far wall. He had to hurry. He slipped the pouch into his waistcoat pocket, and left the shop. The shop bell tinkled as he closed the door. Next time, he was in town he'd order a ring for Kitty to replace the one that was stolen. He slipped down Cow Lane and into Camp Street then turned into Church Street. He didn't see the man with the close-set eyes following only a few paces behind.

Out of breath, Jim entered St Marys. Several men sat at the long slab table, near the altar. Father Whooley sat at the head. The good father beckoned Jim to join them at the table, but the seats either side of Father Whooley were taken, unsure, Jim hesitated.

A man greeted him, and introduced himself as Leggett. "Welcome, you must be Healey." He stretched forth his hand. "The Father mentioned you would be joining us."

"Did he?" Jim replied, the corner of his mouth lifting slightly. He wanted to say, cocky beggar, but he didn't know these men, they may think him irreverent, and be offended. God help him, he'd have to be on his best behaviour.

"Take a seat," Leggett said, pointing to a chair next to him. "This is Getty, and that's Jenkins," Leggett introduced Jim to the two men. A small barrel of ale had been brought to the table for the occasion. Jenkins offered Jim a drink.

Jim licked his parched lips. "Tea will do nicely"

Frank Getty whispered to Jenkins. "The man is a teetotaller."

Jenkins whispered back, "We can't have that, can we. Let's have a little fun," his eyes glinted. "Let's put a something special in his tea?"

"Aye, that'll be a laugh, Ned."

The men went outside to boil the billy over an open fire. Jenkins scooped tea leaves into the billy and left the water to steep. He emptied a large slug of vodka from his hip flask into the teapot and gave the brew a stir. Chuckling to himself, with great pomp and ceremony he carried the teapot back into the meeting house. Getty followed, grinning inanely.

Jenkins placed a tankard in front of Jim and the teapot beside it, and took his seat, watching like a cat does a mouse.

Father Whooley called the meeting to order, he began by announcing how much had been raised by the parishioners, then told them how much the diocese in Dunedin would commit. He believed all going well, the building work could start next spring. The timber would be sourced from the Head of the Lake timber mill and the stone from Alexandra.

Jim had been listening to the speeches for some time. He poured himself a tankard of tea, raising it to his mouth swallowed and licked his lips. He frowned, and took another sip just to be sure.

Jenkins nudged Getty's elbow, "Seems to like his tea."

Jim drank the pot.

Marnie kept her hood up and her head lowered They stayed below as the steamer chugged its way across the lake. Jack told those near them that his wife was feeling ill but assured them she'd be fine once they were ashore. To Marnie it seemed an interminable age before they reached the foot of the lake. Disembarking, they walked ungainly down the gangplank, and along the wharf, arm in arm. The water licked the stony shore. Their boots crunched noisily as they walked across the gravel road to The Ship Inn.

Marnie stood awkwardly beside Jack as he signed the register in the names of Mr and Mrs J Healey but the man on the desk never gave them a second glance.

Jack asked if there was any transport headed South to which the hotelier replied there was, but the wagon driver was as unreliable as the weather.

"Both a liar and a drunkard," he grunted contemptuously, depositing their bags in the airless room.

The room had a bed, a wardrobe, and a pitcher stand squeezed into a confined space. The room was so small Marnie thought they would barely be able to pass one another or open the wardrobe without falling on the bed.

"The wagon is scheduled to leave in the morning at 7am. Be ready, here's hoping he will be," the proprietor said briskly, closing the door.

Jack hoped the hotelier was bluffing. They needed to catch a wagon. They weren't far enough away from the Madame's long arm yet.

Marnie unbuttoned her cloak. "I'm stifling hot," she complained. She tugged off her gloves. "I suppose we can't open the windows for fear of being eaten."

"It's not the sandflies you have to watch out for," Jack teased, a wicked glint in his eye. He threw her on the bed. "Now come here, and fulfil your martial duty."

"Oh, you beastly thing," Marnie pretended to fight him off. "You are an absolute terror!"

He grinned. "A terror, am I? Then let me terrify you darling. It's going to be a long wagon journey and I won't get you to myself for well over a week, maybe two, so let me have my wicked way."

"I love you," Marnie said kissing him on the nose.

He laughed. "Oh, that terrifying, am I?"

The meeting was a rowdy one with everyone putting in their pennies worth. The table was littered with differing opinions, but all thought a proper convent school was necessary. Although the supplies weren't going to be too problematic, they agreed with every able-bodied man away at the fields, they would be hard pressed to get labour to build the facility

"Then we may have to roll up our sleeves and volunteer our services," Jim said.

Father Whooley glanced up at Jim, his eyes narrowing in suspicion, he noticed there was a slight slur in Jim's speech. He frowned. Jim's movements seemed exaggerated. Had Jim been drinking? Had he planned it that way?

The meeting drew to a close, and one, by one, the men left the church. Concerned, Father Whooley suggested Jim stays the night at his abode rather than venture up the canyon alone when dusk was approaching. But Jim steadfastly refused, saying that Mary would need him at the hotel. He was on dangerous ground; it was slippery beneath his feet. If he stayed a moment longer, he would find a myriad of drinking holes to visit. Disappointed and unable to persuade Jim to stay, Father Whooley said his goodbyes.

The air was beginning to chill, but the light was still good, and if he was lucky, he would make it back to the hotel before dark. By then he'd be stone cold sober, and Mary none the wiser. He hadn't drunk a drop for nigh over a year and now he could feel the liquor charging through his veins, triggering the age-old thirst. Jim clutched the pouch in his waistcoat pocket like an anchor. If he didn't get back to the canyon soon, he'd go to a tavern and drink till he could not stand. He weaved his way to the stables, picked up the horses and set off for home. Riding Nugget, he led Thistle alongside, he had a strange feeling he was being watched, he twisted in the saddle but unable to see anything. He told himself he was being ridiculous, but his skin prickled none-the-less. He batted the notion away thinking Mary's superstitious nonsense was making him edgy.

Jim redistributed his weight in the saddle, grateful the horses knew the way home, he let them have their heads. There was a lonely stretch of road before the junction and he could see the jagged line of grog shanties in the distance marking the site of Arthurs Point. Jim licked his lips, he had the taste all right, he must get home before he succumbed to the pull of the grog.

The wharf had been too crowded to get to them. Someone had to pay, and that tall, gaunt man was as good as any. Bill felt under his jacket for the leather that sheathed his weapon and followed the man, first to the livery, then to Bennett's forge which solidified his suspicion that they were in it together. He followed the man, went to the jewellers and then to the church and waited outside for his chance. He waited three stinking hours in the hot sun. Finally, the man came out, but there still were too many people around for him to strike, so he followed, biding his time.

After collecting his horses, the man sat awkwardly in the saddle. Drunk, Bill thought, pleased. He ducked into the livery and paid the stable-hand for a hack. He asked where the man who owned the two horses came from. The stable hand thought nothing of telling Bill the man was Healey, of Long Gully.

Bill took a shortcut and reached outskirts before Jim. He hid in the flax and waited, his fingers twitching in anticipation. Should he beat the bastard, or stab him? He heard the sound of the horse's hooves approaching. Even in the growing gloom the rider was recognizable, sitting a little slouched and lopsided in the saddle and leading a second pony. Bill's fingers curled around his baton as the rider passed him. He would need to move fast or the opportunity would be lost. Batten in his raised hand, he dug his heels into his horse's flanks and charged out of the bushes.

Healey twisted in the saddle trying to get a look at his attacker, but dulled by drink, his reactions were slow. Bill struck from behind, levelling a blow that unseated the rider. The horses whinnied and reared. As he fell, Healey let go of the reins, and somehow had the presence of mind to pull his feet free from the stirrups so he wasn't dragged. But he landed poorly and tumbled down the into the shallow, icy creek. Losing consciousness, Healey lay face up in the creek, the water softly burbling around his ears.

Healey's horses didn't stray but stood nobly nearby nibbling at the grass, waiting for their fallen master to rise. Bill peered over the bank at his victim's inert body resting in the artery of water that traversed the heart of Queenstown.

He may not have captured Marnie but someone paid the price, and he didn't even need to dirty his knife. If the knock-on Healey's head didn't kill him, the ice-cold water would. He would tell Madame that he'd killed Jack Healey, one Healey was as good as another, and she'd be none the wiser. Bill rode back to town a happy man. Justice was served a Healey was dead.

Darkness fell and the temperature plummeted. Jim lay unconscious in the creek all night. He was found in the morning by a passing digger, but by then the frostbite had taken hold, and his fingers were turning black.

Chapter 19   The Crying Wind

Mary was convinced something was wrong. She woke up in a slick of sweat. When morning dawned, she insisted Pat go down to Rees. He told her she was overreacting but secretly, he too, feared the worst. Jim had deserted them once before, what was to stop him doing it again? Pat rode down to Queenstown his stomach curdling with worry. He didn't visit his usual haunts but instead went straight to the priest's house and hammered on the good Father's door. The housekeeper opened it and let him in. He didn't offer his name, just told her it was urgent, he needed to see the priest. Niamh told him the Father was a busy man and to wait while she let the Father know he was there. A few moments passed before Father Whooley entered the room, he stood before Pat, his placid face gaunt.

"I'm afraid I've got bad news," he told Pat. "Jim fell from his horse and spent the night in the creek. He is in the infirmary suffering from the effects of frostbite."

Taken aback, Pat asked, "What? How?"

Reluctant to say, Father Whooley used discretion. "A digger saw the horses grazing on the roadside and went to take a closer look. He found Jim in the water. He managed to pull Jim out, and with a struggle he hefted him over his horse's back, then riding the other horse, he took Jim straight to the infirmary. Knowing Jim and I were friends, Doctor Martin sent Jim's horses here for me to stable until you came..." Father Whooley trailed off, his voice paper thin.

A ripple of fear travelled the length of Pat's spine. "Is he?"

Father Whooley shook his head sorrowfully. "He's alive, but in a bad way. He suffered a nasty knock to the head, and a couple of his ribs were broken in the fall. The doctor is doing his best."

"Why didn't you send for..." Pat was having difficulty understanding.

"I wanted to see him before I raised the alarm."

"And?" Pat pressed.

Father Whooley hung his head. "He's not good, I'm afraid."

Pat gulped. There was not a moment to spare, he must see his father. "Send word to Dan. Tell him to meet me at the infirmary."

"This very minute," Father Whooley promised.

When Pat arrived at Doctor Martins infirmary, the doctor's wife looked at Pat with pity in her eyes, and he resented her for it. She led the way to the surgery, opened the door for him, then left without a word. Doc, was bent over Da, his stethoscope on his chest. Pat froze. The doctor motioned to him to come in. Pat stood looking down at his father, unable to believe his eyes, Da looked shrunken, his tanned skin was white, hard and rubbery to the touch, and his fingertips black. Pat wished his family were there to keep vigil, he needed them to pray for a miracle, for the saints wouldn't listen to a mocker like him.

Dan was uneasy. He had a strange sense of foreboding and didn't know why. He came inside out of the hot February sun, and shut the door hoping to block out the baking heat. The warm wind sang a mournful tune as it whistled under the door. The hut smelt of dirt, smoke and sweat, but it felt empty without Yankee and Harry there. He sat wearily down on an upturned crate and mopped his brow with his kerchief.

His mates had gone to stock up on stores and took Tu with them. If they got waylaid in a tavern or two, they wouldn't be back until dusk. Any chance for a bit of solitude was usually to be enjoyed but for some reason, Dan felt lonely. He missed Yankee and Harry's light-hearted banter and Tu curling up at his feet, his expectant dark eyes ready and watching.

Dan decided to lift his melancholy by singing an old Irish sea shanty. He had a voice like gravel but there was no one's ears to bruise. He'd sung the first few bars when there was a pounding on the hut door. Dan picked up the axe handle and walked stealthily to the door, he opened it a crack. A scruffy boy stood there, panting, his cheeks red from running.

Dan frowned, he put the axe handle aside and stepped outside. "What do you want?" he demanded.

"Are you Dan...Dan...Healey?" the boy puffed.

Guarded, Dan cautiously asked, "Who wants to know?"

The boy wheezed. "Is yer father... Jim Healey of Long Gully?"

"Aye. Why?"

"Better come quick, Father Whooley says to tell you - yer father has had an accident. He's at the infirmary."

Wasting no time, Dan saddled his horse. He pulled the lad up behind him and told him to hold tight as they rode into Queenstown. He dropped the lad outside the newspaper office, gave him a shilling, then rode over to Doctor Martin's Infirmary. He knocked loudly on the door.

Mrs Martin opened the door. She had a sharp nose and quick lips. "There's sick people here who need to rest, and you knocking like the blazes is enough to disturb the whole street," she grumbled.

Dan apologized. Hat in his hand, he respectfully asked to see James Healey.

Her face changed, and there looked to be something like sympathy in her eyes. "Follow me," she said, leading the way.

She opened the door and Dan could see Doc Martin standing over Da, his brow deeply furrowed. Da lay swaddled in blankets like a babe, and Pat was kneeling beside the bed, praying. He looked up at Dan with red-rimmed eyes.

"I'll leave you be," Mrs Martin said quietly. Her retreating footsteps echoed hollowly as she walked down the hall.

Dan stared down at his father's waxen face in horror. Shocked, he asked, "What happened?"

Pat told him the story. "It's not the bump on his head what's going to kill him," Pat added bleakly. "Doc reckons he'd be all right if it was just that, it's the exposure that is shutting down his organs."

Dan fell on his knees, crossed himself and made all kinds of rash vows to God.

They listened to Jim's ragged breathing, it seemed like the only sound in the room. Knowing he was beat, Doctor Martin gently laid his hand on Pat's shoulder. "Take him home, son, we don't expect him to last the night. The Father's been and already given him the last rites."

Pat crumbled, his heart breaking like soft slate. God, oh God no. There were bridges that needed mending. Words that needed to be said. He needed time, now it was too late.

"Don't leave me again, Da," Pat whispered brokenly in his father's ear.

Save for the slight rise and fall of his chest, Jim did not respond.

Dan's voice cracked as he said, "We are going to have to take him home to Ma."

Pat nodded, dashing away his useless tears.

Practical by nature, Dan said, "I'll ask the newspaper boy to find Yankee. Meg will need him."

"Aye," Pat agreed.

Dan rode to Bennett's forge to see if he could borrow a wagon or suchlike. Shocked by the tragedy, Bennett readily agreed, and gave them the use of his wagon. Hitching Thistle and Nugget to the cart, Dan thanked him profusely and went back to the infirmary where he paid the bill in full. The doctor's face was grim as the boys carried Jim out using an old blanket as a stretcher. They loaded him gently into the wagon. Jim was white, stiff and cold and his fingertips were black with the frostbite. Eyes sunken in his skull, Jim's breath came and went in short ragged gasps.

Dan felt like he had eaten rocks and they were stuck in his gullet. "Do you think we'll make it in time?" he asked the doctor.

Doc looked at him with apologetic eyes.

"Pray we do." Pat flicked the reins.

The wind was against them, taunting them. Pat drove the cart along the trail while Dan followed on Goldie. Pat pointed out the spot where Jim was found.

Dan scratched his head. "It's hard to believe. Da is such a good rider."

"Nugget must've been spooked by a weasel or a rabbit," reasoned Pat.

They rode the packer's trail and in parts where the track was wider, Dan rode alongside, hoping to see the slight rise and fall of his father's chest. Pat stopped frequently to check Jim 's condition.

They were opposite Castle Rock when Pat pulled up to take another look. He climbed over the back and put an ear to Jim's chest. There was no movement, not a sound, not even a gurgle. The grief-stricken look of horror on Pat's face told Dan the worst. Pat drew the sign of the cross as tears flowed down his ruddy cheeks and into his scruffy beard. He covered his father's face with a blanket, and Jumped down off the wagon. There was no longer any need to hurry. Pat sat on a patch of tussock and stared bleakly into space. Sniffing, Dan wiped his nose with the back of his sleeve and sat beside his brother.

Distraught, the brothers sat side by side by the track, a long time, not speaking, the weight of their grief almost threatening to break them. They had lost their father, again.

Rising, Dan said, "Come on, let's take him home to Ma."
And the wind cried.

Mary checked the washing, there was a warm wind like a whispering ghoul coming up the gully, the washing would be dry in no time. She went back inside and attended to her chores. Anxiety was eating her alive, she wished Pat would hurry up and return. Although she loved the pub, without her children, it felt empty.

Thank heavens for little Grace. Mary went to check on the child. The babe was still sound asleep in her crib. Mary sighed, and closed the door carefully.

Then she heard the sound of horse and cart rumbling in the distance. Mary thought it must be Dusty and went out to the porch to investigate. When she spied her horses pulling an unfamiliar cart and Pat driving them, and Dan riding behind like they were in some sort of procession, her chest tightened.

Mary steadied herself placing one hand on the veranda post, she waited until the cart pulled up outside the hotel, and Pat applied the brake. Her eyes flitted between her sons but neither met her gaze. She held her breath, and gripped the post. Her mouth dry.

His tread heavy on the veranda steps, Pat soberly removed his hat and placed it over his heart.
Mary's eyes flicked past him to the cart where Dan stood, his head bowed.

"Where's your Da?" she called to Dan, her voice suddenly shrill.

Pat mumbled to his hob-nailed boots. "We brought him home to you, Ma."

Mary flew down the steps. Lifting her skirts, she clambered aboard the cart and removed the blanket. Jim's lifeless eyes stared up at her.

"No!" A long keening wail pierced the air as she fell on Jim's body. His skin was the colour of candle wax, cold and rubbery to the touch. She shook him.
Dan didn't try to restrain her but waited until she went limp.

"Ma," Dan began quietly, "there is something in his jacket pocket. A pouch of some kind."

Mary dug her hand into Jim's pocket. She drew out the small velvet pouch, she opened it found the gold band and read the inscription, *love remains*. Mary choked back and sob and clutched it to her heart.

Beaten, Pat sat heavily on the front porch steps. There were so many words to say and now he'd not have the chance. Why had he thrown opportunities away to the four winds as if time did not matter. They were dust, time was short, and he'd wasted it.

Head bowed, Dan stood alongside the cart, leaning against it for support while his mother grieved. His dream of having a united family was as far away as the moon from the sun. He'd hoped that he could keep family close, so he'd feel like there was an anchor in the stormy sea of life, and now with Da gone, that hope was lost.

For her sons' sake, Mary composed herself, wiped away her tears and covered Jim. Climbing down, she instructed the pair to carry Jim to her room. Struggling with Jim's leaden weight, the boys carried him up the steps, through the house and laid him on the bed. They stood like statues while Mary stopped the hands of the clock, and pulled the curtains. They watched while she bathed her husband's body, put pennies on his eyelids to keep them closed, rolled up a small towel and placed it under his chin. Kissing his bluish-grey cheek, she combed his hair and beard. Then arms tightly wrapped around her body as if holding in the hurt, Mary sat down in the rocking chair beside her husband's lifeless body and scolded him.

"Blame fool, I told you not to go but you wouldn't listen," she muttered darkly, a rush of anger igniting passion.

Pat and Dan watched their mother's emotions change as rapidly as the river in flood. Always strong, always capable, she looked tiny and fragile, like she was made of eggshells. They waited for her to tell them what to do.

Mary told Dan to put a sign on the door. For the second night in living memory the hotel was closed for the evening. The first was the night Annie died. Now Jim had gone to join her, and baby, William, the stillborn child, and the unborn of their union.

Grace woke up and let out a loud cry reminding them she was still there. Dan went and got Grace out of her crib and held her close as if he was frightened of losing her as well. When he returned to his mother's bedroom, he put Grace down. As if sensing something, Grace waddled to the deathbed and kissed her grandfather's lifeless hand. Dan and Pat felt like soldiers without weapons, helpless, the battle lost.

Fretting, Pat wished Meg would hurry up, Ma needed her there. Where the hell was she?

Needing something to do, Dan chopped wood for the fire, brought the washing in, he gave Grace a bread and butter sandwich, and made them all a pot of tea. He brought more chairs into the room and they sat in silence, their thoughts clamouring to be heard.

Time wore on, and the candles burned low and guttered in their holders. Mary threw her sons blankets, they would hold vigil that night, they would sleep in the same room and keep Jim company.

"Ma," Pat began, "the funeral…"

Mary lifted her head. "I want him to have a good coffin, there's money enough for it."

"There will be no way to get word to Jack," Dan said glumly.

Mary nodded. "I will send a letter to the Riverton Post Office - they will call in there eventually."

"What about Kitty?" Dan asked, his voice hoarse.

"I'll send a telegram." Mary wished she had never let Kitty go. She needed her here now like never before.

Dan and Pat felt the unsaid words. Their mother needed comforting; she may look like she was made of iron but the little woman had clay feet.

Pat thought seeing his Ma angry was far preferable than seeing her sad. He shook his head vigorously. "Can't believe Da died of the bloody frostbite," he said, dully.

Mary had the presence of mind to change Grace, and give her a bottle but she didn't make dinner, and no one else felt like eating. Mary allowed Grace to curl up beside her grandfather on the bed, the sight reminded Mary of the night Annie died and grief washed over her in rolling black waves.

The candles had been replaced and the new ones almost burnt to stubs by the time Meg and Yankee arrived. It was a risk them travelling in the dark, but one they were willing to take. His arm about her shoulder, Yankee brought Meg in to see her father. Meg fell on her knees and wept. Crossing herself, Meg offered prayers for the dead. She held her father's cold hand in hers and kissed it. Her long brown hair came loose and hung down her shoulders. Yankee knelt beside her, his own heart breaking to see her so devastated.

Pat had hoped Meg would bring comfort but he could see Meg was too distraught to offer any.

Finally, Meg lifted her head. "How?"

Pat sighed. "The priest said he was thrown from his horse, hit his head when he landed, rolled down the bank and spent the night unconscious, face up in Horne Creek. He didn't drown, it was the cold that killed him. He didn't regain consciousness after the fall." Dan and Pat carried in the small table. Pat poured five glasses of whisky and placed the unstopped bottle in the middle.

Pat picked up his glass. "To James Patrick Healey."
They raised their glasses and drank. Meg coughed as the amber liquid burnt her throat.

Pat refilled his glass. "Now what, Ma?"

"Life goes on," Mary shrugged. But life without Jim would be hard and the claim would be worked out eventually.

Pat ran his fingers through his scruffy beard. "I will continue to work the claim." He reached across and patted his mother's hand. "We will be fine, you'll see, Ma."
Mary weighed his words, doubtfully. Could she count on him? Pat was unreliable. Dan was the responsible one, but Dan had his own life to live, it would be wrong of her to ask him to give up his life to help her. She'd run the hotel on her own before and she could again. But she was worried, with miners disappearing in droves, how long the hotel would remain profitable? And how long before the gold ran out?

Meg glanced sideways at Yankee. "Ma, do you want me to stay?" she offered.

"Nothing needs to change, I can manage," she assured them. "I'll be lucky if the pub can find enough patronage to keep me busy."

No one dared to challenge Mary, a fighting spirit was easier to bear than a broken one.

The clock struck midnight. The candles flickered and went out.

Chapter 20   Shadows

As a sign of respect, the mining community afforded Mary Healey privacy and didn't visit the hotel for three days, but every time they opened the front door there was jars of pickles or jams, bread and honey left by those wanting to express their remorse. Mary spent that time cocooned within herself in some sort of trance. Endless chores forgotten, she sat numbly besides Jim staring into space. With the school being looked after by a child's mother until her return, Meg was pleased to be able to stay at the hotel and busy herself with the cooking, cleaning, and minding Grace.

For three days the family sat with the corpse telling stories, singing songs, lamenting their loss and drinking toasts to their good father's memory. Harry came to help with the burial. Backs bent with grief, shovels on their shoulders, the four men trudged the path to the Skippers cemetery to dig the grave.

Catherine Asterly never left the terraces without her husband but when she heard the tragic news of Jim Healey's passing, she asked Lord Asterly and Lottie to mind the children while she rode to Long Gully. She found Mary on the front porch staring absently into space. Mary woke when Catherine tethered her horse to the hotel's hitching post. Without a word, Catherine climbed the hotel's front steps, and sitting beside Mary she simply held her hand.

Tears pricking her bloodshot eyes, Mary said, "I told him not to go. I told him I had a bad feeling but the pig-headed fool wouldn't listen," she said bitterly.

Catherine squeezed Mary's hand a little tighter, and nodded.

"I thought it hurt when I lost him the first time, but having him back and learning to love again then lose him hurts worse, and this time it's forever." Mary gritted her teeth. "And I'm angry, angry with him for leaving me and angry with God for taking him."

Having suffered loss herself, Catherine knew that this was a time for listening.

"I hope you understand," Mary said her throat tight with dried tears.

"I understand," Catherine assured her.

They sat there a long while.

Finally, Mary roused herself. "I can't leave everything up to Meg, I have to be about my business."

Promising to visit shortly, Catherine embraced Mary, said her goodbyes and rode home.

Jim Healey's funeral was held at the Skippers Cemetery. Out of respect for his widow, miners from all over came to farewell him. Jim was buried beside his beloved Annie. Mary instructed the telegram office to wire Kitty and the Riverton Post Office on the day of the funeral. She thought it wrong to bury him without all his offspring present but it couldn't be helped. They would have to make do with their last memories, and hold those dear in their hearts

The weather was inclement. The sky, the colour of slate. Catherine weaved her way through the mourners and passed Mary a black veil to wear. Mary thanked her and donned the veil she didn't want anyone to see her feeling weak. Dressed all in black, Mary felt like a crone, her heart in tatters and her life was in ashes.

Jim would have expected her to be strong, and carry on, and she wasn't about to disappoint him now. Numb, Mary stood tall with her head erect during the eulogy while Meg quietly shook with sobs beside her. Mary fingered the gold band on her hand, *love remains*, a message from the grave. He was dead but their love would live on.

Holding the ropes tight, with Pat and Harry on one side, and Yankee and Dan on the other, they carefully lowered Jim's body into the freshly dug earth.

Fighting back tears, Father Whooley said, "Ashes to ashes, dust to dust..."

Mary stepped forward and picked up a handful of soil. She let it fall loosely through her fingertips onto the coffin.

Pat threw the first shovelful of dirt onto the coffin then Dan. Yankee and Harry followed suit. The men filled in the grave while Mary silently watched, her body as taut as wire. When the last shovel of dirt was patted into place, Mary placed a smooth round quartz stone on the head of the grave, and made the sign of the cross, then walked away. It started to spit. Meg raised her eyes, to the skies, were the angels crying? Meg added her stone, then one by one, the others placed their stones building a small cairn as a memorial. The miners followed behind Mary; a slow solemn procession made their way back to Long Gully. Harry poured water from a flask on his hands, and ran his wet hands over his head to wash away the spirits. Dan, Harry and Yankee fell into step at the rear of the procession but Pat remained.

"I'll catch up," he told them.

Pat put down his shovel and sat cross-legged on the grass. He patted the fresh soil as tears slid freely down his face and mingled with the rain. Angry, Pat raised his fist to fight an unseen power. Why not me, God, why not take me? he demanded. Why couldn't he save the others by sacrificing himself?

"You left me again, Da. This time for good. I never got to tell you I love you. It's not fair to lose you twice. How could you leave me again, you old bugger?" Pat looked up at the heaven's half expecting a reply but the wind pushed clouds across the broody sky and ignored his broken cries. Pat sniffed and dried his eyes. "Let's have one last drink together old man." Pat took out his hip flask, took a good slug and poured the rest on his father's grave. "I solemnly promise to take good care of Ma for you, Da. I can't do more than that." He sighed stood up, wiped his hands on his moleskins, turned and headed for home.

Harry didn't stay the night; he went straight back down to Moonlight. Father Whooley didn't join them but instead sat in his hut, blaming himself for Jim's death. It was his duty as a Priest to keep what was said in the confessional a secret. He had been so devastated when he realised Jim was drunk, he'd wanted to shake him, a year of hard work destroyed in a day. But yesterday he discovered the truth. Fearing he'd been the cause of Jim Healey's death and seeking absolution, Jenkins had come into the confessional and admitted he and Getty had laced Jim's tea with alcohol.

"Must have made him unsteady in his seat," muttered Jenkins.

He had been so angry he had wanted to slide the screen across, grab Jenkins by the throat and bash his head against the confessional wall. Instead, he thanked God that Jim had not willingly sought alcohol, and Mary needn't know her husband was drunk when he fell from his horse. But God help him, his soul was still troubled by the knowledge if he hadn't asked Jim to be a part of the church committee, Jim would still be alive.

That night anyone who wished to toast Jim Healey's memory was welcome at Long Gully. The hotel was fit to bust with miners, who although they hadn't drunk with Jim, said they admired and respected the man just the same. They told stories and sang ballads until late.

One old timer said, "Your husband was afraid you'd give him a right roasting when he got home, so he thought he'd save you the trouble, and turned up his toes and let Saint Peter do it for yer instead." Knowing his jest to be kindly meant Mary forced herself to smile. There was dancing and singing, toasting and speeches all around her but she felt hollow. He was gone and nothing anyone did, or said, would ever bring him back.

Hoping that exhaustion would help her sleep, Mary danced, poured drinks, wiped and cleaned glasses. The miners stayed on to the wee hours, finally the last patron left, shuffling sadly away into the yawning night. Alone in her bed, feeling spent, Mary thought how life had gone full circle, eighteen months ago she lay in this same bed wondering if Jim Healey were alive and wishing him dead. And now, now, he was dead, she wanted him alive, lying next to her. Hugging the pillow tight, she cursed him and wept.

Chapter 21   Valley

Kitty had just returned from Mass and was about to turn the key in the boarding house door, when a young dark-haired boy in uniform suddenly appeared.

"I have a telegram for Miss Katherine Healey. Does Miss Healey reside here?" he asked politely, tipping his hat.

"A telegram?" Kitty repeated, with a sinking feeling in the pit of her stomach. She frowned. "I'm Katherine Healey," she said taking the envelope from him.

Expectantly, he waited, hand out.

Fishing in her bag, she placed a coin in his palm.

"Good day to you, Miss." The boy bowed.

"And you."

Kitty closed the door. Hands trembling, she tore the telegram open. DA FELL FROM HORSE STOP BURIED 4 FEB STOP STAY STOP.

The telegram fluttered from her hands. Kitty stared at the offending scrap of paper on the tiled floor. What day was it? Today was ...too late, the funeral had already taken place. Weak at the knees, Kitty sat on the stairs, her mind whirling with shock. Da was an excellent horseman but then she supposed even they fell. She should have been there with her family to mourn her father's passing, and to comfort her mother. They needed her, and she needed them. If she had stayed at Long Gully then maybe this wouldn't have happened. It was selfish and wrong to go to Dunedin. But she couldn't go back home. To go home would be to admit defeat. She'd fought to get here, and worked hard to prove herself worthy. She was being noticed and been given better jobs, and making a name for herself.

After what seemed an age, Kitty plucked the telegram off the floor. The telegram said STAY, Ma had said that on purpose. Kitty was surprised her mother didn't insist she come home immediately. She must write. Clutching the telegram tightly to her chest, she wrapped her arms protectively about herself, and climbed the stairs to her room. Da dead, she could scarce believe it. She took off bonnet and gloves and placed them on the duchess, she stared down at the dent on her finger where her ring used to be. First, she'd lost his ring, now him. Gentleness and mercy, Kitty snorted, life was not gentle or merciful, life was perilous and uncertain. She curled up on her bed and cried herself to sleep.

A week passed. Kitty liked the distraction of work; it kept her too busy to mourn. Kitty knocked at the side entrance of the grand home named Pembroke House. She stated her name and business to a maid and was waved to a pew in the cloak room where she sat, her sewing basket on her lap, waiting to be called. Awed by such grandeur, Kitty's eyes took in every minute detail; it was everything she could do to stop herself from gaping. It was rumoured that the house boasted thirty-seven rooms but apart from the hallways she would possibly only see only one or two. The housemaid, Miss Grant, a thin-faced, haughty looking woman with a severe part and tight bun, came to get her and to show her into the sitting room.

Miss Grant announced Kitty's arrival in a clear, crisp voice. "Miss Healey from the dressmakers to see you, Miss."

Kitty's heart stopped. She clutched the handle on her sewing basket tightly. Beside Miss Georgiana sat Mr William Burns.

"Kitty!" William exclaimed, leaping up.

Georgiana's head turned sharply. "You know this young woman?" she asked, arching an inquisitive black eyebrow.

Flustered, he corrected himself. "Miss Healey. Yes, I do."

Ignoring him, Kitty ducked her head. "Miss."

"Thank you, Grant, that will be all. I will call you when I need you," Miss Georgiana dismissed her servant.

Nodding stiffly, Miss Grant closed the double doors behind her.

Miss Georgiana glanced from Kitty to William and back again. "How do you know one another?" she asked, watching Kitty curiously with her cat-like eyes.

Kitty kept her eyes lowered and waited for William to explain.

"We met in Skippers. I am acquainted with Miss Healey's family." He sat down again.

"Really? You didn't mention being in Skippers Canyon to me," she said.

Bet he also didn't mention being engaged to both my sisters, Kitty thought meanly. She felt plain and poor. Georgiana Pembroke was beautiful. She had luscious raven black hair, a fair complexion, lashes that brushed her cheeks and exquisite blue eyes. She could see why William was taken with her.

Kitty approached the woman. "Miss, I was sent," she broke off, then continued, "I was told you needed some needlework done."

"Yes, it's only a hem. We are having a ball here on Saturday night and my dress is too long, I don't wish to trip," Miss Georgiana said matter-of-factly. She looked Kitty up and down. "I have been told

375

you are rather adept with a needle. The head dressmaker assured me you will do a fine job."

"Yes, Miss, I will Miss," Kitty nodded. She tried to smile but her face refused to cooperate.

Georgiana arose. William got quickly to his feet.

"If you will excuse me, William, I will go to my dressing room and change into my gown. You can wait if you wish, but I'm sure you have more important things to do."

"Yes, yes. I will visit you at a more convenient time, Georgiana." William bowed politely.

Georgiana then turned to Kitty, "Wait here. I will send Grant for you when I'm ready. Good day William." She swept out the room in a rush of blue silk.

Burn's gaze shifted back to Kitty; his eyes softened. "I was sorry to hear about your father. I read about his accident in the newspaper."

Kitty turned away. "I am surprised to find you still in Dunedin Mr Burns. I thought you were making your way to the West Coast. I can plainly see why you changed your mind."

"Business keeps me," he said.

She turned back sharply. "Does she know she is a business proposition?" Kitty meant to be cutting.

"That was unnecessarily cruel," William replied, recoiling.

She narrowed her gaze. "Cruel? I would have said honest."

William touched her sleeve as he passed by. "I meant it when I said I'm sorry," he said and left the room.

Cheeks burning, Kitty turned to find Miss Grant watching her with interest.

"Follow me," she said turning on her heel.

Kitty gripped her sewing basket tightly and followed the straight-backed woman along the great hall and up the long, sweeping staircase. She had meant to hurt him, she wanted to scratch his eyes out and watch him bleed.

Chapter 22   Retribution

Weeks passed and Mary found herself going through the motions, but her heavy heart made the days feel endless. Pat knuckled down to work, and though he spent most nights cozied up with a bottle, as far as she could tell hadn't been visiting whorehouses or opium dens. She received a letter from Kitty, who shattered by the news, said she would come home if needed, however the tone of the letter suggested she would prefer to stay on in Dunedin if permitted. And a letter from Meg, saying she was settling in nicely to life at Riverstones Station, and enjoying teaching the shearers and Chinese cook, to read and write. But still no word from Jack, and that was a concern, she had no idea if they had made it safely to Riverton.

One afternoon Dusty arrived at the hotel, his leathery face alive with excitement. "Mary! Mary!" he called, clumping heavily up the front porch steps.

Mary's heart leapt. Perhaps Jack had sent word, and all was well.

Dusty was waving the *Otago Witness* like a flag. "Mary! Mary!" he called.

Irritated by his lack of respect for a house in mourning, Mary rebuked him. "What the devil are you shouting about, man?"

Dusty handed her the newspaper. "They've found him!" he said triumphantly, pointing at the headline. "Charlie Butler has been arrested! He's being held in Dunedin jail."

Mary stared at him in disbelief, then at the newspaper in his hand.

"He's to be tried there," Dusty said, pointing at the article.

Mary read the headline.

Notorious Pick Axe Murderer Captured

Charles Butler alias Champagne Charlie has been apprehended. Discovered hiding in the McKenzie Basin, he will be tried at the Dunedin Court on March the third 1866 for Murder, Attempted Murder, Arson and Theft.

It had been well over a year since Charlie torched the hotel and tried to kill them. Jim was unable to see justice done but while she had breath in her bones, by God she'd have justice.

Dusty blurted in eagerness. "I reckon you'll be called to testify."

"I reckon I will," Mary replied, her chin set in determination. "And I'll be damned if any bugger will stop me." She gave Dusty back the newspaper then rolling up her sleeves, she said, "But before I go to Dunedin to make sure the scoundrel hangs, let's unload these here stores."

ABOUT THE AUTHOR

Michelle Kelly lives in Auckland, New Zealand, in a cute little cottage she calls 'The Writery'. Originally from the Deep South, she still considers herself a Southern girl at heart. She always wanted to be a writer but it wasn't until her boys went to school, that Michelle enrolled in a correspondence writing course where she wrote her first and accidental novel. The assignment was to read a 50,000 word novel and write a synopsis. Michelle wrote a 50,000 word novel! The surprised Tutor marked it, and told that she should try and get it published. It has sat in the bottom drawer gathering dust ever since but Michelle says, who knows maybe one day 'Blood Money' will make it on to the bookshelves.

Renowned for being a plant killer, Michelle is proud of the two best things she ever grew, her sons, Paul and Mike. In fact, it was her sons that inspired Michelle to write her first published novel 'Payback'. Enjoying their pre-teen years, she wanted to create a snapshot of that time in their lives, and so wrote a novel loosely based around the boys Roller Hockey team. The publishers didn't think the sport popular enough, and told her to rewrite the novel, and change the sport. Stubborn to the core, Michelle refused and wrote a new novel using the same characters. Payback became a NZ Post Finalist in 2009. Since then, family and friends have been afraid that something they may say or do will end up in a novel. She says, they have every right to be worried!

Michelle's historical novel, 'Riverstones', came to her in a dream but she says the sequel 'Scattered Stones' was more of a mundane work it out while walking on the beach process, but says, it helped to have a framework to build the new plots on that lead into the final book in the series.

Michelle's next big project is to write the screenplay for the Riverstones series so she can showcase the beauty of the Central Otago landscape to the world.

Michelle says how the saga began...

I had an idea for a historical novel that was percolating in my coffee pot brain but wouldn't flow onto the page – a condition called Writers Block. Then, I had an ear operation and as I was coming out of the anesthetic, I had the most amazing dream. A dream so real I felt I could almost touch the wood paneling on the walls of the Long Gully Pub.

But the process was all back to front. I wrote the book, then spent hours in the library researching before finally visiting the place. Travelling into Skippers Canyon was a family adventure. My brother-in- law, sister- in-law, nephew and I drove into Skippers canyon in a small 4WD jeep filled to the gunnels with camping equipment. It's a harrowing, heart-stopping road definitely not for the faint hearted. We stopped at Long Gully, the site where Riverstones is set, and where the remains of the old hotel's chimneys can still be seen.

That night we camped by the Skippers schoolhouse, and the next day we set off to find the ghost town Bullendale. I've never been good at directions, or taking them, we walked for 6 hours, crossed the river at least 80 times, and have yet to find Bullendale. Had we kept walking, I was convinced we would end up in Hokitika. Next time I go in, I'm taking someone who knows where they are going which should save several hours walking, and the soles of our shoes.

I wish I could be a prolific author and pop out books, but for me writing the Riverstones series has been an elephant pregnancy. I've spent hours at libraries, looking up Papers Past on the internet, and visiting museums trying to get a feel and knowledge of the past so the novel would be authentic. I hope I have achieved that. During that time, I discovered so many incredible stories I wanted to write them all, but couldn't, and so I concentrated on Mary Healey's story and Riverstones was finally born.

Scattered Stones continues the Healey family saga but fear not, their journey isn't over and the third book in the series, Sticks and Stones is well underway.

Also by the author:

First in the series -

Riverstones: published 2014 available from Amazon.com in Paperback and Kindle or ask for it at your local retailer.

Third book in the series-

Sticks and Stones - published 2021 available from Amazon.com in Paperback and Kindle or ask for it at your local retailer

e: michellekellyauthor@gmail.com

www.michellekellyauthor.com

www.ingramcontent.com/pod-product-compliance
Lightning Source LLC
Chambersburg PA
CBHW072110250626
47159CB00007B/2379